'Brilli*ant*, brilli*ant*, bri her child, stressing the syllable. 'Why, yes, of c Brilliant. She is our jev just look at her eyes, at the diamond's light in them. She must keep the White Tsaritsa for ever in the family – if only in her eyes and in her name.'

'Madalena, my darling, you're crazy! Brilliant! For a name?'

'Yes, yes, it's perfect for her. Brilliant – Brilliant Curnonsky.'

Vitya's smile lit up his hollow eyes. Well . . . why not? It did contrast well with the ancient aristocratic surname. Why not give her a magical dimension, he mused, staring out at the snow, hardly daring to think of the gathering momentum of terror that had cast the dark shadow of Stalin across the land . . .

'Brilliant . . . Brilliant . . . ? Yes, it is wonderful. Let it be so. Let us give her some beauty and some magic – if only in her name!'

AUTHOR'S NOTE

Brilliant and Galina are two Russian women, one representing the West, the other the East, but for all they understand of each other's lives they could have emerged from alien civilizations. The legendary flawed diamond, the White Tsaritsa, ominously divided and belonging to two opposing cultures, is symbolic of a Russian yearning for a spiritual wholeness that seems fated to elude them. Galina's eventual appointment to the Congress of People's Deputies holds a ray of hope for the future.

The idealistic struggles of early revolutionary women such as Alexandra Kollontai, Nadezhda Krupskaya and Inessa Armand, to try to establish real equality in Soviet women's lives, was a dismal failure. Modern Soviet women feel they are liberated in name only; liberated to carry the dual burdens of work both inside and outside the home, without having achieved any real share in the power structure. They have been exploited by a system which has demanded everything but returned nothing. The Soviet Union's present uncertain path towards democracy under President Gorbachev will most certainly see the emergence of Soviet women as a new force – they have learned hard and bitter lessons and they will want to get it right this time. An exhilarating and challenging prospect; but how can modern woman 'get it right' – in any society – given the chance to start all over again with new rules and a new social contract between men and women? Perhaps the Utopian dream of perfect equality between the sexes could emerge as Russian woman's triumph and reward for the long years of sacrifice and disillusion.

PROLOGUE

'Madalena, *milaya maya* – my darling – you're crazy! Brilliant! For a name?'

'Yes, yes, it's perfect for her. Brilliant – Brilliant Curnonsky.'

Vitya stood at his wife's bedside, his etiolated shadow climbing the walls of the lamplit room, and silently pondered the name that was to be so irrevocably linked with his daughter's destiny.

Madalena hugged her new-born child and stared with fierce pride into eyes of the purest, clearest blue. Vitya, his hands shaking with tiredness, had kept his promise and delivered her. The shadow of cholera stalked the town and only one supply doctor had been sent to help him with the epidemic at Perendpelo.

The precise geographical demarcation of the straggling township, whether to the right or left of a meandering line on a map of Europe, had been haggled over for centuries by Poles and Russians. Most often the Russians got the upper hand, but it was a devoutly Catholic community which clung to the traditions of its Polish ancestors. Besides, the Russians were barbarians and the brooding forest that stretched away endlessly into Russia beyond the girdle of the river signified for them the great divide, the Christian from the Infidel.

Vitya rubbed his fist across his eyes and bent his head over the baby girl, then combed his fingers through his hair in a gesture of weariness and resignation that touched Madalena's heart. She knew that this provincial town with its *poshlost*, its narrow-minded bourgeois mediocrity, tormented and frustrated him. He had been forced into vol-

1

untary exile, to leave his post as Professor at Moscow University, when his political activities made life in the capital too risky. It had not seemed unnatural for Victor Curnonsky to move there after his marriage in 1950 and his father's death. For generations the Curnonskys had lived in Perendpelo where his father had been the Oblast's doctor. A complicated escape plan had been set up to spirit the family away to the West and safety should the danger become too great.

Suddenly Vitya lifted his head and fumbled deep inside his pocket. He pulled out a twist of tissue paper, yellow and intricately crumpled with age. Slowly, with respectful care, he folded back the crumbling sheets and took out a diamond ring. Madalena gasped and held her breath as he held it to the light.

A small oil lamp burned dimly in the corner beneath the niche of the Virgin, but the room was flooded with the blue light of a full, palpitating moon that had turned the snow-covered fields into a landscape of surreal beauty. Every star blazed into infinity and the diamond caught up their intensity, throwing out such an other-worldly beam that Madalena's heart chilled in awe, then soared in exultant celebration of its beauty.

'*Da, da*, brilliant, Curnonsky brilliant – there's the diamond, the Curnonsky diamond. . . .' Madalena breathed. 'The White Tsaritsa! Your mother's ring. Vitya! It's . . . it's quite fabulously beautiful.'

'Yes, Lenochka, my darling,' Vitya's voice choked and became husky, 'I've been thinking for a long time that you ought to have it . . . because I love you . . . and you have given me a gift more precious than any diamond. Mamasha always meant it for my wife, and nothing is safe from confiscation now. So I took it from the chimney place this morning . . . and now . . . now you must always, *always* keep it with you!'

Vitya took her hand and slipped the ring on her middle finger. Madalena raised her arm, arching her fingers in a graceful curve to catch the preternatural column of moon-beams searing through the window.

'On your tiny hand it looks like a make-believe ring, the stone is so ridiculously large. But well, it *is* a fairy-tale in a way, that ring, you know.' Madalena nodded. The story of the White Tsaritsa, stranger and more improbable than any fable, had entered Russian folklore, was known and embroidered upon throughout the length and breadth of the land, by a people addicted to *skazhky*-telling around the stove of a winter's evening.

'It's strange to think the stone wasn't cut and polished until 1913. The twins, my father Anton, and Uncle Grigor, and that amazing ceremony in St Petersburg.' Vitya chuckled. 'The Slavophile versus the Westerner! Uncle Grigor, huge and cleanshaven, standing for the West and progress, wanting the superstitious "heart" that flawed the stone removed. Father the doctor, huge and bearded, on the side of orthodoxy and preservation, finally agreeing to the cutting. Then the high drama of the public cleaving, so tricky the diamond could have shattered into a thousand pieces, successfully dividing the stone into two halves.'

'And so Anton kept the flawed half for himself. It's uncanny, but it is just like a tiny heart inside . . .' Mada-lena spoke as if to herself.

'Thank God, Father had the sense to hide his ring down here at Zhelenaya Roscha. Though the Bolsheviks fired the house in 1917 they never found the ring – a diamond can resist any heat, of course – and it was presumed lost in the sack of the capital. Poor Uncle Grigor! Whether you're superstitious or not, he seemed to have lost his talisman. The New Soviet State didn't waste any time in appropriating his perfect half of the Tsaritsa, after he was shot for Menshevik sympathies.'

A slow smile of pleasure transformed Vitya's haggard features as he watched Madalena's fascination with the ring.

'All that extraordinary beauty waiting to be released by

man. That's why I have always found the diamond so magical, quite unique among precious stones. Diamonds have this strange alchemy with man, without his special skills there would be no piercing beauty, no blue fire in their icy heart. Man and light! Diamonds need both. When the stones have been cut and polished into their myriads of facets, the light does the rest!'

Vitya's smile was tender as he watched the jewel on Madalena's twisting fingers weave a sparkling pattern around the baby's head.

'Yes, as a doctor, the combination of man and nature has always fascinated me. I've been in love with the White Tsaritsa since the first moment I saw it on Mother's hand and she showed me the mysterious flaw deep inside. I can still remember my shock at that unearthly beam. . . .' He shook his head and smoothed a stray strand of fine blonde hair from Madalena's forehead.

'Its enormous value goes without saying, of course, but we could never realize its worth here. It'll be security for you in the West when you . . . when we can finally go away together.'

The child followed her mother's moving hand and the pinpoints of light from the brilliant-cut facets danced in the depths of her pale eyes. Suddenly, dramatically, with a turn of Madalena's wrist, the blazing blue fire from the adamantine heart was caught and bathed the baby's head in an aura of supernatural light.

'Brilli*ant*, brilli*ant*, brilli*ant* . . .' Madalena crooned to her child, stressing the word, the Russian way, on the last syllable. 'Why, yes, of course! Brilliant! We must call her Brilliant. She is our jewel, our own precious diamond; just look at her eyes, at the diamond's light in them. She must keep the White Tsaritsa for ever in the family – if only in her eyes and in her name.'

'Madalena, my darling, you're crazy! Brilliant! For a name?'

'Yes, yes, it's perfect for her. Brilliant – Brilliant Curnonsky.'

4

Vitya's smile lit up his hollow eyes. Well . . . why not? It did contrast well with the ancient aristocratic surname. Why not give her a magical dimension, he mused, staring out at the snow, hardly daring to think of the gathering momentum of terror that had cast the dark shadow of Stalin across the land. He shivered and turned his gaze back from the cold external light to the glowing face of his young wife, gilded in the honeyed rays from the icon lamp, cradling her child in protective arms.

'Brilliant . . . Brilliant . . . ? Yes, it is wonderful. Let it be so. Let us give her some beauty and some magic – if only in her name!'

'Touch them! Go on – touch them! They will be yours, all of them, the fabulous Chardin jewels will all belong to you . . . when you marry me!'

Jean-Claude's voice was soft, insistent in Brilliant's ear among the darkened jewel vaults of the Maison Chardin. It was four in the morning, they had eaten at L'Archestrate and danced at Castel's. He was madly in love with this ravishing blonde American who spoke perfect French with an endearing Russian accent, who knew more about jewels than he did, but more, much more than that, had an aura of recklessness about her, an entrancing wildness, a tantalizing hint of the untamed Steppe that made his conventional French temples throb and the blood course through his veins in a way he had never known. She had style – the sort of style he prized above all else in a woman – and he desired her to a degree that shattered his urbane composure. There had been other women of course, mostly older than himself, attracted by his appealing boyishness; Jean-Claude had inherited the soft dark hair, grey eyes and straight nose of his Breton mother.

As a rule his exquisite relationships with women of a 'certain' age involved cultivated conversation, well-chosen food and wine and carefully selected locations for the act of love itself. Jean-Claude always felt a certain detachment, seeing himself from the outside, an actor playing a perfectly judged role. But now this Slav beauty had come to tempt him, her vibrancy had touched an unknown erotic chord and he was determined to have her, and to make her his wife, and let her beauty and knowledge enhance the name of Chardin.

He had heard about Brilliant Curnonsky, of course. Her name was well known in the trade, synonymous with breeding, education – albeit an American one – and a remarkable diamond 'eye' that had already earned her the reputation of a master diamantaire. But it was her reputation as a woman that intrigued him – she was said to be aloof, even frosty, and immune to masculine blandishments. Even more surprising, thought Jean-Claude, as he grew to appreciate the warmth of Brilliant's personality, there were no apparent shadows from the past to tarnish the shining image.

Brilliant had come to Paris in March to organize the autumn collection for Zylos of New York. She was staying at the Ritz – fruits of my new-found success, she had sighed ecstatically, wallowing among vast monogrammed sheets and more obscenely fluffy towels than she and her mother Madalena had in the whole of their linen cupboard in New York – and was lunching with Jaime Ortiz, the Madrid buyer for Zylos. Her head was thrown back when he first saw her, laughter setting off the curve of a perfect cream throat and strong wicked teeth. A cloud of pale hair cascaded over her shoulders and merged with a buttercup linen suit.

'This is Jean-Claude Chardin, of Maison Chardin, of course – he pops in here for a worker's lunch . . .' Jaime introduced them in a laconic fashion, irritated at the unwelcome interruption. Something fathomless in Jean-Claude's eyes appealed to her; gentle yet cool, he was handsome in a sensitive Gallic way, so different from the rugged American good looks she was used to.

In the days that followed they were inseparable. A mutual passion for precious stones brought them together and forged a common bond, acting as an unconscious aphrodisiac and giving Brilliant's relationship a dimension that was new to her. Brilliant was as intrigued by the apparent contradictions of Jean-Claude's personality as he was by hers. She sensed an inner conflict and emotional economy that she thought might be the result of a strict

7

French upbringing. She felt instinctively that he needed her. When she was with him it was as if complicated protective layers were being shed from his brittle outer shell and he was falling in love for the first time – and becoming vulnerable.

As for Jean-Claude, from the moment he had seen her face, etched in spring sunlight, he had felt a pull towards something he found very difficult to express, or even acknowledge. That diamond image, shining bright? Was that the key to his attraction, Jean-Claude wondered in a moment of cynical introspection. It was as if Brilliant herself possessed the positive qualities of the diamond; it was not merely a glossy aura, and through her love he could become . . . well, he could be different. Perhaps he could acquire some of her attributes by association; through her he could change and grow, he could become all the things a part of himself still ached for – if he let that symbolic light flood in.

Jean-Claude was in no hurry to take her to his bed. He wanted to savour, as a connoisseur, this extraordinary sexual excitement she roused in him. He set about his conquest, painstakingly applying the same meticulous attention to detail he gave a new collection, supervising the props and stage effects of the developing affair with a zeal he had never yet matched in the act of love itself.

Flowers – from DuLaurier's, naturally – arrived in great swathes to make a bower of her room at the Ritz. He had crossed the Pont Notre Dame to the Marché des Fleurs at cock's crow to choose a bouquet to match her eyes, a dazzling shimmer of blues ranging from the palest blue-tinged white of carnations through myosotis, columbine and forget-me-nots to the deeper hues of delphinium and foxglove.

The fastidious Jean-Claude supervised the arrangement of the immense basket of blossoms and the finished product really did shimmer and refract the light, like the finest diamond, with the multi-faceted shades of blue and white focusing at the centre in the intense blue fire of wild cornflowers.

The next day another prodigious arrangement arrived, in creams and pinks as a tribute to her fairness, and nestling at its heart was a Fabergé egg filled with caviar. He had discovered her passion for the egg of the sturgeon, preferably of the Beluga kind, and always from Russian waters.

One night at a small table laid romantically *à deux* in the window recess of her room at the Ritz, she had paused, a silver spoon heaped with the pearly delicacy halfway to her lips, her eyes darkening with appreciation across the ice bucket.

'All this is totally unnecessary.' She waved airily at the finely chopped onion and egg yolk, the ethereal melba toast and mountains of crushed ice, sophisticated accompaniments to the eating of caviar. 'As a Russian I consider them just fillers, the sublime creaminess should be savoured on its own, preferably in enormous quantities. Yes, I will have some more champagne . . .' She laughed huskily as she touched her tulipe glass against his. 'I sound revoltingly indulged, don't I, but caviar is one of the few luxuries I enjoyed as a child. My ridiculous Aunt Dolly used to send kilos from Paris – she had no idea, thought it must be the one thing we were missing in the New World. If only she'd sent some winter socks.'

He smiled as he carefully refilled her glass.

'Ah, yes! Your relatives – Comte and Comtesse Litvinov – and your other aristocratic connections.' His eyes brightened. 'And your own title, of course – Comtesse . . .' He looked slightly uncomfortable as she shot him a glance of scornful surprise. 'Well, you know how it is in certain circles, especially in Paris, everyone knows how everyone else is connected, you will find your "noblesse" can be of great value here.'

She put down her spoon and stared. Surely he couldn't be serious?

'My noblesse!' She threw back her head and gave a

throaty unaristocratic guffaw. An erotic charge shot through his veins, but he frowned. On occasions she showed an irritating tendency towards levity over the important issues. He watched her greedily swallow another spoonful of caviar.

'I only found out I had a title by accident – when I was about fourteen. I went with Mother to an incredibly boring émigré get-together to raise funds for charity. Neither of us wanted to go, I remember. An ancient gentleman in a mouldering frock-coat – straight out of Pushkin – came up and kissed my hand and there were tears in his eyes, real tears, imagine. "Countess Curnonsky," he murmured as he bent over my calloused little paw, "you have inherited the family diamond in your eyes. . . ." ' She chuckled and raised her glass with a flourish.

'Calloused hands . . . *mais pourquoi* . . . lovely hands like these . . . ?' He frowned and took her free hand gently in his, studying the palm in disbelief.

'Oh, they were pretty calloused in those days.' She caught her breath as he brushed the hollow of her palm with his lips.

'I used to get up at five and work at anything I could set my hands to, stacking crates out back of the corner shop, delivering papers . . .' She shivered. 'Agony that, on cold mornings. I preferred the grease and sweat of the deli, I'm a mean hand at the pastrami and coleslaw routine. It didn't matter as long as it brought home the bacon.' She withdrew her hand, wiped her mouth matter-of-factly on her napkin, then her face broke into a wide grin.

'Good Lord, don't look so horrified! It wasn't as bad as all that – at least not as bad as it was for some of the kids in our neighbourhood. Mother had talent, real talent, she turned our shabby apartment into an exquisite salon with her own hands.' She smiled wryly. 'Not that those ghastly kids she taught appreciated its refinement, murdering the French language with their strangled vowels. It was the

10

pushy mothers I loathed the most, so arrogant and bullying. I tried to protect her, get her to stand up for herself. They ranted and raved over their dress orders, swearing that Mother had got the measurements wrong, they had said a twenty-eight-inch waist and she had made up a twenty-four. . . . "This frock has no pzazz – no detail! Would you please put a little more trimming on it and make it look like *real* money was spent on it. . . ." ' She mimicked a heavy nasal twang.

'At night we worked on the dress orders. First she rubbed almond oil into my hands, she said I was ruining her fine fabrics. When I was too tired to hold the needle any more she sent me to bed. I could tell from her red eyes next morning she must have sat up half the night. But she never complained, she thought we were just so incredibly lucky.'

Brilliant sighed and took a quick sip of champagne. 'You know, I have a Proustian affinity with smells, I have only to catch a whiff of hot chocolate and I'm back there in that warm room, sewing so close to Mother that our arms sometimes touch, my flower-sprigged bowl is under my nose and her soft voice murmuring – she had a real gift for *skazhky* – that's our Russian story-telling.'

She raised fervent eyes. 'She could have done so well in *haute couture*, she had such taste, such style, but she adamantly refused to get a job outside.' She looked down at the tablecloth, toying with a few crumbs of toast. 'She never felt really happy with the English language, we only spoke French or Russian at home. She always had this thing about being there when I came back from school, otherwise life wouldn't . . . wouldn't be "in order" – *v poradotchky* as Mother put it . . .' Her voice choked and her eyes filled. In the nostalgic Russian phrase all the cherished warmth of her mother's home came flooding back with disturbing emotional force.

He squeezed her hand comfortingly. 'And your father? I know it must be difficult for you to talk about him?'

She returned the pressure of his hand. 'Not really. You

11

see, I never knew him. Vitya was killed in 1953 when I was just a baby. But for my mother he's still very much alive, she talks about him – or with him – every day.'

'She must be very proud – I've read a lot about his work for the Stalin resistance.'

'Yes, Vitya was a remarkable man, and selfless too. Mother said she knew he was going to die from the moment he handed over the ring.'

'The White Tsaritsa?'

'Yes. He gave it to Mother the day I was born. Pockets of resistance like ours were high on Stalin's hit-list, so when the net started to close in we were spirited over the border, and Father was supposed to follow later. He never made it – he was ambushed by six men in grey and shot on the spot.'

'So then you managed to get to your aristocratic relatives in Paris?' His voice was gently probing.

'Not immediately. Mother escaped done up like a farmer's wife, with the ring sewn inside her blouse and me bundled up in a shawl. We were with a party of mourners who had permission to cross the border for a relative's funeral. We waited at Uncle Lyuba's house – and waited and waited. Mother told me that when friends came to break the news about my father she felt sorrier for them than for herself – their grief was so real – that was typical of her unselfishness. She said she pressed her hands against the White Tsaritsa inside her blouse, harder and harder until the stone marked her flesh, gritting her teeth so she wouldn't cry out. Everyone had been so kind, she couldn't weaken for their sake and mine. Finally we followed the escape route westwards from one safe house to the next, ending up in Paris.'

She was silent for a moment, staring into space.

'But why didn't you stay in comfort in Paris? What made your mother go to America?' For Jean-Claude such a move was totally incomprehensible.

Brilliant shrugged.

'Our relatives weren't well off – they seemed to live by

12

scrounging, Mother said. She didn't like artificial society life and wanted to use her artistic training in the West, without interference from the family. A week or so with Prince and Princess Torlovsky, the Count Litvinovs *et al* and she'd quite made up her mind. My Aunt Dolly Litvinov was very attached to Mother. She saw us off at Cherbourg, Mother dressed to the nines in a new wardrobe of aristocratic cast-offs. Dolly was wildly romantic, she waved us off in floods of tears at the quayside, swathed in ancient sables. The sight of the young heroine off to the New World with a baby clutched to her bosom was too much for Auntie and she had to be assisted to a cab by a couple of porters.' Brilliant's wicked smile instantly transformed her face. 'Then . . . Mother sold the White Tsaritsa to Joel Vanderberg in New York . . . for practically nothing.'

'Aha, the infamous villain of the piece! Adamantina certainly pulled off a coup, acquiring that legendary diamond so easily, the envy of every jewel house in the world.' Jean-Claude's eyes narrowed with curiosity as he saw Brilliant give an involuntary shudder.

Adamantina! Brilliant still remembered the chill she had felt when she first heard the name. She had been twelve and Madalena had taken her to the Adamantina showroom on Fifth Avenue where the White Tsaritsa took pride of place in an International Diamond Exhibition organized by Joel Vanderberg. She had hung back, dazed by the opulence of the room and the smell – at once expensive and repugnant – of the strange crowd pressing round her. Only when her mother had pushed her closer, so that her nose pressed against the glass, had she forgotten everything and remained so long in a spellbound trance that Madalena, laughing, had had to shake her arm and pull her away, her breath was misting the showcase and her awed expression drew patronizing smiles from the well-heeled clientele.

'But it's really ours, Mother, that ring! You told me so yourself, that Joel Vanderberg cheated you and gave you practically nothing. It belongs to the Curnonskys – it should never have gone out of the family. It's so beautiful, I want it more than anything I've ever wanted in the world!' She had clasped her hands and closed her eyes, nearly stumbling down the subway steps as they left the luxurious cocoon of the showroom and plunged into the cold reality of the winter rush-hour in New York.

Madalena had clutched her hand and pulled her close, frowning as she looked down at the rosy face beside her, a face already promising the beauty that was to come.

'Shhh. . . . You mustn't feel so strongly about things like that – it's just a stone, after all. Material things don't matter, we're together, we survived because of the money from the ring. We have been lucky, many people had nothing when they came to America, nothing.'

'But Mother, how are we so lucky? You're always working late into the night, your eyes get so red. Why, you only said yourself, yesterday. . . .' She had broken off, ashamed, but her fists had clenched with helpless anger as Madalena's hollow eyes clouded.

'A fabulous stone like that should belong to the people, everyone should have a chance to see it and to share its beauty.'

Madalena's voice had been firm. She had been deeply impressed by the American Ideal, what it represented to penniless immigrants like herself, and the freedom and equality that formed the basis of the Constitution. 'If America doesn't work, then the world won't work!' was one of her favourite expressions.

But for Brilliant the White Tsaritsa became an inspiration and an obsession and night after night she begged Madalena to repeat its story. Joel Vanderberg became the villain and acquired, in Brilliant's overheated imagination, all the attributes of Beelzebub himself. Her name, her childhood, the ring's history and her destiny were so irrevocably linked that she would have no rest until the diamond was back again in Curnonsky hands, or at the very least, out of the unscrupulous Vanderberg's.

She felt that the diamond had haunted her for the thirty-three years of her life, and had undoubtedly been the inspiration for her career as a diamantaire.

'But Brilliant,' Jean-Claude continued gently. 'Your mother, Madalena, must be very proud of what you have achieved. She must be more . . . more comfortable now – now you're in better circumstances.'

She stared at him in silence for a moment, across the gulf of background, culture and experience.

'Better circumstances? Of course, much better. Though it's still not quite the lap of luxury, I've managed to move her, not without a struggle, to an arty little pad in SoHo. She loves it though, she says it reminds her of her student days. In fact she's become quite girlish and bohemian again. She spends her time at lectures and galleries and gives the occasional lesson, but strictly to pupils of her choice.'

'She was very fortunate, then, to have a daughter who could provide for her so well.' With Gallic practicality Jean-Claude considered the subject satisfactorily closed.

'No, I was the fortunate one. She gave me love and security, helping her gave my life shape and purpose. It certainly got me started on the work ethic: how else would I have had the ambition to get where I am today, embarked on my "brilliant" career?' She flashed a mocking smile at her own pun and helped herself to more caviar.

'Your career? Ah, of course . . . the jewellery.' He sat back and smiled at her vibrant face. He pressed his fingertips together. 'Why shouldn't you have a career, it's not demeaning, even for someone of noblesse.' He leaned forward confidentially. 'You know, my mother worked as a mannequin and then as a vendeuse for the House of Patou. To work for such a craftsman is an honour in France.'

She looked at him reflectively. Yes, she had heard of his mother, the unfailingly elegant Marie-Laure, with her famous monthly 'salons', rivalling the *grandes dames* of the eighteenth century in their cultivated refinement.

'Your mother is . . . very special, isn't she?' For no particular reason Brilliant experienced a pang of anxiety.

Jean-Claude's eyes immediately took on a guarded expression.

'Special?' He made the word sound as though it were an insult and Brilliant felt embarrassed, almost naive. 'My mother is a very cultured and intelligent woman – yes, I suppose you could call her special.' He gave a stiff smile. He never, ever spoke to other women about his mother. That would be unforgivable. But Brilliant looked so uncomfortable that he relented slightly and the warmth came back to his eyes.

'I hope you will meet her quite soon,' he murmured. 'Now! More champagne?' Sensing the effervescence of her mood evaporating, he was quick to refill her glass. He smiled reprovingly as her pink tongue curled round another spoonful of caviar.

'You must save a small corner for the special dinner I've arranged at Jamad. I only intended this as an *amuse-gueule*, you know.'

He propped his elbow on the table and rested his chin on his hand, a pose he knew was becoming.

'Tell me about this diamond "eye" of yours. I've heard in the trade that it is uncanny, you can spot the four Cs – clarity, colour, cut and carat – at a distance of twenty yards and across a crowded room!' He smiled, but his eyes betrayed his interest. This eye, and her ability to drive a hard bargain, had already earned her a formidable reputation in tattling trade circles.

'It's nothing I've consciously worked on, it must be a gift . . . it comes so easily I've always taken it for granted.' She shrugged dismissively. 'Even as a child I was drawn to precious jewels in some inexplicable . . . compelling way.' She looked at him carefully, choosing her words, watching his reaction. Could she tell this man of her

16

obsessive drive, could this at last be someone who might just possibly understand?

'I wanted to get a job straight away, to make things easier for Mother, but she insisted I went through college. We had endless arguments about it, ending in tears and great wringing of hands. Then I won a scholarship to Parsons and seemed to find my niche, jewellery design – they discovered my "eye" – so I realized I'd better put it to good use and I got my first job with Reinot, in New York. Speaking French was a great help, of course.'

And her looks, too, he thought, watching her expressive features, not realizing the emotional effort it cost her to speak about herself, to release some of the pent-up frustration she had kept in check for so long.

'You would be an asset for any company you worked for . . .' His pulse throbbed as he thought of the men who must have desired her.

'Incredible that you have escaped marriage for so long . . .' he mused, as if to himself, then stopped as quick colour flooded her face.

He glanced towards the richly canopied hotel bed. The intriguing enigma of her personality, a rich sexuality promised by her looks juxtaposed with the slight but definite aura of frigidity she emanated, had roused him to a pitch he found hard to control. But his instinct warned him to tread warily. This woman was a rarity, a challenge and an inspiration to him as a connoisseur of beauty. If the rumours he had heard were correct she could be very hard to win. Some of the less gallant of her frustrated admirers had been heard to mutter that she had no heart at all, that it had been frozen into a replica of the diamond for which she was named, or even that her sexual proclivities lay elsewhere. This element of the elusive and bizarre only added fuel to his ardour.

'I'm so sorry, *chérie*, forgive me! I didn't mean to sound unchivalrous. But a woman like yourself, *si charmante*. . . .' He shrugged helplessly, for once his Gallic cool flustered. 'But really, you must have had to beat off hordes of prospective lovers. Ah, but then, you wanted your career.'

She smiled at his embarrassment. 'Please, there's no need to apologize. I'm used to hearing the same thing. What! No husband? But remember I was raised in the United States where men have other things on their minds besides amorous adventure – whereas here in Europe. . . .' She smiled mockingly and stroked the long stem of her glass in silence. Could she really tell him what she had told no other person, not even her mother, something her fierce pride and hurt trust had pushed to the back of her mind?

'You are probably wondering whether I'm capable of love, or perhaps you think I may be cold. . . .' She spoke almost to herself. No, on the contrary. Every inch of her long, languorous body had thrilled to Robert's touch. She had been ready to give up everything in willing adoration, to lose herself body and soul in him.

'There is no mystery. It's very simple, hackneyed even, the classic case of the young girl crossed in love.' She smiled wryly. 'But I took it very hard. But really, now! My adolescent adventures must be the last thing you want to hear.' She looked down in silence at the pools of lamplight that turned the wet Place Vendôme into an enchanted fairy circle.

'You are quite mistaken, *chérie*, anything that concerns you is of interest to me. You must tell me about this . . . this adventure. You are a woman of the world, surely you didn't expect me to think you still a virgin?' He squeezed her hand encouragingly.

She looked at him in surprise. The champagne had mellowed her. Perhaps she should voice some of the emotional hurt of her first experience of love, if only as catharsis.

'His name was Robert McEnerny Firbright III. He was at Stamford, I was at Parsons. I met him at a college ball. He was just embarking on an amorous career that has

18

since become his life's work.' She smiled tartly. 'Are you sure you want to hear all this?'

'I insist! This Robert . . . No doubt he was ruggedly handsome in an American way?' He seemed intrigued, even titillated by the prospect of sharing her experience.

'Oh sure, he was good-looking! At his christening the good fairies lavished all the preppie gifts on him with abandon – *old* New York money, he was at pains to tell me, absolutely top drawer, film-star profile, adonis build, shoulders *this* wide, tousled flaxen hair. . . .' Her mouth twitched at Jean-Claude's rapt expression. But – amazingly – she was enjoying herself. Putting her experience into perspective with such acerbity had shattered the long-standing spell.

'I was too infatuated to notice that the good fairies had held back on strength of character,' she went on, 'that the spoilt selfishness would develop into a ruthless ego. I knew about the intellectual laziness – it was his athletic prowess that got him into Stamford – all literary interest was labelled pretentious among his set, but he had great charm, an endearing boyishness. Our physical attraction was incredible, we grappled like young lions for one long, hot summer in a cottage on Cape Cod. We were idyllically, ecstatically in love, never out of each other's sight – or bed for that matter – for any length of time. . . .'

A pulse was beating hard at Jean-Claude's temple as she continued.

'I was the happiest of women – you see, I'm an old-fashioned romantic at heart – planning the details of our new ménage, how secure and comfortable I could make my mother, then the holidays came to an end. Robert had failed his exams, and wasn't going back to Stamford. He had a place in his father's stockbroking company which one day he would take over. I stayed on at the cottage to pack up, then followed him back to the city at the end of the week. Do you know,' she smiled with nostalgic pleasure, 'I remember so clearly the new suit I wore that day . . . the day. . . .' Her voice faltered, she swallowed, then carried on in a firm voice. 'The day I decided to surprise him and carry him off to lunch on my first day back. It was early September, there was a nip in the air as I flew up the steps of the Firbright Building. The blue suit was Mother's creation. I wore a silk blouse tied in a stock at the throat with a pearl pin – quite the young executive, I thought. I went up unannounced and found his door, admired the impressive nameplate, then a pretty secretary bounced out and I got a glimpse of my golden boy shooting his cuffs and straightening his tie. . . .' She paused, staring out of the window, but Jean-Claude said nothing, willing her to go on.

'It was his eyes I remember most, so changed, so cold.' Her hand clutched instinctively at her throat. 'He stared as though I were a stranger, as if we had met for the first time, demanded to know what I was doing there, then – taking pity on me, I suppose – sat me down and patted me on the shoulder like a Dutch uncle.

' "You see, Brilliant," he said, "it was just a holiday romance, Father and Mother have other plans for me, the family name and all that. . . . You must understand, for the moment I have to toe the line, I owe it to them not to disgrace the Firbrights." Sublety was never his strong point.' She smiled drily.

'So that was that. Somehow I managed to leave the room po-faced, then I wept my heart out in the ladies' room of the coffee shop next door. The owner must have thought I'd died in there. Hours later I walked home across the city a changed woman. It's easy to laugh now, but at the time it hit me hard. I was very proud you see, but vulnerable. I never even told my mother what happened. I suppose I wanted to save her the hurt she would have felt for me. So. . . .' she spread her hands expressively, 'I threw myself into my career, treating the opposite sex with the indifference I thought they deserved, and now I suppose I have earned the reputation of an ice-maiden.'

Far from feeling like an ice-maiden at that moment,

her heart seemed to be filled with warm amber honey that flowed through her veins and inflamed her to the finger-tips. A great burden seemed to have lifted and she felt eager, compelled even, to love again. She looked at the courteous man beside her. He was so considerate, so ready to listen, to understand.

'And you, Jean-Claude. . . .' Brilliant gave a shrug, slightly embarrassed and not sure how to go on. 'Well, all these questions about me and I know nothing about your . . . well . . . about how it happened that you're not. . . .' Whatever way it came out it sounded flippant and prying, which was not at all what she intended.

Jean-Claude's eyes took on an expression that she found difficult to read.

'Of course, my darling, you want to know about me. I am really a very straightforward person. Until recently I lived with my parents, mainly for financial reasons.' He laughed. 'That's the way the parsimonious French keep their children on the straight and narrow. Then two years ago, when I was thirty, some trust money was released and I bought my own apartment. I was always too tied up in the family business to take any relationship seriously. Naturally, I am not inexperienced' – her heart missed a beat as he squeezed her hand – 'but I never met the right woman, I have never fallen in love and now the miracle has taken me completely by surprise. . . .'

With a supreme effort of will Jean-Claude turned his back on the Louis Quinze bed.

'Come now, you need attention, stimulation – the whole of Paris is here to divert you. You have to forget the past, and I am here to help you do just that!'

Jean-Claude hurried to help her on with her coat and Brilliant, shivering as his lips brushed the nape of her neck, was quite sure that more than two people anywhere in Paris that night would constitute a crowd, but instinct and experience warned her to tread warily with this man. No philistine here, but a Parisian of cultivated refinement,

21

almost Oscar Wildean in his pursuit of good taste, demanding simply nothing but the best.

After dinner at Jamad she declined his invitation to dance or drink at any of the clubs frequented by his *bon-chic, bon-genre* circle. Pleading an urgent desire for fresh air she drew him along the quais of the moon-dappled Seine. The whispered sighs of generations of lovers rustled through the ancient ivied walls above their bench, her head inclined as if by magic to his shoulder and his hand reached up to caress her hair. She turned towards him, shadowed eyes full of mystery. The roving searchlight from the Île de la Cité caught her upturned face in its silver beam. Jean-Claude cupped her face in his hands in disbelief.

'Your eyes! In this light, they are extraordinary . . . so like the facets of a diamond it is uncanny. Everything about them, the colour, the clarity. . . .'

She smiled, the guard she put up automatically with men who paid her extravagant compliments long since dropped.

'Yes, so I've been told. My eyes and the White Tsaritsa are one and the same. At least I've inherited the family jewel – if only in my eyes!' She laughed ironically.

'Yes, it is true,' he murmured, 'you do have that magnificent diamond there, but even so, the tragedy is yours. Losing a legend, the Curnonsky talisman passing out of your family – why, it's part of Russian history.' His voice was passionate.

She sat upright, eyes alight. 'I didn't think you knew so much!'

'Of course I know, who doesn't? That *Time* magazine article was a pretty impressive piece of reporting.'

An issue of *Time* earlier that year had featured the White Tsaritsa in a stunning colour photograph on its front cover, with a lead story to coincide with the World Diamond Fair in New York. The article was necessarily vague about the earliest origins of the famous lump of crystallized carbon. Rumoured to have been found in the sixteenth century by a peasant on the banks of the Tura river in Siberia, it had soon found its way into the aristocratic Curnonsky family. Apart from its enormous size – four hundred and five carats – its claim to fame was a unique flaw, a speck of dark blue at its centre that seemed to be in the shape of a tiny heart.

The legend grew in Russia that the diamond had magical properties, that its 'heart' of goodness and truth preserved life and brought good fortune to all who possessed it. It became the talisman of the Romanov dynasty, on loan from their Curnonsky cousins, and helped safeguard the continuation of the Imperial line. The stone was forsaken by Nicholas II, the last Romanov, who preferred the occult influence of Rasputin for his spiritual guidance, and it was split apart to remove its flaw by a sceptical Westernized Count Curnonsky. Four years later the Red Flag fluttered from the Imperial Palace towers of St Petersburg and the last of the Romanovs faced a firing squad in Ekaterinburg.

'You know, I would give anything to find out the real origins of the diamond; I'm sure there is something mystic and romantic there. . . .' Brilliant laughed, slightly shame-faced. 'I can't explain it to anyone, least of all to myself, but there is a connection somewhere between me and the White Tsaritsa – a magnetism – a link with someone from the past. It has always haunted me. People think that my interest in the family jewel is purely commercial, but it isn't, it's stronger than that, it's part of me – I am that diamond. . . .' She paused, willing him to understand. He took her hands in his.

'Brilliant, *mon amour*, you never need explain to me. I understand – completely! I assure you I would have felt the same, if the jewel had passed out of our family.' Jean-Claude's sentiments were heartfelt. Wars, deaths and marriages could come and go – but family inheritance was sacrosanct.

'Never mind what happened to the White Tsaritsa in the mists of the Middle Ages, its recent history would

23

have won it the Légion d'Honneur here in France,' he continued. 'After all, Peter the Great was supposed to have been inspired to build St Petersburg, the Wonder of the North, where the diamond pointed him.'

Story had it that the Westernized giant of a Tsar was hunting snipe in the Gulf of Finland when his party struck camp on a low hillock overlooking a swampy plain. The enormous Imperial sword, set with the White Tsaritsa, lay on a low silken stool. The slanting rays of the sun disappearing over the horizon caught the great diamond in such a way that it seemed to catch fire, gushing great streams of blue light that flooded over the valley.

Peter, so the story went, straddled in a camp chair before the fire, shot forward as though electrified. His eyes followed the dazzling points of eerie light, took in the wide bay with its creeks and inlets, the River Neva flowing broadly out to the Gulf of Finland, then he sprang to his feet.

'*Svyataya mecta*! The Holy Place! Here I shall build St Petersburg, my wonder of the north. We have been guided to it by divine intervention – my sanctified new capital of All the Russias.'

Brilliant smiled.

'Catherine the Great's story is my favourite. You know she had a penchant for giving her lovers gifts for services rendered to the royal bed. Ivan Preobarensky's performance must have been pretty impressive, because he got the White Tsaritsa sword, scaled down for a mere mortal of course. When he got his marching orders, she managed to get the sword back in time to wave it over the revolutionary masses in front of the Imperial Palace. The power of the legend was so great that the crowd crossed themselves and departed, giving our Catherine time to pounce on the ringleaders. From then on there was no looking back. The White Tsaritsa was given the equivalent of your Légion d'Honneur, placed on a special plinth in the Imperial Collection and brought out to protect the monarch in times of need. Of course Nicholas II had no time for the legend, it was all *babushka* claptrap, and he agreed to hand it back to the Curnonskys on condition the stone was cut in two and the fateful flaw removed, to put an end to the mystique surrounding it.'

'Did you know that in 1913 my great-grandfather, Philippe Chardin, went to that cleaving ceremony in St Petersburg?' Jean-Claude's eyes gleamed. 'We still have letters in the archives that he sent home with his impressions. It must have been amazing! Diamantaires and cutters came from as far afield as New York and they had the time of their lives, if Philippe's anecdotes are anything to go by.'

'Isn't that extraordinary? There is a link between us then, through the White Tsaritsa. Our great-grandfathers must have actually met in St Petersburg in 1913.' She sighed. 'And to think that was the beginning of it all.'

'The beginning of it all?' He raised dark brows.

'I mean, the cutting ceremony took place just before the war. Tsar Nicholas refused the perfect half of the diamond for his Tsarina and it went to Grigor, the older Curnonsky twin by half an hour. It was considered too dangerous to try to cut the flaw from the rest and my grandfather, Anton, who never wanted the cleaving anyway, was tickled pink to have his half with the mystic flaw polished and set into a gold ring identical to Grigor's.'

'Mmmm. . . .' Jean-Claude's eyes were thoughtful. 'I saw the White Tsaritsa only a few months ago in New York, in pride of place in the Adamantina showroom. It made a most unusual impression on me. Even discounting the extraordinary legend, it does have an uncanny aura, something almost supernatural. When you look deep into it and see the flaw, just like a heart . . . I felt a shiver run down my spine, in spite of myself.'

Brilliant stared, heart beating. Something inside her seemed to melt, to open . . . and to expand.

'The perfect half is still in Russia, isn't it?' Jean-Claude took her hands in his. Brilliant continued to stare as if seeing him for the first time, then nodded slowly.

'Yes, it's in a museum in Leningrad. Mother always wanted us to make . . . to make a pilgrimage, but I put it

25

off. Somehow I just couldn't bring myself.' She shrugged. 'After the Revolution the Bolsheviks took the ring as part of the New Treasure of the People and Grigor was shot, he had thrown in his lot with the wrong side. Anton hid his flawed half behind the chimney at Zhelenaya Roscha, in Perendpelo.'

Jean-Claude caressed the contours of her cheek.

'That diamond is part of your destiny – I feel it as strongly as you do – and it is not too late to change things, for justice to be done.'

His words stirred in her a great longing, an inexplicable anguish, in which an aching desire to love and be loved were irrevocably linked with her diamond – could there be some hope, was it possible that all her dreams might one day become reality?

By the end of that enchanted week her feelings were in turmoil. She was sure that he cared for her and was beginning to hope that he might actually love her, but she also realized intuitively that he was in no hurry to let a physical relationship intrude. Jean-Claude wanted the object of his love to be suitably adored and shown to its best advantage – by surrounding her with beauty they would arrive together at a heightened consciousness which would increase the intensity of their feelings. . . . Or so at least she reasoned as she sat across the table at L'Archestrate that evening – maddened by now with desire and wondering if he was ever going to sweep her up in his arms and into his bed, if those lips that so appreciatively savoured the Château de Tracey '67, that had so sensitively and articulately wooed her, would ever do wonderful, unspeakable things. . . .

They were finishing a meal which had been like a symphony, *Le Grand Menu en petites portions*, eight tiny courses of the most exquisite food imaginable, each one complimenting the last, subtly sauced and artistically presented, yet so light she felt merely satisfied and aesthetically content, just as she would now – and her eyes narrowed to smouldering fire – if he were to whisper urgently. . . .

'Brilliant, Brilliant, *chérie*, wake up! I want you to come with me right now, this minute, quickly!' He was laughing and shaking her hand. 'I want you to experience something quite, quite wonderful. . . .' Was this the moment, then? Her knees shook as the waiter pulled back her chair and she stood up, tall and slender, smoothing down a midnight-blue dress that followed the graceful outline of her body.

But the taxi turned into the Place Vendôme and not towards his apartment in the Marais, and they were soon in a *belle-époque* elevator plunging down into the depths of the earth – down, down, towards the celebrated vaults of the House of Chardin.

In the plush-lined compartment Jean-Claude pressed her compliant body close and brought his mouth to her ear, but his urgent whisperings were not exactly what she might have hoped for.

'Darling, did you do your homework, you know, the little red book I gave you yesterday?'

She shook her head. *Chardin – Joailliers des Rois de France* still lay unopened on her bedside table.

He clicked his tongue reprovingly and she felt like a negligent schoolgirl.

'You must read it! It concerns the family.'

When they left the elevator Jean-Claude asked her to stand still, so she waited obediently, unable to see in the velvety blackness. He flitted bat-like through the darkened vault for what seemed an age, then suddenly switched on a blaze of spotlight. Instinctively, she put up her hand to shield her eyes, almost blinded by the dazzle from tray after tray of peerless diamonds hastily spread out on the baize-topped tables.

'Run your fingers through them, exult in them – millions of francs worth of them. Which stone would you like for your engagement ring? Touch them! Go on – touch them! They will be yours, all of them, the fabulous Chardin jewels will all belong to you . . . when you marry me.'

2

It had seemed quite simple and inevitable then to choose
a diamond for her ring of alliance, an alliance which in
the years to come would bind her more to the House of
Chardin than the man whose life she had promised to
share.

She had not known what stunned her most, his words
or the diamonds, or quite what to concentrate on first.
Delighted with the effect of his proposal, Jean-Claude
took her hand and said gently, 'Brilliant, my dearest, I
love you. I am asking you to marry me. You must pick
your own diamond – and I can't think of anyone better
qualified to do the choosing!'

She was enough in love, enough under the diamonds'
spell to accept – and leave the vault with a perfect fifteen-
carat gem tucked casually into her pocket.

It was natural afterwards to go quietly and wordlessly,
bodies entwined, hearts thumping with anticipation, up
the rickety staircase of his house in the Marais. Jean-
Claude had recently bought the magnificent old mansion
only a stone's throw from the sixteenth-century Hotel
Particulier owned by his parents.

'I've done nothing to it yet except on the top floor,
there will be an elevator eventually,' he explained as they
toiled their way breathlessly upwards. At last he pushed
on a heavy oak door and, extricating one arm from their
embrace, illuminated a charming circular room, built in
one of the ancient turrets. The walls were hung with ivory
watered silk, the high ceiling was tented and the enormous
bed draped and hung with the same silk. Dignified walnut
furniture stood on rugs faded with time, spread over the
original wooden floors.

Jean-Claude led her towards the window and turned out the light.

'This has to be seen in the darkness,' he whispered. He pulled a heavy cord attached to the massed silk which shrouded one semi-circular wall. Like a theatre curtain opening on a stage set, the thick drapes swung slowly back to reveal the impact of the Paris night, the Île de la Cité, Notre Dame resplendent in its floodlight and the whole of the magic city, incandescent and shimmering, at their feet. She stood at his side, enchanted. Without a word he began to undress her there in the dark, so softly that she shivered at the feather brush of his fingertips. Holding her breath, she felt the cool current of air as her dress fell at her feet.

She remained as though frozen and he turned her towards him, outlining the tender curves of breast and thigh against the luminous Paris sky. He drew her gently to the bed which yielded invitingly to the pressure of their bodies.

'No ordinary bed this,' he told her smugly much later, 'but a bed of great experience! It was once the amorous couch of the courtesan Ninon de Lenclos, the legendary "Grande Horizontale" of the Belle Époque, who still relished lovers at the age of ninety.'

His lovemaking was as his courtship – elegant, controlled and spectacular. His lips sought hers, then retreated, sought hers again and then wandered from the warmth of her returned pressure to seek fresh fields of exploration. As an insect flits from flower to flower in search of the perfect nectar, his mouth tasted her, tantalized her, aroused her, seemed about to settle and was gone, until – maddened with desire – she held his head fast, but he gently freed himself and still as tenderly and rhythmically, his long smooth body barely brushing hers, with the consummate skill of a musician, played her fortissimo and pianissimo. As soon as her yearning body yielded to his insistent caresses he retracted, only to lead her on again, playing every erotic chord in her body until she

29

moaned for him to stop and pleaded with him to enter her.

A piercing ray of sunlight woke her, streaming over the pillows and turning the spreading strands of her hair to molten gold. Jean-Claude, elegant in a cashmere dressing gown with a Paisley cravat, hair smoothly brushed and smelling of vetiver, was looking down at her and smiling.

'Good God!' She pulled up the satin sheets and retreated into the pillows at the brisk tap on the door, then her face flushed a deep pink at the memory of the night's voluptuousness.

'Put the tray down over there please, Fabrice! My fiancée and I will breakfast by the window.' The manservant deposited the silver tray of fragrant coffee and brioches on the table and exited with polished aplomb.

Brilliant soon realized they had become betrothed in the old-fashioned sense of the word, and the reckless feeling of abandon induced by her momentous decision of the night before soon gave way to more sober reflections, as Jean-Claude began to outline her responsibilities as a future member of the House of Chardin.

It was with some trepidation that she returned to the Ritz, packed her suitcase and sent a cryptic message to Zylos that she was off to the country in pursuit of an important contract. She picked up the book *Chardin – Joailliers des Rois de France* from the bedside table and tucked it dutifully into her handbag. That very afternoon they left for Treilhan, lovely, verdant Treilhan, to meet the family and tell them of their happiness.

Brilliant fell in love with the Manoir de Treilhan at first sight and it was always to be the only real Chardin home for her. Jean-Claude's Breton grandparents lived there – Grand'père Ambrose had worked for Chardin in his youth, but only briefly and unwillingly. His real passion had been horses and his stud-farm at Treilhan, with its low ceilings and open hearths, still had the feeling of a gentleman farmer's estate of the seventeenth century.

On the autoroute, seated next to Jean-Claude at the wheel of his modish Bentley, Brilliant perused the Chardin book, in between sneaking sidelong glances at his insouciant profile that made her heart pound.

She soon came to realize that a sense of humour and the Maison Chardin were not compatible.

'Good God! They were a crafty bunch, your ancestors. As skilled at survival as making jewellery!'

He frowned in distaste and she felt immediately that she had made a gaffe, impugning the Chardin name.

The succinct little book informed her that the Chardin renown stemmed from Honoré de Chardin, court jeweller to Louis XIV. Honoré's skill and sumptuous workmanship assured him a secure place at Louis's court, and after his inspired creation of the sunburst design, which became the Sun King's official emblem, he was assured of a title as well. Louis conferred on the new Comte de Treilhan some obscure lands in a remote rocky corner of Brittany, where the sea teemed with fish and the gulls cried endlessly over flinty fields rushing steeply down to the sea.

Honoré was an extremely astute man as well as the greatest jeweller of his age. He knew that what Louis required both of him and his work – conspicuous opulence – should be allied always to a certain classical restraint in his craft as in his private life. This good taste and common sense permeated every aspect of Honoré's life. He married the gifted daughter of an ancient Breton family to run the manoir he erected on his estates. The Comte escaped the carnage of the Revolution by living the life of a country squire at Treilhan, closing down the family business and sending his two sons to find their fortune in Martinique. Ten years later the older brother returned with a stunning Creole wife and a bevy of dark-eyed babies. The younger Chardin remained in Martinique, bought sugar plantations and prospered. His family were related by marriage

31

to Josephine de Beauharnais, the lovely Martiniquaise who later bewitched Napoleon and became his Empress.

During the Third Empire, the fortunes of the Chardins, reestablished in their shop in the Place Vendôme, were once more consolidated. Josephine's love of fine jewellery was legendary and she honoured Pascal Chardin with more titles and land in the distant Auvergne.

They had survived. Common sense, hard work – an element of luck – seizing the opportunity. . . . Brilliant swallowed and glanced at Jean-Claude. A premonition, fear for the future, gripped her as they turned into the long drive of poplars that led to the gates of Treilhan. Was she being foolish, what did she know of this handsome young man so masterfully pointing out the sights of the Chardin estate? Would she survive as an individual, or would she be swallowed up by a ruthless enterprise that did not tolerate failure?

They had arrived in the gently gathering dusk. The studded front door swung open to greet them and all her doubts were swept away in the warmth of Ambrose and Amélie's welcome, the barking of excited dogs and the delicious smell of peat fires and new-baked bread. Old Paulette, the maid who had come to Treilhan as a young girl, wiped the tears from a face as wrinkled as a last year's pippin and showed Brilliant to a charming muslin-decked bedroom, next to the master's suite in the west wing.

But nothing in the first hectic week of love had prepared her for Marie-Laure. The devastating Marie-Laure! Jean-Claude's mother had arrived as Brilliant was dressing for dinner. Her chauffeur-driven Mercedes scrunched to a halt in a wide arc on the gravel and she sprang out and went straight to her private sitting room, after greeting her in-laws with a perfunctory kiss. She sent immediately for her son.

'Shut the door! This conversation will, I hope, be private.'

When her son had surprised her with the news that she

should come at once to Treilhan to meet his future wife, Marie-Laure had been in her salon with the Duchesse de Teizay and could not give proper vent to her feelings.

'And why does this meeting have to take place at Treilhan and not in Paris? I suppose you think your grandparents will give this wild idea moral support?'

Jean-Claude shut the door and then turned the key in the lock, his lips pursed in a caustic smile. He looked at his mother with an expression of veiled sensuality and she knew that nothing had changed. Her son still belonged to her.

'Maman, I did it for you! Brilliant is of noblesse and then there is the matter of the diamond, to which she could have a legitimate claim and might one day manage to acquire.'

Marie-Laure's eyes flashed.

'For me!' She vaguely remembered a past conversation about an arranged marriage for convention's sake, but this . . . to an American . . . 'Noblesse! A penniless émigrée.' But there was grudging acknowledgement in Marie-Laure's voice. The Curnonsky name was a respected one and the French relatives were sought after in the right circles. 'As for the diamond, she can hardly inherit it, and you are in no position to buy it.'

Jean-Claude lowered his eyes. Like most children of old French families he was kept on a tight financial leash. Strict laws of inheritance ensured the integral survival of ancient property.

'But you will see, Maman, she has style, and something . . . something indefinable. . . .'

'You will soon tire of that. Come here, Jean-Claude.'

He went compliantly, succumbing to the erotic thrill of the forbidden which had started when he first learned that what he did with his mother was wrong, and because it was wrong it had been irresistible. Before that, when she had roused him as a child, it had seemed natural, and only later had it become a drug and an obsession.

'*Nounours*, come here!' She loosened his tie with her

33

elegant oval-tipped fingers. 'How can you have sex with her, it will be vile and vulgar.'

'Maman!' He shifted and glanced at his watch.

'We have time.' She smiled softly as her fingers found his flesh. 'She will have to learn to wait for you, *n'est ce pas*?' She patted the couch at her side. 'You will have to convince me . . . or else I may be very angry with this . . . this Brilliant.'

Ah . . . yes! Jean Claude closed his eyes. His mother, ever elegant, ever refined, knew how to please him. Marie-Laure's mouth relaxed into a triumphant smile. Her son still belonged to her. She was not ready yet to give him to another woman.

Brilliant, putting the finishing touches to her toilette, hummed cheerfully as she brushed her hair and twisted it into a chignon at the nape of her neck. There was something about the Mary Poppins decoration of the room that made her feel sixteen again, and virginal. She smiled wryly, but it was true. Maybe it was the effect of an engagement – there was something old-fashioned and formal about it – and she even caught herself wistfully regretting that she hadn't come chaste to Jean-Claude's bed.

She looked at the little secretaire with its neat arrangement of crested writing paper and envelopes. She would sit down after dinner and write and tell her mother all about her engagement. She felt so ridiculously happy and optimistic, she wanted to embrace the world.

She put down the hairbrush and slipped on the demure silk dress she considered becoming for a first meeting with one's future mother-in-law, then clasped a simple row of pearls around her neck. One last glance in the looking glass was reassuring. She looked nervous, but tasteful and well-bred.

She was leaving her room when she heard Jean-Claude's voice in the hall below. Her heart was beating fast and, feeling suddenly anxious, she leaned over the banister and called to him softly. Her voice trailed to a whisper and a strange fear tugged at her heart. She pulled back into the shadows and watched, pale-faced and silent.

They were walking away from her down the galleried hall, arms entwined and heads together, whispering intently. The young woman's head rested intimately on Jean-Claude's shoulder, his hand stroked her arm as he explained something. The woman lifted her head and looked inquiringly up at him and Brilliant recognized with a shock the same profile, the same eyes and set of precise, finely moulded features, the luxuriant, not-quite-black hair. Of course! His mother, the famed Marie-Laure. But so young, so almost indecently girlish, her posture so like a lovesick maiden's. . . . Brilliant was gripped by an inexplicable anguish and her mouth was so dry that she had difficulty calling out his name, loudly this time, as she stepped forward into the light and started down the stairs towards them.

'Jean-Claude!'

The engrossed couple whirled round to stare at her and – surely she didn't imagine it – they drew protectively closer and Marie-Laure tightened her grip on his arm.

'Maman, this is my fiancée, Countess Curnonsky.'

Brilliant smiled, but felt an unaccountable chill. Why had she not obeyed her primeval instincts, which in her case had always been infallible, and simply turned, fled and left them? But she loved him. She, Brilliant Curnonsky, who had never given a thought to fighting for a man, found herself entering into a grim battle with another woman, caught up in a treadmill from which she could not escape. Beautiful Marie-Laure in her precise Saint-Laurent clothes, ankles trimly together in their Gucci shoes, dark hair tied back with a flat bow from the perfect oval of an impassive face, muttered a barely audible '*on va voir*', when Jean-Claude introduced his future wife. Brilliant felt a stranger to them both as she took Marie-Laure's outstretched hand.

'My dear, my son has been telling me all about you and the reality is even more beautiful than the description!'

Marie-Laure felt disposed to be charitable, although her other hand increased its pressure on her son's arm. Her eyes swept the American woman from top to toe. Yes, she had breeding, she would do. She was beautiful, of course, but she had something more – she could quite understand what Jean-Claude saw in her. There was an indefinable aura of mystery, a hint of a secret locked away, a haunted quality that touched the heart yet at the same time intrigued. If she had been a woman whose proclivities lay *that* way she might well have been interested. She would have to get Marguerite de Launay to look her over.

'We must go and eat, Paulette is getting anxious about her souffle!' Marie-Laure relinquished her grip on her son and tucked her arm confidentially through Brilliant's. 'How fortunate to have a daughter-in-law named for a diamond.'

Her chatter was designed to put Brilliant at her ease as she led the way to the dining room. Perhaps she should let her son marry this American. They could work out a marriage settlement to exclude her. It would help curtail the influence of Boy de la Broussaillère and Jean-Claude's other artistic friends.

The proximity of Marie-Laure and her cloying chypre scent gave Brilliant a sensation of suffocation. She glanced imploringly over her shoulder at Jean-Claude who followed behind them, but his face was impassive. Then all was bustle and candlelight and appetizing smells as Amélie, scented and rustling in grey taffeta and old lace, a simple gold crucifix at her throat, shepherded them into dinner.

The painful memory of that meal often came back to haunt Brilliant in the months to come. Ambrose and Amélie presided at opposite ends of the table and she sat alone, feeling like a plaintiff in the dock, facing Marie-Laure and Jean-Claude. Marie-Laure's conversation, elegant and erudite, started out with the general and progressed to the particular. Without sacrificing one whit of the requirements of good taste she somehow contrived to extract a myriad of personal details of Brilliant's background and private life. Brilliant's flesh seemed to be on fire and her mind a confusion of conflicting impressions. Her overwhelming recollection was a sense of irrational shame; a humiliating suspicion that she was somehow competing for Jean-Claude's affections. Marie-Laure seemed to be conducting a flirtation with him in front of her eyes, or was it just her excessively artificial style? The fond looks, the melting smiles, the playful raps on the wrist – I must be going mad, thought Brilliant, perhaps I am just extraordinarily on edge. Later, much later, she came to realize the significance of those first impressions.

Towards the end of the meal Brilliant put her hand to her throbbing head and Marie-Laure was instantly solicitous.

'Brilliant, my dear, we are being so selfish. It is such a delight to have you with us that we are forgetting you must be tired. It is such a strain to meet one's future in-laws. . . .' She leaned forward and pressed Brilliant's hand. 'I haven't forgotten how it was for me!' She beamed at Ambrose and Amélie. 'We must let you get some rest, what must you be thinking of us?'

Brilliant smiled shakily. Perhaps she was just overtired and emotional. That would explain everything. She let herself be led off to bed by Amélie, who fussed around the room checking on her creature comforts. After smiling assurances from Brilliant that all was well, she kissed her fondly and left her to a night of fitful sleep.

Marie-Laure left the next morning to join Honoré, Jean Claude's father, in Paris, to play hostess at one of the sumptuous soirées for which she had become renowned, and with her went any cloud that might darken Brilliant's happiness.

The grandparents adored her, as did old Paulette, gratified at her excellent appetite. It was hard to leave after those few blissful days, she had so completely fallen under Treilhan's spell.

There were two letters waiting for her on a silver salver when she returned to her room at the Ritz. One was from Stavros Zylos, devastated that his talented protégée had thrown in her job, albeit for an illustrious marriage. The second was in meticulous copperplate writing on crested writing paper, from Honoré Chardin, in the Rue du Parc-Royal.

In his letter Honoré begged her, in engagingly informal language, to forgive him for not being at Treilhan to welcome her into the Chardin fold. He was suffering from an attack of gout, which made travelling an agony. He would be delighted if she could call tomorrow, Thursday, for a glass of forbidden champagne before dinner. He apologized on behalf of Marie-Laure, who had an early engagement with the Orléans family and could not be present.

Just before seven the next evening, Brilliant was shown into the elegant salon of the Chardins' eighteenth-century house in the Rue du Parc Royal by a servant whose livery bore the *fleur-de-lys* crest of Marie-Laure's Breton family. The room looked empty and Brilliant frowned. Honoré had stipulated between six-thirty and seven, but Brilliant, perhaps subconsciously, had delayed her arrival to avoid the possibility of meeting Marie-Laure.

The weather had turned colder and a light rain was falling. Feeling chilled, Brilliant approached the log fire crackling in the grate. Hidden from her by the broad back of a wing chair, Honoré was dozing, his leg raised on a low stool and a silver-topped cane in his inert hand.

With his prematurely silver hair and high-coloured cheeks he resembled his mother Amélie, and looked what he was, a country gentleman who had lost his way into the Rue du Parc-Royal.

Honoré had been 'caught' very young, while on a summer vacation from university in Nantes. He had been twenty and desperately shy, rather half-heartedly attending a course at the Faculté des Beaux Arts in order to appease his parents. At eighteen Marie-Laure, the daughter of the neighbouring Comte de Bassenet, was already age-old in womanly wiles. Her father was impoverished *ancien* gentry, but Marie-Laure desperately wanted to shine in society, and that required money. She was slender, dark-haired and quick-witted, with a deep musical timbre to her voice. Honoré was captivated and the families were delighted at the match. At first he adored her, but after the wedding and the birth of the son she so badly wanted she treated him with cold indifference, lavishing all her attention on the male heir. Marie-Laure had been quick to realize that Honoré had no real interest in running the Chardin business. As the years passed she had become the company's driving force, together with her son Jean-Claude, who inherited in full measure the social snobbery, passion for detail and acquisitiveness of the de Bassenets.

Brilliant coughed gently. Honoré opened his eyes effortlessly and looked at her without surprise.

'My dear, how pathetic to be caught snoozing like an old dodderer! It's these beastly pills I'm taking – make you doze off at the drop of a hat. Here, could you give me a hand, the leg gets very stiff, sitting about like this.'

She helped Honoré to his feet and he grasped her hand, then leaned heavily on his cane.

'I'm not normally decrepit like this, you know. Spry as an old goat, usually. The attacks last about a week, I'm just over the peak of this one now.'

He stood with his head cocked on one side and appraised her critically but not unkindly, with a shrewd eye used to judging horseflesh.

'Hmmm . . .' he said at last, his pale eyes twinkling. 'I have to hand it to the young fellow – if he found you, he can't be all that bad . . .'

Brilliant raised her eyebrows and then laughed with him.

'Ring that bell, would you, m'dear! This calls for champagne. Strictly forbidden, of course, like all the other good things in life. Can you imagine, no white wine, no strawberries – no lobster! What else is a Breton to eat?'

'No lobster!' Brilliant looked appalled.

'You love it too? As a boy my job was to look after the lobster pots at Treilhan. I'll get some sent up and Aubin'll cook for us. He's from St Brieuc – knows how to do it the only way – à la nage.'

As the footman served the champagne, Brilliant looked discreetly around the room. It reflected Marie-Laure's impeccable if unimaginative taste, from the Toile de Jouy curtains to the precisely placed objects on Louis tables.

Honoré intercepted her glance and grinned.

'Know anything about horses? Take my glass and go through that door, my dear.' He motioned with his head. 'I'll hobble after you. It's the only place I'm allowed to spread myself around a bit. You couldn't imagine a horse's rump in here!'

Brilliant offered to help, but Honoré independently refused a supporting arm.

'Good God, Brilliant, you've made me feel better already. Tuck the bottle under your arm, we'll take another glass in there.'

Honoré's study bore flamboyant witness to his passion for bloodstock. Oil paintings and framed photographs of favourite mares and rosetted prize-winners crammed the walls, bronzes of proud stallions sat on the bookcase and piles of *The Field* and *Courses et Elevage* were stacked up on the floor.

'That's me at Quimper in '47 on Barsillac!' Honoré pointed to a photograph of a jockey crowned with glory in the winning enclosure. 'I used to do a lot of point-to-pointing. Wouldn't think so to look at me now.' He patted his comfortable stomach.

Brilliant peered at the yellowing photograph. She could almost taste the salt spray on the handsome young jockey's lips, feel the texture of the sun-bleached hair, could sense the tautness of his chest muscles through his open silk shirt. She smiled at Honoré and he looked pleased, gratified that she had seen him as he was, in his golden prime.

'That's Sanharad, isn't it?' Brilliant studied the oil that had pride of place over the chimney piece. As a result of a brief acquaintance with an English peer who owned an illustrious stable she had become knowledgeable about racehorses, and her interest in breeding had lasted much longer than the relationship.

'Yes! He was bred at Treilhan.' Honoré looked at Brilliant with new respect. Oblivious of the time they chatted over the rest of the champagne of bloodlines and brood mares, of stallions and stable-mates, until the servant tapped and announced that Honoré's dinner was ready.

He looked at Brilliant regretfully.

'I would have asked you to dine with me, but my son gave me one hour only, you're expected elsewhere, I believe?'

Brilliant nodded and an unaccountable lump rose to her throat. Honoré had touched her with the warmth of his welcome, for the first time she really felt she was joining a family. But there was something else, too, that her intuitive nature was quick to sense – Honoré was lonely. As she prepared to leave he took her hand in his.

'We need new blood and common sense in this family, my dear!' His voice was gruffly sincere. 'I welcome you with all my heart, and wish you every happiness.'

He watched her go with sadness. Why should he have doubts, she was so very much in love. But Honoré instinctively recognized in Brilliant the woman he could have had, the passion of a generous nature doomed to run aground, as his had done, on the treacherous rocks of cold egoism. As for Brilliant, she found in Honoré, who was to become a lifelong friend, the embodiment of the spirit of Treilhan.

3

And so, four months after they had met, with the conflicting blessings of the family, Brilliant and Jean-Claude were married, not fashionably in Paris but in a magical summer twilight in the family chapel at Treilhan.

She wore a wonderful dress which floated round her like wisps of moonlight, its smoky white chiffon swirling and undulating in an invisible breeze, scattering streams of starlight from its tiny crystal beads. On her head she wore a little high-pointed diamond coronet with a gauzy veil billowing round her face. She wore diamonds in her ears, around her throat, at her wrists and in her hair – she was literally showered with diamonds from the fabulous Chardin collection, with, of course, Jean-Claude's magnificent ring on her finger. In the candlelit chapel she was dazzling; thousands of prisms of iridescent light etched her in an aureole of enchantment.

She was astonishingly lovely that night, and her mother, watching in the shadows, shed tears for her vibrant warmth, her touching happiness. Madalena had arrived from New York a few days earlier and declared that she had found her second home, so immediate was her rapport with Ambrose and Amélie, so great was her approval of Treilhan and its sturdily independent way of life. Her greatest wish for her daughter had always been that she would find – and inspire – a great love, as she had had with Vitya. Over the years Madalena had watched her daughter mature from a gauche teenager into an assured young woman, and as a mother she knew the heartache that Brilliant had often tried to hide.

When she had received Brilliant's letter telling of her engagement, the first of a rapturous flood of correspondence in which Brilliant described the depth of her love for Jean-Claude and her bliss at becoming part of the House of Chardin, Madalena's happiness had been muted at the knowledge that they must live so far apart. She had revealed nothing of her own disappointment, but sent her daughter letters full of love and encouragement.

Madalena felt that her whole life had been devoted to this joyous moment, to see Brilliant married on the arm of the man she loved. Yet – and she glanced across the chapel to where Marie-Laure stood at Honoré's side – with the intuition of the child-like and inherently good, Madalena sensed the presence of evil. Since Marie-Laure's arrival at the family dinner last night Madalena's peace of mind had been shattered. What could she do – what should she do? But also, with the instinct of the idealist, Madalena recognized something else. She knew that Jean-Claude, who, as Madalena watched, took Brilliant's hand and placed on her finger a plain band of gold, was drawn to her daughter not from love alone but from need. Brilliant's love could help him, protect him from this mother whose influence she instinctively felt to be harmful. Surely, this altruism had always been part of Madalena's philosophy of life? In spite of herself, Madalena struggled with gnawing feelings of anxiety and doubt. She shivered. With the lengthening summer shadows the air of the chapel was growing cold. What could she do but watch and wait and pray for their happiness?

Marie-Laure, subtly elegant in pale grey with a sweeping hat, held the beaming Honoré's arm and watched the ceremony with narrowed eyes. Maybe it was better this way. As it was inevitable Jean-Claude should marry one day, all to the good if it were to an outsider, an American, not one of their own kind. Her revenge, being protracted and almost imperceptible, would give greater satisfaction.

The newly-weds spent the honeymoon off the Breton coast at Belle-Île, in a tiny cottage belonging to Ambrose and Amélie. It was perfect, thatched like a beehive, white-washed and oakbeamed, with a gigantic muslin-draped fourposter to which young Natalie, commissioned from the village to cook and clean for them, brought steaming coffee and warm croissants every morning, modestly averting her eyes from the two beautiful bodies so close together under the covers.

Together they spent long summer days combing the wild rocky beaches and coves for molluscs, and Jean-Claude taught her how to eat oursins, best collected after the full moon – to break the spiny outer shell cleanly in two and swallow the palpating urchin in one gulp; head back, savour it, inhale it, the essence of the sea in one prickly half circle.

Soon after their arrival they were caught in a fierce squall in Jean-Claude's boat and arrived back to the cottage chilled and exhausted. Brilliant spent the remaining days of the honeymoon nursing him through a high fever. Her bedside manner had never been put to the test and she administered the doctor's orders of cooling drinks and light blankets, secretly marvelling how his chiselled features, wanly reclining against pillows of crisp Breton lace, contrived to look stylish even with a temperature of one hundred and four.

The honeymoon, she recalled, had not been memorable for its sexual activity, but rather for its tenderness and companionship. Certainly she had no reason to complain about his appreciation of her selfless care. When they returned to Paris and threw themselves into plans to finish the apartment in the Marais, Brilliant found the effects of his chill seemed to linger; it had a debilitating effect on his virility and it was some time before he made love to her properly again.

Her new life in Paris as Madame Jean-Claude Chardin took up all her time and attention; for the present she was happy and there was much to learn. Their social life was more formal than that to which she had been accustomed in America, and the Chardins regularly entertained a socially prominent circle. To her amazement she found something of an anachronism, the French aristocracy, was alive and flourishing. The Revolution might never have been. She found it necessary to learn the etiquette of placements and introductions; woe betide the upstart who introduced a Marquise to a Duchesse – or should it have been the other way around, she never could remember.

Then there was the family business to learn, and Brilliant, bored with discussing swatches of fabric and paint effects with interior decorators, threw herself wholeheartedly, at Honoré's invitation, into learning the Chardin operation.

A close understanding soon sprung up between Brilliant and Honoré, based not just on a shared interest in bloodstock and gastronomy, but on something much more fundamental, a mutual antipathy towards Marie-Laure. It was always understood between them but never articulated and their meetings, in Honoré's club in Paris or at Brilliant's home, were always arranged to exclude her.

As if in revenge for her husband's high regard for Brilliant, Marie-Laure became even more possessive of her son. She would call him up at inconvenient hours of the evening, often just after they had sat down to dinner, and imperiously demand his presence, pleading the most feeble of excuses – a headache or a message that had not been passed on. Brilliant was for the most part understanding. She remembered the close relationship she had had with Madalena, and tried to imagine how she would feel if an only son were lost to marriage.

The first year passed quickly enough, absorbing the Chardin business, flying to Tel Aviv, Hong Kong, Bombay, centres of the diamond trade, living, loving, thinking precious stones. This was a love affair more genuine than the real one that was even now expiring before her eyes.

Jean-Claude never seemed to recover from the enervated sexual state of their honeymoon. Never again were they to reenact the eroticism of that first ecstatic night. She came to loathe his soft caressing hand on her arm,

45

his unfathomable eyes that promised her everything but gave nothing. She could not understand at first and became by turns demanding – exploring his body with a thousand provocative caresses – and patiently acquiescent, waiting passively for him to want her. But he was happy to lapse into a comfortable intimacy, sharing her bed and her life like a faithful hound. There were rare times when she felt him roused against her as she lay turned away from him in the early morning, and he would enter her forcibly, but she had been made rigid by the anguish and constraint of the relationship and could not respond, lying motionless, her face bathed in tears.

Equally disappointing as her relationship with her husband was the realization that she was unlikely to have any real influence on the running of the House of Chardin. Her abilities as a buyer, her phenomenal eye and her flair for design were used to advantage, but the cabal were careful to exclude her from any policy-making decisions.

Quite soon after her marriage she had rushed into the showroom in the Place Vendôme, late for a lunch appointment with Jean-Claude, full of enthusiasm over her new designs for the Duchesse de Cressay's baguette diamond collar.

'Monsieur Jean-Claude is in a meeting.' The receptionist pouted through Bardot lips. 'He sends his apologies, but will be with you presently.'

Brilliant smiled her thanks and turned her attention to some alterations in the window display. Why did she have the feeling that all the showroom staff were Marie-Laure's harpies . . . ? She made some mental notes on the shop interior, small improvements that jarred against her commercial instincts.

The House of Chardin was the epitome of French conservatism, with a clientele that read like the Almanac de Gotha, but it was losing ground to the jewel houses which had opened their doors to a wider public, new money, without losing a whit of their prestige. She frowned and shook her head as she witnessed an example of what she called the Chardin Freeze-out Policy happening in front of her very eyes.

A slight Frenchman in his early forties, black hair receding over a bony skull, obviously wishing he had never set foot over the Chardin threshold, was being given the treatment by Denise, their leading vendeuse. The silent scorn on her intricately made-up face was worthy of Marcel Marceau as she took in her customer's diffident request, which Brilliant, just out of earshot, could not quite catch.

'Denise . . .' Brilliant was at her side in a second and managed a taut smile. '. . . I didn't quite hear Monsieur's request, but I just wanted to remind you of our new items in a more interesting price range . . .' For a dangerous moment two pairs of eyes flashed, then Denise gave a pained half-smile.

'But . . . Madame Chardin . . .' The man's small black eyes looked desperately from one to the other like a cornered fox.

'No, no, Denise! I insist.' Brilliant smiled disarmingly, then turned her attention to the Frenchman. 'Perhaps, Monsieur, you could describe the sort of thing you have in mind? We have a most varied range of merchandise.'

'*Mais oui, Madame!*' His face broke into relieved creases as he blurted out: 'You see, my wife . . . I need a very special gift . . . at last she has given me the child for which we've waited so long . . .'

Brilliant quickly spirited him away from Denise's glacial environs and soon had him happily inspecting a tray of the small pieces she had specially commissioned for just such a customer.

'A Chardin never serves on the shop floor!'

She turned to find Marie-Laure's eyes, two splinters of ice, inches from her own. A stab of apprehension gripped her. She looked slowly from Marie-Laure's venom to Jean-Claude's stare of disapproval.

Like a naughty child summoned back to the nursery, she followed obediently behind them to the office, where they closed the door on the smirking satisfaction of the shop-floor staff.

'I am sure, my dear, you must have temporarily forgotten who and where you are?'

Brilliant began to giggle uncontrollably as Marie-Laure's face darkened and contorted.

'Whatever your circumstances might have been in America, we do ask you to consider the family name while you are here.'

Brilliant continued to laugh helplessly as she looked from one outraged face to the other. Jean-Claude extricated an immaculate handkerchief from his breast pocket with one elegant movement of the wrist and handed it to her.

'I think you had better sit down, *chérie* . . .' There was real concern in his voice. '. . . I have been wondering lately if you haven't been under too much strain . . .'

'No, no – I'm quite all right.' She dabbed at her streaming eyes, secretly horrified at the violence of her emotions, first the cold anger that had swept over her and now this hysterical mirth. She sat down at the desk and looked at them levelly. She was composed now, her former anger under control, but no less evident.

'Marie-Laure, we are simply losing out to other houses – Cartier, Tiffany, even Van Cleef's – by not selling to a more varied clientele. Our staff aren't trained in customer relations – by just a change in basic philosophy, a new approach, we could double our sales and improve our staid image.'

'Our image!' The words were an outraged hiss. 'We will never turn ourselves into one of those emporia, selling trinkets just like Woolworth's. Do you think we want people to come in off the streets?' Her voice rose to a small shriek. 'We would rather close shop than change our philosophy, which is catering to our own class of clientele.'

Marie-Laure swept out of the shop to keep her lunch appointment with the Comtesse de Paris, leaving Brilliant chewing her lip in irritation. Later that week she took Honoré into her confidence, explaining to him the need to change, even if out of basic egalitarian principles. To her disappointment he merely spread his hands and said gently, 'My dear, even if I did agree with you, which I mostly do, there is nothing – but nothing – I could do against them.' He shook his head sadly.

She soon came to realize that Jean-Claude's passionate interest in her appearance was an extension of his own persona; he regarded her as a showpiece for the House of Chardin. Dressing in couture clothes, premières, the Opera, first nights, fashionable parties, eating out at the right restaurants, seeing and being seen became an indispensable part of her life.

Jean-Claude loved the razzmatazz of the couture fashion shows, where front-row seats were always reserved for the starry young couple. After the Saint-Laurent spring extravaganza in the February of the second year of their marriage he took her, as he often did, to lunch at the Espadon Restaurant in the Ritz out of sentiment for their first meeting and, not least, because it was the venue of the *haut monde* who meant so much to him.

Aristide Jouissac, theatre critic of *Le Monde*, and his actress wife Sylvette LeMarre had also been at the show and were joining them for lunch. She and Brilliant crossed the foyer to the ladies' room, Sylvette filling her in with the latest bits of salacious gossip from the Comédie Française.

Sylvette was one of Brilliant's favourite Parisiennes. Born in the Auvergne, she had the Auvergnat's tough stockiness of frame and bony obstinate skull, for all that it was adorned with the best couture clothes and exquisite make-up, and the most enchanting little vixen's face, slanting green eyes, tip-tilted nose and a laughing, generous mouth.

She had the Frenchwoman's devastating ability to combine ruthless practicality with shameless coquetry which, together with a reputation as a *grande amoureuse* and not inconsiderable talent, had made her one of the Comédie

49

Française's most sought-after actresses. Critics raved over her Manon and her Marguerite; Marivaux might have had her in mind when creating the part of Silvia.

Sylvette bobbed down next to Brilliant in front of the low dressing-table mirror, licked her fingers and pulled a few curls from under her toque, twisting them adroitly around her temples and nape, preening this way and that, so obviously delighted with her reflection in a *belle époque* suit that Brilliant smiled with pleasure.

'You're like a cat that's finished the cream! That colour really suits you.'

Quite by accident the two women were wearing clothes whose mood recalled the turn of the century – Brilliant in a jewel-green velvet suit, straight skirted and deeply belted, with luxurious fur at wrist and neck; Sylvette's chestnut curls tucked under a black astrakhan toque, her curvaceous little body displayed to full advantage in a Russian hussar's jacket, deep red, with astrakhan collar and black frogging marching down the middle.

'Brilliant, *chère*, you must have seen him – Serge Meyrac?' Brilliant nodded, she had caught a glimpse of Sylvette's new director in the foyer as they came in.

'He's here lunching with old Sanceret of *Figaro*, but he's shaking him off quickly and we're meeting at the theatre to go over that difficult bit in *Phèdre*. He has the most amazing chest, like a barrel, and *tout poilu*, absolutely all over – hair, I mean – his back, backside, everything, so primeval, *n'est ce pas?*' Sylvette threw back her head in a great sensual guffaw, revealing the strong column of her throat and a row of even, greedy teeth.

There was some perplexity in Brilliant's answering smile. Aristide was as perfect an Adonis as one could hope to meet, if a trifle studied in his manners and toilette, like many Frenchmen she knew. Women flattered and pursued him, actresses went in fear and trepidation of his more acerbic reviews. In public they were the ideal couple, loving and supportive, much in demand socially, yet Sylvette consumed men as other women would chocolate, carelessly yet compulsively, apparently suffering neither guilt nor surfeit.

As the two women crossed the restaurant to their table on the heels of a hand-hoisted waiter, there was a murmur of recognition. Sylvette nodded here and there to acquaintances and, no doubt, thought Brilliant, who for some reason felt curiously deflated and detached, to several ex-lovers as well, to judge from the avidity of the male faces turned towards them.

The two men were deep in conversation, their faces a few inches apart, and they sprung to eager attention as their wives reached the table. Brilliant smiled ruefully at the warmth with which her husband greeted Sylvette. At first she had been jealous of the attention he paid every pretty woman he met, or man for that matter. Now she had come to realize it was part of his character; the winning charm, the fulsome package he was at such pains to cultivate.

She remembered that lunch for the aching emptiness she felt inside, amid the smart lash of Aristide's acidulous gossip and the toing and froing of the decorative world; for a sense of loss, of love longed for but always elusive. She remembered it too for the final caressing gesture of Aristide's, that somehow angered her with its intimacy and complicity.

They were leaving the foyer after the meal, pulling up collars and girding themselves for the bitter wind that whirled flurries of snow across the grey expanse of the Place Vendôme, when Brilliant glanced back, looking for Jean-Claude in the vestibule.

In the corner, his profile sharply etched against an ebony caryatid, Aristide helped Jean-Claude with his overcoat. His face, over her husband's shoulder, came close, smiled and whispered, brushing his ear with his lips. His hands, white against the dark cloth, smoothed the shoulders of the coat in one studiously intimate gesture. Jean-Claude turned on him the engaging, boyish smile. Brilliant, face burning, pushed her way out into the wind.

Was that all it was, just cloying sweetness, meted out to everyone, just his charming ways? She knew now, at least, that she received only her share, no more than that, of the carefully controlled emotional machine that was Jean-Claude Chardin.

One freezing March day three weeks after this incident, when a lingering layer of snow had frozen hard and turned the Place Vendôme into a giant skating rink, she arrived early at the Ritz for a lunch appointment with a plebeian client contemptuously passed on by Marie-Laure.

That week the hotel had organized a prestigious antiquarian book seminar, being held in conjunction with an exhibition of rare medieval books at the Petit Palais. Brilliant was amused to see knots of venerable professors, academicians and collectors chatting in the elegant nooks and corners which normally housed the city's mondaines. Many of them were American, and it was heart-warming for her to pick up the accents of home. She descended the small staircase to the downstairs ladies' cloakroom to check in her coat. As she passed the little booth next to it she overheard one such American on the telephone, obviously having difficulties with the language. She paused, not wishing to be inquisitive, but intrigued by the title of the book he was haltingly requesting.

She recognized it, thanks to Madalena, who had often laughingly quoted its pages as an antidote to modern feminist thinking, as *The Domostroy*, a medieval Russian treatise for women. In this venerable tome the Monk Silvester had set down the code of behaviour for Russian women – seclusion in the women's quarters, the *terem*, and a life of chastity, passivity and prayer. She could not see the man clearly, he had his back to her, a book was clutched under one arm and his head was down in the booth as he strained to catch the words on the other end of the line.

On an impulse she lingered, then approached the booth. The man looked up blankly and held the receiver away from his ear.

'Can I help? That is to say, I couldn't help overhearing

52

the name of the book you want – I know it – it's *The Domostroy*.' She stood, her coat over her arm, her cheeks burning slightly for no accountable reason.

He frowned, not understanding her at first, but when she repeated herself and he realized that she was not French, his face relaxed into a smile.

'You know it? Marvellous! I've got a copy here with me but I understand Pertuis Fils have the original by Silvester himself – the only other one is in the Hermitage. If you could just explain on the phone that they should hold it and I'll be there immediately . . . There's someone else after it . . .' He glanced apprehensively over his shoulder.

Brilliant laughed and took the receiver. 'I'd love to help!' Within minutes she had asked Pertuis Fils – Madame Pertuis had social aspirations and was a crony of Marie-Laure's – to bring the book to the Ritz.

The tension left the man's eyes and he smiled.

'You know the business well – I'm afraid I'm still a bit of an amateur! Are you representing a company?' How ridiculous of him – if she knew all about the book, she was probably after it herself.

Brilliant shook her head.

'No, no, I'm nothing to do with books. I'm here because I married a Frenchman . . . and . . . and I live here,' she finished lamely.

What eyes she had! Startling, heartbreaking eyes. They reminded him . . . he stared, trying to remember, then his heart contracted as he recalled the time, so long ago, when that diamond had first captured his imagination.

She felt uncomfortable under his appraisal and picked up her coat from the chair where she had left it. It was not the presumptuous physical inspection of the Frenchman, but a sad searching look that struck a nostalgic chord.

The American was tall and strong-featured, dark-haired with greying temples. She thought he might be a professor, as he had the slightly distracted air of the academic.

They both stood staring at each other and Brilliant could have moved on – but she did not want to go. Later, trying to rationalize the emotions of that brief encounter, she could only assume it was a sentimental craving for another kind of life, towards another kind of man, that had drawn her so much to this stranger.

Perhaps considering his silence ungallant, he asked tentatively if she would care for a drink, and, having twenty minutes before the arrival of Hervé Blanchard from La Baule, from whom she hoped to extract a particularly attractive order over lunch, Brilliant accepted.

As they sat alone in the small salon next to the Restaurant Espadon, a message arrived which reassured him.

'Monsieur Hillman, a gentleman from Pertuis Fils called to say he will be with you in half an hour.' Mr Hillman grinned broadly, his smile transforming the rather severe lines of his face. They talked about the exhibition at the Petit Palais, which she had seen, about her knowledge of the Russian book from her mother and about New York, where he lived. There was time for no more before the bell-boy's discreet hovering and his message, 'Monsieur Blanchard is waiting, Madame Chardin.'

Mr Hillman's eyes flickered and he glanced down at Jean-Claude's engagement ring and the plain band of gold on her finger.

'How stupid, we didn't introduce ourselves – and now you have to go.' He stood up and took her outstretched hand. His own hand was calloused and, seeing her slight frown, he apologized. 'I've been doing a lot of work on some land I bought in New England, it makes a change from my sheltered working life!'

Yes, a cloistered academic, a good family man, farm somewhere up in New England, cultivated friends, solid values, a faithful husband . . . all the things she might have had – had her life worked out differently.

Mr Hillman still had hold of her hand and was watching her intently. Suddenly, for no apparent reason, she moved forward and kissed him – why she did it she never could imagine. Her arms reached out for him, her lips miraculously found his. Not that he held back – no, to say that he merely responded would have been an understatement, and for Brilliant, used to the *délicatesse* of Jean-Claude's embrace, to be kissed so thoroughly by a man who really meant it was a novel experience. When he finally let her go his eyes were inscrutable.

He did not seem embarrassed when she stepped away, confused and wishing the ground would open up and swallow her. He just gently pressed her hand and mumbled a goodbye, his eyes telling her how much he wished that she did not have to go.

Whatever had possessed her to do it? It had nothing in common with wanting a man in the manner of Sylvette Lemarre – she had no lack of admirers of the dilettante kind. Was it an attraction towards him, specifically him, or just a man of his kind, a real man – however wide the parameters of that definition were? At any rate, she would never know. Never know what had caused this extraordinary effect.

She turned to find Hervé Blanchard waiting, titillated to have found the young Madame Chardin in such a compromising situation. She gave him a very difficult time over lunch which stimulated Hervé enormously. He put in an order for three important pieces for his mistress's birthday and later even Marie-Laure had to admit that Brilliant had a winning way with clients.

Jean-Claude spent the next weekend at Treilhan breaking in a new colt. The weather was bleak and Brilliant had decided not to go. Honoré was at Vichy for a cure and she felt listless and downhearted. On Sunday morning she received an urgent message from Ambrose. Jean-Claude had had a riding accident – nothing serious, a pulled muscle, possibly some broken ribs. He was being driven straight to the Polyclinique in Neuilly – if possible he wanted to be fit enough to attend the Sight in London on Monday morning. The Central Selling Organization allowed prestigious clients to view stones – known as 'goods' – which had been specifically requested in advance, once every five weeks at a 'sight'.

Brilliant arrived at the clinic a few minutes after Jean-Claude. The doctor confirmed Ambrose's diagnosis; nothing serious, but he would not be fit to travel for a few days.

'There's nothing for it, you must go in my place.' Jean-Claude smiled wanly and threw a long-suffering glance at the adoring young nurse hovering at his side. 'I'll telephone Henry Myers at the Trading Company first thing, so he can expect you. The box we've ordered is for Hervé Blanchard, so it's very personal to you. Women *are* allowed in the Diamond Company, you know!' He smiled at the surprise on her face.

At first she protested, but Jean-Claude continued to insist. He had seen her eyes light up and knew that it would be a personal triumph, the fulfilment of a lifelong ambition.

Later that morning she was packing a suitcase for London when she found she had mislaid her address book. She turned everything out of a drawer in her secretaire when a single sheet of ivory writing paper fluttered to the floor. Its *fleur-de-lys* emblem, Marie-Laure's family crest, stared up at her. She recoiled from its familiar blazon as if from a snake, and realized, in a sudden flash of insight, just how much she feared the influence of Jean-Claude's mother. The words swam up at her and as she held the paper to the light she could see the impression of the date from the first page: 30th September, two months after their wedding.

. . . something you will have to go through, a beastly thing, a mistake, but I understand now, and forgive you, and it will never come between us. Our life, our own special 'way' can never be affected. She may suspect, so be careful, my darling, because she would never, never understand. It is two months now since you went away from me and I have suffered such

56

pain from our separation. But then came your letter and I knew all would be well again and you would soon fly back to me, my handsome *nounours*. Don't worry, I can arrange everything. It is not advisable to think of divorce just yet, she will be hurt and toweringly angry – I think she has more 'character than you give her credit for – and may not be happy with the terms of the settlement. But a fool who doesn't read the terms of a wedding contract deserves the little that she gets! No. Far better to wait and let time do its work. You and she will naturally grow apart, for with her obvious sort of looks and vulgar sensuality she will inevitably commit *une faute* which will make the whole business easier to settle amicably. It troubles me of course to have . . .

Brilliant let the paper drop as though it held some noxious substance and wiped her hand down the side of her skirt, unconsciously trying to remove any trace of contact. A slow flush spread over her cheeks and she clutched at her ribs as though warding off an invisible blow. She had loved him so much, given herself to him completely, so convinced that he loved her in return. They were two women scrapping over a spoilt, handsome child who couldn't possibly love either of them. Marie-Laure Chardin, how much she had to answer for, that poisonous woman. What had she done to her son? And the wedding contract. Did Marie-Laure think her such a fool not to have read it? She was simply too proud to care; in fact her independent spirit had been shocked by such a prosaic document. A contract drawn up before marriage as to the precise distribution of the spoils should there be a breakdown was somehow unspeakably Gallic. She had preferred to pretend to be ignorant of the fact that in her and Jean-Claude's 'contract' instead of the usual '*séparations des biens*', had been inserted a trivial sum in full and final settlement. She remembered the look of contempt on Maître Boucicault's face as he handed her the pen to sign, looking from her to Jean-Claude and then back to Marie-Laure's impassive face.

She picked up the telephone, dialled a number and

jumped at the proximity of Marie-Laure's deeply melodic voice.

'Of course, Brilliant, my dear! You can come over now – is anything the matter? You don't sound well. Don't worry about Jean-Claude, I've just come from the Polyclinique and I have arranged to have him convalesce here while you are in London. Have you had lunch, can I offer you something?'

Feeling suddenly gauche and ridiculous, Brilliant mumbled barely audibly, 'Oh . . . er . . . nothing much . . . just coffee . . . and maybe fruit – I'll be with you in under an hour.'

She replaced the receiver, sat down at her desk, put her head in her hands and for the first time since her marriage began to think seriously and sanely about her relationship with her husband.

Forty-five minutes later, make-up carefully reapplied, dressed in a svelte black suit with an imitation ocelot collar and muff, a sweeping cape of the same fur over her shoulders, she got out of a taxi in the courtyard of the Hotel de Merri in the Rue du Parc-Royal. The liveried manservant opened the grilled door, took her cape and ushered her quickly through the small octagonal hallway, up a graceful curving staircase to the first-floor salon where she had first met Honoré. The air was heavy with the scent of burning apple logs from the Treilhan orchard. Marie-Laure sat in a deep armchair by the fire, a pink-shaded lamp behind her. Her face, upturned in greeting, was bathed in a rosy glow from the half-drawn apricot moiré curtains.

She motioned Brilliant into a chair opposite, facing the full impact of the piercing March light streaming through the casement. Brilliant smiled grimly. She had never felt so much in command of herself as at this moment. Settling back in the upright Louis Quinze chair she arched her back and with one graceful movement slipped off her jacket and shook back her hair – an economy of gesture that enabled her to show off the beauty of her bosom, the luxuriance of her hair and the luminosity of her skin, as, deliberately turning her face to the harsh light, she made sure this woman knew she feared not the minutest inspection.

Marie-Laure dropped her eyes – Brilliant had scored her point – and with fluttering hands indicated a small table set at her side.

'You must be hungry, my dear – it's well past lunchtime. It is most important to eat well at midday, I abhor this "grabbing a snack" which is creeping in even over here. The French have always eaten their main meal at lunchtime and remained slim; all the calories are metabolised by the day's activities. But as you said "just a little fruit," I sent Jacques to Chaumet's, but it seems such a little nothing for such a bitter day.'

Brilliant suppressed a gasp at the 'little nothing' of fruit heaped on a silver salver. Hothouse peaches – in March – and blushing amber-skinned apricots, strawberries and cherries from heaven knew where, still with their stems and green leaves attached, were heaped with mangoes, papayas and pineapple, passion and kiwi fruit, while mangosteens and lychees peeped from nooks and crannies of the luscious pyramid. She could imagine Marie-Laure, hands gently clasped, giving the servant urgent instructions. And Jacques would have lovingly hand-picked each fruit, queening it in the store. That man loved to spend his employer's money and should truly have lived in a more flamboyant epoch. He deftly served coffee. They have got the 'best' silver out for me, Brilliant thought. Eyes down, concentrating on a few cherries and an apricot, she missed not one movement, from the servant's white-gloved hands to his mistress's unconsciously tapping foot.

'You won't have any more? But you've not eaten a thing. Have a petit four, they're from Fauquet's, the best *friandises* in Paris. I can't tempt you? That will be all, thank you, Jacques. We will serve ourselves.'

Jacques withdrew with a flourish, closing the double doors behind him.

'You will join us for Easter at Treilhan, won't you, my dear? Paulette is so looking forward to you coming, she says you are the only one in the family who really enjoys their food; cooking for you is such a pleasure, you have such a healthy appetite. We de Bassenets never had good digestions, you know.' Marie-Laure looked down at her own child-like frame and non-existent bosom with satisfaction. She considered it *grossière* for a woman to be well developed.

Brilliant stared at her for what seemed like a long time, and in fact was miles away in a long reverie of freedom, of the idea of release from the confines of this artificial life that suddenly seemed so odious. As though waking from a numbing sleep she turned slowly in her chair to Marie-Laure, who was beginning to lose a little of her *savoir-faire* in the face of this poised, strangely brooding woman.

'No, Marie-Laure, I'm not going to Treilhan, this Easter or ever again. I'm leaving Jean-Claude, I've quite made up my mind. I'm leaving him to you, that's what you want, what you've always wanted, what you've always schemed for. I thought I wanted to keep him at all costs, but now suddenly, I don't care any more! But, my dear mother-in-law, he will never be yours, and you, of course, know precisely why . . .'

Marie-Laure's cheeks mottled an unbecoming red and she pushed her hands down on the sides of her chair, then suddenly sank back, her eyes guarded.

'Brilliant, we are so fond of you, my dear. You are saying terrible things . . . You are tired, overwrought, whatever has made you think like this? Honoré has been asking too much of you; you must wait, rest, go away for a while – just think things over calmly.'

'There is no need to think things over – everything is suddenly dazzlingly clear. Don't concern yourself about the marriage settlement. Naturally, as a Countess in my own right, I did not insist on the *séparation des biens*' that you left out of the contract. Any amount you might see fit to offer me would be merely inconsequential.' Marie-Laure's mouth twisted and her eyes went dark.

Brilliant rose slowly to her feet and pulled on her jacket. In slow-motion she saw Jean-Claude and Aristide Jouissac and that single smooth, caressing gesture. 'Yes, everything is perfectly clear to me, now . . .'

Marie-Laure jumped up and reached out a restraining hand, but Brilliant was through the double doors and down the corridor without a backward glance. As she reached the head of the staircase a door hurriedly clicked shut and she caught an unmistakable whiff of vetiver. So he had been there, listening, summoned already from the Polyclinique by his mother, expecting confrontation.

She felt light and slim as she ran down the stairs; what had she eaten? A few cherries and an apricot. Think of anything, anything – admire the chandeliers, the eighteenth-century silk wallpaper, anything to hold back the tears stinging in her eyes. How could she have been such a fool? She had loved the man, married him – he was her husband. The word was suddenly odious to her, she felt duped, defiled and agonizingly empty; the longed-for love had been a phantom she had never been able to grasp.

'No thank you, Jacques, I'll walk – it's not far.' And holding her head high – out of the corner of her eye she sensed a twitching of the upstairs curtain – she wrapped her cloak round her and walked swiftly down the ancient street. The tears she had held back could not come, she would not cry for him. They fell inside her, on the fresh wound where the hurt was, each tear a memory, each tortured contraction a requiem for the love that had never been.

4

It was the matter of an hour to put into two suitcases the few things she wanted to take from her life with Jean-Claude. Instinct told her that he had no intention of disturbing her. There was no need for stealth; a confrontation would not be in his civilized scheme of things.

To the housekeeper Gaby, who stood biting back the tears, her shrewd eyes betraying her knowledge of the situation, Brilliant gave a hasty story of needing a week's rest as she telephoned for a taxi. She started to scribble several notes to Jean-Claude, but each one seemed more trite than the last. How could she say all she wanted in a few curt words? He had heard enough and needed no explanation; anything more would only develop into recriminations.

In a daze and acting purely on instinct, she arrived at Charles de Gaulle, paid the taxi driver, bought a ticket to London and circumnavigated the paparazzi who fastened like leeches on a face as potentially gossip-worthy as hers. She went through immigration and sat in the departure lounge, clutching her handbag containing her passport and a few thousand francs tightly in her lap.

What had she done? Through the haze of pain and disillusion came another jolting and disturbing realization. She was absolutely penniless. Well, not quite, she gave a wry smile; give or take the few jewels she had taken with her – relatively penniless. Certainly without the lucrative job she had held down before becoming Madame Chardin. She would have to go to work. That was no problem, she relished the idea of independence, getting her nose down to the grindstone, immersing herself in problems other than her own. She stared down at the engagement ring on her finger and her eyes misted over. Goddammit! She had absolutely no reason to wallow in self-pity.

A man had arrived and was sitting opposite her, right in the middle of a row of empty seats. Her vacant eyes met his inquiring ones. She uncrossed her legs and smoothed down her skirt. It would be so easy to go off with a man like this, good-looking, affluent – use him for a while. Why not? Use him as she had been used. She had no need ever to be lonely again. Yet she wanted to be alone. Her gaze swept coolly over the half-smiling traveller, over his exquisite suit that whispered Armani, Gucci shoes and Burberry raincoat, Hermès briefcase and *Financial Times*, and repressed a giggling desire to find out if his underwear was designer labelled as well. Then she rose and went to find a seat by herself, tucked away in the corner of the bar.

She held a glass of cognac in the palm of her hand and inhaled its heady bouquet. There it was again – that diamond image! Her ring's reflection was caught up in the golden liquid swirling in the glass and gave out a thousand prisms of blue and burnished flame.

Why had she married Jean-Claude? She had loved him – yes – but wasn't part of that love what the French called *interêt*, part of their mutual fascination for diamonds? Had she not cherished, in convenient corners of her heart, a secret desire that one day she would be in a position of enormous wealth and power, wealthy enough to acquire for her family their own diamond, the fabulous White Tsaritsa?

It was a dream, a reverie that had flitted in and out of her consciousness during the two brief years of her marriage without being fully crystallized. Now, with the loss of that dream came the full realization of the aspirations she had nurtured, together with a sense of shame that she had done so. Like a naughty child who needs to be loved in spite of herself, Brilliant thought of her mother, of the unswerving warmth of Madalena's love, and felt a redoubled pang of emptiness and remorse.

Her mother had died six months after her marriage to Jean-Claude and the shock of her death had cut like a knife into Brilliant's conscience. For Brilliant knew, in her heart, that Madalena had never really got over her leaving home. She had lived just for her daughter – Brilliant had given her the strength and motivation to fight her daily battles against a hostile world. Madalena's decline had been very gradual. Brilliant went to see her in the house she had bought for her in New England; she had looked for all the world like a prosperous WASP matron, but she had become very frail, the fight had gone out of her. A month later Brilliant learned that she had died of complications after bronchitis. Brilliant tightened her grip on the cognac glass and bit her lip. She imagined how Madalena must have felt as a bewildered immigrant entering an alien civilization, sole supporter of a tiny baby, all her hopes pinned on that one ridiculous diamond. After a lifetime of sacrifice she had left her mother alone to be with Jean-Claude.

The flight to London was called and Brilliant walked down a rabbit warren of impersonal corridors to gate number twenty-four, where she was shepherded on to an aeroplane with cool efficiency and without so much as a whiff of the air outside.

Out of habit she went straight to the Savoy. Most diamantaires put up there, though Jean-Claude was sometimes fickle, preferring to be nearer Jermyn Street and his tailor in Savile Row. While reception checked out her favourite suite overlooking the river, she leaned her elbow on the polished desk and looked around the opulent foyer. Everyone seemed to be with someone; couples met and embraced, walked off arm-in-arm or sat together on sofas, heads close. Potential couples sat and eyed each other warily through the palms, under cover of tea or cocktails, *Tatler* or the *Standard*.

'Good evening, Madame Chardin! It is good to see you again. A telegram has arrived for you from Paris. Monsieur Chardin is not unwell, I hope? We will have your bags sent to your usual room straight away.' The head receptionist, a Breton, voiced his concern as he handed her a telegram. 'It is quite some time since we've seen you, Madame! We shall do everything we can to make your stay a pleasant one.' His brisk welcome veiled the curiosity in his eyes that she had arrived alone and without her usual reservation.

Crumpling the paper in her hand as though it contained something shameful she followed the bell-boy to the lift. Alone in the room she kicked off her shoes, rang room service for coffee and Fernet Branca – the brandy had given her a headache and affected her digestion – then sank on to the bed and opened the telegram from Jean-Claude.

'My dearest Brilliant, have you gone mad? I love you. Arriving London tomorrow evening. Am distraught. Jean-Claude.'

She thought of him composing the telegram, searching for the right words. The French *désolé* made her smile. No doubt he was desolated, like an inconsolable child, for in many ways he had come to depend on her completely. There were several more flights to London that evening, but his desolation was not the kind to send him rushing to Charles de Gaulle tearing out his hair. No, he would still be in Paris in the morning, checking with Dr LeBossier when it would be prudent to travel, then he would pack an immaculate suitcase and tie up loose ends with the housekeeper.

She dropped the telegram on the table. Her feelings were curiously ambivalent. On one hand she felt detached, as though the distance of the Channel had alienated her from his influence; on the other the wound was still fresh, searing, if she let her thoughts turn inwards. He would come seeking her here tomorrow evening, she could not avoid him for long. He would plead, cajole, the Chardins had a position in society to consider, they should stay together in their old sweet companionship. He really would think her mad to give up such a comfortable relationship.

She clasped her hands behind her head and stared up at the ceiling. Then there was the problem of the Sight at the Diamond Trading Company in the morning which, if she were really honest, she desperately wanted to attend. And why not? It would be her last obligation to the House of Chardin and she would fulfil it admirably, she thought with fierce pride. At least she would have the satisfaction of reaching that pinnacle of achievement before the reality of a new job began in earnest.

She groaned, rolled over and looked at her watch. Seven-thirty. She would check out in the morning, and move into a small apartment for the time being. The thought of seeing Jean-Claude again filled her with panic, from which she deduced she could not trust her emotions. Thoughts revolved in her head for the evening, planning it like a condemned man his last meal. She would go down to the foyer and get the newspapers and magazines, look up the property for rent, have a long luxurious bath, a light supper in her room, perhaps some of the excellent television she had missed in France, and go to bed with a good book, at last her own woman. Not the sort of evening to set the temples athrob with anticipation, but one that she might have to get used to. First of all she would go out and walk along the river for a bit, to clear her head.

She rose from the bed, went to the window and pressed her forehead against the cold pane. The opalescent lights along the Embankment shimmered in the river; lighted specks of unseen craft moved slowly through the black, heavy tide. Her head felt better now and she was hungry. Quickly brushing her hair in front of the glass she imagined she looked different. She peered closer – no, only a little tired and slightly drawn. A flush burned high on her cheekbones, her eyes glittered. She shrugged her shoulders and grinned at her reflection. 'Far too robust for La Dame aux Camélias, my dear, you're not exactly the pining type.'

Carl Vanderberg put the telephone down on Andrew Kramer, searched in his pocket for a cigar case, drew out a Bolivar, spent an unconscionable time cutting, preparing and lighting it, then settled back in an aromatic cloud of smoke as he contemplated his evening.

Normally the programme Andrew, his London partner, had suggested would have delighted him. Early drinks in the pub, theatre, supper in Covent Garden and then, if the night were fine, the walk back to the Savoy through the quiet streets he loved. But he had refused, pleading another engagement.

Perhaps there was something wilful in the wind, certainly March was the most unsettling month, still a nip of winter in the air yet the buds were bursting, getting ready for the great renewal that he envied nature – so unfair to find oneself visibly deteriorating inside the same cracking carapace.

Not normally a vain man, at forty-five Carl was just becoming conscious of his own mortality. As he had dried himself off from the shower in the reflection of an unkind mirror, he saw the flesh of his well-muscled back had not quite the same springy resilience, his athletic frame had begun to thicken imperceptibly round the waist, fine lines at the eyes and mouth had ceased to be etchings and were now well scored in the canvas, and as for his thick dark hair, it had been greying since his twenties. A day of taking stock, today his birthday . . .

He looked at the thick tip of ash hovering on the end of his cigar; the slightest movement would dislodge it and blow its cindery pieces into oblivion, upset the delicate convoluted balance that made the whole. The desire for change was deep within him, and perhaps that was why he had first phoned Kirsty and then Andrew.

Kirsty's gentle Scots voice had fought to conceal a tremor when she told him it didn't matter – she understood – would he call her as soon as he was free? He might have felt better if she had screamed and shouted, made a fuss, as most American women of his acquaintance would have done, he reflected. Kirsty was so modest, so self-effacing, he had wanted to shake her, yell at her, 'Hate me! Despise me! I have been using you for two years and now I'm dropping you.' But it was true that she understood, her quiet intellect told her that this big unhappy man had only wanted a temporary haven that women such as she seemed born to provide. Since his divorce Carl had sought out women like Kirsty, gentle, undemanding, balm to the heart and ego. Like a convalescent waking up to find a lingering illness cured, a mysterious inner chemistry suddenly altered, yesterday's balm of Kirsty no longer soothed but irritated, incompatible with his changing condition.

The solid wedge of concertinaed cigar ash finally trembled and fell on to the table. On an impulse Carl decided to throw on a sweater, go down for a rummage through the bookstall and enjoy the luxury of being incommunicado, a couple of whiskies, a steak and a good claret – then oblivion.

He locked the door behind him and started down the corridor, which was faintly redolent of a century of high-living and with the proportions of a more generous age. A tall woman with a mane of pale hair walked briskly ahead of him, rounded the corner to the elevators and disappeared. There was something about the erect way she carried herself, the energy of her walk, that made him quicken his step. Maybe this time it was her. Then he checked himself and strolled the last few yards to the elevator. The woman had gone, like so many of the visions glimpsed since that unexpected embrace in Paris, phantoms seen across a street or in a crowded restaurant, tantalizing him with a likeness to her, sometimes disappearing before he could check her out, always leaving him with hopes unfulfilled.

He searched the foyer, checked the bookstall, then the

restaurant, and finally made despondently for the bar. The swing doors taunted him with their vacant revolutions into the cold night air.

'Yes, I'll have a malt whisky, Terry. Make it a large one!' He grinned with resignation at the Irish barman.

'Countess Curnonsky, you have inherited the family diamond in your eyes . . .'

'Touch them! Go on – touch them! They will all be yours, all of them, the fabulous Chardin jewels will all belong to you . . . when you marry me.'

Jumbled words and images from the past drifted through Brilliant's mind as she paused in the doorway of the Diamond Trading Company and took a deep breath, widening her nostrils to unravel the heady atmosphere of this all-male preserve.

It was a strongly masculine scent, a particularly potent brew, that gave her the sensual thrill of forbidden pleasure, its curious bouquet a combination of leather armchairs, Havana cigars, starched linen and the indefinable but powerful tang of money.

The roomful of men in front of her had come, to use the trade vernacular, for a 'Sight' of their box, a packet of diamonds with a minimum cost of two hundred thousand dollars, while the half dozen or so wealthiest among them were about to stump up between five and twenty million.

She clenched her fists to stop the tremor in her hands. A vision, long since buried, rose and taunted her – the émigrée girl, awed by the opulence, the lights, the crowd, pressing her nose close to the showcase to catch her first glimpse of the Curnonsky Diamond – their diamond.

In the second that she paused in the doorway she saw her life as an uncertain pathway leading to this one threshold of achievement. Why then the inexplicable panic? Was it only nerves, or a presentiment of something ominous that was yet to come.

Resisting the urge to turn and run, she followed Henry

Myers, the managing director, towards a group of men deep in conversation by one of the soaring windows. Her appearance produced a silence so profound, transfixing men in mid-sentence and gesture, that across her heightened senses flickered another image, straight from a Russian fairytale, of Vassilia the Sorceress, who had the useful knack of turning men to stone with one piercing, fateful glance.

A woman in the Diamond Trading Company? While it was not unthinkable or even unprecedented – the male-dominated world of diamonds had no edict that particularly excluded women – to attend one of the Sights which were held ten times annually in London was the ultimate accolade of the industry, a sign that this most insular of worlds had finally acknowledged a superior cutting edge. Some diamond houses had been known to send an elderly woman member in the past, but now here she was, a gemstone among the boart . . .

Carl Vanderberg, released from his transfixed state, roused himself and moved closer. It *was* her, the woman from the Ritz, but to find her *here* of all places . . . Henry's eyes gleamed. It took a lot to elicit emotion from these hard-hearted diamond men. Not even last year, when he had he seen slapped a surcharge of twenty-five per cent on the boxes, had he seen such a frisson of dismay ruffle the urbane feathers of their composure.

'Gentlemen, I want you to meet a new member, and such a decorative one, too. Madame Brilliant Curnonsky Chardin, Jean-Claude's wife – I think you need no further introduction. Carl Vanderberg,' Carl stretched out his hand mutely, 'is of course from Adamantina. This is Tom Sikowski of Star Trading, Bernard Wolfe here of Winston's, Danny Joel of Diamond World . . .' Henry quickly went round the group and introduced other members as they drew nearer, intrigued.

Yes, yes, of course, Brilliant Chardin! The men's eyes narrowed and they began to relax. The name was known to everyone in the trade, a diamond 'eye' of legendary repute. Brilliant – all diamantaires, many of them of mid-European origin, knew – was the Russian for a cut and polished diamond, but her beauty and well-documented exploits in the press had made the details of her strange name, her early life and her marriage to an eminently eligible French jeweller, household knowledge.

Good Lord! Mr Hillman. Brilliant shook his hand mechanically. The man she had kissed at the Ritz. She had not forgotten his name, it was imprinted on her memory, together with all the details of that unfortunate encounter. But Henry Myers had introduced him as Carl Vanderberg of Adamantina. Oh no, surely not, surely it could not be true?

Brilliant managed to murmur, 'Mr Vanderberg? Why yes, we have already met. When you were . . . when you were someone else,' she finished lamely.

Carl Vanderberg met a challenging gaze and his heart contracted with the memory, so astonishingly like that extraordinary diamond. A murmur of voices roused him and with quick embarrassment he let go of Brilliant's hand and turned to meet the amused expression of his colleagues.

A Slav princess, straight from the pages of Russian fable, thought Carl, mesmerized by a look that held his levelly, and seemed to hold mysteries he would never fathom. The beauty of the legendary diamond had surely been bestowed on her like a magic gift. The fairest of women in the truest sense, ash-blonde hair, translucent skin – but it was the eyes that one remembered, clear as mountain water, a sparkling blue that could deepen in shade from glacier to indigo with the colour of the sky or the intensity of her mood. The diamond's ice and fire meet in her face, he mused; ice in the modelling of her nose and chin, fire from the wide mouth, the way the big eyes tilted slightly in the high cheekbones, hinting at earthly pleasures among such spiritual fairness.

He saw Henry Myers try to guide her towards the door but she was stopped in her tracks by newcomers hurrying from their Sight rooms on the wings of the sensational news of the female arrival. She turned to him again and this time – did he imagine it? – a look of anger flashed at him, sharp as a laser, from those compelling eyes.

The pulse at Brilliant's temple had become an insidious drill of pain; she longed for quiet, to be alone with her own turbulent thoughts.

She turned and left the room abruptly, graciously refusing Henry's offer to escort her to her Sight room. He had shown it to her earlier, at the far end of a deep-carpeted corridor. Her heart was beating unexpectedly fast, her palms were damp, her hair hung heavily round her shoulders. So that was Carl Vanderberg, alias Mr Hillman. Mighty Adamantina himself, head of the largest and most important jewel house in the world. Vanderberg – a name she respected even if she had come to despise it. He had disarmed her with that sad, searching look in Paris – how that ridiculous, regrettable kiss must have amused him. Carl Vanderberg, of all the men in the world! She grimaced. An unfair blow seemed to have been aimed in the direction of her ribs. The past had a devilish trick of turning the screws at the most inopportune moments. Now was hardly the time to go over all that . . .

Caught off guard, she was struck by the anguished expression on a woman's face – her own – glimpsed in the glass doors at the end of the corridor. Always, in the depths of her consciousness, she was convinced there was something – someone – from the past who was close to her, anxious to communicate, trying to impart some knowledge she would find out if only she tried hard enough. Just when she thought she was solving the enigma, a fog descended and the image of the great diamond rose up to taunt and tantalize her. Instinctively she turned away. Her eyes held such a disturbing resemblance to the diamond that she was sure people would guess at the obsession she tried to hide from the world. Just occasionally someone seemed able to see into her soul, as

Carl Vanderberg had done, and she felt naked in front of him, and deeply ashamed of her secret.

Vanderberg. Why should he have any more understanding of what drove and inspired her than Jean-Claude had done? Her mouth compressed into an uncharacteristic line of bitterness. Not surprising that the tall American's eyes should show curiosity and complacency, with the White Tsaritsa flaunted in pride of place on a pedestal in the Adamantina showroom. He was probably gloating at her discomfort right now – meanness tended to run in families – and his unspeakable Uncle Joel had certainly raised it to an art form, persuading her guileless mother to part with the diamond for so little. Well, Carl would find out that her daughter was made of sterner stuff. She pushed open the door of her room. Better get on with the job she was here to do – she sensed the competitive antennae that were out to judge her performance within these hallowed walls.

The small square room had north light only, like all the cells used for a Sight. There were neutral blinds at the curtainless windows and the bland, off-white decoration of walls, carpet and furnishings was especially chosen not to distort the assessment of a diamond's colour and clarity.

She had already worked out with Jean-Claude the specific requirements for the five-million-dollar contents of their oblong cardboard box, rather like a shoe-box. It included specials for Hervé Blanchard's important order, large stones for the annual Spring Show, and what was over would be used for infill items. Not that the name of Chardin was associated with infill items – it had a justifiable reputation for the quality of its workmanship, achieving in its dazzling pieces that difficult combination, faultless style with luxurious opulence.

A box represented above all a selection, which had to be accepted in its entirety. Brilliant knew that the stones could not be rejected merely as being unsuitable for one's house prestige. In fact she had been keen to persuade Chardin's that the smaller stones, of excellent quality –

the Diamond Trading Company could be relied on to maintain standards – were useful as part of their collection. A man choosing a costly piece for his mistress could negotiate an eternity ring or earrings for his wife as the bargain part of the whole transaction.

'The box is just like liquorice allsorts; you have your favourite ones, the ones you know are going to be there, and some you don't want as much. But it simply isn't done to refuse any,' Honoré had told her. He had been her mentor in the early days at Chardin when she first displayed her gift for grading stones. Last year, Honoré told her, the Diamond Trading Company had given the diamantaires permission to leave out two stones – unheard-of leniency. This year the economic situation had improved and trade had stabilized – it was the lot or nothing.

Lovingly, and with infinite care, she began to unwrap the stones from their twists of blue tissue paper and set them out in groups on the black baize-covered table. She hummed almost inaudibly to herself, a sound like a kitten's contented purr. Lost in a private world, she leaned forward in intense concentration. Her eyes, focused on the stones, took on the diamonds' gleam, their hardness; her rapt and passionate gaze exchanged sparkle for sparkle, fire for fire. She was in the self-induced, semi-ecstatic state that the proximity of precious stones roused in her, something akin to erotic satisfaction.

She had finished unwrapping the stones now and they lay spaced according to colour and carat along the top of the table. Her quiet humming ceased, the intensity of her concentration increased and her gaze transfixed, so that the stabbing rays from the gems became a thousand quivering prisms. An hour of communion spent with her diamonds that claimed her totally, mind and spirit.

She was so totally absorbed that the neighbouring church clock chiming the hour made her start and shake the table of diamonds. She glanced at her watch, her first wedding anniversary present from Jean-Claude. A wafer-thin square of gold, its black mother-of-pearl face was bare except for the bold strokes of two faultless diamond hands, a perpetual reminder of his exquisite good taste. One o'clock, and she was hungry.

The intense concentration of the last few hours had sharpened her appetite. She had planned to join a school friend now working on *Vogue* for the launch of a new scent, but somehow the prospect of the media crowd at lunchtime did not appeal. The diamonds had put her in a reflective mood. She wanted to be quiet, alone or, better still, with a soul-mate, someone she could relax with, be herself. She began to replace the stones rapidly in the little twists of blue paper and put them back in the box.

Carl Vanderberg, pacing the nearby vestibule, glanced impatiently at his watch. Twelve-thirty. Surely he had not missed her? He had quickly examined the contents of his box, but could not get Brilliant Chardin out his mind. How extraordinary but also how fortunate that they should meet in the Diamond Company. Ever since their meeting in Paris he had felt uncomfortable about his concealed identity. He frequently used the name Hillman when travelling in his search for rare books, and what had started out as a desire for anonymity – he had been loath to use the levers of wealth in bookish circles – had become a pleasant necessity when he found he could escape through his alter-ego into a less materialistic way of life. And now, to be truthful, was he surprised that those remarkable eyes had dismissed him with such evident contempt?

The White Tsaritsa had never directly been his concern, even if it was now ensconced in the Adamantina showroom in New York. Yet Carl felt a pang of sympathy and something akin to conscience when he remembered Uncle Joel's story of the Vanderberg appropriation of the famous diamond.

Joel, a notoriously hard driver of a bargain in a business

75

noted for its toughness, had been more than a little proud of his coup. Madalena had not thought to take the ring elsewhere, there was no question of shopping around, since to the man in the street the Vanderberg name and diamonds were synonymous. If he had offered Madalena a ridiculously low price, that was all part of the business. Who was to know, in the uncertain post-war years, whether another Thirties'-style slump would not come along. There was very little big money around then, and Joel had hung on to the White Tsaritsa, knowing that when the time was right he could sell the stone and make a killing.

Joel Vanderberg had learned his craft the hard way. His older brother Bernard, Carl's father, the leading diamond dealer in New York, had lost everything in the great crash of 1929. He had played the stock market heavily and made a fortune, but every single penny was tied up and lost overnight. Bernard had bought a farm in Kentucky with the first big money he had ever made and after the crash he moved out there with his wife and young daughter to breed horses and lead a rustic life.

This was the hardest thing to understand. How could a man, a Jew, born and brought up on the East Side of Manhattan to live, breathe and dream the diamond business, simply forget about it all and potter around his farm with a battered hat on the back of his head and a permanently contented grin on his weathered face? All that was missing was the straw in the mouth. It was too much, he had gone off his rocker, of course, the shock had permanently unhinged him and as a good brother who had personally managed to hang on to what he had got, Joel made it his duty to keep an eye on Bernard's boy, born in Kentucky some years after the crash.

Diamonds run in families and in the blood, so at thirteen Carl was packed off to a distant cousin in Antwerp to learn the business from the bottom. He spent the first year sorting out boart – gravel-like industrial diamonds – before he was allowed anywhere near the real gems.

Joel had never married, and as Carl grew into a gangling youth with heavy brows over intense watchful eyes, his uncle gave him the benefit of his enormous expertise, together with whatever gruff affection he was capable of.

One day shortly before his eighteenth birthday, when Carl was with him in the grimy apartment he still kept on the lower East Side, Joel delved behind books and papers at the back of a shelf and unlocked the door of a safe with his clawed, arthritic fingers.

'I want to show you something that will be yours one day.'

Joel was already troubled with stabbing pains in the back and sides, and had begun to rethink his personal conviction of immortality.

Suddenly, there it was, totally unexpected and start-lingly magnificent, a ring with a great diamond that exploded in fierce rays of light, filling the dingy room with unearthly glamour.

The two men, one gnarled and swarthy, the other a pale stripling whose bony shoulders were slightly rounded with the rapidity of adolescent growth, were fused in common admiration as their heads met under the Angle-poise lamp clipped to the baize-topped table. This had been Carl's first glimpse of the White Tsaritsa and now, as he thought of Brilliant sorting her box so near him, it seemed that destiny had linked him to this woman, and the ring that now reposed in Adamantina on Fifth Avenue had forged a common bond. But it was his now, and the knowledge was somehow bitter-sweet.

Yes, no doubt old Joel, dead these twenty years now, had been a wily scoundrel, but he had lived as he had preached, hard and frugally. He had amassed an astound-ing fortune and the year before his death had made Ada-mantina into a public company, with the youthful Carl as chief executive and substantial shareholder. A further twenty per cent stake went to another nephew, the reclusive Max, son of Joel's older brother Jacob who was killed in a road accident soon after his honeymoon. Jacob's wife Ruth had married again and moved to a religious farming community. From what they heard of Max he was ideologically opposed to the iniquity of the diamond business, but content enough to receive his not inconsiderable regular dividend.

Through a series of judicious mergers Carl's flair and expertise had built Adamantina into the empire it was today, but somehow right now Carl could not get that story of Joel's out of his mind. He recalled bitterly how Joel loved to tell of his acquisition of Madalena's ring, how his coup gave him so much satisfaction.

'Do you know, Carl,' Joel had told him, 'of course, I was astounded to see the size of the ring on her finger, but what surprised me even more was the hand! It was meant to wear that jewel, a slender aristocratic hand, roughened a bit with hard work and deprivation, flaunting that ring so carelessly and proudly!' Carl's heart contracted and his downcast eyes suddenly focused on the vision of another slender hand outstretched before him.

'I've come to say goodbye. It was interesting to find out who you really are,' Brilliant told him as he shook her hand. 'I have evidently interrupted some deep, dark train of thought.'

'Yes, you did, but in the pleasantest possible way.' A broad smile spread slowly over his face, deepening the lines in his cheeks. 'You've caught me hanging about playing the young swain, waiting to invite you to lunch. And to explain myself. I always travel incognito when I'm rare-book collecting – that's my hobby. I prefer to remain anonymous, but every now and then it catches you out. Vanderberg – Hillman . . . it's a kind of bad translation, you see. I thought perhaps we should talk about certain things we . . . we have in common.'

'Nicely put, Mr Vanderberg. I can tell you're a skilled diplomat as well as a jeweller.' It was good to feel so waspish, good to feel a release of tension. She had already declined Henry Myers' offer to join a group for lunch. This meeting promised to be very different.

'I'd be delighted to lunch with you! I have a very good appetite and it's way past my lunchtime. In Paris the stroke of twelve is sacrosanct. But if you don't mind I need to stop at the Savoy first, to put a call through to the bank.'

'Of course. We could eat at the Grill – I'll arrange it while you're phoning.' Carl hailed a cab and they discussed the neutral subject of Paris restaurants until they approached the forecourt of the Savoy. Before the taxi stopped Carl thought it prudent to inquire about Jean-Claude.

'Henry told me your husband is ill – nothing serious I hope? We've often met at a Sight.'

Brilliant stared at him, thinking hard. Carl seemed a considerate man, one who might be a useful ally right now. She really ought to forget that stupid incident and her obstinate antagonism because of his uncle, the family connection. But – and the thought suddenly struck her – he *was* practically family, associated as they were through the White Tsaritsa and linked for ever by his possession of the diamond.

'No, nothing serious. But this is my last job for Maison Chardin. Jean-Claude and I are not together any more.'

Her chin went up and her eyes took on a defensive expression. It was the first time she had spoken of her failure out loud. The doorman opened the cab door and she stepped out ahead of Carl. As they walked in silence to the crowded elevator he glanced at her stony profile. He had heard of them ecstatically in love, this must be just a lover's tiff and she needed a shoulder to cry on. Oh, well. . . . He had no desire to play the father-figure to a lovesick young woman, particularly when there was a French husband behind the scenes.

'If you give me fifteen minutes, I'll meet you in the bar.'

Brilliant smiled and hurried to her room where she dialled the bank and arranged payment, due within seven days of the Sight. Only then could the goods be despatched, in tough cardboard boxes bearing the DTC's seal, a box so prestigious that she knew it could be sold just by showing the company's invoice. Two years ago the DTC's boxes were changing hands at twice the Syndicate price. They stopped that game in Antwerp and Tel Aviv where all incoming boxes had to go through a central delivery office, which opened and delivered them personally to the Sightholders in sealed envelopes. The DTC withdrew invitations to Sightholders they felt had been guilty of encouraging speculation, suggesting banks reduce their credit. Ever since, all Sightholders had to account for their precise needs – a policy which made Honoré lament, 'We are no longer customers, but employees of the Syndicate!'

When she joined Carl at the bar twenty minutes later it did not matter a damn about the state of her marriage. She wore a black dress that set off her luminous skin and hair, wonderful diamonds at her ears and throat; she had shed her former sadness and delivered a thousand-volt sparkle so that every male head in the room turned as though pulled by an invisible force.

She chose to give very few details of her decision to leave Jean-Claude, just enough for Carl to read between the lines and understand the deadly finality of the step she had taken. Later, over lunch, the germ of an idea began to sprout in his mind when she told him of her intention to throw herself back into her former career.

'Was the box all you expected?' he asked, curious, as most of his colleagues, to know if her much-vaunted eye was a reality.

'Yes . . . and no! I had asked for some specials, we have a client – a billionaire builder. . . .' she made an involuntary grimace at the memory of Hervé Blanchard's presumptuous eyes. '. . . who wants a beautiful set – three important pieces – for his lady love. The stones they came up with were superb, just what we wanted. We also asked for matched sets for earrings, we're doing a roaring trade at the moment, and they were fine, of super quality. But

80

I had to mention to Henry as I was leaving that two of the stones passed as Fl flawless weren't Fl at all. Of course, its difficult for me as a new girl to bring up something like that – *un peu* presumptuous, *n'est ce pas?*' Her broad smile dimpled one side of her cheek and exposed even teeth. 'But equally I didn't want him to think I can't recognize any lapse in standards.'

He looked at her in admiration. Yes, the word had filtered through – everyone at the Exchange knew what everyone else was doing, thinking and buying – and he was impressed. She had been right. There was no point in beating around the bush with a reputation like hers.

'Shall we talk about the White Tsaritsa?' he asked gently.

'I thought you were never going to ask, it's obviously been bothering you ever since we met. . . .' She stopped, surprised at her own sharpness, a patch of colour burning high on her cheekbones.

'As well it might – if I were to voice your own sentiments!' The sharpness in his voice matched her own, then suddenly he relaxed and shrugged his shoulders.

'You know, I was terribly afraid that you wouldn't accept my invitation to lunch, and we would never have the opportunity to set the record straight. I know you think my Uncle Joel had all the attributes of Shylock himself, but the business deal was a straightforward one. Your mother needed the money and times were bad in the trade.' he held up his hand as her eyes flashed dangerously – 'and I can assure you, that however hard a nut he was, the White Tsaritsa meant an awful lot to him.'

She looked down, biting her lip, then made an effort to smile.

'Well, the past is the past. . . . Besides, you weren't directly implicated in it. Tell me about your Uncle Joel, what was he like, what did he tell you about the ring?' She clasped her hands and as he answered her questions, Carl became more and more despondent as he began to realize why she had accepted his lunch invitation with such alacrity.

'I'll never forget my first glimpse of the White Tsaritsa. I was just a boy, we were in his office. I think it was the first time I really saw the shattering fire at the heart of a diamond and understood its charisma. . . .' Carl spoke mechanically, disturbed by her rapt expression. He had met many diamond-obsessed women in the course of his work, but with Brilliant that fascination seemed to consume her totally.

'But my mother? What did Joel say about her, what was his side of the story?' Carl felt a stab of quick compassion, but the obsessive direction of her questions together with her scarcely veiled hostility depressed and also irritated him.

'I didn't think our lunch would turn out to be such a major inquisition.' He smiled drily as he motioned to the waiter.

'I'm so sorry, I must appear so . . . so . . .' Brilliant shook her head, at a loss for words. 'I know you must think I'm motivated out of revenge, or greed, or even worse . . .' she took a sip of wine . . . 'but the reason I care so much about the White Tsaritsa is something quite apart from me, I can't explain, it's almost beyond my control. . . .' She stopped as Carl raised inquiring brows, remembering the time, not so long ago, when she had confided her innermost feelings about the diamond to another man, only to have them ultimately betrayed.

Carl experienced another pang of regret. The woman struck a deep mutual chord, of love longed for but never quite attained. She had a vulnerable quality about her that touched him and yet . . . there was still a gulf between them that she was very careful to maintain.

'But Brilliant,' Carl's voice was gentle, 'your mother, Madalena, she is happy now, she must be glad of your splendid marriage, you have been able to make her life more comfortable.'

Brilliant's eyes clouded over.

'Mother died last year, six months after I married Jean-Claude. She came to France for the wedding, looking wonderful, she was over the moon with happiness for me. But . . . but her life had always revolved around me, and after I left she must have given up the struggle. She went into a decline – I knew nothing about it – and she died quite suddenly, after an illness. And to think that . . . that I wasn't with her at the end . . .' She swallowed hard. 'The funeral was the most awful experience. Jean-Claude couldn't come, the new collection was being shown, I felt so . . . so alone. Worse was knowing that between Jean-Claude and me, after just six months . . .' She broke off in confusion as Carl frowned. While the waiter removed their plates she made a conscious effort to control herself and commented matter-of-factly, 'The real reason I'm so avid for information is that I'm thinking of researching the White Tsaritsa's history. I want to try to find the forgotten archives in Russia, then perhaps get someone to help me edit them.'

Carl was thankful that the conversation had taken a less emotionally charged turn.

'That's a marvellous idea and I'd be the first to support you! Look, I know it's a sensitive issue, but we should try to put the past behind us. When you next come to New York I'll give you all our cuttings and files, I'd be glad to help you in any way I can.'

Again he gave her that searching look that seemed to see right through the hidden shadows.

'I knew there was more than mere acquisitiveness in your interest; you know in our world of glitzy consumerism it's so easy to be disillusioned. It's a world I was born to, but in many ways have little taste for . . .'. His voice trailed off and he laughed apologetically, unwilling and unused to reveal more of his feelings.

'Glitzy consumerism – I've never ever thought of it like that. But then I've always had my feet very firmly on the ground. Part of my philosophy of selling beautiful stones is that they should be available to everyone, through a wide variety of prices.'

She leaned confidentially across the table.

'You see, I've always had this crusade about the "demystification" of jewellery selling – out with the fear of the rock shops where only oil money or superstars dare to tread – and in with the man in the street and educating him for all you're worth about the possibilities at the lower end of the market.' She paused for breath and Carl chuckled. He had heard about her genius for selling, her technique a blend of inspiration and manipulation, but to see the fire in her eyes as she expounded her theory was to thrill to the electrifying reality.

'I couldn't agree with you more – those are precisely my own beliefs. I have been thinking of instigating a whole new approach at Adamantina. . . .' He studied her thoughtfully.

'I only wish they'd felt the same way at Chardin. . . .' She bit her lip and looked quickly away.

'Brilliant, while you've been talking I've been thinking things over, and in case you think it's merely fortuitous, I can assure you I never make business decisions lightly.' He smiled the broad smile that transformed his stern face and deepened the lines around his eyes.

'What you just said about wanting to "demysticize" the whole business of jewellery selling – well, that's precisely what I want to do in New York,' Carl continued. 'The girl who runs the Adamantina showroom has finally persuaded one of my richest clients to marry her. She deserves it, bless her, it's been a ten-year campaign – but she's leaving at the end of the month. There are one or two potential successors lined up – it's a very special job, requires a real knowledge of the trade, social poise, business acumen, plus it gives an opportunity to use your design skills. Valerie worked very closely with all our top designers, hers was the final decision on many of our top-selling pieces. I can't think of anyone as well qualified as you to handle the job – that is if you'll take it on, of course. But even if we agreed on a specific timespan, it would tide you over a difficult period, get you away from Europe. . . .'

To get away. . . . Even as Carl was talking, her heart gave a great lurch of anticipation. She could leave for New York straight away, she smiled wryly – like Cinderella, she had a deadline – just disappear into anonymity, back to the dear adrenalin-producing hustle of that extraordinary city.

'I take it it's signed and sealed then?' One look at Brilliant's shining eyes was enough. Carl reached over and took her hand in a firm handshake. It was not until they were leaving the restaurant that the thought struck her. Adamantina – the White Tsaritsa, she was actually going to work alongside it . . . and Carl. It was important to get the record straight from the very beginning. She turned and said to him at the door, 'I think you'll find me a pretty tough business partner, Mr Vanderberg.' She smiled and walked ahead of him to the hotel's airline reservations desk.

5

Galina ran into her office, out of breath, just as the telephone started to ring.

'Is that the Museum of Tsarist Treasures in Leningrad? Can I speak to Galina Alexandrevna Signorin, the director? This is New York calling!' The man mimicked a heavy American twang.

Galina immediately recognized Arkady's voice.

'Arkady! You bastard! I'm late, I've no time to fool around.'

'So I noticed. I've called twice already. As the new director, I really think you ought to take your responsibilities more seriously. . . .'

'Shut up, Arkady! I'm not in the mood. Sasha's got a bad cold, I didn't know whether to take him to school or Babushka Leila's. . . .'

Arkady clicked his teeth in sympathy.

'Leila's, I hope . . . she'll love spoiling the little monkey.' Arkady's mother was a tower of strength in Galina's harassed life.

'Arkady, I've got piles of paperwork to get through, what do you want?'

'I want to talk about our Exhibition of Tsarist Treasures. I've just received the go-ahead from the Ministry, and that means a trip to New York to set it up. Adamantina are financing everything – think what that means for you? Aren't you excited, *dorogaya maya*?'

'We . . . e . . ll – yes.' Galina tried to sound enthusiastic. At that moment Masha, her assistant, set down a steaming glass of tea and another stack of paper on her desk. Galina felt mortified to be still in her coat at 9.40 a.m. She should be setting an example. And the realities of life in Leningrad in April – the buses late because of the thaw, her good coat spattered in mud, two curators down with flu, which meant she wouldn't have one free half hour in the day to stop – were far more pressing than a dream of New York, which might not even come true.

'Listen, Galya! The Americans are businesslike – they like things organized down to the last match-stick. I'll come over at eleven and we'll discuss it, all right?'

'No, no, Arkady! Make it later, come at twelve, I've too much work.' Galina's voice was firm, she wasn't going to be dictated to by Arkady.

'Does that mean we have to eat in your foul canteen?'

'It doesn't mean you have to eat at all – I've having lunch at the Dom Kino.'

Galina put the telephone down and sighed. She was as keen on this exhibition in New York as Arkady, in fact the whole idea had been hers. Ever since she had come to work as a young curator at the museum, she had dreamed of staging a magnificent event with her beloved Tsarist treasures. Her flair for the theatrical had conjured up the drama of the setting and the depth of her scholarship had ensured the authenticity of its historical content.

Arkady, as director of Russelmaz, the Soviet diamond ministry in Antwerp, had helped her present her idea to the authorities. Then he had gone straight to Adamantina, as the most prestigious diamond house in the world, to sponsor the exhibition in their New York showroom, and what had started out as an impossible dream seemed about to become a reality. But Galina was understandably anxious. She knew nothing of the financial problems of staging such an event, she was an historian and not an entrepreneur. Arkady had swept away all her doubts. She was to leave everything to him.

She hung up her coat and frowned with annoyance as she inspected the mud spattered along the hem of its long skirt. She would give it a good brush once it had dried out. It was one of her best discoveries from the *Commissiony* shop, where you could always be sure to find a selection of antiquated clothing. The coat was full-skirted and tight-waisted, and Arkady said it made her look like an extra from *Zhivago*. . . .

Arkady! It seemed she had been in love with Arkady all her life, from the first time they played together under the limes in the Summer Garden, in the beech woods at Tverskoe or at Pioneer Camp in the Caucasus. When her family had moved out to Vishnev after her father died their paths had diverged for a while and they had met again at university. Arkady, dazzled by the metamorphosis of his pigtailed playmate into a pert young beauty, had pursued her as single-mindedly as a botanist with a net. They had become lovers and after a rapturous summer of sexual awakening, swore to remain inseparable.

But Arkady's devotion had been short-lived. She had found that he was attracted to all things beautiful as inexorably as *babochkas*, summer moths, are attracted to lamplight on a June night. In many ways his love was sincere, but it was love of acquisition and conquest that motivated this man of passion, not tender consideration for the object of love itself. Arkady had not deceived her . . . he told her he could never be faithful. He loved her but . . . he needed to be free.

She had married Slava Sigorin out of hurt pride. Slava and Arkady had been rivals for her favours at university and Slava had thought she had chosen him. At the wedding Arkady had proposed the toast, smiling at her over the rim of his glass with his pale eyes that seemed to be able to see into her soul. She had tried to shut him out of her heart during the years of her marriage, but as Slava's best friend he was a frequent visitor to their apartment.

After the divorce Arkady had tried to storm his way into her life again, sending a single cornflower, 'their' flower, sheaves of poetry or some memento of their summer of love together. She had teased him gently with what she thought of as sisterly affection, convinced all feelings from the past had fled with her marriage to Slava.

Eventually he seemed to believe her. Whether she believed it herself was another matter.

She took a gulp of tea and started on the pile of paperwork. Her career brought her great pride and fulfilment, although it had been hard at first, reconciling the long working day with motherhood. With two children and no live-in *babushka* life sometimes seemed impossible, though things were easier now Alyosha was going to the *Detsky Sad*, the state kindergarten.

There had been days when she felt she could not cope, when her predecessor, Igor Platonov, catching her running down the corridor, dishevelled, late again, had called her into his office for another humiliating homily on the responsibilities of a lady curator. Perhaps she was finding the job too much for her? But she had stuck it out, written her thesis and one or two well-thought-out papers, then Igor Platonov had been promoted elsewhere and they had offered her his job.

Working among the fabulous jewels of the Tsarist Collection was reward in itself, but the stifling bureaucracy irritated her, with its enormous piles of paperwork that were shifted from government department to department and demanded more and more of her time. It was all so unnecessary. Every time she tried to simplify things she received reprimands from on high. They accused her of trying to take short cuts, to save time, all typical of a woman. Galina was anxious to succeed and this was the first time a woman had occupied the post of director. She knew that she had to try harder than Igor Platonov and for the moment she was submissive. But she would make changes, they had to come.

She tried to concentrate on a letter from the Ministry of *Khozaistva* – Domestic – concerning supplies. They said the museum had had its quota of lavatory paper and must wait six months for more. Didn't she know there was a nationwide shortage of paper, even for newsprint? Galina sighed. She thought it unacceptable for a prestigious museum to have the neat squares of cut-up newspaper suspended on string that were a feature of many office lavatories.

Masha brought more tea and they discussed the day's programme. Galina prided herself on getting more work out of her curators, mainly women, by adopting an informal, friendly approach. They were all supportive of each other, and there were less days lost to illness than in the days of Igor Platonov.

Masha had left notes on her desk for a lecture she was giving that afternoon on the jewels of Godunov's court. She leafed through them idly but her thoughts wandered to Arkady's impending visit.

Adamantina and the White Tsaritsa! Extraordinary the part fate played in one's life – or was it simply fortuitous that Arkady had gone straight to Adamantina? It could not be just coincidence that the Russian part of the White Tsaritsa – Grigor's perfect ring that had been acquired by the Soviet state – was on permanent display in her museum.

Arkady had visited the Adamantina showroom in New York earlier in the year and on his return had helped her display their ring to greater effect. It was now dramatically presented in a darkened cell with a single searing spotlight, and Galina had dreamed up the idea of a tape playing atmospheric music in the background.

'You've been watching too much Tarkovsky!' Arkady had sniffed when she first made a presentation – the music had metamorphosed into the clashing of swords, violent screams, conspiratorial whisperings – intended to evoke the historical background of the diamond, the *Smutnaya Vremia*, the Time of Troubles. But he had had to concede that it was effective – and popular. Galina's gradually revamped Museum of Tsarist Treasures, and the White Tsaritsa in particular, was now one of Leningrad's main tourist attractions.

It was now eleven-thirty and Galina had got through half the papers, most of them trivial, spent time on the telephone and organized her staff. She leaned back in her chair, folded her hands behind her head and looked around the room. It was dreary and anonymous. Apart from a photograph of the boys on the desk there was nothing to show that this office belonged to her more than Igor Platonov. She was going to have to make quite a few changes.

Her eyes rested on the capacious bag containing the manuscript Arkady had brought from the Archive Museum yesterday. Fedor's love story, the finding of the White Tsaritsa. She had read it in bed last night and it was still fresh in her mind.

She shivered involuntarily. Her thesis had been on medieval jewellery and the Time of Troubles was familiar to her, but she could still agonize with Elizaveta Romanov as a mother, she could still share her suffering as she watched her only son Fedor Curnonsky leave for exile across a war-ravaged Russia. The spectre of civil war, the possibility of another, even more catastrophic Time of Troubles was very real to Galina. Never a day passed without her waking to fears for her own sons' future.

Fedor's touching journal, started in the painstaking Cyrillic script of the schoolboy, ending on his deathbed as a revered elder statesman in Michael Romanov's court, was the stirring testimony of a bloody epoch, but even more, through Fedor's life of selfless devotion to his country and his Tsar, it was proof of the enduring quality of the human spirit.

Galina imagined that a lad of fifteen would have to grow up very fast in the summer of 1603. For three successive years there had been famine in Muscovy, a total failure of the harvest. Boris Godunov had seized power after the death, rumoured not to have been from natural causes, of Ivan the Terrible and Anastasia Romanov's sickly son. Witchcraft, sorcery, treason! The Romanovs were found guilty of all three and hounded to distant exile. The destructive reign of Ivan the Terrible was nothing to this new wave of class hatred and revolt that plunged Russia into an era of chaos – the *Smutnaya Vremia*.

Fedor's epic journey from Moscow with his father Ivan and their Romanov supporters would have been enough to turn any youth into a hardened man before his time, thought Galina. Fedor had been plucked from his bed in the middle of a terrifying night of murder and arson, when all Moscow reeked of smoke and blood. Hideous screams rang from the Kremlin walls as he cowered under furs in the sleigh; his father had whipped on the horses and he had glimpsed the hand of his mother, Elizaveta Romanov, raised in ghostly benediction before she, in her turn, had fled to seek sanctuary in the Novodevichy convent.

In the course of that nightmare flight over the Urals, across a motherland torn from end to end by desperate civil war, Fedor had witnessed the depths of man's inhumanity to man. Yet his spirit remained remarkably unscathed; he had inherited his mother Elizaveta's introspection and he often wandered away from the Romanov exiles' camp towards the river Tura, where he found the two things that were closest to his heart, Aisha and the extraordinary, shimmering stones.

To the veiled Tartar women Fedor was a curiosity, with his hair as pale as ash bark and his disturbing eyes that seemed to absorb their colour from the changing skies. Eyes that were hypnotic, that made you afraid to look into them, eyes that hinted of special powers, but, hush, they had been warned never to talk about Fedor's 'second sight'. For Aisha, the wife of Taras, the Tartar Ataman, it was an honour to care for Fedor, the son of Elizaveta Romanov, a noble lady of royal blood. Fedor had come to the Tura as the winter snows were melting; by the time the Siberian sun had reached its intense midsummer heat he had become fluent in the Tartar language.

Fedor had fallen in love with Aisha with all the passion of his romantic, impressionable heart; and Aisha, inured to the rough embraces of her huntsman husband, had lost her heart to this sensitive youth who read to her from the Cherdoran, composed verses in her homage and bought

92

her whimsical love tokens, collected in his daily wanderings along the Tura. Lovely, laughing, entrancing Aisha . . . Fedor had watched her shyly, his heart swelling with pride. At sixteen she was scarcely more than a child herself. She was the most beautiful of the nomad Tartar women, her dance the most undulating, her stories the most spellbinding. Aisha, his Aisha . . .

Galina relived Fedor's emotions, through the vivid pages of his journal, the day he had found the White Tsaritsa – the day he realized he would never see Aisha again. It was the day the messenger had come, wraithlike from the dust of the Steppe, and woken the exile camp from the heavy sleep of dawn. At last the call to Moscow had come! The Romanovs had rallied to the Pretender's call to defeat the usurper Godunov. Amid the cries and halloos of the exiles' joy, Fedor, grief-stricken at the thought of leaving Aisha, had rushed blindly from the camp and run until he collapsed, exhausted, in a little gully.

Fedor stretched out his hand towards the dazzling stone, straining to reach it in the dried-out gully. *Bozhe moy!* It had to be an *almaz*, one of those pebbles that made Aisha catch her breath – hush, not to tell anyone, they were the property of the Tsar – that sometimes turned up on his wanderings along the Tura and were duly presented to her in bashful token of his love.

But this *almaz* was miraculous! As oval and solid as a curlew's egg, as clear and sparkling as mountain water – Fedor turned it over in his grimy fingers in intense concentration – but there, deep inside, was a tiny speck, a little heart, a leaping flame! A slow smile spread over his prematurely adult face. He would give this heart to Aisha as a token of his undying love. He stared as though hypnotized into the heart of the diamond and it seemed to calm him. The pounding at his temples stopped and the tears dried on his cheeks. Tomorrow the Romanov exiles started back for Moscow, he would leave the Tartar camp and Aisha, perhaps for ever. His eyes, blue as the Siberian skies, seemed to assimilate the purity and intensity of the stone and in that moment he assumed the responsibilities of manhood. Behind him lay the horror of the Time of Troubles, the flight from Godunov's charges of sorcery – all because of his gift that must always remain a secret, his way of seeing into the past and the future, inherited from his mother, the famous Romanov 'second sight'.

Before him lay his destiny, now irrevocably linked with this miraculous diamond – he instinctively knew it and lowered his head piously, eyes closed. Vivid images of the future sprung up in his head, the flash of a diamond-encrusted sword-hilt, a coronation chalice held high, a jewelled crucifix on the breast of a dying Tsar. A sudden splintering crash nearly burst his eardrums, dizzying his senses – a weapon flashed, the diamond was cleft apart, Russia was in chaos. He doubled up in pain and clutched his heart as though the wound were real. He opened his eyes with an effort and cradled the diamond reverently in his palm. He solemnly gave it the promise of his protection, though he could no longer look into it for fear of what he saw.

Extraordinary Romanov eyes, thought Galina, looking at the photograph of Brilliant Curnonsky that Arkady had given her, that were handed on through the generations, together with that troubling enigma of destiny. Galina looked closer at the colour photograph, torn from the pages of a glossy magazine, and pursed her lips. She was a *krasavitsa chudesnaya*, an amazing beauty, Arkady had told her, and she could see that for herself. It wasn't just the looks, but the *soignée* grooming, the clothes, the jewels, the elegant man at her side that stamped her as a creature from a race apart. She was married – Galina had specifically asked, although that had never stopped

Arkady in his pursuit of female conquest, she thought wryly.

Galina pushed the picture away with sudden venom, stood up and went to the rickety cupboard where she kept items for a hasty toilette. The door, when opened, hung askew on a loose hinge and revealed a square of cracked mirror. She surveyed herself critically. Men used to whisper *krasavitsa* when she passed – but that had been years ago, before Arkady, before Slava, before Sasha and Alyosha . . . But she was still the same to the outside world. She lifted her heavy chestnut hair off her shoulders and piled it on top of her head; it was inside she had changed, she was . . . she was. . . . Galina could not put her finger on how she had changed, but now she had the responsibility for her children's lives and had no time for their chauvinistic *krasavitsas*.

She took the brush from the shelf, swung her head down and brushed her hair hard, then flung her head back again. She looked wild, exotic. . . . She thought of Arkady and quickly twisted her hair into a soft heap on top of her head and pushed in a few hairpins. She put *kompakt* on her upturned nose and filled in her generous mouth with cheap pink lipstick. She rubbed over her lips with her little finger to blend it and then licked them to make them shine. It would do. She looked pale but it suited her, it made her eyes look darker and her winged eyebrows more pronounced.

'Arkady Ilich Tverskoy!' Masha announced Arkady with a great fluttering of eyelids. He was a minister, one of the intelligentsia, but much more than that, he knew how to twist a woman round his little finger; the bastard, thought Galina, as she dismissed Masha with a curt nod.

'Galya *maya*! How lovely you look.' Arkady gave her the familiar triple kiss and she stepped hastily back, away from what she used to call his 'tartar' smell – hard male flesh and leather.

She smiled, gratified, in spite of herself.

95

'I'm going to lunch with Zina – at the *CineCentre*. I had to make an effort.'

'Zina? Hmmm.' Arkady frowned. Galina knew he considered Zina a bad influence, that he was jealous of the men she might meet through her. Zina was a close friend, almost family – well, it was impossible to describe Zina. Someone she couldn't get rid of would be more accurate. They had lived together in Vishnev and gone to university at the same time. From their earliest teens Zina had been her mentor in the ways of the world, always the apogee of modishness and latterly a true Russian libertine. But now Zina's driving ambition, talent and looks had taken her to the top of her profession; as the actress Zinaida Azerova her face beamed at Galina from hoardings and bookstalls all over the capital.

'You look pale, Galya. You're not worrying about Sasha, are you? I called in just now at Leila's and he's having the time of his life.'

There was tenderness in Arkady's voice and Galina flushed with unexpected emotion.

'Thank you, Arkady, that was kind! I'm sure he'll be all right. It's just that he coughed nearly all night and kept me awake. Now – we'd better talk about business as we haven't much time.'

She paused, while Masha sashayed in with two steaming glasses of tea, and frowned as Arkady's appreciative eyes followed her exit.

'What that girl's doing working in a museum, I can't imagine!'

Arkady laughed. 'I agree. This is no place for pretty girls. Did you do your homework?' He inclined his head towards the bulky bag with Fedor's manuscript.

'I read it, yes. The story is familiar to me, through my thesis on medieval jewellery, but the original is . . . spellbinding!'

'And Brilliant Curnonsky – or Chardin as she is now? Here's a packet of clippings about her – with details of her life, her new job with Adamantina, everything you need to know.'

'Everything I need to know? Arkady, I'm only historical adviser to this exhibition. I imagine I shall meet this . . . this Brilliant, and get to know her in due time.'

'Ah, but I haven't told you about my plan for the White Tsaritsa. The most staggeringly simple way to get it back to Russia. Where it belongs, Galya. The mystic stone – our future depends on it!' He gripped her arms and sat her down on the chair.

'Listen, while I tell you. You see . . . when I heard that Brilliant Curnonsky was working at Adamantina, I was puzzled at first, and then began to put two and two together . . . Why was she working there? And then I had this miraculous plan. . . .'

After Arkady had finished explaining, Galya looked elated, but shook her head.

'It seems perfect, and somehow – I agree with you – justified. But do you think you can persuade her?' Galina got up from the chair abruptly and went and got her coat. 'At least I don't have to be part of it. My job is strictly with this exhibition. Remember that, Arkady!'

He sprang to her side and helped her on with the coat, his mouth coming close to her ear.

'Without your support, I'm lost, Galya,' he said softly, his lips brushing her hair.

She tossed her head and moved away, her lips trembling.

'Enough of that, Arkady. But . . . but I wouldn't do anything to stand in your way . . .'

She turned her back and, as she adjusted an astrakhan toque on top of her piled-up hair, she watched Arkady in her compact mirror. His slanting green eyes narrowed in satisfaction and his lips pursed in a gratified smile.

She whirled round and faced him. 'Bastard! God help her – our compatriot Curnonsky!'

On the steps of the illustrious Dom Kino, Zina was signing autographs in a desultory fashion, her tumbling red curls just visible between a lavish fox fur hat and enveloping ankle-length coat.

'You're late, Galya!' she snapped. 'And it's brass monkey weather!'

'Don't give me that! You've never been early in your life. What happened? Kolya throw you out again?'

The two women fell on each other's necks with undisguised affection, then arm-in-arm, chattering ten to the dozen, entered the dining room reserved for stars and their guests.

6

Marie-Laure opened the window of her private office in the Place Vendôme and took one or two unaccustomed deep breaths of fresh air. Normally she avoided contact with the great outdoors and exercise in particular as it only expanded the chest. But today she felt tense and provoked. There was a niggling question of etiquette to resolve, apart from the unpleasant conversation about the deplorable state of Chardin sales that she had had earlier this morning with Honoré.

The problem of etiquette concerned the meeting with Yasmina Said and Comtesse de Tarn Riberac. As a matter of protocol she always received Adèle de Tarn Riberac, being of 'the blood', in the salon reserved for titled clients. But Yasmina Said was an upstart, a Lebanese adventuress to whom Marie-Laure had no intention of giving preferential treatment. Adèle would understand, of course, she would soon accept the reason why this meeting had to be in her office – one glance at Yasmina would be enough.

Marie-Laure lingered a minute longer by the open window, grudgingly acknowledging the miracle that nature was working on the chestnut trees around the *place*. Luxuriant sprays of blossom had burst out overnight in delicate pink and white and the fresh green foliage cast dappled shadows on strolling Parisians savouring the April sunshine.

It was one month since Brilliant had left their lives – Marie-Laure pursed her lips in a wry smile – whether or not for good it was impossible to say. That her defection had been to another jewel house, Adamantina, their arch rival next door in the Rue de Rivoli, had made the whole thing more understandable and taken the culpability from the Chardins' door. Marie-Laure had hinted at scandal –

who knew what Carl Vanderberg had offered? But to her chagrin she could not prove a thing. Yet Jean-Claude had been quick to blame her. Marie-Laure twisted the tassels on the silk curtains between her fingers. He was quick to accuse her of conniving, of driving Brilliant away with her open hostility.

Jean-Claude had been inconsolable. He had pursued Brilliant to London and then lost track of her. She had simply seemed to disappear into thin air. On Marie-Laure's advice he had gone off to the South Pacific for an extended holiday and in Bora-Bora he had seemed to forget Brilliant and find new interests. He had returned three weeks later, thinner and rather sallow, with a talented native boy he wanted to project into the world of design, and a new interest in perfume. He had been dazzled by the seductive scents of the isles and talked of nothing but patchouli, vanilla, ylang-ylang and musk. Then he had turned his back on the jewellery business and immersed himself in the production of the house scent 'Chardin', to be launched in June. While Marie-Laure was glad to pursue new sources of revenue, she was concerned that they no longer worked closely together and she was having to turn more and more to Honoré for financial advice. But more, much more than that – she gave the curtain a savage twist – her son had changed towards her. He no longer needed her, they had grown apart.

As she watched, a black limousine with shaded windows drew up outside Maison Chardin and the chauffeur held the door for the occupant to alight. Marie-Laure's lips tightened in a supercilious smile.

Yasmina Said. What extraordinary ostentation! Marie-Laure peered discreetly from behind the curtain as Yasmina smoothed down the skirt of a chic black suit and started up the marble steps of the Chardin entrance. Possibly twenty million francs' worth of diamonds were distributed about her small person; diamonds on her ears, at her throat, on her lapel, on her fingers and at her delicate wrists. All of her own design and of the very finest quality – Marie-Laure had to grant her that. The most coveted stones from the African mines found their way to Yasmina's base in Sierra Leone, the centre of the diamond 'submarine' trade. Yasmina's business was, on the surface, strictly legal; her uncle Jamal Said was one of Koidu's 'Big Four' who were allowed a legitimate export licence. She was the enormously wealthy widow of Jamal's nephew and had spread her tentacles far and wide to set up as an internationally renowned designer.

Yasmina created for the super-rich and scornfully refused to work on stones of under twenty carats. Owning a genuine Yasmina had a certain cachet in the trade, and as well as 'new' money, some of Europe's oldest families were numbered among her clientele. This had been the carrot that had enticed Marie-Laure to invite her to Maison Chardin. They had met at Nadine de Rothschild's Russian Easter party and Yasmina had sparked off her avarice by mentioning the Sierra Siren, a fabulous new five-hundred-and-fifteen-carat diamond just found in the marine terraces off Sierra Leone. But much more importantly, Yasmina had referred to Brilliant working in New York as Carl Vanderberg's assistant, and had let slip her curiosity as to whether or not this was just a sabbatical.

As for the Comtesse de Tarn Riberac, Adèle was one of Marie-Laure's most valued customers, and had been invited to meet Yasmina as part of a desperate bid to boost sales and acquire the Sierra Siren. Adèle was looking for gems to replace a priceless stolen parure of ancient family diamonds. The theft of this parure had been the stuff of much spicy gossip in the popular press just after the New Year. The French criminal department had held a young house guest of the Tarn-Riberacs, who was rumoured to be Adèle's lover, as number one suspect. Adèle and Guy de Tarn Riberac had separated for a while, adding fuel to the speculation, but all seemed to have been settled for the best, with the case against the alleged lover dropped and the Tarn-Riberacs back together again.

Marie-Laure suspected the truth to be otherwise, of course. She knew Adèle de Tarn Riberac too well to think of her charitably. Her major crime had been indiscretion – she had nearly been found out – but everything else was ephemeral and the Tarn Riberac marriage and the family jewels were still intact.

'Madame Said has arrived, Madame Chardin. Shall I show her in?' Marie-Laure's secretary tapped at the door and inquired softly.

'Of course, Chantal. And tell Philippe to bring in the Pol Roger in half an hour.'

Marie-Laure sat down quickly at her desk and busied herself signing papers. She looked in an abstracted way as Yasmina made a striking entrance, with her small dark head elegantly poised and carmine lips parted in a studied smile.

'Yasmina! How good to see you.' She pushed the papers away and got up from the desk. 'One has so much work . . . I almost forgot our appointment.'

The two women exchanged frigid kisses and Yasmina's shrewd eyes swept expertly over Marie-Laure's desk.

'Of course.' She peeled off her black leather gloves. 'The Comtesse won't be late, I hope? I have an early lunch with Suki Alanos.'

'No, she is punctual as a rule. I'm also expecting my son, Jean-Claude, who is involved in all our business decisions. Ah, *voilà*! Here he is.'

Marie-Laure's face lit up as Jean-Claude slipped soundlessly into the room and she waited, chin raised expectantly, for his kiss. He embraced her perfunctorily and hurried to take Yasmina's hand after their introduction and hold it the obligatory fraction from his lips.

He turned to Marie-Laure with a frown and glanced hesitantly in Yasmina's direction.

'Maman, Father has just told me to give you the message. A shareholders' meeting has been convened for tomorrow. It has been arranged at the request of the Comte de Nemours.'

'Oh.' A spasm of irritation crossed Marie-Laure's face. 'I have been invited for the de Crecys' weekend in Deauville. . . .'

'It is important, Maman.' Mother and son exchanged meaningful glances.

'Nothing serious, I hope . . .' Yasmina had crossed to the window and was tapping her gloves against her palm as she looked down discreetly at the *place* below.

'I think our Comtesse is arriving now,' she observed. 'At last we can get down to business.'

Adèle de Tarn Riberac swept into the room, excusing herself for being late, wearing an Hermès *tailleur* not unlike an equestrian costume which set off her slim hips and rider's thighs to perfection. A small hat with an eye-screening veil was perched on her head; she wore delicate pearl earrings, an antique diamond brooch and the Tarn Riberac engagement ring.

Marie-Laure embraced her with warmth. Here was real class and aristocratic restraint.

The introductions were brief, Yasmina and Adèle exchanged glances of appraisal.

Yasmina ceased playing with her gloves, sat down in the chair offered by Jean-Claude and crossed her knees fastidiously. She recognized in Adèle de Tarn Riberac a woman of mettle and said matter-of-factly, 'I think we should come straight to the point. I have the Sierra Siren at my disposal and naturally all the other houses are after it. The stones cut from it – and I envisage four or five major gems – will be my designs. That is part and parcel of the transaction.'

'That means we must first find the customer?' An ironic smile hovered round Jean-Claude's mouth.

'Yes, unless you have the resources to buy the Siren and sit and wait.' Yasmina's reply was dismissive. 'I don't need to approach any of the great jewel houses. I have an Arab client who is obsessed with legendary stones who wants to keep the Siren in its entirety. But to do my friends a favour – and because I passionately want to

103

design superb jewels from such a staggering gem – I am willing to talk business.'

Marie-Laure nodded her acceptance. 'Well, the Comtesse needs very special stones for her new parure – you read no doubt about the theft of the family jewels . . . ?'

Adèle pushed the veil back from her face and coughed lightly.

'This, of course, is a family matter. Although we have received the insurance money, certain relatives are proving a little . . . uncooperative. The purchase of new diamonds, the style and the jewel house is not just my decision alone. Others have to be consulted. There has been talk . . .' she paused and looked hesitantly from Marie-Laure to Jean-Claude . . . 'of going to Adamantina.'

'Adamantina?' There was deathly silence in the room after Marie-Laure's breathless exclamation.

Yasmina looked around with relish.

'Would it be indiscreet to ask if the Comtesse de Tarn Riberac knows of your daughter-in-law's "situation"?'

Marie-Laure looked flustered. 'It is quite all right . . . we can talk openly . . . Adèle is one of us – practically family.'

Adèle gave a taut smile of acknowledgement.

'You see,' Marie-Laure turned towards her, 'Brilliant is at present working for Adamantina – there has been a lovers' tiff – it's all most unfortunate.'

'Most unfortunate.' Adèle's smile was condescending. 'Well, I came here to see Madame Said in order to keep all my options open. But the family have already approached Adamantina, in fairness I have to tell you that. I pride myself that I have always been loyal and completely honest with you in the past – that was partly the reason for coming here today. Now I will leave you to discuss business with Madam Said.'

'But . . . but Adèle . . .' Marie-Laure's voice was almost a wail. 'I've ordered a little refreshment – a glass of Pol Roger . . . ?'

Adèle shook her head. 'No thank you. The *régime*, you know!' She patted her flat stomach. 'I have to go, I shall miss my appointment *chez* Hermès for a new riding saddle. *Au revoir*. No, no, please don't bother to show me out.'

Marie-Laure turned her back on Yasmina after Adèle had gone and looked at Jean-Claude in desperation. The defection of one of her most valued clients to Adamantina – the prospects for Chardin looked appalling. She clenched her fists and swallowed bitterly. She knew perfectly well that the decision to go to another house was the strong-willed Adèle's – and hers alone. The American jewel house was not so *au fait* with the details of her recent scandal and were consequently easier to manipulate. Marie-Laure had been temporarily upstaged in the game of conniving. But Adèle would live to regret it.

'Adamantina? How interesting that Brilliant Curnonsky should have chosen to go there. It can't be just coincidence that they have the White Tsaritsa.' Yasmina's voice was spiteful.

'Coincidence?' Marie-Laure felt her nerves stretched to breaking point. 'I don't think any of it was coincidence. Carl Vanderberg obviously appealed to the vulgar side of her nature, which had become quite marked. There was more to it than a business deal, although she is his so-called assistant . . .'

'*Maman!*' Jean-Claude turned pale and clenched his fists.

Yasmina rose abruptly from her chair and tapped her gloves on the desk.

'I doubt that very much. You see, Carl Vanderberg and I are engaged.'

'Oh?' Marie-Laure gave her a scathing look of disbelief.

'Oh, yes! For more than a year, in fact, there has been an understanding between us. And the White Tsaritsa is all but sold to my Arab client. I certainly think your daughter-in-law has got her wires crossed if she has gone to Adamantina for any ulterior motive.'

Jean-Claude threw his mother a glance of triumph.

'You see, Mother, what did I tell you?'

'Be quiet!' Marie-Laure held up an imperious hand to silence him. For a second their eyes met and Jean-Claude's held an expression that made her shiver.

Yasmina had been intent on picking an imaginary piece of fluff from her black sleeve. Suddenly she turned astute eyes on Marie-Laure.

'You know, of course, that there have been rumours in the market-place of Adamantina going downhill? That Carl Vanderberg runs the empire too autocratically?'

'Really? I had heard otherwise, that they were doing very well,' Jean-Claude replied coldly.

Yasmina clicked her tongue.

'No diamond house is doing well right now, as you probably know yourselves.' She looked shrewdly from one to the other. 'But I heard from one of Adamantina's major shareholders that there is talk of merging with a European house with the prestigious name and clientele to carry them through a difficult time. . . .'

'You mean . . . you mean . . .' Marie-Laure's eyes grew wide.

'Precisely! I only leave you with the thought . . . that Adamantina could become a pawn in your game . . . a liaison between yourselves and Adamantina, with your daughter-in-law and the White Tsaritsa thrown in – what would you say to that?'

7

'Jewellers to the World' read the sign on the imposing portals outside Adamantina Incorporated on Fifth Avenue. The doorway was intentionally imposing, making it a big event for most people to venture over the threshold. That is, until Brilliant Chardin had made her much-publicized improvements.

'We'll have to call out the riot squad soon, to control the crowds on the sidewalk,' Carl hissed in a stagey aside as she brushed past him in the lobby, a clipboard under one arm and her face set in anxious lines.

'Yes . . . well – they're out there all right, but are they coming in? And once they're in, are they getting the right treatment? I've got Molly with her Irish smile in the lobby hiving off the big spenders into the Inner Sanctum, but the layout in here isn't all I would like it to be, though I suppose in the end it's all down to the staff. I've been interviewing all morning and it's heart-rending. I want to hand the job to everyone, so many of them are nervous and really keen. I want them all to succeed, but – ' her face broke into a resigned grin – 'in the end I have to be ruthlessly pragmatic and pick the ones I know can sell, without looking down their noses at anyone.'

The sweeping changes to the shop front on Fifth Avenue had caused a fascinated buzz of interest from early morning to long after the last weary wave of shoppers had trudged home. The three famous eye-level street windows had been changed into soaring floor-to-ceiling showcases, opening up the shop inside to the inquisitive world and serving as an ever-changing source of entertainment.

'What bait have you dreamed up for the centre window this week?' Carl's mouth twitched at her harassed expression. Brilliant had hit on the idea of using the middle window for a crowd-luring display; at that moment a craftsman was seated at his bench under the spotlight, oblivious to the noses pressed to the glass mere inches from him, honing the facets on an emerald-cut diamond.

'I think I'll continue with the craftsman theme for a while, using different processes in making the finished piece – I want folk to realize that jewels aren't just inanimate objects, but have real people behind them, from the beginning to the very end of the line.' She glanced at her watch.

'I have to fly, Carl, I have a customer in there who has asked for me personally – "highly recommended", he says.' She gave him a conspiratorial wink.

'I was just going through myself.' Carl opened the door to the Inner Sanctum, where the wheat was separated from the chaff, the serious customer with the wherewithal to come up with the ten-thousand-dollar minimum was hived off from the casual shopper with only a few hundred dollars to spare.

Inside this sumptuous small salon Brilliant welcomed an awed couple, Herbert and Sandra Groser of Des Moines, while Carl, with a slight nod of greeting, made his way to his conspicuous desk at the rear of the room.

An impressive Venetian-glass chandelier was suspended from the ceiling of the lofty octagonal room but its light was subdued, no window allowed daylight to penetrate and the perpetual twilight was pierced by a sophisticated system of spotlights. The walls were hung with dove-grey moiré velvet, the same velvet-covered the fat tub armchairs and banquettes and a deep carpet of charcoal-grey diamond design muffled all jarring noise. Four antique desks were arranged around the curving walls, each one presided over by a sober-suited salesman. By each desk hovered a young woman assistant who bore pieces for inspection to and from the tightly guarded strongroom. A few discreet showcases on the wall tastefully displayed a handful of jewellery, in order to give full impact to the *pièce de résistance*.

On a dark podium in the centre of the room sat the White Tsaritsa, completely sheathed in shatter-proof glass, with a mechanism that could retract it into the bowels of the earth should any disturbance sound off the alarm. One concentrated beam of light from the heavens probed the secrets of its brilliance.

Towards the back of this padded amphitheatre at a desk on a raised dais Carl Vanderberg presided, undisputed king of New York diamantaires. Carl had personally controlled the extensive dealing and manufacturing side of Adamantina since Joel's death. Joel had never been one for outward appearances, but his spirit lingered on. Not in the decor and style of the new Adamantina showrooms, but in the unique excitement, taste and flair that permeated the Adamantina empire and had earned it its premier place in the jewellery hierarchy.

Brilliant shook Herbert Groser's great ham of a hand, then Sandra's scarlet-taloned one, and ushered them to the privacy of a corner banquette. She drew up a chair for herself and took out a small notepad, glancing towards Carl on his dais. Carl scanned the piece of paper passed on by his clerk and gave Brilliant a quick nod. Then he entered Mr and Mrs Groser's details in one of his notebooks. Carl had inherited Joel's little red account books which held details of every client and every stone sold since the Forties. He appreciated Joel's claim that his whole life was there. He had only to receive a phone call from a client, pull out his books and, while chatting about his vacation, could quickly check on the client's purchases for birthdays, Christmases, anniversaries, special achievements, discreet presents for girlfriends . . . In fact Carl had become a close friend and confidant of most of his regular clients and knew more than they did of their special needs. Often a man would call him: 'Look, Carl, it's my wife's birthday next week, I haven't any time, could you mail me some ideas – you know – something really special!'

Well, mused Carl, she had a pair of $100,000 earrings

last birthday, perhaps she would like a bracelet to make up the set – he had one that would be a good match for $130,000. In case that wasn't suitable he would mail with it a baguette-cut diamond ring at $85,000 that he noticed she had admired on her last visit. Carl knew that the client would keep both and everyone would be satisfied.

Carl's little red books read like a personal history of some families. He had insight into a great deal of personal knowledge about a man's lifestyle, but was known for his discretion and integrity.

A certain amount of selling and rebuying took place, of course, usually to the good for Carl, when an upwardly mobile wife sought to upgrade her jewellery as well. The changing moral climate too, with one in two marriages ending in divorce, meant there were many repeat brides who wanted to get rid of the old engagement ring and could afford a better one. The divorcées tended to confide in Carl, 'This ring is a much better one. . . .' by the same token making an unconscious comparison with the ex-husband.

An almost sexual aura of excitement surrounded Carl Vanderberg on his lonely throne, and he would be the first to admit that he was turned on by a fine diamond, 'like a cool glass of the finest champagne, sexy and sparkling!'

At some time or other most of the really 'big' stones had arrived at Adamantina for an offer. The famous six-hundred-carat Namibia Golden, the two-hundred-and-fifty-carat Brasilia Star from San Antonio in Brazil, even historic stones from the Maharajahs' collections like the Jhandir and the Ajati Princess, four centuries old, had found their way on to his books.

Kings and queens were among his customers: Farouk of Egypt, the Shah of Iran, Sheikh Yamani of Saudi Arabia, tycoons like Onassis who paid three million dollars for a flawless pale blue diamond of one hundred and fifty-five carats from the Premier Mine in South Africa, for which Carl had originally paid $300,000.

The royal Saudis were excellent customers, as the law

of Islam made it obligatory for a man to treat all his wives equally. Therefore many a chastened sheik had returned with the million-dollar gem he had bought for a new favourite, only to change it soon afterwards for four identical ones at half a million each. Film stars and show-business clients were particularly drawn to Carl's salon; his glamour and excitement, the elusive star quality were things they recognized and understood. Elizabeth Taylor, in the heyday of her jewellery-buying sprees, had returned with a new husband to trade in a gift from a previous one and significantly increased the value of her new purchase. Carl was intrigued by the psyche of the women who coveted precious stones. Hardly able to control their emotion, their eyes misted over and their voices became husky with craving once seated at an antique desk inside the Inner Sanctum, face to face with a choice of his most fabulous pieces.

Brilliant inclined her head closer to Mr and Mrs Groser, poised the pencil over her pad and asked a few preliminary questions.

'Do you have a particular piece of jewellery in mind? A ring, say, or a bracelet? Then we can get down to the type of stone and after that, of course, the value.'

'Hmmm . . . Hmmm . . . Herbie? Herbie! *The jewellery!*' Sandra gave her husband a vigorous nudge. Herbie seemed to be paying more attention to the socialite blonde in the grey outfit who was serving him, peeking down the front of her dress like he'd never seen charlies before. The man was behaving like a dumb klutz, grinning like a Cheshire cat into the woman's big blue eyes. Sure, she was good-looking and had that something Sandra found it hard to put her finger on, that irritatingly elusive and hard-to-counterfeit quality, real High Class.

Herbert had made it big in Des Moines in the bathroom fitting business – water-closets to be precise. He had inherited his grandfather's workshops and discovered a cache of original Victorian lavatory bowls in an outhouse. Some of them were innovative, with musical seats that

111

responded to the user's pressure. They sold so well that Herbert had copies made. One closet led to another, television coverage helped. Soon he was mail-ordering nationwide, the king of the Victorian water-closet. Herbert became a local celebrity, the 'musical water-closet man', but Sandra had other ideas and wanted to escape the plebeian associations.

They had moved three times in the last year, each time to something more compatible with her social aspirations, and now she had 'discovered' jewellery. The real social lionesses of Des Moines were covered with the sort of thing she used to buy fake, diamonds as big as quail's eggs on their fingers, chandeliers in their ears. Some were economical and shopped around, but she had been told, quite unequivocally, that if you wanted the best you went to Carl Vanderberg at Adamantina.

As Herbert was still strangely silent, staring at the blonde, Sandra continued, 'Mrs Lorelei Jameson from Des Moines is a customer of yours, she recommended me. She says you're way and ahead the best and I want a baguette ring just like hers.'

'Now, now, Sandra gal!' Herbert stirred sheepishly into life. 'What we're looking for, Miss, Miss . . er . . . Chardin, is a ring of the highest quality – absolutely flawless – that'll be a good investment. Size doesn't matter so much, we just want the best.'

'I see!' Brilliant smiled at them both and sat back, closing her notebook decisively. She liked Sandra Groser's direct approach. Here was a woman who wanted her money to show. To hell with the investment! Husbands like Herbert were more unusual in the United States, where the marketing of diamonds proved something of a sex study – the men wanting size and the women wanting quality. Brilliant found that in Europe diamonds were often an investment for a rainy day, whereas the Americans, true romantics at heart, had a sentimental approach to the buying of their gems.

'If you would just come over to the desk and sit down,

I'll inform Mr Smithson of your particular requirement and he will help you further. Just one small point – do you have any price ceiling for your purchase?'

The million-dollar question, and it always got them where it hurt. Herbert clutched a region where his wallet might reasonably be expected to be, went a little glassy-eyed and then recovered his poise. In this atmosphere of rarefied elegance, such directness went down as well as a belch at a tea-party.

'No, no, of course not – just show us a nice selection.' Good, that meant 'give me a ladder to climb down on, by showing me some smaller stones.' Mr Smithson's black-dressed assistant was sent off to the vaults with a marked request form signed by Miss Chardin. Brilliant excused herself, saying she would return towards the end of their presentation, and left Sandra and Herbert to relax a little. They sat back, let out an almost audible sigh of relief and looked around the room as if for the first time. The initiation ceremony over, they took in the groups of two or three gathered round the desks, intent under the spotlight, poring over the lustrous gems in the velvet trays. The padded walls seemed to muffle all sound except for a low murmur of voices and the gentle swish of the assistants' silk dresses as they crossed and recrossed the room.

Brilliant had seen Carl glance at his watch, leave his chair on the dais and walk to a small door almost hidden behind draperies on the far side of the room. She knew he had an interview at four-thirty with Arkady Tverskoy, the representative of Russelmaz, the overseas diamond division of the Soviet government. Plans were afoot for a joint Soviet/American venture, an exhibition in Adamantina of pre-Revolutionary Russian jewellery, which Brilliant had taken up with great enthusiasm. But now it was four o'clock and time for his tea – Carl was a man of punctilious habits during office hours – and she had taken to joining him at this hour to talk over the day's business.

She pressed a buzzer at the side of the door, which opened soundlessly to let her in. The office was small and cosy, wood-panelled and lamplit, a refuge from the feminine world outside. Carl sat in his leather armchair by an open fire, a butler's tray exquisitely laid for afternoon tea at his side. Brilliant had dissolved into laughter the first time she had seen him in his 'English' room, tea-strainer poised over a Spode cup, but then Carl's taste and his unabashedly sybaritic nature, taking the best from many cultures and fitting them into his urbane lifestyle, were just two of the many things she was beginning to learn in these first two months of the job.

She sat down opposite him by the fireside and took the cup he offered. Carl's sideways glance approved the spread of her long fingers round the cup as she drank, warming them in that curiously feline way women have. She kicked off her shoes and wriggled her toes towards the flames. She was so obviously at ease in her employer's presence that Carl practically expected her to purr at any moment. He had been ruminating on the disturbing forecast in diamond futures and his preoccupied face softened.

'You look good today! I've ordered your favourite – home-grown strawberries.' Besides some delicate cucumber sandwiches, the tea tray held a bowl of strawberries and some thick cream, in an antique Georgian creamer of elegant contour. Outside their hermetically sealed world the pale green foliage of late May tossed in a cold east wind.

'Yes, I'm feeling pretty pleased with myself, thank you.'

She took an extra large berry from the dish and bit into it, exposing the luscious pink and white perfection of its interior. 'We've had four new clients today who've probably spent one million dollars between them, pretty unevenly distributed though – Sheikha Ib'n Aziza spent over half of it – and there's still one more fish out there I'm going to reel in any minute now.'

Carl smiled at her undisguised pride of achievement. He knew many women involved in the rarefied world of selling big stones, but he had never met one like this. He could not have wished for a better assistant, but he sometimes wistfully hoped she would let up, talk of something other than business. Yet however hard he tried she steered the conversation back to her consuming passion.

He was relieved that she seemed to have put her separation from Jean-Claude and her pending divorce right out of her mind; it had not been mentioned since her departure from London. They had settled quite easily into a comfortable business relationship based on mutual trust and respect.

He was astounded at her knowledge of gemstones, especially diamonds. She could tell with uncanny accuracy the carat and clarity of a diamond a woman was wearing across the room, and she carried her loupe with her at all times to peer and pry around the competition. It was her eye he valued when there was any doubt as to the quality of an expensive stone. Whereas his own knowledge had been slowly acquired through necessity and careful coaching after nearly three decades in the family business, Brilliant's seemed to be an inherent gift, an extraordinary talent that developed quite naturally out of fascination for her subject.

When she first arrived she had seemed completely unconcerned as to where she should live, even protesting that a room in a small hotel would suit her fine, but he had taken a lease on an apartment in a brownstone on 53rd, ten minutes' walk from the Adamantina building. As far as he knew she had very little social life. Friends from her college days sometimes looked her up for lunch, but from the number of reports, projects and designs she presented him with each morning, the evenings must have been devoted to work as well. When she expressed a strong interest in the financial side, he let her have access to the books. She pored over them for a few days and then came back with a most professional in-depth proposal for increasing sales.

'Listen, Carl!' she told him over the teacups, following the morning presentation of her report. 'I think we should get the Ayers people here and find out the direction of the new De Beers advertising.'

Carl smiled and nodded, he had been thinking along those lines himself. Adamantina's position in the diamond retailing world meant that they had a lot of clout with De Beers, and therefore with N W Ayer, the advertising agency responsible for all De Beers advertising and market research in America.

'We all know it's women who want diamonds and men who buy them, or we think we know that, because we are preconditioned.' Brilliant warmed to her subject. 'Well, an awful lot of things have changed over the last decade. There are more women in executive jobs who not only buy their own diamonds, but can afford to give them to their men. I think we should aim a whole new campaign at women to buy for men, and for men to buy for themselves. Diamonds for men! It opens up a whole new potential. Except we've got to exorcize the Diamond Jim Brady image, the feeling that a gentleman doesn't wear diamonds, that it simply isn't elegant. Well, it damn well can be elegant if the designs are right and the advertising's great.'

'Good thinking.' Carl was watching her attentively. 'But how do you intend to get it across to the red-blooded males?'

'Well, I was thinking of using real people in the ads, famous faces, craggy and familiar – politicians, writers, judges, footballers, that kind of thing – all wearing their diamond pins, cuff-links, moneyclips and so on. It wouldn't be difficult to get them, De Beers is such a prestigious name and most people are tickled to death to appear on a whole page spread, great advertising for them if they've got any sense. I know I could sell the idea, anyway.'

Carl laughed and nodded in fervent agreement.

'If you couldn't sell the idea, then I'm damn sure no one can!'

Brilliant continued. 'Just imagine the increase in turn-

116

over if you could get the men enthusiastic enough to buy a little something for themselves when they come in, or better still, get their girlfriends spending. Besides, since my single girlfriends swear there's hardly a heterosexual male left in New York, we had better start pushing the men buying for the men. But in the end it all comes down to design. You remember that little Japanese guy who won the De Beers International Diamond Awards last year – the $25,000 grand prize – nearly all his fantastic stuff was for men, tremendously aesthetic, elegantly modern but not boring. In fact, I seem to remember the Japanese walked away with four of the ten prizes. Well, Akiko arrived in New York yesterday on a research grant and I say we snap him up immediately. He's already had several juicy offers.'

'Good God! What are we waiting for? Get on the phone and book him immediately. Ask him to dinner tomorrow, it's one way to get you away from the account books.'

Carl sipped his tea and watched her over the rim of his cup, chuckling in that spontaneous way she had, delighted that things had gone her way, as she dialled a number and left a message.

'He's at a museum somewhere, but I've left him an offer he can't refuse!'

Carl looked at his watch. 'The Russian invasion will happen any minute. I've met Arkady Tverskoy before, but he's bringing a companion this time, none other than the important lady curator of the Museum of Tsarist Treasures. I can just imagine her, can't you? An earnest heavyweight in a blue Crimplene suit. Now – as you're the one with the Russian connections and were so enthusiastic over this idea in the first place – I'm going to leave most of the interviewing to you.'

Brilliant replaced her teacup on the tray and looked at him levelly.

'Do you know, I'm beginning to think that Carl Vanderberg can actually be intimidated by women.'

117

'That's not fair – well . . . perhaps only women of a certain type.'

Brilliant smiled. She felt with Carl, she liked to convince herself, as she would with the older brother she had never had. Involved through the shared 'blood' of the diamond, close through a mutual commitment, yet with none of the sexual overtones that had often dogged her relationship with former employers.

Carl was a professional first and foremost and she respected that, a gentleman in all his dealings. She knew, for instance, that this Russian woman coming now would be given as much time, courtesy and consideration as he would give a customer spending half a million on a special gem. He had been cool and watchful with her at first, not surprising, she supposed, given her background. But now she found him relaxed and easy, a perceptive man with a quick self-mocking wit, covering a very private inner person. She did not know why she had so many preconceived ideas about the way he would be, a sort of snobbish European arrogance, which crumbled into grudging admiration as she found out more about him.

She was intrigued to observe the man she had mistaken for a professor at their first meeting in Paris at work in such a sophisticated setting. But she found that her first impressions had not been entirely wrong. She noted with amusement that his air of academic abstraction seemed to bring out the protective instinct in his female personnel and he appeared unaware of the 'aphrodisiac of power' that his position as head of Adamantina automatically conferred. Despite the apparent unworldliness, she soon found that Carl was no slouch when it came to business matters. He ran his enterprise with all the benevolent rigour of a medieval statesman; hard-working himself, he commanded devotion and loyalty from his workers, no detail was too small to escape his attention and his consideration towards his staff was exemplary.

She had been in New York only a couple of weeks when one Saturday he helped her move into the apartment he had found for her on 53rd. He expressed surprise at the almost Japanese asceticism of her furnishings.

'It's not that at all, Carl, it's just that I don't have the time or inclination to decorate with a capital D, and I'm certainly not going to compete with the American ladies who make it their life's work. A few rugs, floor cushions and huge plants suit my mood of the moment. If I see another Louis Quinze chair I think I'll scream.' She had laughed apologetically, suddenly thinking that his place was probably crammed with it – yes, pale colours and silk lampshades and French provincial this and that. Nothing wrong with it, of course, except it summed up the over-stuffed, artificial lifestyle she was so thankful to have escaped.

'After all this exhausting work I'm ravenous and I'm going to cook for you. I went to the market this morning and came away with a basket of goodies, too delicious not to use straight away,' Carl told her.

'Good Lord, you're not a foodie, are you!' There was real concern in her voice.

'No! Nothing so compelling. I'm greedy and I like to cook, an accomplishment I think all men should acquire, if only out of self-preservation. I like to experiment with tastes and flavours. I might eat something somewhere and try to reproduce it, but I'm not a basic cook, good old apple pie would defeat me, much to my sorrow. No, I guess like many men I can do a little flamboyant this and that with a sauté pan or wok, or cook myself breakfast and that's that.'

'Thank heaven for that!' Her sigh of relief was heartfelt.

So he invited her to dinner at his apartment off the Village, and shortly after eight Brilliant found it felt good to be sitting in an oak-framed chair *chez* Vanderberg, sipping an expertly made Margarita, listening to Pava-rotti's sublime *O te cara* and watching Carl's energetic chopping movements through the kitchen archway.

Of course his home would be like this – now she was here she felt annoyed with herself for thinking otherwise.

It was a substantial town house built around the turn of the century in a block of other similarly worthy edifices, most of them turned into elegant apartments. The ambiance Carl had created for himself was so European that she might have imagined herself in a friend's pleasantly bohemian Paris apartment, or perhaps it was more reminiscent of Vienna or even pre-war Prague. It had a delightful un-American shabbiness; threadbare and lived in, each object or piece of furniture had been chosen for its intrinsic beauty, regardless of its splendid state of decay.

There was a certain theatricality, a grandeur, in the sheer size of the drawing room, with its frayed Aubusson wall hanging and velvet curtains crumpling to the floor at the three windows, drapes as thick and heavy as stage curtains, the plush rubbed away in places, each tassel of the fringe as broad as her hand. There were deep sofas and regal armchairs, the brocades still retaining glimmers of their former glory, ancestral portraits and hunting scenes, blood-dark and conceived on a heroic scale, wall-to-wall books at one end of the room and a much-used ormolu desk. As the evening was cool, a hickory log fire smouldered aromatically in the wide fireplace.

Everywhere there were books, books and more books, evidence of his passion. When she expressed surprise – volumes tumbled from small tables, tottered in piles on the desk, lay stacked up on the floor or acted as doorstops – he laughed deprecatingly.

'Yes, I should have had a musty old bookshop, it's my antiquarian nature. It all started when I was a kid and found my first old volume on a stall in the flea market. I had just read *Huckleberry Finn* – frowned on now for racist reasons – ' Carl raised amused eyebrows – 'and it made a great impression on me. Nosing around among some old comics and annuals I suddenly found this tattered old volume. As I leafed through the yellowed pages I remember my excitement mounting . . . then I found it . . . in bold strokes of a thick pen the inscription, "To Seamus Scanlon in loving appreciation of your friendship – Mark

Twain". That was the start of it. Now I reproduce that first excitement regularly, the musty smell of old pages sets my heart beating – will this be a lucky find, will my detective work have paid off?' He shrugged and laughed.

'Anyway, it's harmless and inexpensive enough. The whole point is, you see, you are the one who makes the discovery, the one who finds the forgotten treasure. The book's value goes without saying of course, but that isn't the motivation for me. Take a look at that volume over there . . .'

He gesticulated through the archway in the direction of his desk, releasing a spray of finely chopped parsley from a formidable-looking knife. '. . . You might be interested in it, it's French. a Ménagère, written about 1740, must have come over with the early colonists – *Le Maître Cuisinier Pours des Ménagères de France*. I've been struggling through it with the aid of a dictionary, and it gives an amazing insight into the mores of the time, the lady of the household having her finger on the pulse of life, as it were. If I had more time I'd like to translate it, I don't think it's been done. The other day at Le Trinquant, one of Pierre LaValle's dishes was so like one in the Ménagère – he said it came from his grandmother – it was incredible. This little book has been hiding its light under a bushel all these years, while the Nouvelle Cuisine boys think they've got it all sewn up!' His face was alight with an enthusiasm for his subject that she had never seen displayed at Adamantina.

She pulled herself out of the depths of the armchair and crossed to the desk. The Ménagère was on a stand with a powerful light directed at the page: '*Myettes de Veau avec les Cèpes de Forêt avec Son Persillade*'. Hmmm . . . it did sound a bit like a sample from the Nouvelle menu but . . . and her nostrils quivered, it smelt exceptionally good. She wandered towards the kitchen, but Carl barked a warning.

'Don't come near me, I'm not that confident, things are at the scraping off the floor stage!'

Brilliant laughed and went back to her chair, perched on the arm and sipped her drink. She had gleaned a few official facts about him. He was divorced from a South African diamond heiress; the marriage had been short, no children. He was a prominent member of the Art Collectors' Guild. He farmed extensively in New England and Arizona.

'Well, you're always full of surprises. And the farming too. How do you reconcile all this . . .' she waved her hand around the apartment . . . 'and that . . .' She gesticulated vaguely in the direction of Fifth Avenue.

'Ah, well, you see, I'm really very nouveau riche.' He had evidently come to a more relaxed stage of the cooking process, and took his whisky tumbler in one hand, wielding the wooden spoon with the other.

'I took my father's words to heart – "Never put your trust in man or a diamond".' He seemed to think that anything so artificially maintained in price, as diamonds undoubtedly are, is an extremely risky business. He encouraged me to put my faith in the soil, "Mother Nature'll never let you down". That's not true, of course, either.'

Carl smiled wryly and she warmed to him. He was so quick to contradict himself, as though some fastidious inner voice was constantly criticizing, saying, 'that's presumptious crap and you know it'.

'I've always thought there was a touch of the Renaissance man about Carl Vanderberg, sitting up there on a dais, more medieval than modern in his "compleatness" . . .' she mused almost to herself, as the clatter of the finishing touches in the kitchen drowned her voice.

'À table – à table!' he called triumphantly. 'Have you ever noticed, that when men cook it's absolutely imperative you drop everything immediately and pay homage to the "creation".'

She walked quickly through to the dining room which led off the kitchen. Built on a less grandiose scale than the drawing room, it achieved intimacy from its warm colouring: worn amber silk on the walls, magnificent tawny curtains falling heavily to the floor, rich colours of Persian rugs on polished parquet that gave off the wholesome smell of beeswax and clover. Although it was not yet dark, he had lit the tapering candles in the wall sconces and the candelabra in the centre of the vast cherry-wood table.

'I thought there was no point sitting at opposite ends of the table, although I'm convinced it was the distance they kept at mealtimes that made old-fashioned marriages endure.' Carl strode briskly behind her carrying a laden tray.

He never talked about his marriage, although waspish allusions to the married state were commonplace, and she chose not to ask. There was a tacit understanding between them on this delicate subject. He seemed to have a handful of close women friends – she had come to admire his skill at handling some of the more persistent. She often took calls for him, knew most of them by name only, and was amused at the varying degrees of coolness with which they treated her.

He had laid one corner of the table with an elaborate display of old silver and glass that would have done justice to a royal banquet. With an equally regal flourish he seated her in a high-backed chair where the leaping flames from the fire could warm her. The morsels of veal with their wild mushrooms were every bit as tempting as their aroma had prophesied, and as they sipped a miraculous Montrachet he talked a little more about himself as a diamantaire.

'Whereas you, Brilliant, are a "natural" by instinct and inclination, I was merely thrown into the business by the family connection. Uncle Joel spent a decade trying to mould a rebellious country boy into a sharp city slicker, with varying degrees of success. He certainly taught me all I know about precious stones, but the other experiences I preferred to acquire at my own pace, and I'm sure I'm still a learner. There are certain aspects of the diamond

123

business that I found pretty hard to take . . . still do for that matter.'

At that moment the telephone rang and on his return he seemed thoughtful, his ebullient mood had gone as he told her, 'There has been a problem with a consignment at customs, a mix-up with the papers or something. I have to go immediately.' He looked so grim that she stared at him in surprise.

'I'm sorry, Brilliant, I didn't mean to sound so brusque. I've spoiled your evening. It's just that . . .' He seemed about to confide in her, then hesitated and fell silent.

'Well . . . it can't be helped . . .' Brilliant was still surprised, and if she admitted it, more than a little disappointed that the evening should end so abruptly.

Later, reflecting on that meal, she felt that for all he seemed open and spontaneous with her, underneath Carl's perceptive self-criticism and witty asides lay the deep reserve of a very private person, with an impregnable facade that would prove very hard to crack.

8

Carl's treasured Joseph Knibb longcase clock chiming the half hour made the tea tray rattle and brought them back with a start to the preoccupations of the present and the imminent arrival of their Russian guests.

A discreet buzz at the concealed door announced George, their major-domo, who stuck his head round and announced staccato:

'The Russians are here . . . ahem . . . that's to say Mr Tverskoy and Miss er . . . Miss . . . er . . . here to see you, Mr Vanderberg.'

Carl stood up abruptly.

'Oh yes, of course! Show them in, would you please, George.' He straightened his tie automatically and moved towards the door.

Brilliant also stood up and waited expectantly, a flicker of amusement on her lips at the wary expression on Carl's face.

The door shut behind George and opened again just as swiftly. A young woman stepped briskly into the room followed by a tall man. The wariness vanished from Carl's face and stupefaction took its place. So much for Carl's heavyweight lady curator in blue Crimplene, was Brilliant's dazed reaction once she had recovered from her initial surprise. An apparition in a close-fitting violet ankle-length coat, fur-collared and cuffed *à la Tsarina*, chestnut hair upswept and tucked under a little purple toque, stretched out both hands in greeting and smiled broadly from under a coquettish spotted veil.

Brilliant clasped her gloved hand mechanically and then turned to the man. She had the impression of dark blond unruly hair, high cheekbones and a certain controlled ferocity in the slightly tilted eyes. Except for the modern cut of the Russian's Italian suit, she could have sworn she had entered another age. The tall stranger took her hand in his, brought it expertly to within inches of his lips while his eyes burned into her with disturbing intensity. A supercharged shock of emotion ran up from the tips of her toes to the roots of her hair and then down again. It was the most extraordinary sensation she had ever felt and she wanted it to last for ever. He let go of her hand and it fell back at her side. She continued to stare uncomprehendingly into his eyes as though he was about to tell her something of vital importance. Carl's laugh intruded into an almost strange hypnosis.

'Well, I can honestly say I've never been proved so wrong in my life! As Brilliant will tell you, Miss Sigorin, I had conjured up an entirely different mental picture of you. I feel as though I've been set up – Arkady, you could have given me a hint about the ravishing curator.'

The man she had been introduced to as 'Arkady Tverskoy, Russia's Number One in Diamonds' smiled.

'Yes, Galina is my hidden asset on this trip! I love to watch the expression on people's faces when I introduce her – "Have you met the curator of the Museum of Tsarist Treasures . . ." You see, we're looked on as curiosities, a different species, they never know quite what to expect and stare and pry as though we were from another planet.'

And from another planet they could have been, thought Brilliant, still strangely silent, staring at the couple. There was an indefinable uniqueness about them which she found impossible to explain. It puzzled her during the first few hours of her acquaintance and, later, brooding on the intensity of her reaction, she could only put it down to precisely what Arkady had just said. They were the same species, yet different. There was a spontaneous energy about them that came from a different time, different values, different concepts, as though they had been held in a time warp and had suddenly emerged.

'Please call me Galina Alexandrevna.' Galina slipped off the retro overcoat and handed it to Carl. 'Or better still

Galina, if you don't find it too informal.' She smiled at him as she sat straight-backed in the chair he proffered, lifting her veil with a graceful feminine gesture a million times more erotic than the baring of acres of flesh.

'I've always loved the romantic sound of Russian names – the way they roll off the tongue. Is there any protocol about what I should or should not call you?' Carl sat beside her and inquired with the eagerness of a teenager.

'Oh, yes, it is very clearly defined.' Galina's voice was low and musical, her English excellent, although slower and more heavily accented than Arkady's. 'To call someone Mr or Mrs is very formal, but we would never dream of calling a superior or older person simply John or Bill as you do. Using the patronymic is a mark of respect, it is always used when addressing someone in public . . . so you see all the Anna Arkadinas, Ivan Ilichs and Nikita Semyonichs of Russian literature are not just an anachronism.'

'Is it usual in Russia to be so fluent in English? It speaks volumes for the sad state of our language teaching.'

Arkady and Galina exchanged amused glances.

'Oh, no, we were very privileged, we went to Spetz-school together, that's a specialized school where all the teaching is done in English. Only I was a model pupil, Galina was too busy doodling on her notepad to take much in.'

She glared at him and assured Carl, 'Arkady was the most appalling tease and terrible . . . I think you say . . . swot . . . you have ever come across.'

'So you've known each other a long time . . .' Brilliant spoke almost to herself.

'Since pram-time! Our mothers were best friends. We used to dribble together in the Summer Gardens.'

Brilliant laughed with the others, experiencing a feeling of strange relief.

'I must say, Galina, I was surprised too. You're not quite what anybody would have expected from a museum curator.'

127

Galina's smile revealed an expanse of healthy even teeth.

'Oh, I dress fairly normally for work, you know! A long skirt might get caught in the Underground doors. But I have always had a passion for old clothes, anything old come to that, and I'm always rummaging in the Commissiony – they are our second-hand shops. In fact it's the only way to dress with taste in Russia if you have no access to foreign goods.'

'It's hard to find her at work these days. The job's a sinecure, she's always away "researching" some arcane titbit or other, except now I know that's a euphemism for tracking down the nearest jumble sale.' Arkady had taken a seat opposite Brilliant and seemed to be assessing her as he spoke.

Galina looked indignant. 'The job is easier now I'm director of the museum, but that's because I took over from a man. Before, when I was the dogsbody I had no time at all to spend with my children.'

Carl got up reluctantly from Galina's side and looked at his watch. 'It's getting late and I want to get the contract signed, Arkady. Let's drink first to the exhibition's success, and then I'll leave you with Brilliant for a few minutes if you don't mind, Galina.'

Carl crossed the room to a drinks cabinet cunningly concealed behind some panelling and when he returned with a bottle of champagne and some glasses the others were talking in Russian. Brilliant replied rather heatedly to a remark of Arkady's, then Galina smiled quickly and said something that made them all laugh. A quick stab of alienation twisted at Carl's heart and he remembered that sense of pain he felt as a teenager, when his closest friend came down from university with WASP colleagues and the intellectual conversation excluded him; he was outside an elitist club whose membership would always evade him.

'Your Russian has the merest trace of a French accent, so delightfully pre-Revolutionary, you would be welcomed with open arms by the Soviet *ancien régime*!' Arkady inclined towards Brilliant in mock gallantry, his eyes gleaming sardonically.

Brilliant's chin went up. 'I didn't think they still existed, I thought you had done a fairly thorough job of extermination.'

A muscle twitched at the corner of Arkady's mouth. 'I am Count Arkady Tverskoy, our lineage can be traced to the first Romanov court, Countess Curnonsky.' Brilliant flushed, the appellation tripped off his tongue as easily as if it were in common use.

'Believe me, I am not joking,' he continued. 'Social snobbery is alive and well and still flourishing in Russia today. Certain of my relatives consider themselves more aristocratic than any European nobleman.'

'That's a particular set-up I for one crossed the Atlantic to escape,' Brilliant snapped. 'And now you are destroying my fond illusions that at least one reasonably class-proof society still does exist.'

'Bravo, Brilliant! But I think Arkady's real snobbery is of an intellectual kind, more of which you'll doubtless come across later . . .' Galina intervened quickly, rolling her eyes heavenwards in mock alarm, so comically that it defused the situation and they all laughed.

Carl's momentary struggles with the champagne bottle sent the cork catapulting across the room and in the bustle to fill glasses and drink toasts Brilliant had barely time to reflect that if Arkady was protective of Galina, she was scarcely less so of him. . . .

'To the winds of change that sent you to us – to *glasnost*, *perestroika* and the success of Gorbachev!' Carl raised his glass. There was silence as they drank, four pairs of eyes over the rims of their respective glasses expressing varying degrees of optimism, scepticism, indifference and resignation.

'That's as political as we're going to get for the moment.' Carl smiled wryly. 'Now let's get down to the signing. Brilliant, you'll be pleased to know, everyone is agreed for the end of November.'

'Is there any significance for this particular time?' Galina drank quickly and put her glass down on the table.

'Yes.' Carl smiled at her. 'Great commercial significance. It's going to get people into the showroom in the weeks before Christmas, that's when we have our biggest sales.'

'Oh!' Galina murmured politely, looking a little nonplussed. It was evident that any connection between the exhibition and commerce had not directly occurred to her.

'Yes,' Brilliant rejoined with enthusiasm. 'It's going to be a marvellous opportunity for us to launch our new line, which has a rather Byzantine feel – you'll love it, Galina. A very talented Spanish girl did the designs, I'll show them to you later. Talking of design, we have to think about advertising. De Beers are sponsoring us, so we have serious money to spend on the campaign. We can go over-the-top Russian,' she grinned sheepishly, 'I mean, really capitalize on it being so . . . so. . . .'

'So much "the flavour of the month"?' Arkady smiled. 'It hasn't escaped our attention, certainly not if you tune in to the BBC World Service, as all English speakers do. If it's Russian it's "in" . . . what did I tell you about coming from another planet? We have sent telexes to De Beers in London and Johannesburg, but as they can't keep an office here, how can we discuss these promotional ideas?'

He knows the answer to that question as well as I do, thought Carl, getting up to refill the glasses. There is not much about the trade that Arkady Tverskoy of Russelmaz doesn't make it his business to find out, so what is he trying to prove . . . or who is he trying to impress?

'You'll have to do it through Ayers as normal.' Carl looked at Arkady levelly. 'You see, Galina, it's rather a unique relationship. Because of the American anti-trust laws, De Beers, as a mining monopoly, cannot show their faces in the States. So from their dizzy heights on the forty-first floor of the Avenue of the Americas, the advertising agency acts as big brother. The De Beers executives can't even visit the Ayers offices in New York, the trust-busters are always on the lookout and all meetings have to be held in London. It's good spy-thriller sort of stuff, isn't it? Though I've heard that quite a few De Beers people take a "vacation" in New York, and lunch at "21" is considered neutral territory. First thing in the morning we'll get Ayers in here and have a conference, you'll be able to see the real creative McCoy at work. Right! Shall we go into my office, Arkady? We'll be back shortly – keep the champagne flowing.' Carl motioned Arkady to follow him.

'Oh, by the way, Carl, I nearly forgot,' Brilliant called after him in concern. 'The Grosers are waiting for me back there to finalize their sale.'

'I'll put a call through to Molly, she's more than a match for our Herbie. Let's go, Arkady.'

Arkady brought his heels together and inclined slightly, his eyes swept over the two women as though it were unbearable to tear himself away, before following Carl into a private den just off the panelled room.

'Some more champagne?' Brilliant took the bottle from the ice-bucket. Galina quickly tucked her feet under her chair so that Brilliant would not see them. Too late, the American had noticed the state of her soles. So what – she had refused to wear the other choices open to her, those boots for kicking tanks in or the hopelessly out-moded court shoes. At least these little Louis-heeled slippers, circa 1910 her practised eye reckoned, did not offend her taste or detract from her *touyalet*.

As Brilliant bent over and refilled her glass, Galina could smell her expensive scent, redolent of amber and leather, see the fine blonde down on her forearm, feel the warm current of air displaced by that thick curtain of pale hair as it fell over her face. She was beautiful; Galina pursed her lips, more in confirmation than in approbation; yes, Arkady had been right. He had briefed her carefully before they left, there had been photos. He had never met Madame Chardin, but a file of press cuttings had presented a picture of Carl Vanderberg's assistant that had filled Galina with trepidation. But now here she was, and not the slightest bit intimidating. Warm and even vulnerable, with compelling eyes, Fedor's eyes, that marked her out as having a special destiny. What if she had that 'second sight' of her ancestor. She will sense me a fraud, come here to spy. . . . And the White Tsaritsa? When shall I tell her that the Russian half is in my keeping? Damn that Arkady and his devilish scheming.

Ah, there's a real woman, my mother would have said! Brilliant glanced at Galina obliquely as she replaced the bottle on the table. She would have approved the seductive grace, the taste and individuality that made Brilliant feel suddenly unimaginative and artificial in her designer 'uniform' of that season. Galina's hair was glossy with health, her fine natural skin was spattered with freckles across a delicious upturned nose and her mouth moved expressively when she spoke. The face of countless Tanyas and Natashas whose dark-fringed eyes had gazed mournfully at her from the archives of the Soviet screen. Yes, she is utterly charming and uncontrived with it – no wonder Carl is entranced. She smiled wryly. She had never seen her employer show the slightest reaction to any female blandishments up till now, in fact it had always intrigued her that he remained so apparently impervious.

'I love this room, Carl's furniture, it's just my style. He has excellent taste.' Galina looked around the room with approval, a hundred unanswered questions buzzing round her head. 'I've always felt happiest among old things, so you see the museum is my idea of heaven.'

'Do people still have antiques in Russia? I've seen exquisite things in glossy books.'

'Not any more, most things were destroyed in the Great Patriotic War,' Galina continued in Russian. 'Though some old families managed to hang on to their furniture. You can pick up odd bits and pieces in the countryside if you're dedicated enough – I've a friend, the husband of . . . of someone I know, who has a fabulous *dacha* just outside Moscow that looks like the set of *A Month in the Country*. His Peter the Great fireplace is the pride of his life.'

Brilliant smiled. 'I heard you mention your children. It must have been difficult to leave them?'

At Galina's deep sigh, Brilliant knew she had touched a raw nerve.

'You're right. Sasha's six and Alyosha's only four, and I've never left them before. My mother came up from Vishnev to look after them, but I worry all the same. . . .' She frowned and was silent for a moment, her fingers plucking at a tassel on her bag. 'And you, Brilliant, do you have a family?' Galina quickly recovered her poise.

'Me? Oh no, I don't.' Brilliant lowered her eyes in front of Galina's inquiring gaze, not before she had seen mirrored there surprise and something more, could it be concern? A little spark of self-pity welled up in her and then an inexplicable resentment. She felt suddenly conscious of her thirty-five childless years and her flat unproductive stomach.

She stood up, went over to the desk and picked up a sheet of paper.

'When Carl comes back we'd better fix on a time to go over the exhibition schedule. It's very important to have a professional attitude – I'm afraid you've rather held us up with signing this contract – these things are usually organized a year in advance.' Brilliant's tone was sharp, almost patronizing. . . . Then she stopped, hating herself. She had used her position, her sophistication to deliberately put Galina in her place. Galina made her feel further ashamed with her reply.

'Oh, I know we were late making certain decisions. . . . You've no idea how much persuading it took on Arkady's part to get me here, not just because of the boys, but I hesitated. . . . I had such doubts about coming to the West. I felt inadequate, inexperienced in the ways of big business, all the complexities of setting up an exhibition like this were so daunting – even though my part is only on the historical advisory side. Arkady kept telling me I had to come, he needed the support of my museum, of course, but he wanted me to see America, to have a break, a rest. . . .'

Seeing the look of inquiry in Brilliant's eyes which any woman would recognize as a question mark as to their personal relationship, Galina, try as she might, felt her cheeks turning slightly pink to avoid giving anything away.

'Arkady has this tremendous brotherly concern for me, you see. We practically grew up together until my early teens when my father died and my mother moved to Vishnev. Then we met up again at university. . . .' Galina spoke lightly, her eyes avoiding the American woman's. How despicable, how can I lie to myself as well as to her. . . . Why do I want to tell her everything, with those extraordinary eyes that compel me to trust her? She went on brightly, 'So you see, he thinks it gives him proprietorial rights to cajole, bully and interfere in my so-called career.'

There was a pause, an unspoken emotion flowed for a moment between them, then Brilliant said gently, 'Arkady was right, you had to come – the exhibition was your idea, I believe?' Galina nodded. 'Don't worry about the organization. We really have everything under control. There are just a few formalities to go over – a few changes in the exhibits. . . . Then you must enjoy yourself, go mad in New York! I'd love to help you . . . tell me what you'd like to see?'

Galina looked a bit bemused.

'Well, as it's my first visit to the West I've really no idea. I just want to soak up the atmosphere . . . it's always something of a culture shock for us. You have to treat me gently, I shall probably wander round a few museums on my own in a daze. Oh, of course! The compulsory shopping – I have some requests – and there's the boys, I've just glimpsed toy shops so far from taxi windows, but I can't wait to start buying.' At the mention of the boys Galina's wide brown eyes lit up her pale face with a radiant maternal glow.

'Right, toy shops it'll be, cosmetics, clothes, shoes. . . .' Brilliant diplomatically kept her eyes above floor level. 'We can have a field day tomorrow afternoon, when business is over. I'm already excited . . . where to go . . . toys . . . FAO Schwartz is the place. I love shopping for toys. I hope . . . oh, God! I hope one day it will be for my own children. . . .' This last remark came out in one breath and so unexpectedly that it momentarily rendered her speechless. Not the sort of thing she could ever imagine saying in brittle American tones to a compatriot, but in her own emotive language, to a Russian whose eyes she had just seen fill with suppressed tears, it seemed right, it was moreover true, her heart had at last articulated a desire she had long kept silent.

Galina was fighting to control her own emotions. 'I'm sorry . . . so sorry . . . I feel such a fool. . . . You see it's Sasha's first day back at school. . . .' Galina blew her nose and looked up, smiling shakily, the tip of her nose quite pink. 'I'm worse than he is, he always cries the first day. But it's not just that, I honestly think I'm a bit tired and overwrought. You've no idea what it does to come here, how it shakes the soul in a fundamental way.' They both laughed.

'I knew our Russian soul would have to come into it somewhere . . . or is it just a euphemism for emotional weakness – I've often wondered?' Brilliant sat down and laid her hand on Galina's arm.

'No doubt about that in my mind.' Galina's eyes were sparkling again, the tears drying on her flushed cheeks. 'Brilliant, you truly are Russian, how can it be that you've never been back?' Brilliant shook her head and said nothing.

'But your heart, your feelings . . . you can't deny your motherland. At least to see it and feel its lifeblood, the warmth of that much-vaunted soul. Oh, I know the past . . . your father. . . .' Galina had been warned by Arkady to be tactful, but suddenly only the truth seemed acceptable. '. . . but you can't deny your roots, to find out what you're really made of.'

Brilliant smiled regretfully.

'I know, I know. Where's my curiosity, if nothing else? But somehow I've always been afraid to embrace the Russian experience. Afraid that the immensity of it all, emotionally, might engulf me. Yes, I really think it's been like that. But who knows, perhaps time has changed me, perhaps now I should make the pilgrimage. There are things I need to see and find out. . . .' Galina seemed to know everything about her, that was evident. It was like talking to a Russian alter ego, she understood her mood, anticipated her every response.

'That's just what I was going to talk to you about, Brilliant.' How fortuitous that it should come about like this. She had thought it would be difficult, and Arkady had told her not to say anything, to leave it to him. 'You know that I am curator of the Museum of Tsarist Treasures – actually my university thesis was on medieval jewellery – so I am an authority on your . . . on the Curnonsky Diamond.'

'The White Tsaritsa! Did you see it when you came in?'

'Of course. That was part of *our* pilgrimage. You can imagine our emotion, face-to-face at last with that stunning symbol of our history, the fateful heart. . . .' Galina was silent for a moment, deep in thought. 'Brilliant, in my museum I have the other half of the White Tsaritsa – it is our *pièce de résistance*, it draws more visitors than anything else. . . .'

'The White Tsaritsa – you have it there?' Brilliant stared at Galina as if she were telling her some impossible untruth.

'Why, yes, you know it became part of the Soviet People's Collection after the Revolution, then during the

136

difficult days of civil war and the New Economic Policy it was hidden away, perhaps the government were afraid its charismatic power might be used against them. During the thaw Khrushchev opened the museum – not for any love of culture, more as a means of earning hard currency. Tickets for the museum are on sale at all the Intourist desks in the big hotels, it is one of their biggest earners. We were sure you knew we had the White Tsaritsa's twin when we first wrote, then we wanted to surprise you and bring it, but the authorities gave us a big "*nyet*". With the legend of the heart, you see, it is very special. Superstitious or not, every Russian thinks there's something magical about that stone, and so it would be somehow bad luck to let it go out of the country. But we want to copy the dramatic way you've displayed the stone here and. . . .' she smiled quickly '. . . and make a synthetic copy of it, to take its "heart" back to Russia. So I am spying on you a little, if you like, we need to turn the ring into our star attraction.'

'What do you think it is, the flaw inside, the tiny heart. . . .' Brilliant wasn't listening to Galina's museum talk, but clutched at her arm compulsively.

Galina answered her with the informed ease of the art historian.

'A small speck of crystallized carbon probably, but it is extraordinary, from some angles it looks just like a tiny blue flame leaping upwards. There is something unique, almost supernatural about its fire, it's easy to see how the legend grew. . . .'

Just then the door of the small study opened and Arkady entered the room. He glared at them suspiciously, like a big cat about to pounce.

'Everything's signed. What are you nattering about like old babas? What, crying is it, *devushka*, what's the matter?' He looked more angry than concerned, seeing traces of tears on Galina's cheeks.

She looked confused and Brilliant put in quickly, 'We were talking about children, Arkady, and . . . and personal things.' She felt a flicker of unexpected anger. She wanted to exclude him, she resented his bold eyes that swept over them both with such presumptuous arrogance. 'Old babas, indeed!' Then he laughed sheepishly and became all charming naivety, begging to be forgiven, as Carl joined the group and made a rendezvous for the morning.

'So it's a reception tonight for you two with the Ambassador, very grand!' Carl smiled broadly at Galina. 'If you're not fixed up tomorrow night perhaps you could join us for dinner? It's Akiko, isn't it, Brilliant? He's a talented Japanese designer we'd like to employ – so we can make the evening an international affair. Anyhow, let's finalize it in the morning. Arkady, before you leave, I'd like you to meet our managing director. . . .' The two men walked ahead of them and were soon talking to senior members of Carl's staff.

The lights were out in the showroom as the two women passed through, except for one celestial beam illuminating the White Tsaritsa on its pedestal. They made straight for it, as though drawn by a magnet.

'So, this is it, the twin of our legendary diamond. It's quite, quite breathtakingly beautiful – but sort of spine-chilling at the same time. It surpasses even my imagination!' As though talking to herself Galina pressed up to the glass and misted it with the involuntary exhalation of her breath, then she turned to Brilliant.

'Brilliant. . . .' To Galina's surprise her voice came out almost as a sob. 'I know how you must feel . . . how it must hurt you. When I read the story of the White Tsaritsa my heart went out to you. But then, when you came here to work for Carl, I have often wondered – was it just coincidental, or was it really the pull of that diamond?'

Galina's quest for the truth always triumphed over the need for diplomacy and Brilliant laughed as she patted her gratefully on the shoulder.

'If you really want to know, I never even thought about it.'

'Arkady showed me the *Time* magazine cover story and it really gripped my imagination, started me off thinking about a thesis, or a book on the White Tsaritsa. I got very excited about it, but then pressure of work made me shelve the idea.'

Brilliant's eyes were as dazzling as the prisms of light in the diamond as they blazed at Galina.

'Would you . . . Could you really do it? It would be a dream come true for me! It's such a part of me, something I can't explain . . . But I think you understand.'

'Ladies, ladies, I'm shutting up shop!' George's insistent voice boomed through the distant gloom.

Galina pressed Brilliant's hand. 'We'll meet tomorrow then?'

'Yes, here first thing, then the rest of the day's our own.'

The two women exchanged complicit smiles, behind which so much was left unasked, unheeded and indeed unknown in the deep complexities of the female psyche.

9

On the way back to the Dodge Plaza Hotel Arkady was in ebullient high spirits.

'Marvellous! Marvellous! It went so well. You impressed them, my little dove. What were they expecting, some thirteen-stone woman-tank?' He turned in the taxi and hugged her compulsively. 'Huh, we have beauties, too – real women, soft yet strong, not their ersatz, neurotic man-eaters.'

Galina laughed at his infectious pleasure after signing the contract. She loved to see him like that, so buoyant and effusive. His moods could be mercurial, elated one minute, utterly downcast the next. She stole a look at his flushed face and his thick ruffled hair. He looked nineteen again, and her heart turned over with an emotion she thought she had long since buried.

'What do you think of her – our compatriot? What did I tell you, an amazing beauty – *krasavitsa chudesnaya* – even more than the photos promised.' Arkady gazed distractedly out of the taxi window, a muscle working in his jaw.

'Yes, yes, such a beauty, truly enchanting.' Galina's nose wrinkled as it did when she was amused in a cynical way. For all she was used to his *krasavitsa chudesnayas*, her stomach tightened with the stinging bile of envy and she wanted to throw herself into his arms and scream at him: Love me, Arkady! Love me and only me! But she gripped the fabric of her handbag with a ferocity that turned her knuckles white and concentrated her attention on the seething sidewalk humanity observed through a veil of unshed tears.

When they were in the corridor outside her room, Arkady advised her earnestly, 'Wear that dress again

140

tonight, Galya, it suits you so well.' He peered anxiously at her pale face. 'Take a bath now and have a little rest – the bathrooms are quite something, huh? I'll come for you in an hour.' He caressed her cheek with the palm of his hand. 'You're tired, little dove – rest now – and don't worry, everything will be fine.'

She smiled tartly as she closed the door behind her and leaned against it wearily. 'Wear the same dress. . . .' Arkady knew as well as she did that it was the best in her meagre wardrobe. He had been over her clothes with her before their departure, clicking his tongue over the unsuitability of some, exclaiming over the originality of others. He was fastidious about her appearance, seeing her as an extension of his image of a Russian of superior taste.

She sighed as she sank into the limed-oak replica of a Louis Seize armchair and kicked off the dilapidated shoes. The holes in the worn soles seemed to stare at her like accusing eyes. What the hell! What on earth did anything matter? How could she possibly compete with Brilliant's gloss, sophistication, or worldly assurance. *Krasavitsa chudesnaya, da, da*, there was no disputing that. But she was warm and *simpatishna*, too; how could she really dislike her? She was exactly the woman she would have chosen for Arkady had she been asked – mettlesome, intelligent, of Russian blood. Yet resentment welled up in her. What can she know of our lives? What does she know of a system that saps at one's energy and morale with each insidious day?

She picked up the photograph of the boys she had placed on the desk and stared at it dispassionately, even coldly. What did she know of the change motherhood brought to your heart and your horizons? You were never free again, as men could be free. The maternal mix of love, anxiety and suffering held you trapped in an emotional stranglehold far more powerful than the uncertain bonds that exist between the sexes.

A slash of red light from the neon sign outside the

window fell across the boys' faces like a wound and she shuddered – perhaps an omen, a portent for the future? Quickly, superstitiously, she replaced the photograph on the desk with a whispered prayer. To Galina and her contemporaries the threat of war was very real, a numbing dread kept alive by the unforgettable experiences of a whole older generation of bereaved women. The twenty million fathers and sons lost in the Great Patriotic War had left the women of Russia not only to weep but to work, to stoically till the soil, rear their infants and rebuild a new society from the devastation of the old.

Galina paced the room, in the grip of an inexplicable anxiety. This, her first trip to the United States, had done nothing to allay deep-rooted primeval fears. It was true, a certain cynical disposition told her, that now President Gorbachev needed to deflect money from the arms race to put more food on Soviet tables, he perceived the Americans as loveable and friendly again. Yet the Americans' volatility and superconfidence could be interpreted as a lack of responsibility. She felt that anything could happen in this crazy country and it filled her with foreboding. What could they understand of the dark forces stirring in her country, of the complexities of a nation that for so long felt itself inferior and on the defensive, and who at last saw a way of breaking free?

Bozhe moy – God help us! Galina longed for the arrival of Arkady and the promise of a slug of vodka before the evening's torture began. Torture because Galina hated socializing of the formal sort, chit-chat with people she didn't know, had nothing in common with and probably would never see again. She looked around the room almost in desperation; it was beginning to turn into a prison.

The feeling of unreality to which she always succumbed in new places, with nothing of her own to relate to, threatened to overwhelm her. She went quickly into the bathroom and ran the gargoyle tap over the bath. Unbelievable, such a bathroom! When they had arrived this morning, Arkady had been jubilant at her astonishment.

A Roman fantasy of marble pillars, spouting dolphins, soap by the urnful and a statue of Aphrodite in an elevated niche. Most certainly over the top, but who was she to complain? She struggled with one of the little plastic bottles of bath foam and squeezed it below the dolphin's gaping mouth, watching in delight as a quivering mountain of soap bubbles rose up and almost obliterated the bath. She felt a trifle guilty. She should save all the little jars, goodies and giveaways that were distributed around the room and she would ask Arkady for his. A man had no need for all that paraphernalia.

She took off her dress of deep violet crêpe, with tiny pleats *à la* Fortuny. That dress had been the find of her life, hidden for years in the attic of a friend of her mother's . . . whose mother in turn had been a lady's maid to a lady who travelled, possibly even to Paris. Perhaps the dress was a Fortuny – there was no label. Galina could not authenticate it, but she felt instinctively it had to be a creation of the master.

She turned the dress inside out and took a hanger from the wardrobe. A slight problem here, as once removed the hanger had no hook at the top. Galina frowned but, used to improvisation, soon had the dress hanging up on the shower-rail, the hanger secured with a laddered pair of tights. As the steam from the bath began to work on the creases, she squeezed a wash-cloth nearly dry and sponged a mark near the hem, then rubbed around the arm-holes and neck, looking closely at the fabric. It was becoming threadbare under the arms, but then nothing would withstand the light in here. She screwed up her eyes at the battery of spotlights, worthy of an auditorium. She studied the stitching inside her dress with admiration – such skill, such perfection. She had a mental picture of the little *modiste* who had toiled over it, intermingled with an overall romantic view of a leisurely and refined Paris in the first decade of the century.

A discreet rapping on the door made her start and think of Arkady. It couldn't be time. . . . She glanced down at her modest regulation Soviet underslip. Whoever it was at the door this was hardly a garment to be seen in. She grabbed the pristine white towelling robe from its hook, slipped it on and opened the door a crack. An elegant middle-aged woman passively returned her stare of inquiry.

'Can I turn your bed down, madam?' The woman smiled pleasantly. 'Your room, madam. I've come to prepare it for the night.' She ticked off the room number on a report pad and enunciated carefully.

Galina allowed the chambermaid into the room and watched her obliquely, while making a pretence of tidying up some of the clothes she had left strewn over the chairs.

'Hallo, I'm Ida!' She was fashionably coiffed and made-up, dressed in a flower-sprigged shirtwaister with a row of pearls around her neck. 'I'm assigned to this floor so I'll be looking after you during your stay.' Ida smiled and Galina smiled shyly back. Looking after her. What was she supposed to do? She could certainly have done with a *babushka*, a live-in granny, to look after her at home, but here in this lap of luxury it hardly seemed necessary. Ida started to turn back the bed with a briskness at odds with her elegant appearance, extracted two small objects from her pocket and placed them on the pillow. She disappeared purposefully into the bathroom with a pile of towels and tossed out the ones Galina had barely used in a heap on the carpet. She came back clicking her tongue and carrying Galina's dress.

'Just saved it in time, honey. The hem was just catching the water. I'll hang it in the closet now, it'll all fall out nicely. I turned off your tub for you. Call me if you need anything, just dial 14. There's a hair-dryer in the right-hand closet drawer. . . . Have a good evening now!' Ida swept out with a cheery smile and a bundle of used towels.

Galina swallowed. Such pampering was hard to get used to. She went over and peered at the pillow. The two small objects were chocolate hearts, one white, one dark. She

144

picked them up and transferred them carefully to a pocket in her carry-all.

Help, nearly seven o'clock! Arkady would come for her in twenty minutes, there was no time for the leisurely soak she longed for. In the bathroom she threw off the robe and the ghastly slip, but the Fortuny was so thin modesty demanded it. She stood there in her viscose knickers. The light was cruel but Galina wasn't too displeased with what she saw. The frantic running of her busy life and a natural disposition had kept her slim. Her breasts were still like two halves of an apple, high and firm so she never needed to wear an ugly Russian bra. Only a very slight slackening of the skin on her flat belly bore testimony to her two children. Her legs were long with well-placed muscles, taut and firm from much walking and an aversion to the Leningrad transport system.

She shampooed her hair in the bath with another little jar she had found by the basin. She felt less extravagant now, as Ida had replaced all the goodies she had so carefully hidden away in her bag. She draped herself in the vast bath sheet and hunted for the hair-dryer. She hummed cheerfully to herself as she hung her head down between her knees and swung her long hair to and fro in the hot current of air. This marvellous machine was so efficient, her hair would be dry in no time. This was one of the things to put on her shopping list . . . well, maybe not. She would have to see if there was any money left when she'd bought the computer and the essentials for the boys.

Quickly now, into the Fortuny. Galina knew the dress became her and her former feelings of gloom completely disappeared. She began to look forward to the evening.

I'm in New York, the indescribable charisma of that name. . . . A pulse of excitement began to beat at her temple. What Zina would have given to be here; she had plied her with lists of shops, restaurants, the *chicarny* places to go. Would Zina have wasted one moment moping about feeling lost and inadequate? No – 'Enjoy it!' had been Zina's imperious command at the airport, so she had better pull herself together and not let Arkady down.

Back in the bathroom again, her hair swinging loose, she peered close to the glass for a quick touch of lipstick, *kompakt* on the moist nose – some new cosmetics she just had to buy. She had never critically examined herself under such a light in her life. Suddenly, springing along her parting, gleaming in the spotlight, were grey hairs, several of them . . . she looked through her hair in utter disbelief. *Vot* – well, that was that then! She had suddenly grown old without noticing it. Grown old without ever having known love. Her life was passing her by on a treadmill of work that she could never, ever get off.

Arkady's irritated voice at the door broke into the panic of her thoughts.

'*Devushka!* Are you there, can you hear me? Open up, quickly!'

Arkady's arms were full of glasses, a bottle and various titbits.

'What's up?' One shrewd glance was enough. 'You need a drink, Galya *maya!*' Arkady's voice was concerned. 'You'll get over it – the reaction to the West. It's normal, all Russians have it . . . you'll soon become as hedonistic as the rest.'

He poured a generous glass of vodka and held it out.

'Drink, my darling!' His voice was stern but his eyes dwelt on her anxiously. 'Down in one, now! There, in thirty seconds you'll feel like pulling down the Empire State Building.' He waited impatiently while she drained her glass.

'Put your hair up, Galya, with your swan neck you have to . . .' While she obediently twisted it up in a glossy coil and secured it with pins he wandered absent-mindedly round the room.

'What do you think of the decor? . . . such bourgeois conformity.' He threw a scornful glance at the painting

146

over the bed, a still-life in tasteful peaches and cream that echoed the colours of the curtains and upholstery.

She glared at him impatiently over her shoulder as she fiddled with a brush, intent on disguising those devastating grey hairs.

'Why are you so damn critical of everything they do? Do you suppose for one moment that we have some sort of God-given monopoly on taste and refinement? Anyway, there's nothing wrong with this room, it's elegant and original. I like it!'

'Original, huh!' His eyes gleamed maliciously. 'Poor Louis Seize must be turning in his grave at the plagiarism of his style – of course, they have no culture of their own so have to copy slavishly . . .'

'You're impossible. . . .' She wheeled round and aimed the hairbrush at his head. He fielded it neatly and grinned broadly.

'There – you see, no more sadness! I love to see you get mad. Now there's colour in your cheeks and sparkle in the eye.'

She tossed her head and smiled ruefully. It was true, he continually teased her, deliberately made her angry; their relationship had always been stormy. But she knew that behind Arkady's facade of cynical levity was hidden an unshakeable belief in his own troubling convictions.

'Good vodka, export only.' He poured them both another glass. 'I've saved the Dubrovka for that fat-cat Beriosonov at the Embassy. What a sinecure he's got. It may have softened him up physically but in here,' he tapped his head, 'he's as sharp as a laser. Has to be, to have hung on here so long, so watch out! We don't want anything to jeopardize our project.'

Galina said nothing, but rummaged in the depths of a cloth bag for her jewellery.

'I had a meeting with Tessorian before I left, he'd just flown in from Akademgorodok. The replica will be as spectacular, as perfect as the original, flaw and all. The Minister kicked up a stink about the price, synthetics cost

147

almost as much as the real thing, but I managed to persuade him of the amazing amounts of currency it would earn the museum. . . . Plus another small ace I had up my sleeve.' His eyes glittered with satisfaction. 'It was an offer he couldn't refuse!'

'When did you discuss it with Carl Vanderberg?' Galina was fastening an amber bracelet at her wrist.

'I haven't,' he said. She looked at him in surprise. 'That's to say, I mentioned the idea *en passant* when we arranged the exhibition. First things first. Now we've signed the contract and have his confidence we can relax. He seemed very vague when I mentioned it, but possibly because our beautiful compatriot was at his elbow and there must be some undercurrent of passion between them over it, huh?' Arkady grinned. 'What do you think, that she hates him and is working for him to sabotage his operation, or she's obsessed and wants to be near the ring, or hopes to get a rich customer to buy it for her?'

'None of those things.' Galina was tight-lipped. 'I asked her.'

'You asked her?'

'Yes, and she said she hadn't really thought about it . . . and I told her about the replica and she was very thrilled.' The last words came out in a rush as she saw Arkady's eyes darken.

He got up abruptly and clenched his fists. He searched her face silently for a second, then embraced her impetuously, once, twice, three times on the cheek, in the fervent Russian triple kiss.

'You did the right thing, Galya. Aha! Thrilled, was she . . . ?' He poured himself another drink gleefully. 'Now Carl will be putty in our hands.'

'You think so?' She stared at him curiously. 'I liked him very much, he's kind and, well . . . rather introverted – an *intellectualny*. Not at all how I would have expected a New York jeweller to be.'

'You liked him?' Arkady glowered at her suspiciously. 'Don't judge a book by its cover. Besides, businessmen

148

here don't all look like Armenian racketeers. Of course they can be *intellectualny*, but that doesn't stop them from being racketeers.'

He laughed as her chin went up. Then he drained his glass, his expression changed to one of mellow confidence and he came and stood by her elbow. His voice lowered to a fierce whisper.

'You know why I want that replica so badly, Galya *maya*. To the devil with the museum and foreign currency! Do you think I care a damn about such bourgeois concerns? That diamond is the symbol of Russia, it must be reunited. It is the soul of our nation that was torn apart at the time of the Revolution.' Galina stepped aside and moved the bottle away from his outstretched arm. She knew and feared the bouts of wild drinking that were triggered off by his moods of elation.

'Now, devil take it!' Her cheeks were flaming. 'It's the vodka talking! I was just telling her that our Russian soul was a euphemism for moral weakness and now you are blaming it all on a diamond.'

He grasped her hands convulsively but she shook them free.

'Don't push me away, dear one. You love that legend as much as I do, the story of its mystical heart of truth – a Russian heart, Galya. All right, we have the perfectly cut twin, but the important part – the part that would make us whole again – is here, in New York, in this alien culture that would never understand what it means to us. To the Russians the White Tsaritsa whole again would become a symbolic pilgrimage. It would reawaken our national pride lost through years of bungling and demonic leadership and point us towards a spiritual rebirth. We are poised culturally between East and West, we could never live as they live. We must choose our own path to salvation, with our own Russian values.'

Galina had heard this all before. She found the amber necklace she was seeking at the bottom of the bag. She sighed in exasperation.

'You know as well as I do that without the Revolution we would have developed into a democratic nation, we were way ahead of the Americans commercially. Don't try to make excuses for Russian weakness. Remember your own quote, "You can't have slavery without slaves". It's just talk, talk, talk. Eternal moral dilemmas and no action.'

'What good is progress if we lose our soul? Civil war, anarchy, anything could happen if we imitate the West. Just putting more food on the table isn't going to provide all the answers.'

'Well, it might make life a whole lot easier in the meantime, while we contemplate our souls.' Galina grinned as she tussled with the clasp of her necklace. 'I'm much more prosaic. It's women who make up half the workforce yet do three-quarters of the work. They're the ones who're going to force Gorbachev's hand. Well, no more! We've had enough. The new Revolution's going to come from the women.'

Even as she articulated unconscious and unthought-out ideas she became convinced of them, all the more so since coming here. It seemed to her that the women of Russia had been the victims of a staggering confidence trick. She felt a sudden flash of anger at the enormous injustice of it all.

Her voice shook in spite of herself. 'Let's go now, Arkady! I'm tired and you're making me angry. Either we go to this function or we stay here and fight. Can you fasten this necklace for me, the clasp is old and it always sticks.'

She turned her back and bent her neck submissively to Arkady's competent hands. His fingers shook for a second and he had an irresistible urge to kiss that vulnerable, chaste nape. If it were any other woman he would have done so, but he held himself in check. The scent, possibly from the old dress, the suppliant neck stooped to take a jewel reminded him so forcibly of the mother he had adored and lost that he wanted to throw himself at her feet and put his head on her lap. 'Mother, forgive me, I have come home. . . .'

'Have you rung the boys?' His voice was gruff. Had she noticed the tremor in his hands? 'Call them when we get back, it'll be morning, they're eight hours ahead. Tell them you're buying wonderful toys, dammit, you were talking about children with *her*, I've got expenses – so spoil them.'

As they walked along the corridor he suddenly remembered Beriosonov's special vodka that he had left in his room. He fumbled with the key and flung open the door.

Galina's mouth was a perfect zero of surprise.

In Arkady's room the same paraphernalia of limed-oak Louis Seize furniture met her eyes, the same imitation Flemish weave curtains and upholstery, the same still-life over the bed, only everything miraculously transformed at the wave of a colour-magician's wand into shades of blue and green.

Arkady's smile was triumphant. 'Original, eh? You see it's all an illusion, an exercise in the art of appearances, and we are going to beat them at their own game!'

The evening was a trial for Galina, if not for Arkady. Beriosonov had summoned a small group to meet them for dinner; one couldn't help thinking at the last minute, as an unobtrusive foil to the star-turn of Caspar Dodge and his wife Roma.

Even Galina had heard about Czech-born Caspar, a quite astonishing story of property acquisition and business acumen. Now Caspar had made it in so many fields – hotels, hospitals, charitable foundations – the United States had grown too small for a man of his vision and he was turning his hand to patronage of the international arts. She and Arkady were Caspar's guests at the illustrious Dodge Plaza, his triumph of futuristic architecture recently opened on Park Avenue. Caspar was in some way sponsoring the Tsarist exhibition with Adamantina and

De Beers, but Galina was hazy about the economic ramifications.

Dodge's wife Roma was another matter. Roma, the ex-actress, now mid-forties in aspic, saw cultural causes as a great excuse for changing three times a day into different designer gowns, through charity lunches and fashion-show teas to fully fledged gala balls. Roma buttonholed Galina very early on. Enunciating clearly in words of one syllable, she put Galina through her standard interview for foreign nationals. It always made good lunchtime conversation the next day.

While Roma was formulating her questions, to which the only necessary answers were yes or no, Galina watched with mounting repugnance. Roma was impossibly thin, the top of her dress sank into giant saltcellars, pathetic little arms with wasted muscles projected like sticks out of a loft and the transparent skin stretched over a network of veins gave her the appearance of an emerging chrysalis. Only a *tour de force* of make-up gave this face definition and life. But the eyes were haunted and terrified; the eyes of a starving child blazed painfully on Galina as Roma put her inane questions.

Galina wanted to throw her arms round her and say, 'Eat! Eat your fill! Let yourself get a little rounded – he won't love you any the less. Because if you are starving yourself to keep your husband's affection you'd better forget it. Men like Caspar can never be faithful. Once you've accepted that, you can start to live. And I for one should know,' she wanted to add, but Beriosonov came and rescued her, plied her with drinks and attention, pleased that she was so pretty, pleased that the distinguished pair had made such an impression on the Dodges.

At the dinner table Galina was glad of the buffer of a portly banker between her and Caspar Dodge; a foot occasionally brushed hers from an indeterminate direction and his eyes flirted boldly. She found it difficult to meet

Roma's strained expression and longed for the evening to end.

Arkady propounded the bright future of Russia now that restraints were removed, giving them a firework display of oratory and posturing, drunk with his own heady vision of a cultural Utopia. He was nothing if not good value, Galina thought sourly, he should hire himself out to dinner parties as the token mercurial Russian; no need to work ever again in his life. Over the coffee and cognac she managed a terse whisper to the ever-vigilant Roma. A taxi was in order – exhaustion, jet-lag, would she excuse them? Roma seemed curiously relieved and extricating themselves was easy. Lunch with the Dodges was mooted and half-arranged, and they left in an aura of warmth and bonhomie expressed all round.

She was terse with Arkady in the taxi and he hung his head like a penitent child, his shoulders suddenly crumpled and the elation fizzled out of him like a pricked balloon.

'*Gospody!* How you play to the gallery!' She glared at him in exasperation. 'How can you, of all people, possibly believe in that intellectual claptrap? Of course things will be better with *glasnost*, but are we really going to seize our freedom and do what the world expects? It would be truer to say that you are afraid, we all are, of failure; that our Russian pessimism will overcome the will to do what is right. People are already taking the easy way out . . . they've lost faith, not just in government but in themselves.'

He turned to her, his face suddenly haggard and his tragic eyes affirming everything she had said.

'Galya, Galya, don't scold me, *devushka* – I'm afraid, so afraid. . . . We are weak . . . there is a fundamental flaw . . . we are cursed. . . .'

'Sshhh . . . hush now. . . .' She cradled his head on her shoulder, frightened of his eyes and the beating of her own heart. There was no need – she knew the depths of his true awareness, the nightmare of gnawing doubt and inadequacy that underneath the bravado every Russian nurtured, like a canker, in his heart.

As Galina put him to bed, crushed and despairing, her heart ached for the depths of his suffering. But she was unable to help him, how could she? His pain was his own. Hers was her own.

She turned his bedside lamp down low and was tip-toeing from the room, when on impulse she stopped and glanced back over her shoulder. All the pain, all the jealousy, all the suppressed desire of the years rose up in her throat and seemed to choke her. Arkady was already asleep. She had taken off his tie and loosened his shirt and the lamplight gleamed on the tawny skin of his chest.

An irrepressible desire to touch that familiar flesh, to breathe in that Tartar maleness stole over her and she crept back close to the bed and stood looking down at him in silence.

In sleep his face had taken on a touching innocence, a troubling resemblance to Alyosha caught at her heart and she knelt by the bed so that his slightly parted lips were inches from her own. Slowly, incredibly tenderly, she traced her fingers over the outline of his profile without touching him, then ran them down the length of his body as though she could burn the impression on her fingertips. Arkady moaned a little and flung one arm over his head. His lips moved and he mumbled something in his sleep. Could she – dare she do it? Almost without thinking she lay alongside him on the bed and held him in an embrace as tender and fleeting as the brush of angels' wings. In one second of agonizing joy he was hers again, her Arkady. In the beat of his heart and the stir of his breath she became whole again. She could go on living. Maybe life was just made up of fragments of happiness like this?

10

The New York weather had undergone one of its rapid overnight changes. As Galina scampered along Fifth Avenue the next morning in an effort to keep up with Arkady's unrelenting strides she suffered with the rest of the city's workers from the glassy sun and a bath-house humidity.

Zigzagging in and out of the oncoming tide of humanity she risked a glance at Arkady's stony profile and her lips twitched. He had a monumental hangover and had had to leave the breakfast table quickly while she was tucking into her plate of ham and easy-over eggs. What a pity to miss such a breakfast buffet, laid out like the Horn of Plenty, a feast if only for the eyes. But Arkady had declined to look. Oh well, there was always tomorrow. . . . Nevertheless, she had urged him to try the stack of pancakes with maple syrup, but his eyes had beseeched her to be silent. Serve him right for his over-indulgence – she had been diffident with him at first at breakfast, unsure what he might recall of the night before. But he had been dead to the world and remembered nothing of her nocturnal embrace.

'You see – it's already nine!' Arkady looked at his watch in exasperation as a neighbouring clock struck the hour. 'We're late – people here get to meetings on time! Eat, eat, my girl! You have two more days to work your way through the American menu.'

Galina bit her lip to keep herself from laughing.

'I don't think Carl will mind if we're late. . . .' They were nearing Adamantina now. 'He isn't that sort of man. Besides, the meeting was informal – more of a chat and a briefing.'

Her cotton dress from Gemma's atelier swished a cool

current round her bare legs as she lengthened her stride to keep up with Arkady's. She had spent a good five minutes peering out of her bedroom window to see what the locals were wearing – a telescope would have been more appropriate from that height – and was pleased that the black and white Estonian cotton two-piece, a Valentino copy, seemed to be sartorially correct for the morning. The thrill, the pace of New York was beginning to work like a potion on her senses, quickening her pulse and lifting her spirits.

Arkady paused in the Adamantina doorway and wiped his face with a handkerchief. He looked dreadful. She surveyed him critically and then instinctively straightened his tie – still handsome, but whey-coloured, though suffering had always suited his histrionic style, she reflected. Galina smiled grimly as they pushed open the door. She had endured too much at Arkady's hands to waste much time on sympathy.

'Galina, Arkady! What a morning! It's going to be hot as hell. Come through – it's cool in here. Molly will bring us coffee . . . Was the evening a success?' Carl exchanged amused glances with Galina as Arkady quickly subsided into an armchair and accepted a cup of black coffee.

'Brilliant will be with you in a minute, she's going over the vault records. Galina, I'd love your opinion on an antique piece I've been offered. It's difficult to authenticate, but I think it must be your period, or possibly later.'

Their heads were soon bent over a baize-topped table in the corner of the showroom. Galina, looking through her loupe, exclaimed over an exquisite gold brooch in the shape of a bow, the ribbons set with fine diamonds.

'Yes, it is genuine.' She looked up eventually, her voice a little hesitant. 'It is quite late, probably around 1670. . . . It's French – and possibly the work of Gilles L'Egaré. You can tell by the distinctive tulip enamelling and the table-cut diamonds. They used to refer to them as "brilliants", but what we call the brilliant-cut wasn't invented until 1700, by Vincenzo Peruzzi in Venice.'

156

Carl smiled at her in approval.

'Good girl! You certainly know your stuff! That's just what the experts came up with – but now I have a second opinion that I value highly.'

A spontaneous reaction to the chivalrous attentions of an attractive man made her stomach tighten and she fought hard to control the shaking of her hand as she handed back the brooch. Carl examined it again under the loupe, his whole body strained in taut concentration. The probing spotlight etched the strong features of his profile, made the dark hairs on the back of his hands spring up in sharp relief. She was so close she could smell him, freshly showered, but still a scent of dark male, so intoxicatingly heady that she involuntarily stiffened as their shoulders brushed.

She backed away slightly as he put down the loupe and perched on the table, his eyes on a level with hers.

'You have no idea how I envy your knowledge of that Middle period. If I had my time over again I would have studied it – though certainly books instead of jewellery.'

Carl was telling her of his treasured tomes on medieval craftsmen when Brilliant came to collect them for the meeting. He put the French brooch away in its case and glanced obliquely at Brilliant. She looked extraordinarily elated. Last night she had bombarded him with the Russian's proposal for the White Tsaritsa, and while he had been touched at her emotion when he agreed to the replica, he had experienced an ominous stab of foreboding. Now with Arkady at her elbow that foreboding was crystallized into an almost tangible sense of menace and with it a sombre premonition of what fate might hold in store.

Brilliant was happy to keep the briefing short. A warning frown from Carl and a glance in Arkady's direction informed her that his attention span would be limited. After the meeting they inspected the sketches for the new Byzantine collection and then decided enough was enough.

Brilliant smiled at Galina. 'The rest of the day is ours!

157

We're going to be absolutely selfish – buy up the whole town. We'll all meet up again tonight, in the Algonquin at seven.'

She had thought of taking Galina somewhere smart for lunch – maybe beautiful-people watching at Mortimer's, or possibly to be bullied at joints like Elaine's or Pearls – but then it had suddenly occurred to her that Galina might like to see how she lived; to be invited to someone's home was much more personal and she had two whole days left for doing the social rounds.

'How do you feel about lunch at my apartment?' Brilliant suggested as they hit the wall of suffocating air on the street. 'It would be something different, as we're going out tonight. Help! It's so warm, thank heaven for air conditioning.'

'I'd love to see your home, only I don't want you to have to cook and all that. . . .' Galina looked anxious.

'Oh, I won't cook, I'll call in at my local deli – it's fabulous, I promise you won't starve. I live only one block from the shop.'

'Hmmm . . . sounds great.' Galina's nose wrinkled in anticipation. 'I am hungry in spite of a huge breakfast; I couldn't eat a thing last night. . . .' She made Brilliant laugh with her scathing description of the evening with Beriosonov.

They joined the brisk lunchtime trade at Gumbelli's and Galina was lost in a daydream of how different her working life would be if such a cornucopia existed on her street corner. She nodded her head numbly at Brilliant's suggestion that she choose for her. Armed with a crammed paper bag apiece and giggling like teenagers they rushed the last few yards to Brilliant's brownstone and soon had her living-room carpet strewn with plates and packages like some improbable *caravanserai*.

'You've no idea how this makes me feel at home, Russians have a passion for picnicking.' Galina lolled against cushions on the floor and was lost in admiration at the abundance and quality of the food and the size of the apartment.

'I suddenly feel like celebrating!' Brilliant called from her tiny kitchen. 'I don't usually drink at lunchtime – it puts me straight to sleep – but today's special. Carl is all for you copying the White Tsaritsa – so let's drink to Soviet-American co-operation.'

As they clinked glasses Galina confided to Brilliant, her eyes shining.

'You are very fortunate, working for a man like Carl. He strikes me as being totally unselfish – pretty rare in a man. He has such depths of cultural knowledge, at odds with a person in his . . . well . . . worldly position. . . .' Brilliant let Galina talk and her eyes narrowed with curiosity over the rim of her glass. 'He's interested in me as a person rather than where I come from. He doesn't make me feel like an oddity – what Arkady calls the Russian "Christopher Columbus" syndrome! You remember – that famous Ilf and Petrov satire of the Thirties.'

Brilliant chuckled, remembering one of Madalena's favourite stories. A Russian Christopher Columbus fresh from post-Revolutionary Moscow 'discovers' Manhattan – skyscrapers, hotdogs and all – and is treated as a philistine by the 'natives'.

'I promise you won't drag one inquisitive question out of me. Now eat! We need fortification for the work ahead.'

Galina stared hard at Brilliant's bent head as she struggled to open a throw-away container and then piled her plate high like a mother with an army recruit home on leave. There were no dark roots there. Galina stared harder, then sighed. No, Brilliant's hair had none of the tell-tale blackness around the scalp of Russia's peroxide blondes. It was all too disconcertingly natural, and no grey hairs, to boot.

Galina cleared her throat, she had decided to be frank. If Zina had been here she would have milked the last drop of Brilliant's knowledge. What was the point of beating

159

around the bush? After the shock of last night's grey hairs, time seemed to be running out.

'Tomorrow, I'm going to devote the whole day to the museums – after all I am a curator – but after that, I know you'll probably think I'm frivolous but . . .'

Brilliant's eyebrows shot up in genuine interest. Galina let her have her *angst* about the hair, the incipient wrinkles, the dreadful underwear, the non-existent cosmetics and the graceless shoes all in one long plaintive breath.

'Good God! There's nothing there that money can't remedy! Oh, I'm sorry, Galina . . .' she added quickly as the Russian woman's eyes clouded over . . . 'I didn't mean to sound so crass. It's just that . . . that Carl and Arkady had a little agreement over expenses. I don't think your government pays you over and above your salary – so we thought if we could help you out here, in kind as it were, that would be far more welcome. . . .'

Her embarrassment was lost on Galina, whose smile of delight slowly spread from ear to ear. The *quid pro quo* arrangement was part of Russian life and Arkady had already hinted of some such deal here, but to be taken in hand by Brilliant, a benefactor and a fairy godmother rolled up in one, was almost too good to be true.

'Well, what are we waiting for? We had better make a list. . . . Quick . . . how can one afternoon be enough . . ? Lots of women here make shopping their life's work.'

Galina coughed and looked uneasy. 'With all my concern for myself I'd forgotten the most important thing – my computer.'

Brilliant smiled as Galina explained her predicament at the museum. She was accountable for running costs and had decided to stick her neck out and revolutionize the antiquated system that threatened to engulf them all in paperwork. A computer in the computerless Soviet Union would be the answer to all their prayers. She'd worked out the cost and the model she needed and was allowed by the authorities to take it back legally, free of tax.

'It sounds a marvellous idea. So first the computer! And

forget about that hair. . . .' Brilliant called out as she caught Galina eyeing herself disconsolately in the hall looking glass. 'Magda will put you right. She's a friend from way back – a real Hungarian sorceress.'

'Thank God for all that potato salad at lunch – you need stamina for this!' Three hours later they were in a taxi en route for Magda's salon on Amsterdam Avenue – hot, dishevelled but triumphant. It had been a hedonistic *tour de force* worthy of the most luxury-starved shopper.

They had first despatched the question of the computer at IBM and had sent it, packed in three large boxes, back to Dodge Plaza. Toys, children's clothes, shoes, books and records were bought and despatched to the hotel before they had given a thought to more frivolous items. Galina proved herself a dedicated and indefatigable shopper, and confided to Brilliant in one lull for coffee, 'Are you sure it's all right – the money, I mean? I feel it's all a dream and I'm just playing at shopping – please tell me I'm not suddenly going to wake up.' She giggled. 'It's having everything sent that's so strange and irresponsible.'

There had been a slight altercation, their only one, over the Eduardo Ruspoli shoes. Finding themselves on the pavement outside the hallowed portals of the master-cobbler, Brilliant had urged Galina in. Galina had handled his brocade evening slippers with the reverence of Cinderella for the glass slipper and had shaken her head in disbelief – and then resignation. Nothing Brilliant could do would induce her to buy them. They were three hundred dollars a pair. *Nyet!* Galina had shaken her head obstinately. Thinking the day's indulgence – and fatigue – were beginning to take effect, Brilliant had hailed a cab to drive to Magda's for pampering of a different kind.

'Magda's a clever one – I've known her for years.' Brilliant told the cab driver to wait outside a handsome turn-of-the-century building on Amsterdam Avenue.

'When she bought an apartment in this area ten years

ago and opened a salon, everyone said she was mad. Now it's *the* place to live. You'll love Magda, she's larger than life – and down to earth, with the most glorious skin I've ever seen. I'll leave you with her, if that's all right. I've an appointment at five in the Inner Sanctum. She'll bill Adamantina, of course. Until 7 o'clock, then. Enjoy yourself!' She smiled and turned back to the taxi.

'Brilliant!' Galina clutched her arm. 'There's just one last thing. I've hardly any money left and there's a pharmacy over there. I need to buy some tampons, could you take them back for me, do you mind?'

'Why, of course not!' Brilliant agreed, somewhat puzzled.

In the pharmacy Galina filled two giant carrier bags with assorted brands. Speechless, Brilliant quickly paid and commented outside, 'Good God, Galina, you can't be serious!'

Galina, quite matter-of-factly, helped her stow them on the seats under the jaundiced eye of the driver.

'Well, you see, we can't get them at home, only on the black market – or anything else for that matter – and Zina expressly demanded . . .'

'Help! What do you use?'

'Socks. Men's synthetic ones are best, they dry quicker.' Galina grinned wickedly. 'True! A superpower – yet still the Middle Ages. Food for thought, huh?'

Brilliant struggled into the taxi next to the packages and fell back in a heap as she waved Galina away. The Christopher Columbus analogy was rapidly beginning to make sense.

'In the name of heaven! What have you done to yourself, Galya?' Arkady asked through clenched teeth as they crossed the Dodge Plaza lobby later that evening en route to a taxi. Galina stuck her head in the air and chose to ignore him. Even staring straight ahead she could feel the eyes on her. It was novel, it was exhilarating, as though

162

all the drab years had been worth this one intoxicating evening – even if it never happened again she had satisfied a feminine craving that for so long had been suppressed.

'Galya, Galya, is this dress wise?' Arkady's surprise turned to perplexity as he squeezed into the taxi beside her. This new Galina held her head with such disdain, her eyes flashed at him so scornfully that he felt humbled and touched her arm timidly. The seductive scent of the perfume she wore rose from her warm flesh and suddenly, with stunning force, he was struck with the desire to take her in his arms and possess her again, his beloved Galya, to know again that sublime sweetness. . . . He trembled and Galina, thinking he was angry, turned to him, her eyes blazing.

'What do you mean, wise? How dare you! Do you think I have no judgement of my own? I'm sick of your constant comments on what I should and shouldn't wear. At least I'm able to buy what I want at last!'

The effort of controlling his desire was superhuman, a knife seemed to twist inside him and he wanted to hurt her.

'If that's what you want to look like – a whore – go ahead! You're doing it for him – I've seen his eyes lusting after you. Do you think you mean anything to him? You'd just be a whim of the moment . . . he has women here crawling all over him. . . .'

Arkady passed a hand over his eyes and glared viciously out of the window. He didn't know why he felt so angry – or why his anger was directed against Carl Vanderberg. Brilliant didn't care for him, she made that obvious in many subtle ways – or did she? Love and hate were so closely intertwined. He looked down at Galina's foot sheathed in its new slipper, the fine bones visible through the translucent skin like the spines of a fan. Galya, his darling Galya! He wanted to take that foot and cover it with tears of repentance. How could she, with her dancer's grace, ever look like a whore? But in the new red dress that outlined her breasts, touched the two fragile bones of her pelvis and scooped so low behind it revealed the delectable hollow of her back she was dangerously attractive, and he wanted to kill any man who approached her.

'No, I'm sure I don't mean anything to Carl Vanderberg – because he only has eyes for one woman. But if he finds me attractive, all well and good, it'll just help me have the time of my life.'

Arkady clenched his fists and marched angrily ahead of her into the Algonquin bar. He had the novel feeling of not being in complete command of the situation and to his magisterial nature it was utterly exasperating.

He engineered Galina into a chair next to Akiko and pulled up a seat on her other side. The diminutive Japanese designer was resplendent in an updated version of the Samurai costume, with baggy pants and intricate layers on his upper half. After a glass of champagne Arkady began to relax and he turned his attention to Brilliant. The conversation was about Japanese design, which he considered too futuristic to be generally popular.

Carl was keeping Akiko's glass well plied with whisky and seemed to be drinking more than usual himself. Brilliant watched him uneasily. She knew he was worried about the Sierra Siren. This fabulous five-hundred-and-fifteen-carat diamond had recently been mined in Sierra Leone and Adamantina had entered into negotiations for its purchase. Carl had spent most of the day on the telephone to Koidu and now complications seemed to have arisen with the Lebanese dealer who was handling the sale.

'D'you know, Akiko,' Carl raised his glass, 'when I started out in the business the diamond was practically unknown in Japan. Now you have over twenty-five per cent of world sales.'

'Ah, yes!' The little Japanese smiled politely. 'But you see, in my country the quality of the stone is all-important. Dealers search diligently for a ring without a *kizu*, a flaw, because it reflects the purity of the bride herself. Can you imagine the nightmare of Japanese parents, that either the

164

daughter or the ring may be damaged goods – *kizu mono?* The bride must be a virgin, the diamond must be flawless.'

'What about the men, Akiko? Are Japanese men wearing jewellery these days?' Brilliant asked.

'Our battle-cry at the moment.' Carl looked amused and Brilliant's reply was indignant.

'Really, Carl, don't you know that Japanese women control the purse-strings? The man hands over all his salary and then his wife hands him back a spending allowance.'

'Yes, Madame Chardin, that is true.' Akiko's voice was softly respectful. 'But Japanese men think it is feminine to wear a ring, there is real resistance to wearing any jewellery. I even have it myself. And may I add this important point, there is still one occasion when a Japanese lady should never wear her diamond ring – at the tea ceremony. Simplicity is the rule, because it might scratch the tea-bowl.'

'Talking of tea-bowls, while Akiko sat here watching for all you late-comers to arrive, we discussed food, and he's homesick for sushi and sashimi. He's come by way of Santa Monica – that's the Gemmological Institute's training school – and he'll go mad if he sees another hamburger. So I've booked Yorihama's Teppan table, if no one's allergic to raw fish?'

As they made a move to leave Brilliant whispered to Galina, 'You look wonderful, just as pretty as before, only more so.'

It was true. Galina's hair, half piled up on her head and half tumbling around her shoulders, just looked richer and glossier and her make-up was a triumph of barely visible artifice. Her subtly shaded eyes sparkled with new life and definition and her mouth was stained with a transparent gloss as though she had been eating wild berries.

At Yorihama's Carl excused himself for a few moments and went straight to the telephone. Their chef advanced to the Teppan table as a conductor would to his rostrum, bowed low to each guest in turn, took up the instruments

165

Galina, sitting next to Akiko, was initiated into the mysteries of chopsticks and the aesthetics of the Japanese menu.

Brilliant cupped her hand under her saki cup and offered it to Arkady to refill.

'I'm sure this is terribly bad etiquette – a Japanese woman would never allow a man to serve her.' She smiled as his free hand touched hers to steady it.

'Then the men are depriving themselves of an immense pleasure.' His eyes were uncomfortably searching. She swallowed hard and changed the subject.

'Carl's having trouble winding up some business in Sierra Leone. . . .'

'I know. The Sierra Siren is eluding him. It must be galling for a man of Carl's diamond eminence to be frustrated by the Koidu diamond mafia.'

Her eyes widened. 'I suppose I shouldn't be surprised you know all about it. I had thought it was very confidential.'

'Highly unlikely with such a unique stone as the Sierra. I know several countries are after it. The problem with Sierra Leone is that most people prefer to do business by submarine.'

'You don't think the Sierra Siren will come out by submarine, do you?' Brilliant was surprised out of her detachment. Submarining was the trade name for diamond smuggling. A certain amount went on among middle men – but a house like Adamantina was too prominent ever to get involved.

'The Koidu "Big Four" are Lebanese dealers, all of them with legitimate export licences. But submarining is a way of life there, the government turn a blind eye to it, as long as they come out on the right side. Maybe our dealer has had a better offer – rumour has it that it's Jamal Said – and if that's the case there's a woman involved. Carl would be better off getting out there on the next plane – "*cherchez la femme*" and all that.'

166

Carl returned looking thoughtful and sat down next to Brilliant.

'Are you having problems?' she murmured *sotto voce*. 'Arkady seems to know all about it, something about submarining being involved.'

'He does, eh?' Carl looked annoyed, then he relaxed. 'Well, there's nothing new about submarining in Koidu, is there, Arkady?'

'Smuggling? It sounds so exotic and dangerous?' Galina had finally got the hang of her chopsticks and was triumphantly transferring juicy morsels of tempura from bowl to mouth. 'What a fascinating business.'

'It's not as dirty or involved as some of the men would have you believe.' Brilliant had been quick to notice Carl's frown. 'They enjoy playing the "game", it makes commercial life less boring. There are crooks, as in any business, but they soon get rumbled. Only the punctilious can survive, in the trade it's all a matter of reputation.'

'I see!' Arkady laughed. 'All the big jewel houses are whiter than white? We all know the diamond trade smuggles to pay its tax bills. Or to pay for drugs, launder stolen money, and all that kind of wholesome activity.'

Carl savoured the aroma of the strips of Kobe steak sizzling on the grill together with a quantity of plump garlic cloves. He smiled expansively.

'What about the other side of diamonds, Arkady? The KGB constantly pays its agents abroad in diamonds. It avoids changing roubles into dollars. But the main advantage is not feeding money into foreign bank accounts, it might be picked up by counter-intelligence. Sometimes the KGB goes a bit haywire, like the three million dollars' worth of Russian polished that turned up in Bombay just before the election that got Indira Gandhi back into power.'

Arkady looked at Carl coolly. 'You forgot to mention diamond smuggling in the Third World, Carl. Illegal money has been known to help people escape from a crushing political regime.'

Carl shrugged. 'The problem with any smuggling is that it upsets the applecart of De Beers' monopoly, which is basically benevolent and necessary to most producers.'

'I never thought I'd hear Carl Vanderberg supporting anything of South African origin!' Arkady's eyes gleamed.

'That's true! Surprised myself, in fact. I suppose it's the blood of my forefathers flowing in my veins, justifying the whole set-up. It is anathema to me to stomach the South African situation – apartheid, I mean – and carry on business as though it meant nothing. Look – how about a change of mood? Why don't we all go on to Le Privé for coffee and dancing? What do you say?'

Brilliant sensed her approval would set the tone for the others but she shook her head slowly.

'I'm sorry, Carl, you'll have to count me out. I can hardly stand, yet alone shake a leg.'

'Thank you so very much. I'm afraid I have already made an appointment for later,' Akiko answered enigmatically.

'So – that leaves me to play Prince Charming to this gorgeous Cinderella. I hope you're not going to run away before midnight?' Galina had no intention of finishing the evening at such an early hour, and she left on Carl's arm with a broad smile of pleasure.

'You're not serious about going home, are you?' Arkady asked Brilliant as they stood on the sidewalk after saying their farewells to Akiko. 'You just wanted to get rid of them. . . .'

Brilliant laughed. 'Arkady, you're so endearingly presumptuous! I was deadly serious. I am tired, but I'll walk a few blocks with you. I need some air.'

Try as she might she could not get that eager expression on Carl's face as he left with Galina out of her mind. After all, she had made the decision to be cool with him since that embarrassing first meeting in Paris. There would always be the matter of the diamond between them and it coloured their relationship. Galina's talent and charm, her blend of practicality and vulnerable femininity were obviously tremendously appealing to Carl. He had looked so happy. She should wish them well.

She looked up to find Arkady watching as if he were able to read her thoughts.

'I think your employer has never got over his rough handling at the hands of the fair sex.'

'Rough handling? What on earth do you mean?'

'You know, of course, that his ex-wife was a De Beers heiress? Ah, the fair Astrid Breitmeyer, the Star of Jagersfontein. Strong men were putty in her hands.' A muscle twitched at the corner of Arkady's mouth. 'Beautiful but wilful, a legendary horsewoman, she certainly cracked the whip over poor Carl. The Breitmeyers were one of the original Syndicate, old Dutch money, great art collectors and philanthropists. Astrid was home from Geneva being "finished" when she met Carl – I'm sure it was lust at first sight. Astrid felt she had a long way to go and used Carl rather as a testing ground. Carl suffered more, I think, at the hands of the family than with Astrid. They seemed to blame him for the break-up. Anyway, it left him with a fine antipathy for the South African clique. I believe he was quite paranoid for a while.'

'How come you know so much about Carl's private life? I shouldn't imagine he's a man who wears his heart on his sleeve.'

'No, I got it from the horse's mouth, from the fair Astrid herself, when she was sleeping her way round Europe.'

Brilliant glanced at him quickly, but his face was impassive.

'I see! Strange . . . but possible. What happened to this fair Astrid?'

'She was killed in a plane crash. They had divorced by this time. It was only five years ago and Astrid was already on her third husband. She was quite a character, I can tell you, she died as she lived – dangerously – dipping too low over the Iguazu Falls in her Mexican playboy's plane.'

They had reached the corner of the block and Brilliant stopped in her tracks.

'I'll get a cab now. I don't feel like walking any further.'

'No, don't leave! Let's go somewhere and drink some vodka. Come on, I think you need it, *nenagladnaya*.' Brilliant shrugged. Why not? Arkady certainly had an uncanny way of guessing her needs.

'For nostalgia's sake I'll take you to the Russian Tea Room. What! You've never been there? A Russian New Yorker? Shame on you!' He grasped her arm impetuously. She shivered. Something happened to her when she was with Arkady . . . something she wasn't too sure that she liked – it was pleasant, but unpleasant. She was still puzzling over these odd sensations as she slid into a banquette against the deep green painted walls and Tsarist memorabilia of the Russian Tea Room.

'Did you know that Gogol's favourite party trick was pulling his lower lip up over his nose?' Clever Arkady had no intention of uttering a serious word to her that evening. Instinct warned him off the polemics of Russia and diamonds and she could not have wished for a more entertaining companion.

'I have a theory that the food a nation eats reveals everything about its people's temperament.' He summoned the waiter in that semi-rude way she had observed in people from Communist countries. 'What do you deduce from the Japanese restraint? I'm ravenous for food that stirs the blood – *blini* and caviar for a start – with vodka, naturally.'

'I would have thought it had more to do with climate and the restrictions of geography?'

'Not so! The paradox of the English temperament is given away by their love of spice – wars were fought for it, an empire founded on it. No, food is all revealing – maybe I'll write about it one day. The Russians of course have no gastronomy, food is merely an adjunct to strong drink, hence the enormous popularity of the *zakuski*, our hors d'oeuvre table.

170

Vodka arrived in a small carafe ingeniously frozen into a block of ice.

'You must try this red caviar,' he urged her as they were served by a venerable waiter, hands trembling with age. 'The egg of the Siberian salmon is far more delicate than that of the sturgeon. The eggs are larger and creamier, they melt in the mouth like sublimely fishy pearls.'

Brilliant looked around the long, dimly lit room. The pink-clothed tables were packed just a little too closely together but everyone looked happy, the waiters seemed happy, the food was happy, she felt ridiculously happy. Arkady was letting a woman next to him fork into his red caviar, he in turn tried her Eggplant Oriental. The woman was polished and beminked, seated next to a small balding man with twinkling eyes.

'May Cagney and Ernest Lubitz,' Arkady mouthed to her later and she blinked and looked again. 'He just got the Bolshoi on contract – what a coup!' Arkady had an almost encyclopaedic knowledge of what was going on in the New York art world and kept her informed and fascinated with a constant stream of anecdotes and acerbic criticism. 'My work is just a front. . . .' He laughed when she questioned him. 'I can travel. That's all! There you have your answer.'

On the way back to her apartment he seemed curiously depressed, sitting hunched in a corner of the taxi and scarcely saying a word. On the sidewalk outside her door he carried her hand to his lips, as he had done when they first met.

'Goodbye, *nenagladnaya maya*, my beautiful one. I shall never forget these moments with you. It may be a long time before we meet again. Perhaps you are not yet ready for Russia. . . . But please think of me a little – and with kindness.' He walked away without another word.

She felt like calling him back, but something buried deep inside stopped her. Like the Princess and the Pea, she was conscious of an irritating enigma that was elusive

171

and perhaps illusory. She may not have been ready for Russia, but she was even less ready for Arkady.

When he got back to the Dodge Plaza Arkady's first thought was of Galya. He felt smug and sanctimonious. He needed to talk to her. Perhaps he would make her tea in that cunning little gadget he had bought for boiling water in the toothmug.

He rapped on her door. There was no answer. *Chort!* To the devil! She had to be back. He looked at his watch. Two-fifteen. What if she was not yet back? Where in hell's name had that Don Juan taken her? He rapped on the door again and muttered imprecations under his breath. Son of a bitch! A floor waiter with a tray of drinks passed and raised an inquiring eyebrow. Someone stuck their head out of a neighbouring door and told him in no uncertain terms to sod off. He returned petulantly to his room and managed to call her, after much fumbling through the codes on the dial, by way of the reception desk.

Galina lay and stared up at the ceiling, listening to the ringing of the telephone. She knew Arkady was not drunk, just a little depressed and in need of company. Well, let him ring. She had been thinking a lot about her life, lying here in this strange room in the darkness. She was lonely, too, but unlike Arkady she had learned to contain it. She never would have thought it, but she had become strong inside herself. Her job was good, she had the boys. When she got back from Le Privé she had telephoned home and the sound of their voices, their inconsequential chatter – Alyosha had found a dead beetle on his way home – had made her choke with emotion, but had also calmed and reassured her. She was a mother. That was immutable. It gave her life meaning and priority. She loved Arkady. Perhaps she would learn to cope with that too.

She had been Cinderella for one magical evening and even that had carried its own poignancy. Her prince had been charming but when they danced she had felt strange in his arms. A closeness that should have been comforting was merely disturbing, and not because of his maleness. Carl had been attentive and seemed to find her attractive, but . . . something was wrong. It was not just because she felt a deliberate or unconscious distancing – which was good – perhaps what she would have expected from a man of his sensibility. But surely, there should have been some response? She had frowned slightly and looked up at him.

Carl had smiled apologetically, as though reading her thoughts. His arm had tightened round her waist and he had drawn her close. She had sighed, moving with resignation into an embrace that spoke volumes for them both. As she rested her hand on his shoulder his eyes had closed, his nostrils filled with the remembered sweetness of another woman's hair.

Then later, as they talked over coffee, Carl's eyes had crinkled with amusement as he watched her spoon thick cream from the jug like a guilty cat.

'I'm sorry if you find me a bit preoccupied,' he had offered by way of a totally unconvincing explanation. 'I have that elusive Sierra Siren on my mind. I think I will have to leave for Africa first thing. At least I can relax and leave Brilliant in charge.'

'She is an immensely capable woman, isn't she, Brilliant? As well as being beautiful. I liked her a lot.' Galina had sipped her coffee and watched him over the rim of her cup.

'Yes, she's quite some lady! I'm lucky to have her working for me. Just one of those crazy quirks of fate.'

'Like the Vanderbergs acquiring the White Tsaritsa?' Galina's gentle voice had an unaccustomed edge.

'Exactly! Of course, it's common knowledge, and no doubt Brilliant has told you her version.'

'Yes . . . and no. Basically I have only read the *Time* article – which Arkady gave me as homework. I'm fascinated with snippets I have heard here and there – in fact

173

I thought I would like to do a paper on it.' Galina had smiled unassumingly. 'I gave it a mention in a small tome on medieval diamonds I had published in a sabbatical year I took after Sasha was born. Brilliant was very keen when I talked about it.'

Carl had leaned forward eagerly. 'Is that so? You know, it often seems to me that it must be the workings of fate or some nonsense like that which made our paths cross. . . . She loathes me, of course,' he commented drily.

Galina stared at him.

'Well, perhaps it's not quite loathing now, it's become tempered to a gentle animosity!' He had given the self-mocking smile that transformed his face. 'Somehow I feel responsible. I should do something to salve the family conscience, make some effort to stop her actively disliking me, at least.'

Little keys had seemed to turn inside Galina's head as she listened, and finally something clicked. She had smiled, put down her cup and leaned forward confidentially.

'Of course! I understand now – completely. I will do all I can to help. But I will need your co-operation with my studies though. . . .'

She had laughed in spite of herself at the rush of warmth with which Carl had squeezed her hand, then reached across and planted a chaste kiss on her open, astonished mouth.

At last the telephone stopped ringing with a curious strangled bleep. Probably dropped from Arkady's senseless fingers. . . . Within seconds Galina was asleep.

11

Marie-Laure stood on the pavement outside Maison Chardin in the Place Vendôme and examined the showcase window. Good! She gave a curt nod of approval to the window-dresser who was hovering nervously in the centre of the pale velvet frame.

The simple setting – a breathtaking diamond tiara with pendant earrings and necklace below – should give the hordes of ogling tourists an indication of the sort of clientele Chardin catered for. No price tags, of course; they could leave that sort of thing to their down-market competitors. She shuddered and averted her eyes from the monstrosity of hoarding with its garish mural that shrouded Thuilliers on the corner. Building work was under way to convert half of their shop into some kind of stroll-around store selling trinkets. The Place Vendôme was no longer the *ne plus ultra* of taste that it used to be. She looked balefully over her shoulder at the file of camera-laden Japanese disembarking from a coach alongside the magnificent bronze spiral of the Austerlitz column.

Honoré joined her at the window and they stood looking at the display in silence. His face was grave. The financial report they had just received was not a cheering one. A copy had been sent to Jean-Claude and they were waiting for his arrival. A family discussion had been arranged before the formal meeting with their accountants.

Honoré stuck his hands in his pockets in the schoolboy gesture that so annoyed Marie-Laure, turned his back on the window and surveyed the first coachload of the tourists who daily swarmed about the ancient *place*. He liked their cheerful unpretentiousness, the spontaneous way they pressed up against the Chardin windows with bulging, avid eyes.

He shifted his weight on the uneven pavement to relieve the troublesome ache in his thigh. His last attack of gout had left him with constant niggling pain. He had been told by his doctor that his uric acid levels were dangerously high, he should take a cure – in short give up all the gastronomic pleasures that meant so much to him. The prospect was less than enticing, but perhaps Brilliant would join him at Amélie-les-Bains or Vichy? Honoré's face brightened. He would write to her in New York and suggest it. His clandestine copperplate letters arrived regularly on Brilliant's desk, and she adored the wicked wit with which he brought the minutiae of French social hypocrisy vividly to life.

Jean-Claude was late. Honoré whistled through his teeth and glanced covertly at Marie-Laure's stony profile. Since Brilliant's departure his son had seemed to lose all interest in the family business. In one respect, Honoré chuckled to himself, his daughter-in-law had triumphed. Although he missed Brilliant enormously, she had managed to escape. Regretful as Honoré had been, he envied her that liberty and wished her every happiness.

A red Porsche raced into the *place* and stopped with a flamboyant flourish a few yards from their feet. Jean-Claude climbed out in a leisurely fashion. He bent and whispered something to Boy de la Broussaillère who sat in the driving seat. Boy pushed back a lock of blond hair and gave his photogenic smile.

Marie-Laure held up her face to be kissed and felt Jean-Claude's cool lips barely brush her cheek. She changed colour and clutched at his sleeve. Jean-Claude gently shrugged himself free and stepped aside, avoiding his mother's eyes. He pushed a sheaf of papers into Honoré's hands.

'I'm afraid I can't stay – but I have read the report and I have written out my comments in full. There is nothing more I can add!' Jean-Claude began to move back to the car.

'Jean-Claude!' Marie-Laure's mouth opened and shut ineffectually. 'I thought . . .' she managed to continue, 'I thought we were going to discuss the report together?'

'I'm sorry, Maman.' There was just a flicker of insolence in Jean-Claude's eyes. 'Boy has driven all the way from Epernay to meet my parfumeur. We have to decide today on the design for the *flacon*. I will telephone you tonight, before we leave for dinner.'

He was inside the car before Marie-Laure could find words to reply. She turned on her heel and stalked into the Chardin shop without a glance at Honoré. She could not bear his frank blue gaze that lately seemed to mock her. Her forehead was damp – this was appalling! She hurried up the short flight of marble steps to her office and ordered a camomile tisane to settle her nerves.

Much as she hated to admit it, the defection of her daughter-in-law had had a negative effect on her life. To say she had been hoist with her own petard would not be exaggerating. Marie-Laure tapped her fingertips together and stared with loathing at the silver-framed photograph of Brilliant's wedding, which stood among other family pictures on the top of her desk. If only she could turn the clock back to the happy times when Brilliant was there and they had shared him.

Perhaps it was not too late. Would she have to eat humble pie? No! Never that. But a semblance of it might serve her ulterior purpose. Marie-Laure grew pensive. It would all require careful planning of the most strategic kind. After all, she had other things up her sleeve now, information which gave her a superior strategic edge. Marie-Laurie picked up the telephone – there was not a second to lose. Her face relaxed. There was nothing she enjoyed more than breaking the rules. Playing straight was only for fools, and besides, she was beginning to miss the decadent thrill of the forbidden that had been part of her life with her son. Jean-Claude would soon come to heel – she would see to that. But Brilliant would pay for it . . . and working out exactly how to achieve that goal was going to be pure pleasure.

Brilliant was the first in the Adamantina showroom next morning after George had unlocked the main door, turning the serrated key in the metal fireproof door, snapping back a reptilian display of jagged teeth. She paused at the centre plinth and looked for a moment at the White Tsaritsa. This morning ritual always seemed to restore and reassure her. She knocked for a second at Carl's door, quite sure that he would not be there. Not normally an early riser, he seldom appeared at the showroom before ten. She put some documents requiring his signature on the desk, frowned and began to pace the room, arms folded protectively across her chest, as if to keep down the subversive demons of nostalgia and disappointment.

In her mail that morning had been a letter with the familiar French stamp. When she had opened it, the scent of camphorwood from Jean-Claude's Chinese writing desk brought back the room they had shared in Paris with such a sharp evocative sense that tears had stung her eyes and she had bitten her lip.

Jean-Claude's tone was detached. There were just the legal formalities to attend to, it was in both their interests to expedite them as soon as possible. She would receive the draft divorce papers; he understood that as she made no claim on his estate and had waived demands for alimony, the matter could be finalized as soon as the year's obligatory separation was over.

It was not that the letter had revived any feeling for him, on the contrary she was glad that he had initiated the action, it saved her the distress of further communication. But memories of an earlier tender time came flooding back to remind her how empty her heart was, how deliberately she had turned her back on any emotion, healing herself with the soothing therapy of work. It must be just tiredness that made her feel like this; isolated, somehow incomplete. There had never been time to think since the headlong dash from Paris three months ago. But of course there had been time. If she was honest with herself she had never wanted to think. The moment her thoughts turned inwards she reflected on her failure.

Was it possible that she had never really loved him? How could a woman be mistaken about something so fundamental? What did her overwhelming desire to marry him say about her? That her motives were ignoble . . . that her need to be loved triumphed over her common sense . . . that she was superficial enough to be taken in by the sentimental trivia of their courtship. Brilliant knew that guilt and a sense of failure were inevitable consequences of a broken marriage. But she knew equally that even if she had only thought she loved him, and he thought he had loved her, many marriages managed to endure on a far shakier foundation. The circumstances of their marriage had been unusual, to say the least. Brilliant smiled tartly. But why had Jean-Claude turned to her? There was so much that she understood now, even if it was hard to forgive. Her sense of failure was compounded by the knowledge that she could have helped him. If she had really wanted to. If she had really loved him. She found it hard to escape from this dismal cycle of guilt and self-recrimination.

'You'll beat up my antique kelim if you walk any faster!' Carl's voice stopped her in her tracks.

'Oh! You startled me. I was just thinking something over.' The familiar lines of his smile soothed her, she felt ashamed of her fluctuating feelings.

'Such deep dark thoughts that you'll wear out your shoe leather? Brilliant, I've been thinking a few things over myself,' Carl told her. 'My heart is set on that Sierra Siren, but I shall have to go to Africa to get it. There's some . . . well, some slightly irregular business going on which is trickier than I thought. You need a break, why don't you come with me? I promise you it will be quite an experience. Highly educational.' It took an effort for Carl to ask her. He braced himself for the rejection he felt sure would come.

Perhaps if he had not asked her on this particular day of gloomy introspection she might have refused. Her eyes brightened. Yes, a change of scene, she thought, it was one way of putting the past further behind her.

'I think it's a great idea! Molly can manage without us – the new collection is out – so why not? I do need a break, and if there is going to be a scrap over a diamond I can't think of a better tonic.'

Carl's eyes darkened and the blood rose to his cheeks. He could not speak for a moment, then said, 'Right, that's settled then! We should try and get away on tomorrow morning's flight to Jo'burg.'

In the rush of last-minute instructions and organization Brilliant had no time for lunch. Carl had a meeting in his office, so she sent out for a sandwich and was in the Yellow Room at around three, the trade monthly in one hand and a dill pickle in the other, when Molly called to say there was a visitor to see her – personal, a man.

Arkady! He had told her he was lunching with the Dodges – she had not expected to see him, and anyway there had been a finality in his farewell that she felt was sincere. She experienced a stab of anxiety at the thought of seeing him. She pushed away her plate and sprang to her feet, dabbing at her mouth with a napkin. She rushed to the glass and ran her fingers through her hair, shaking out its thickness, then smoothed down some creases in her skirt.

'Brilliant, *chérie* . . .'

'Jean-Claude!' Unexpected and heart-stopping, Jean-Claude's elegant outline materialized in the doorway. In a second he was at her side, his fingers gripped the flesh of her arm and he held her close to his scented cheek.

'Stop!' Her cry of anguish came from the heart and frightened even herself.

'Brilliant!' For a second Jean-Claude's eyes flickered

dangerously, like an animal at bay, then he spread his hands in a gesture of resignation. Molly's head appeared around the door in alarm. In a moment Brilliant felt herself under control.

'It's all right, Molly. My . . . my husband just startled me. We're fine, perhaps we could have some coffee?'

Jean-Claude stood aloof by the fireplace, half turned away.

'Roussalka!' His voice broke with emotion and Brilliant's heart contracted at his tender pet-name, the name of their lovemaking. 'Don't reject me – please listen to what I have to say. The moment I sent that letter about the divorce papers I regretted it. I had to get on the first plane to come here, to explain. I was tormented by not hearing from you, I wanted to spur you to communicate, to recognize my existence. I left you in peace, all these months I waited for you to make up your mind, to come to your senses.' She saw his handsome profile reflected in the glass, the pained tremor on his lips. 'You are still my wife and I still love you. I haven't had one moment's happiness since you left. Believe me, *chérie*, you are the only woman I have ever wanted . . .'

He turned to her, his face a mask of grief in which only the eyes belied genuine involvement.

Calculating and somehow insolent, those eyes gave him away. My God! How could she have been fool enough to think he really cared? Yet . . . somehow she did believe him – quite possibly she *was* the only woman he had ever wanted. Wanted on his own terms, as part of his decadent scheme of things. And it was precisely that shaming and impure love that she wanted to block out of her heart.

'No, you don't love me! Any more than I love you! We should both face up to it and admit it.'

The hauteur in Jean-Claude's face crumpled into pathetic dejection. The weakness of character that had always been latent became sickeningly obvious. He leaned against a chair, suddenly lightheaded. The hurried flight, jet-lag . . . he put his hand to his head.

This conversation with Brilliant was not quite working out the way he intended. Certainly not as his mother had predicted. Marie-Laure had disarmed him with her frank acceptance of the blame for his break-up with Brilliant. She had come to him late at night, wide-eyed and agitated, more emotional than he had ever seen her – and had pleaded for him to forgive her. Things could be changed, they could win Brilliant back again. If it were not one way, then it would be another. He had had to admire his mother's supremely devious mind. Jean-Claude did not for one instance believe his mother's penitence, but he had experienced an enormous sense of relief at their reconciliation. His mother's dominant, consuming love was vital to his well-being. But Brilliant's love was the antithesis of Marie-Laure's. If his mother represented darkness, Brilliant was the light. She spoke to his confused mind of loyalty, honour, integrity – all the things he longed to encompass. She offered him the hope of redemption – without having to do anything about it. He wanted to cling to the straw of survival her presence provided. He did not want to lose her.

'Brilliant . . . please, please, my darling . . . we are man and wife! This . . . this is so cruel . . . Couldn't we talk again, perhaps tomorrow, when you have thought it over?'

'There is no point. Besides, I'm leaving tomorrow for Africa.'

Jean-Claude seemed to rally.

'Oh, really. The Sierra Siren? Carl is not the only one after it. Its acquisition is developing into something of an international incident. But then your benefactor likes to play at God. Who knows, our mighty Adamantina may soon find out he is not as ominiscient as he thinks.'

Brilliant gripped the back of a chair. 'Are you jealous or are you threatening? I know one thing – you can never be half the man he is.'

'As you have doubtless lost no time in finding out. A

182

certain vulgarity – my mother did warn me – has become very evident.'

He stood defiantly, imminent tears choking his voice. Brilliant felt a desire first to laugh, then to take him in her arms and comfort him. He was weak and lost. He was her husband.

She took a step towards him and the next moment he was in her arms. 'Roussalka . . .' His voice was muffled in her shoulder.

'Jean-Claude.' She hesitated, wondering how she should go on. 'Admit that you never loved me – that it was all a mistake. Then perhaps we could be friends,' she swallowed, 'for the sake of all we shared . . .' It was difficult for her to continue.

Jean-Claude lifted his head. It was impossible for him to accept what she was saying. He was going to lose her. And Marie-Laure would be furious at this reversal.

'Brilliant, I believed I loved you . . . even defying my mother . . .'

'Your mother!' A sudden vision of Marie-Laure, terrifyingly real, made Brilliant turn pale. 'And what of her . . . her love?'

Jean-Claude was trembling in her arms.

'Her love . . . that . . . that kind of love was something I can't begin to explain . . . but it is over now!' His eyes blazed with sudden conviction. 'But Brilliant, there is something I ought to tell you. My mother hoped . . . hoped for a reconciliation. Now her anger will be directed against you . . .'

'That is ridiculous! How can she possibly harm me now?'

Jean-Claude made a tremendous effort to control himself.

'I am glad you feel so confident. Whatever you do, don't underestimate Marie-Laure.' He smoothed down his ruffled hair and managed an unsteady smile. 'Well, Brilliant my darling, shall we be friends?' She took his outstretched hands. 'My loss will always haunt me. You are all a man could ever want.'

When he eventually left her, Brilliant sat down and shook from head to toe. Her violent and complex emotions were compounded of grief and regret, but most of all, an overwhelming sense of release. The confrontation she had always feared was over. She sat for a long time, somehow feeling a little of the pain, the sadness and the guilt ebb away. After a while, when she felt calmer, she picked up the telephone and dialled the Dodge Plaza. Galina took her call.

'I just wanted to tell you that I'm leaving tomorrow for Africa.'

'With Carl? Mmmm. Good!'

'I'm sorry we didn't have a chance to see each other again and now it will be a long time until the exhibition. How was lunch with the Dodges?'

'Oh, surprisingly, a lot of fun! The cream between two magical meringues of culture – I'm footsore and museum-shocked.'

'We will be in close contact with you and Arkady anyway. So . . . until November . . .'

Galina's soft voice thanked her, then blessed her and wished her happiness, a Russian anachronism that made her smile unsteadily.

Farewells, farewells . . . there suddenly seemed to have been an awful lot of them. But no more ruminating on the past – there was only the future now, new hopes and new horizons. At the thought of Africa her spirits lifted with a buoyancy she had not experienced for a long time.

12

The African sun struck between the eyes like a slingshot as Carl eased his way through the sliding glass wall of the dining room, out of one air-conditioned civilization into another, ageless one.

'Waiting at the Voortrekker. Hurry!' Brilliant's scribbled note had been brief. It was late – 9.30. Carl had slept in and most of the tables in the shady terrace restaurant were already vacated. In this land of fierce heat most people were up and about their business at dawn.

'Ma'am's over there, in the corner, by the palm-tree . . .' In a few swift strides Carl was at her side.

'Hi – you're late! I've swum, caught up on the local gossip, nibbled a bit of toast and now I'm starving!' Brilliant was lying back in a white wicker chaise longue, wearing a towelling robe. The twisted turban round her wet hair pulled the skin of her temples upwards and gave her eyes an exaggerated slant. In the strong sunlight darker flecks floated in their irises and he noticed how long her wet lashes were, shadowing her cheeks like a child's.

'Let's eat then! I'm as hungry as the eponymous Voortrekker.' Carl stretched out a hand to help her to her feet. The loose robe opened to reveal a body whose curves owed more to the Italian school than to the modernists, clad in a blue bikini. Belting the robe around her and slipping into sandals, Brilliant led the way to the table she had reserved at the front of the terrace.

The Tamananga Treetops Hotel was a glossy new development several miles outside the unprepossessing centre of Johannesburg. A series of neo-native huts were grouped round a central luxurious clubhouse, with every possible facility for the sports-minded tourist or businessman.

The greenery of the complex burgeoned like an oasis

out of the dusty plain. The social centre of this glamorous *kraal* was a meandering swimming pool laid out like a series of lagoons connected by spectacular cascades. The Shangri-La effect was enhanced by a backdrop of palms and riotous plant-life surrounding the Moorish *palanquin* under which they now sat doing justice to the great colonial breakfast.

A huge platter of fresh fruit, papaya with lime segments, pineapple, mango and guava, was followed by a dish of *boerwors* – spiced sausages – with eggs and bacon, plus mealie pancakes. Warm breads in half a dozen varieties, exotic jams and steaming coffee completed the repast.

'Now that's what I call a breakfast!' Carl sighed at last, draining his coffee cup and leaning back in his chair. 'Breakfasts I have known! It's funny how they show up the best and worst of a country's cuisine. I remember the first time I was in France, as a school-kid on an exchange, used to the standard American fare of my youth. The coach stopped at a wayside café just as the sun came up. It was near Annecy, I believe, we had been driving all night. We had wonderful baguettes, I'll never forget them, just baked, with unsalted butter like thick yellow cream, great saucers of home-made apricot jam and coffee in bowls – we thought that very droll – diluted to just the right colour, sugar in lumps . . . It was manna! We famished school-kids ate so much the owner's wife was incredulous – and flattered, too, I suppose. Anyway, it started off a lifelong love affair with France and French food.'

'Me too! Only my French experience didn't come till much later. I finally got to Paris when I was eighteen – visiting Aunt Dolly in the vacation. Suddenly I discovered eating could be a sensual pleasure and an art, not just a necessity for survival . . .' She stopped in embarrassment, then added quickly, '. . . not that Mother wasn't a great cook, only the whole French approach to food was different.'

He nodded and turned his attention to the poolside

186

attractions, a group of pretty girls in bathing suits, possibly airline stewardesses, spreading towels on loungers and oiling themselves in preparation for the day's sun-worshipping.

'Things have certainly changed since I was last around Jo'burg: places like this, plane-loads of tourists . . .'

'When was that . . . your last trip?' she inquired gently.

'Ohhh . . . let's see . . . nine, ten years ago. There were legal details with the divorce to nit-pick over. I always said wild horses wouldn't drag me back! But – here I am of my own volition and it doesn't seem all that bad.' He looked at her quickly. 'I guess time, or circumstances, change everything. I've always flown straight to Sierra Leone or Cape Town and given this place a wide berth.'

'Well, I'm glad you've come back. We all have to do it some time . . . face up to the past.' Brilliant gazed into the hazy distance.

'Just as long as all my skeletons don't come rattling out of the cupboard at once and terrify me to death.' Carl's riposte was straight-faced. She laughed, that lovely spontaneous laugh of hers, throaty and uninhibited, and suddenly he wanted to tell her things he had perhaps never even admitted to himself.

How it had been with Astrid – spoiled and wilful as she was – how he had adored her. Loved her for what Yeats called 'the pilgrim soul' in her. She was a woman who wanted to be liberated but didn't know how, who saw marriage as the only escape from the stranglehold of her strict Dutch Calvinist family. Unhappiness with the limitations of her world, frustration with the waste of her own talent drove her to experiment, to push herself to the limit – drugs, drink, sex – anything to hurt the people nearest her, but most of all to punish herself. A tragically neurotic woman who had burnt herself out like a flame while he stood helplessly by. The inadequacy and shame of that would always be with him. He had not had the maturity or power to hold her. She went on to destroy herself.

Brilliant sat quietly while he spoke, choosing his words

187

carefully, tight, controlled. She was conscious of the burden that the exchange of confidences always places on the receiver. What sort of man took the responsibility for his wife's inadequacy? She sensed he had never spoken to anyone else of this. What had he just said about time, and circumstances, changing everything?

'It wasn't just . . . just the divorce which stopped me coming back.' A muscle worked at the corner of Carl's mouth. 'I had a sort of "uncle", Uncle Ernest – all the diamond world are family – who settled over here. He took me on for a spell, taught me the business from this end. That's how I met Astrid. Ernest was a cranky old sort, he really cracked the whip, but soft as marshmallow underneath. His dream was to retire to a smallholding outside Salisbury and create a miniature New England in Rhodesia, a paradise of security. He was caught up in the Zimbabwe riots . . . and was killed by natives.'

'Oh! I'm sorry.'

'Don't be! Only an unimaginative fool would have done what he did. But I had grown to love him – I was young, it hit me hard. It was just ironic, after years of exploiting the black man, throwing the railroad across his territory and living off the fat of the land, the whites found themselves on the receiving end when the tables were turned.'

Brilliant looked round as if for the first time at the black personnel in their dazzling white uniforms, their slow, courteous smiles, the general air of relaxed efficiency.

'But it all seems so peaceful here, almost paradise!'

'Don't you believe it. No way! Just you try and leave the grounds of this hotel on foot. A forest of invisible guards will rush to stop you, for your own safety. Just make sure you lock yourself inside your car when you travel downtown in Jo'burg, look at the misery and hate on the black faces around you. Go out to the rich white suburbs, I mean really rich, and see how they live – and I'm not talking about the decor. They're all behind ten-foot-high wire fences with Alsatians and electric alarms, the wives and children are shunted around like precious guarded cargo. Have you any concept what it means to live like that? If you were born here you wouldn't know any different and for the most part you'd defend it. If you weren't, it becomes unacceptable to any normal person's sensibilities. Anyway, it's up to you to see for yourself and form your own opinions. Jo'burg and gold are synonymous, so you'd better get yourself down a token mineshaft while we're at it.'

There were a myriad of questions she suddenly wanted to ask. She opened her mouth to speak but the expression on Carl's face stopped her. He had retreated into himself and his eyes were guarded. This was not the time for further confidences, but she did her best to convey, through the warmth of her smile, the empathy of her feelings.

'I'm at your disposal, Carl. This is your territory, where you lead I'm ready to follow.' She tipped her fingers to her forehead in mock salute.

He smile, grateful for her discretion. He pushed his chair back.

'Right! I'll put a call through to Kimberley. Oh, I forgot to tell you. The real reason for stopping here was a summons from on high. Philip Oppenheimer wants a word after the De Beers meeting – I don't know whether I should be flattered or dismayed. You'll meet them all – it will be quite an Olympian gathering.'

The next two days were a maelstrom of activity, which turned out to be mainly social. After the token visit to the gold mine, Carl took her to lunch at the Johannesburg Golf Club, meeting place of the town's white elite. She watched in amusement as sun-ravaged Boer giants clapped him on the back and plump matrons clasped him to their bosoms like the prodigal returned.

Invitations abounded, to golf, tennis, cocktails, dinners – in a couple of days she visited more homes, belonging to more unpronounceable Dutch names, sipped more cool drinks on more manicured lawns than she would have done in a month of Sundays in America. The impression was of one long garden party, each home more beautiful and more luxurious than the last, with more discreetly hovering black servants, more blonde blue-eyed children and – evidently an indication of wealth – ever higher and higher boundary fences.

Carl was much in demand, but whenever he could tear himself away from the attentions of an eager hostess he was at her side, sardonic, amusing, with a caustic gleam in his eye for the butterfly-hued Jo'burg society whose hospitality he so affably accepted.

On the third day they chartered a plane and flew down to Kimberley for one of the four annual board meetings of De Beers Consolidated. Henry Myers, one of the eighteen members, was waiting for them at 36 Stockdale Street.

The meeting had just ended, a pall of expensive cigar smoke still hung over the long walnut table and through the French windows knots of distinguished gentlemen stood chatting among the flowering shrubs on the terrace.

Brilliant was led into a spacious salon, decorated in the grand manner with old Cape Colonial furniture, to be shown the framed cheque for £5,338,650 from De Beers that gave Cecil Rhodes control of the diamond-mining industry in 1888.

'First Philip Oppenheimer would like a chat with Carl in the board room. Then they'll all come through and have pre-lunch drinks with specially invited guests, when I'll introduce you. I've laid on Andy Wilcox, one of our senior executives, to bring you up to date with our developments.' There was a suspicion of a twinkle in Henry's eye.

In due and leisurely time she was introduced to the 'gentlemen'. Julian Ogilvie Thompson, the chairman, was chatting to Antony Oppenheimer, son of veteran Harry Oppenheimer, who had just retired after an illustrious career. Another Oppenheimer cousin, Nicholas, the deputy chairman, talked with Sir Philip, who ran the London business. Then finally she met the Rothschilds, the Barons Elie from Paris and Evelyn from London, to remind her that De Beers' fortunes had been linked with this great banking family for over a century.

'So I've finally met the men who really rule the world's longest running monopoly . . .' she breathed to Carl, as they waited to enter the dining room, summoned by an English butler.

'Yes, look surprisingly normal don't they, considering!'

At lunch she sat between Sir Philip Oppenheimer and Baron Elie de Rothschild. The conversation was as much about wine as about diamonds, the friendly rivalry between the distinguished company's great vineyards in France and South Africa being much in evidence.

She felt on cloud nine returning to the city with Carl on their plane, a euphoria induced as much by pleasure in his company as the high-carat quality of the guests at lunch. The awkwardness she had often felt since that mortifying embrace in Paris seemed to have disappeared and in its place was a new companionable closeness. She would never have thought of Carl as vulnerable, but as he revealed more and more of himself, the public man and the private man seemed to be two completely separate entities.

She found herself looking forward enormously to dinner *tête-à-tête* at the Landrost, so she could draw him out and make him laugh. Yes, that was true, she knew she had the ability to lift his mood, and to see his intense expression poised on the brink of laughter was a pleasure in itself.

They dined well. He introduced her to the best South African vintages of the Landrost's cellar, they talked and laughed and danced until he regretfully called her attention to the deserted restaurant and the weary musicians waiting to close up shop.

Next morning, at the Premier mine, Carl's arm went instinctively round Brilliant's shoulder to steady her. As the Toyota Landcruiser plunged madly through a tunnel fifteen hundred feet below ground she clung desperately to its safety bar.

'I find ladies like the soufflé analogy,' Bob Pearson, the shift-boss, shouted in her ear. 'You see, diamonds were crystallized from carbon in molten material miles under the earth's crust. Then up they came like a rising soufflé when volcanic activity shifted the surface. Liquid kimberlite blows a neat hole, then the gases escape and just like your soufflé, the liquid collapses back into the hole – and there you have it – your diamond pipe.'

'Good God! So the diamonds are just there waiting, like chocolate chips in a cookie?' she gasped, as much with the effort of holding on as against the deafening roar of the tunnel.

'If we can leave the cookery bit out for a while, the answer is yes,' Carl yelled at her ear.

Bob Pearson manoeuvred the Landcruiser into a side-shaft. Half-blinded by a dazzling light, they narrowly avoided a head-on collision with a monster truck.

'That red beam's a laser – it keeps the road-heading machine on a straight track. It slices through the rock like butter, in great three-foot chunks.'

'I'd no idea there'd be so much dust,' Brilliant shouted through her protective mask.

'Yeah, kimberlite's devilish flaky!' Bob boomed above the noise. 'You can't spray it with water, so they use these things like hairnets to hold the roof in, then "garnet" it with liquid cement.'

Carl brought his mouth close to Brilliant's ear.

'Did you know that most of the legendary diamonds of the world – with exceptions, of course,' he smiled, 'have been found in this mine. Over fifteen tons of them. . . . The Cullinan, the Jonker, the Niarchos, the Premier Rose, to name just a few.'

Brilliant was grateful for Carl's reassuring hand on her shoulder in the narrow confines of the dark tunnel. The blue-blackness of the kimberlite obscurity pressed in on all sides; it would be easy for the imagination to play tricks. Would they come out in some time-warped world, discover a lost civilization . . . ? Shades of H G Wells and Jules Verne flitted through her mind.

Nothing so phantasmagoric. Soon a bright pinpoint appeared in the darkness – blessed daylight. They emerged still stooping, and straightened up. She swayed, dazed by the sudden transition from primeval twilight to blinding day. Carl grasped her hand to steady her.

The vast Premier pit lay in front of them. Far above was a circle of blue sky. At that moment, hand in hand with Carl, she experienced an atavistic sensation; male and female, Adam and Eve, they were standing together at the threshold of time. The essence of man, the essence of woman coursed through their veins and united them. Destiny had shaped their path and paired them. A cold sweat broke out on her forehead and she clung to him.

Explosions resounded round her confused brain, Carl was laughing and holding her, shouting in her ear. 'Are you all right? Lean on me! They're letting off explosives over the grizzley!'

Somehow, instinctively, she flattened her cheek against his chest. Her fingers flexed against the muscles of his back and her nostrils inhaled the smell of his flesh. Time passed – moments or perhaps millenia – when she experienced an uncanny sense of the life force that united them.

'Have some of this, ma'am. . . . It often gets 'em, it's the heat and noise, you gotta get used to it. . . .' Bob Pearson was holding a flask under her nose and Carl was staring at her strangely.

'God! How stupid of me. I felt . . . I felt odd. . . . It's the bright light and the noise. . . .' She leaned against the Landcruiser and drank from the flask, disturbed by the acuteness of her sensations, like a replay from the past.

She handed the flask back to Bob.

'Feeling all right now, ma'am?' Bob's eyes crinkled at her. 'Well, that's all there is – back we go. The show's over.'

Brilliant felt somehow tired and dispirited as they tramped back towards the lift.

'It's all so unsentimental,' she confided to Carl as they were hauled upwards. 'I don't know what I expected, but all the dust and bombs, it's so far removed from the glamorous end-product. Also, I thought –' she shot him a quick, embarrassed glance – 'I just thought I might set eyes on a real diamond, you know, glinting there in the dark, waiting to be picked up. . . .'

Bob Pearson smiled. 'That's what they all say! Looking for a diamond's like looking for a needle in a haystack. I've worked at the Premier for twenty years and I've never seen a diamond yet.'

Brilliant looked aghast.

'Come on – I'll show you the day's catch. That'll restore your faith in the glamour of it all.' Bob shook their hands and smiled his farewells at the door of the treatment plant.

'The X-ray machine's made a lot of difference to us since the early days, Carl.' Barend Boshoff, Premier's chief sorter, led the way to the conveyor belt.

'Diamonds are fluorescent, you see,' he explained to Brilliant. 'The X-ray picks out the larger stones, the smaller ones are winkled out on the grease tables.'

Later, in a small office, Barend presented a tray covered with 15,000 carats of diamonds.

'We got these yesterday and the day before.'

'Is that the average output?' Brilliant stared hard at the unprepossessing pebbles, making rough calculations as to their value. 'Do you ever get a day when none turn up at all?'

'Oh no! Nothing as bad as that! Normally we get about 8,000 carats a day, sometimes as low as 6,000.'

'Have you had any real biggies lately?' Carl already knew the answer.

'We . . . ll . . . De Beers don't actually announce the discovery of a big stone. That's up to the customer, who declares it if he wants to.'

'You mean another Cullinan could turn up and no one would know about it?' Brilliant was shocked.

'That's correct, ma'am. Often the customer has his reasons for keeping it a secret. All I can say is Premier's still living up to its reputation as the producer of the Ace of Diamonds!'

'Hmm . . . Sometimes all you hear is a rumour and by the time you've checked it out the stone's already been snapped up.' Carl touched Brilliant's arm. 'It's already dark, we had better be leaving.'

After Brilliant had showered off the dust and joined Carl at the main entrance, he confided, 'I've a small surprise in store for dinner. At least I hope you'll like it.' His brown eyes looked uncertain. 'The restaurant's on our way in to the city – we can go as we are, it's informal.' In the car she dozed, her head brushing his shoulder.

Seated across the white napery from Carl at eight, she found it hard to suppress her amusement. The restaurant was an old gold mine in the prosperous suburbs. At the surface the clientele donned stylish golden helmets for the descent into the bowels of the earth. The old working shafts and implements were as they had been left, only given the Midas touch. Everything – rough-hewn walls, pitprops, chairs, tables, lush candelabra, had been petrified in molten gold – a staggering South African Pompeii. It was unexpected and lavish, but so incongruous it was difficult to concentrate on the gilded parchment menu.

'I'm sorry,' she explained to Carl, 'I think it's spectacular, absolutely fantastic, but coming so soon after Premier and that strange . . . well . . . absurd feeling of unreality. . . .'

He looked apologetic. 'I thought you might find it a shade vulgar, too touristy. I should have booked the Restaurant Winkler, it's very high-style Dutch, more understated.'

'Good heavens, no!' She was quick to reassure him. 'I'm so sorry, I wasn't being critical, I really love it. You know, I still can't believe that Bob Pearson has spent twenty years in Premier and never seen a diamond.'

'Not surprising really, the blue kimberlite's a natural camouflage. In Koidu, you'll see tomorrow, where they're alluvial, people pick them off the streets.'

'Tell me more about the Sierra Siren. What makes it so special?'

'You know yourself Sierra gemstones are the best. They look greenish in the rough, but as you cut, the colour gets better and better. This one's not such a whopper as the Sierra Star they found a few years back – all 968 carats of her – but it's a great big beauty all the same. I've a contact in Koidu, a dealer who's kept me in the picture, but. . . . Well, there are things going on I don't like, so I thought I'd come and take a look myself. Anyway, there's much more to it than that. . . .' He leaned across the table, his eyes alight with enthusiasm. Then she remembered – that ardent expression – it had transformed his face the day he had confided the secret of his beloved books.

'It's the romance of a really fabulous gemstone, the legendary ones – yes, just like the White Tsaritsa – the ones that become part of history, that really excites me! Out of this whole crazy world of diamonds they're the only thing that makes sense. They are the true wonders of nature, their names alone will live on.'

Brilliant's eyes responded to his across the table, matching fire for fire. So the White Tsaritsa really did have a place in his heart. She had often wondered, given his own professed indifference to the commodity he dealt in.

Then there came a moment that she felt, in hindsight, was a turning point in their relationship. His hand, tawny, capable, was resting on the tablecloth a few inches from her own. They both looked down in silence, as though reading the other's thoughts. She knew unerringly that he was holding back, that it was for her to make a move now, that she should somehow take the initiative. His hand trembled slightly on the white cover. Dear God!

Suddenly, with stunning intensity, the memory of Arkady's disturbing touch filled her senses. An unnameable something stirred in her heart and compelled her to remain free. Inches, mere inches from Carl's, her hand flickered and obstinately remained still. She would always look back on that evening with the bitter-sweet remembrance of opportunity irretrievably lost.

13

From the moment they arrived at Koidu airport, Brilliant
found Carl tense and uncommunicative. They had flown
into Freetown the night before and gone straight to dinner
with three local businessmen. It was difficult to assess the
legality of the transactions and Brilliant, feeling superfluous and tired, thought it prudent not to inquire. Carl had
told her to be ready at dawn to fly to Koidu, and in the
morning she stared out of the aircraft window with mixed
feelings at the ravaged scene below.

The landscape seemed to have been devastated by an
annihilating blast from Hades. Pock-marked and pitted
like an enormous cheese, punctuated with the grotesque
roots of toppled trees, the terrain was further blighted
by ugly iron shanties perched perilously on the edge of
crumbling craters. As the pilot circled low over the earthworks she could make out scores of crouching men, half
submerged in water, digging and sifting in a cloud of
malarial mosquitoes.

'Those boys are the illegal diggers, after the best gemstones in the world. There's the mining company's chop-
per over there, they don't even pay attention to that any
more, they all go around with their eyes on the ground,
in the Koidu crouch.' Carl peered over her shoulder.
'They pick diamonds up in the streets and gardens here,
they say the town reservoir's full of them. Tonight this
patch will be covered with thousands of diggers, moon-
lighting to get at the stuff.'

'Why especially Koidu?' Brilliant leaned back in her
seat and closed her eyes hastily as the pilot dipped and
swayed over a crater. 'Why all this illegal dealing?'

'Dealers prefer the colour – and the size. Wouldn't you

be prepared to have a go, if a thousand carats suddenly turned up at the shake of a shovel?'

As the 'fasten seat-belt' sign lit up, the small aircraft banked and headed away from the earthworks over swampland, then straightened up in line with the airstrip.

'A generation back this was just another African village. Even ten years ago it was a shanty town. Now it's got hotels, restaurants – maybe more than a hundred thousand people.'

'Whatever happened to Big Daddy?'

'You'll be pleased to know De Beers carry no clout here. They try, but it doesn't come off. The Lebanese are the real masters.'

The wheels crunched on the uneven surface of the runway and Carl shouted above the roar of the engines, 'The Lebanese give the illicit miners a bag of rice and some shovels, even advise them where to go. They corner all the best stones, De Beers don't really stand a chance. The Africans are involved in a small way, but they sell quickly and haven't got the international connections.'

They taxied to a halt beside the newly painted customs shed.

'The real fun starts with the wheeling and dealing much higher up. The stones are traded hand to hand until they reach the Big Four – the only ones with official export licences. These guys really control the show.'

They stepped out into intense heat. The sky was overcast, a sticky breeze blew dust and debris round her feet. There was an aromatic, spicy smell in the air, and something else, a brooding menace, a premonition of danger. An immaculate young man with a sleek helmet of black hair hurried from the building.

'Welcome, Mr Vanderberg! Mr Said is waiting for you. Did you have a pleasant journey?'

'Hallo, Josef! Fine thanks. This is Madame Chardin, in charge of our New York operation.'

They were hustled with almost indecent speed through customs and while Josef was supervising the transfer of their bags to a waiting limousine – impressive for this part of Africa – Carl confided to her *sotto voce*, 'Josef works for Jamal Mohammed Said, the Lebanese Mr Big in these parts. Word has it that all the larger stones find their way to him, then he off-loads them on the Antwerp market. Some of his operation is official, the Diamond Corporation have three Sights here a year, shared between De Beers, two New York dealers, a Swiss and Jamal Said. I'm going straight to a meeting with him now, strictly private I'm afraid. I'll call your room as soon as I get back.' He turned back to Josef and she slid gratefully into the car's air-conditioned interior.

The suddenness of the African dusk, as always, surprised her. Within minutes it was dark. She had an impression of a main street lined with shops and offices, low-built with wide verandas, then the lobby of the Hotel Monrovie, with its palms, ceiling fans, white-uniformed bell-boys and constant congress of visitors.

Her bedroom was a delight, a colonial throw-back of creaking polished floors, ancient ceiling fan, antimacassars in starched linen on basket chairs and more starched cotton over the narrow bed, crowned with a filmy mosquito net of muslin.

With nightfall the sticky heat was tempered by a cooling breeze which fluttered the gauzy curtains through the mosquito netting. A throb of exotic sounds, insect and animal, African and alien, stirred the blood and drummed an insistent beat at her temple.

She took a shower in the antiquated bathroom, coaxing only a reluctant drizzle of brackish water from the ancient shower head. Feeling an instinctive response to the theatricality of her environment, she took out a dress she had slipped into her suitcase as an afterthought. A siren-song of deep scarlet, one shoulder bared, with a jungle print of white and green, she dimly remembered Jean-Claude's compliments when she had worn it on an exotic holiday. Scarlet high heels and her hair brushed out and held at one side with a red comb completed the *femme fatale* effect. As she walked downstairs her heart beat with a nervous anticipation she had almost forgotten.

'Mr Vanderberg is waiting for you in the bar,' the head receptionist informed her. Brilliant stepped straight into the steaming heat of Sierra Leone's Happy Hour.

An extraordinary clientele, colour-graded from ivory to deep ebony, jostled among a riot of palms and plants in the murky half-light of the long room. Local businessmen, modish and at ease in Coptic robes, lounged alongside gleaming-fleshed women, while their Western counterparts shifted uneasily in basket chairs and ran their fingers inside constraining collars as damp patches spread in the tight creases of groin and armpit.

The noise level was deafening. A shrieking parrot on a stand, the clank of an overhead fan together with the rhythmic percussion of the bar-boys' cocktail shakers formed the background to a babbling wall of voices from every far-flung outpost of the globe.

A table of spruced-up miners out on the town, faces sporting the marks of the odd bar-room brawl, had settled into their last round before moving off to the less restrained environs of the native bars downtown. The heady combination of money and sex – there were several tables with available girls – gave the atmosphere a powerful erotic charge. The women catered for all tastes and pockets and, like the male clientele, hailed from every continent.

Diamond business – and illicit at that – was the *raison d'être* of the Hotel Monrovie. The fast-talking Lebanese, the impassive Chinaman, the perspiring Italian and the gold-toothed African were all here to talk one thing: the illegal exchange of that emotive commodity.

'We . . . ll!' Carl's eyes gleamed as Brilliant walked up to the bar counter. He swung his long legs from the stool and stared at her oddly, his lips compressed.

'I'd been preparing Fritz for Anna Karenina and now we have Some-Like-It-Hot! I'd like you to meet Fritz

201

von Schonenburg, consultant extraordinaire to the Sierra Leone cabal.'

He indicated his silver-haired companion, impeccable in navy pin-stripes and red carnation, with a long ivory cigarette holder held in a surprisingly capable-looking hand. Fritz bowed with exaggerated old-world courtesy.

'*Gnadige fräulein, enchanté de faire votre connaissance.*'

'Relax, Fritz, Madame Chardin speaks English.'

'Oh, I beg your pardon, Madame Chardin. . . .' Fritz looked at Carl, perplexed. 'In the circumstances, I was expecting someone quite different!'

Carl frowned slightly, then turned to Brilliant.

'If there's anything, and I mean anything, you need to know about diamonds in Africa – monkey business or otherwise – Fritz is your man. His grandfather came out before the Boer War, he was pals with Barnato and Rhodes.'

Fritz emptied his glass, bowed again and retrieved his silver-topped cane and panama from their niche under the bar.

'If you will excuse me, Madame Chardin, I have to dash.' Fritz's leering smile revealed a row of rather equine teeth.

'I'm crossing the border tomorrow, as you know.' He darted Carl a meaningful look. 'Winston's buyer will be at the Ducor and we're having "discussions". If I can be of any service while you're here, Madame Chardin, don't hesitate to let me know. My room number is fifteen.' Fritz made a stagey exit, acknowledging acquaintances to left and right with swivelling movements of his hips.

'Fritz has lived at the Monrovie for years, there's nothing illicit going on that he doesn't know about, or instigate.' Carl smiled after his elaborate retreat. 'He had to dash – get it – *dash*, that's the local vernacular for a bribe. Anything can be done here with a little dash, not for nothing is it called the land of waving palms.'

'Why the cryptic remark about crossing the border?'

'The appeal of Liberia is the almighty dollar; here the

trading's done in Sierra Leone pounds. It takes about ten hours to get across the border, except in the rainy season when the roads are flooded. De Beers are there, plus four or five big buyers from the West.'

Sudden shouts and angry voices erupted from a far corner and were followed by the crescendo smash of breaking glass. Within seconds an African bouncer of monumental proportions escorted a flaxen-haired youth to the door. The brawl was over as quickly as it had begun and as Brilliant peered after the protesting Dutchman a woman paused in the doorway and stared at her for what seemed long seconds. Then she began to walk towards them, vermilion lips parted in a smile.

Brilliant looked at the woman with curiosity. She was tiny, but carried her head with the regal bearing of a princess. Her skin had a milky pallor against a luxuriant mass of dark tumbling hair. But it was her jewels, more than the woman's beauty, that had every head in the room craning towards her. A king's ransom in diamonds was hung, draped and suspended from her small person. She seemed to have stepped through a dew-spangled cobweb and the shimmering droplets had remained, scattered negligently about her.

An impressive necklace of pear-shaped stones filled the *décolleté* of a simple black dress and the sash draped around her hips was fastened with a brooch of pendant droplets as big as a saucer. Diamond bracelets, graded in size, climbed up her forearms, pendant earrings swung from her delicate ears and the small hands were weighed down, like a child's wearing its mother's rings. A shimmering spray adorned one shoulder and droplets were scattered in her night-dark hair.

The young woman stretched out her arms to Carl in rapturous greeting. The impact of her dazzling black and whiteness, the myriads of refracted prisms of light and the pungent odour of her exotic scent gave Brilliant a momentary stab of nauseating dizziness.

The woman's laugh was unexpectedly low and throaty

as she reached up to clasp Carl and kiss him fervently on the cheek, swinging her perfumed mane of hair backwards and forwards – once, twice, three times.

'Carl, *mon fiancé*, you have been so long, you are a month late! We even began to get worried about you, my clever one!' Her teeth were white and perfect as she turned happily towards Brilliant, her arm tucked inside Carl's.

'Brilliant, this is Yasmina Said, Jamal Said's niece, jewellery designer and chief ornament to the trade. Yasmina – Madame Chardin, my assistant and diamond-eye extraordinary.'

'Ah, Madame Chardin! Of course I have heard about you. How fortunate to be named for a diamond. What brings you here – or doesn't Carl trust his own eye for the Sierra Siren!' Her dark eyes swept Brilliant from head to toe, shrewd, intelligent; here was no decorative butterfly.

'Oh, I don't think Carl ever really needs to consult me. This was a . . . well . . . a sort of vacation . . . a chance to see another side of the business. . . .' Brilliant finished lamely, looking at Carl, irritated by Yasmina's continuing stare of appraisal.

'Well, you'll certainly see another side here! My Uncle Jamal is one of the few official exporters, but what can he do with all the illegal competition?' Yasmina shrugged her shoulders expressively, setting her several million dollars' worth of diamonds jangling in a cacophony of blue light.

'I see you believe in wearing your product. That is quite an impressive display. Are they your own design?' Brilliant asked.

'Of course! There's no one in the trade who designs on my scale, except Paloma, and she mostly plays with coloured stones. I am under contract to Saks at the moment, but I do have mighty Adamantina interested.' Yasmina gave Carl's arm an encouraging squeeze. 'Although you can imagine, with stones this size, buying an exclusive Yasmina is limited to a millionaire elite. But the jewel I really have designs on is the White Tsaritsa! Re-set in a fabulous parure I have just the client for it. His mistress is the French wife of one of the rulers of the Gulf States. She yearns for it, he would kill for it!' Her eyes glinted maliciously. 'I do so love the romance behind every great sale, don't you, the intrigue. . . . It gives one a delicious sense of power. I gather that for some sentimental reason Carl has so far refused every offer. But this time I really intend to pin him down.'

Brilliant recoiled as if the Lebanese woman had struck her. She stared at Yasmina and the colour drained from her face. She would never have believed it – Carl had betrayed her trust. He had set her up to be witness to a triumphant coup. Buy one legendary jewel, sell the other.

Carl's voice was coming from somewhere distant and his expression was grim.

'Brilliant, I have to go now. I've a long-standing dinner date with Yasmina, broken several times already, I'm afraid. She is going to show me her new designs . . .' Brilliant looked at him sharply but his face was impassive . . . 'so I asked Fritz von Schonenburg to take you to dinner. If that's all right, of course. He's an authority on the Good Old Days, it would be educational for you . . .'

Brilliant felt a spark of anger, which just as quickly changed to cold irritation.

'Really, Carl, I'm not a child! I can fend for myself perfectly well, you don't have to find a minder for me.'

'I don't want you to be alone, Brilliant, that's all.' Carl's voice was so tender that she felt the blood surge to her cheeks.

'Thank you, but really, I'm fine! I appreciate your concern, but I'm quite tired and looking forward to a sandwich in my room and an early night.'

'Well . . . That might not be a bad idea. I'll tell Fritz if I see him in the lobby. So we'll meet at breakfast – and then go out to the diggings.' His face came close and for a second she had the impression he was going to plant a brotherly kiss on her forehead. But he merely whispered,

'Take care!' before leaving with the smiling Yasmina, his arm resting lightly round her shoulders.

Brilliant put down her glass and kicked her heels disconsolately against the bar stool. What to do now? She had never felt less like a sandwich and an early night in her life. The evening she had anticipated so pleasurably had crumbled in her grasp, leaving her disgruntled and sticky-fingered, without having eaten any of the cake. She signalled to the Indian barman and ordered another dry martini. From the corner of her eye she caught sight of Fritz von Schonenburg making a showy entrance through the palm-fringed portals. He came straight to her.

'My dear Madame Chardin, I would be immensely honoured if you could dine with me tonight. I know the most marvellous restaurant, run by a Portuguese, his chef is Goan, I promise you won't be disappointed!'

His approach was so exquisitely mannered that she laughed in spite of herself. Something mettlesome in the old German's eye told her that the evening wouldn't be dull. While they finished their drinks he regaled her with vitriolic gossip about the other occupants of the bar, his faded eyes snapping with pleasure at the unexpected ferocity of her approval.

Sam da Cunha's restaurant was a well-kept secret among the colonial elite of Koidu. Disappointed aspirants got no further than Sam's shabby front lobby in the Asian quarter. The fortunate few, once inside the ornate Portuguese-style room, found themselves in a club for the town's cognoscenti. Fritz's usual table was reserved in a corner, from which vantage point he had a privileged view of the night's proceedings.

'What do you make of our Yasmina, the seductress of Koidu?' Fritz's eyes glittered malevolently over his *thali* tray, the little bowls spicy and aromatic around a central pyramid of fragrant rice.

'Quite breathtaking, but, well . . . incongruous, I sup-

206

pose. What does she do here, all decked out like a Christmas tree? Rather wasted on the local lads, I would have thought. Shouldn't she be adorning the drawing rooms of Europe, or whatever?' Brilliant replied.

'Don't make the mistake of thinking Yasmina a social butterfly. Oh no, my dear, appearances can be so deceptive. She was married at fifteen to Paco Ifraheem, her uncle's partner. Paco died under mysterious circumstances a year after their wedding. There was talk of double-dealing, a rift between the two men. It was an arranged marriage – I don't think Yasmina shed many tears – but it gave her clout as far as her uncle was concerned. She inherited Ifraheem's share and perhaps a few dark secrets . . .' Fritz lowered his voice theatrically, wiped his mouth on his napkin and took a gulp of beer.

'Not too hot for you? Goan cuisine is noted for its liberal use of chili. Use plenty of *raita*, it cools the palate. How else can one explain the enormous influence Yasmina has over Jamal Said? She runs his empire with the velvet gloves on, has the government eating out of her bejewelled hand and is top-dog hereabouts as far as diamond dealing is concerned. Not bad for a young woman not yet thirty!'

'But she doesn't live here all the time, does she? I just can't imagine it.'

'Of course not! She's touting her designs all over the world for half the year – but a business like hers is a tricky one. The shop can't be left untended for too long, and that, I imagine, is where Carl Vanderberg comes in.'

Brilliant felt a stab of pique and with it that strange sense of menace she had felt since her arrival at Koidu airport.

'Look, Fritz! Since the moment I arrived I've felt like a maiden aunt who's had all the exciting bits carefully edited out of the excursion. Just what's going on? Is the government involved in the illicit stuff as well? How does Yasmina get all that wealth – and just where does Carl fit into the picture?'

'Oh, my dear, I thought you knew! Yasmina has had

her sights set on Carl for two years now, but he's a shrewd chap and seems to know how to keep her on the boil. Yasmina needs him, apart from his obvious attractions of course, for diamond credibility. The Saids have a legitimate export licence, but all the big stuff finds its way out by submarine. The government gets none of the revenue and are happy for the crumbs that come their way. There's simply nothing they can do about it – they haven't got the network to control the business.'

'And the Carl-Yasmina thing? She is very beautiful . . . very rich, of course, but . . . well. . . .' She looked at him hesitantly, wary of this elderly intriguer.

Fritz smiled disarmingly.

'Carl is a man of integrity and Yasmina an unscrupulous temptress? But who is using whom? Aha! My dear Madame Chardin – there you have it. That is the question we would all like to find out. We are very vulnerable in Koidu and Carl, though an astute businessman and as anxious as the next for a sharp deal, is too clever a strategist – and has too much to lose – to fall for Yasmina's blandishments.'

'Hmmm. . . .' Brilliant stared at Fritz thoughtfully. 'I used to deplore the De Beers monopoly and think a free-for-all would be more democratic. Right now some of my prejudices could come in for a rethink. When you see the pitiable state of affairs here, you wonder that Big Daddy might not be such a bad thing. At least the profits would be spread around a bit.'

'If you had lived in Africa as long as I have you would take a more liberal view. There will always be pockets of illegal mining, there have to be! As a safety valve and a spur to the open market, but most of all, to give free men the excitement of the dig.' Fritz's faded eyes snapped with sudden unexpected passion, that obsessive light Brilliant had come to recognize as the mark of the true addict. 'I've always been in thrall to the diamond, loved her and hated her, it's in my blood and a hard way of life to get out of. Now I do my best to earn a dishonest crust in this hotbed of iniquity.'

Fritz's attention was caught by something that was happening behind her back and he cocked his head towards the door. Brilliant glanced round. Sam de Cunha peered into the room like a schoolmaster checking his class was in order, then shrank back to allow a many-chinned Buddha to advance to a reserved table. The man was closely followed by three others, equally monumental, with the sleek Josef she had met at the airport bringing up the rear.

'There you have it! A hypothetical shift in diamond-power from De Beers to the Third World. Jamal Said – with Patali from Bombay, Peskov from Leningrad and a tribal patriarch from Namibia.'

Brilliant watched discreetly over her coffee cup as the heavyweight group were seated amid much fluttering attention from Sam.

'You seem to know an awful lot.'

'It's my business to know what's going on – my livelihood, my life itself, depends on it. There's enough money at that table to cause De Beers real problems. Your employer Carl Vanderberg is not with them. Curiouser and curiouser. . . . He had an appointment with Miss Said, but should have been at this Summit. Has something happened . . . has she deliberately detained him?'

Brilliant put her cup down with a sigh. 'Look, if you don't mind, I've had enough intrigue for one day and I'm ready for bed. There's nothing more exhausting than feeling you've fallen into a slimy pit, with no one willing to give you a hand out.'

'I am so sorry, my dear, your impressions of Koidu will be beastly and that simply won't do. I merely hoped I could amuse you.'

Fritz called for the bill, impervious to the spark of annoyance in Brilliant's eye. As they left the restaurant she said to him, 'Fritz, since I came here I've been "taken care of", haven't I? Is it on behalf of Carl or Jamal Said?'

'Such blunt questions are always difficult to answer and if they had been put by a man would be considered very bad form.' Fritz tucked her hand under his arm and, quite unperturbed, guided her to the waiting taxi. 'As I said, your business here automatically becomes my business. You are looked after, "taken care of", as you put it, but woe betide you, my dear, if it were otherwise. Now, to come to the question of sides – Carl or Said – I will leave that conundrum to you, unless you like to consider there are no sides, each is part of the other's activities. Remember, Carl is a man of undisputed integrity, one of the few New York dealers the Big Four trust. We know he has a professed antipathy to the South African regime and carries no great torch for De Beers. We also know he has set his heart on acquiring the Sierra Siren, which is Yasmina's alone to dispose of. Yasmina has doubtless named her own terms, but whether or not Carl is prepared to fulfil them, remains to be answered. I have known men throw away marriages, careers, reputations, everything – for a stake in a beauty like the Siren. I leave you to ponder the implications. Carl was not among the guests at dinner. Negotiations with Yasmina must have come to a mutually gratifying conclusion.'

Back in her room the heat was stifling. The mosquito net proved inadequate, the flask of water covered with a smeary glass was tepid, the ceiling fan squeaked relentlessly and the floorboards in the adjoining room creaked under the weight of its restless occupant. By morning the charm of colonial simplicity had worn decidedly thin.

Dawn found her pale and hollow-eyed at the breakfast rendezvous with Carl. He eyed her shrewdly across the table in the noisy restaurant off the lobby – business got under way early in Koidu – then reapplied himself energetically to his bacon and eggs.

'Didn't sleep too well, huh?' He pushed a cup and saucer towards her. 'Have some coffee, it'll soon pull you round! Sleepless nights are the norm at first, it's the humidity, you soon get used to it.' His almost indecent

210

cheerfulness was harder on her nerves than the reticence of the day before.

'No, I didn't sleep. I'd rather have tea, thank you. Was the evening successful?'

'Successful? In what respect? Interesting, entertaining. . . . Yes, certainly that.' The waiter came to take her order and Carl poured himself fresh coffee.

'You are ready to leave, I take it?' He studied her carefully, his eyes narrowed. 'Get some breakfast under your belt and you'll soon feel a new woman.'

She sighed. 'Please, Carl, spare me the hearty stuff. I presume you came here, apart from a long-overdue visit to Yasmina, to purchase the Sierra Siren? Or so you'd led me to believe. Did she let you have it – if you'll excuse the unintentional coarseness of the expression?'

'I can tell Fritz has been gossiping. . . .'

'He was an amusing minder, wonderfully waspish, just like a bitchy woman.'

'Exactly, and just like a bitchy woman you should take what he tells you with a large pinch of salt. His deviousness is a byword.' Carl put his cup down sharply. 'Look, Brilliant, I don't think I owe you any explanations. As an intelligent woman I thought you would have judged me better. Yasmina lives in a world of fantasy. She collects "fiancés" on her travels round the world as other women collect souvenirs. Yes, she has often spoken of buying the White Tsaritsa, but she knows it's not for sale, any more than I am. She negotiated me an amazingly good price for the Siren – on her own terms, of course. Those terms were very personal.'

'Oh?' Brilliant raised inquiring eyebrows.

'She reserved the right to design the four or five important gems we hope to get out of the five-hundred-and-fifteen-carat rough stone. They will all be genuine "Yasminas" – sold through Adamantina, so she'll get the name plus a percentage. I'm well satisfied – Adamantina will get all the publicity and . . .' he smiled a trifle smugly '. . . I managed to beat off Van Cleefs, Boucheron, Chardin, to name but a few!'

In spite of her recent chagrin Brilliant felt pleased for him. So Yasmina was just an irritating means to an end. . . .

'But you won't be keeping your legendary gemstone whole? I just thought you might have it cut and keep it. . . .'

'In place of the White Tsaritsa? Well, think again! It won't be standing next to it on a twin pedestal either. Much as I'd love to keep the legend whole, I don't think the shareholders would stand for it. Let me tell you something, Brilliant.' He leaned across the table, his eyes hard. 'I'm in this goddamned business to make an honest crust, but the day Adamantina sells the White Tsaritsa is the day I throw in the towel!'

She had never seen him like this. She looked down in embarrassment, a curious lump in her throat.

Carl pushed his chair back abruptly.

'Sometimes, Brilliant, you have to look a little further than the end of your nose. There are aspects of this case that don't concern you and I won't have them disclosed. Not yet. That's all I'm prepared to say for the moment.'

He made an effort to appear off-hand.

'I don't think the diggings are for you this morning. I was going to take you to see an old friend of mine, Duncan McNab, he's nearly eighty. Been out in the bush all his life, panning the tributaries, a real picturesque old fellow. I guess he might just be around next time I call. . . . Let's get you out of the noxious air of Koidu, there's something about this place that breeds trouble. The Siren's going to be delivered personally – by Yasmina. That was part of the deal.'

'Hmmm. . . .' Brilliant pursed her lips and folded her arms. 'Lloyd's must throw a wobbly whenever she forays abroad, glittering like the Adamantina catalogue. She must be well-nigh uninsurable.'

The thought of Yasmina, the atypical tourist, decked

out in her diamonds was suddenly so comical that they both smiled together, then laughed heartily in a kind of pained relief. But for Brilliant the damage was done. She watched Carl covertly through her lashes as they left the restaurant. The game had changed. There were predators now for her diamond, predators like Yasmina, suddenly emerged from the jungle to permanently destroy her peace of mind.

14

At Antwerp's airport the impressive illuminated sign announced 'Welcome to Antwerp: World Diamond Centre'. As Carl helped Brilliant into a taxi it was hardly necessary to tell the driver where they were going. The majority of passengers from the packed international flights went straight to Pelikaanstrasse or the adjoining side streets of Rijfstraat, Hoveniersstraat or Schupstraat. Among these back streets clustered over five hundred diamond dealers, manufacturers and wholesalers, bolstering the city's claim to the world title.

To step into this cosmopolitan diamond world was to step into a mini-state within a state, a haven of security from strict government vigilance and zealous police surveillance. Here the diamond fraternity liked to feel they were a law unto themselves and prided themselves on the confidential nature of their transactions.

Every diamond-producing country had its own representative, including African 'submarine' dealers who felt quite at home in Antwerp's no-man's-land. The Russians were in evidence too. Russelmaz, where Arkady Tverskoy was director, had its office on the second and third floors of a nondescript block in Lange-Herentalsestraat. De Beers' eight-storey office block was situated just opposite – much to the amusement of Antwerp's diamantaires, who assumed they kept a wary eye on each other's movements.

Grobbendonk, a village on the rural outskirts of Antwerp, was an unlikely venue for exotics such as Yasmina, come to supervise the cutting of her master-stone, and Brilliant, lost in her own diamond dreams – the two women's beauty contrasting like light and shade. Carl watched them somewhat apprehensively. It had not been his idea for them to meet – far from it. And by all indications it was going to prove a controversial gathering. Arkady Tverskoy sat a little apart from the main group, his eyes as alert and watchful as a cat by a fishpond.

'Bruting' a diamond . . . Brilliant wondered. Why such a harsh term for turning a lifeless stone into a beautiful jewel . . . ? She watched as Peter Verhoet honed the clamped gemstone into an eight-sided emerald cut, to accentuate the quality of the finished diamond.

Beauty and impregnable strength too, she thought. From the corner of her eye she was acutely aware of Arkady's head turned in her direction.

At first Brilliant had refused Carl's invitation to accompany him to Antwerp at the beginning of July for the cutting of the Sierra Siren. Yasmina had arrived in New York two weeks after their meeting in Koidu and delivered it with the maximum of fuss to the Adamantina showroom. Two eunuch-like bodyguards of impressive proportions accompanied her everywhere, taking turns, it was rumoured, to cat-nap through the night outside her room at the Pierre. They made a striking contrast to her air of fragility, although anyone less vulnerable than Yasmina it would be hard to imagine. Her visits to the showroom to discuss design turned into near routs and rebellion by mortified staff, infuriated by her imperious demands and overbearing manner.

But Carl had continued to try to persuade Brilliant to go. She really should visit Antwerp, he argued, as Peter Verhoet had already started work on an important commission for her new French client. Carl had made it quite clear that Yasmina would be following later – alone – to supervise the creation of her own designs. For the moment business in New York detained her. Then the impossible had happened. Carl ran a distraught hand through his hair as he sensed Yasmina's eyes on him and heard the insistent morse-code of her carmine fingertips on her handbag. Brilliant had communicated with Arkady Tverskoy at Russelmaz and Antwerp had suddenly become the focus of her existence. Not to be left out, Yasmina had orchestrated a major change of itinerary which made the Netherlands her first port of call.

Brilliant tried to concentrate on the diamond taking shape on the lathe. She clasped her hands to stop the tremor in them, recalling the emotion of Arkady's welcome. She had not ceased thinking about him in New York, but had tried to put him on hold in the back of her mind, together with the sense of unease that his memory evoked. But then she had recalled – Antwerp! Russelmaz and Arkady . . . and it became suddenly imperative to see him again. He had seemed surprised when she had telephoned – would it be possible to meet? He had appeared hesitant when their eyes had met, then all misgivings had been swept away in the emotion of his greeting. The colour had gone from his face and she had felt him tremble when he took her hand and held it to his lips.

Now Arkady's eyes seemed to be willing her to look at him. She clasped her hands tighter, concentrating on every precise movement on the lathe. Only a diamond can cut another diamond. . . . The image was mingled with disturbing thoughts of Arkady – either split it asunder or cosset it tenderly into shape, with a mind-shattering power and precision that is quite unique.

Peter stopped the drill and wiped his forehead. He looked at Brilliant and smiled, as though reading her thoughts.

'I managed to beat off a lot of foreign competition to get this great big beauty for my drill. The larger industrials are all being snapped up by the space programme.' He looked rather accusingly at Arkady.

'The space programme?' Yasmina looked at the attractive, enigmatic man who had introduced himself as 'Arkady Tverskoy – Economic Adviser to Sovexport, based at Russelmaz.'

'Yes, that is perfectly true, Miss Said. We are constantly on the look-out for large perfect stones, together with the Americans,' Arkady assured her.

216

'I had no idea such thrillingly large stones were whizzing round in space!' Yasmina gasped. 'It is a market, *mon cher*, that opens up staggering new possibilities. In what capacity do they use these fabulous gems?'

'The windows of the space probes have to be transparent, but able to stand up to unbelievable stress. Diamonds are the only answer,' Carl replied.

Yasmina's eyes became bemused.

'Just imagine! One's personal diamond porthole. Most definitely first-class travel.'

'Here she is, ladies and gentleman! An embryo emerald-cut diamond!' Peter Verhoet's thick Flemish accent proudly announced the end of the first stage of bruting.

'*Fait voir! Mon Dieu, c'est magnifique!*' Yasmina quickly extracted her loupe and bent over the work-bench. Despite exchanging amused glances with Carl, Brilliant slipped off her stool and stood elbow to elbow with the Lebanese woman beside the table. The two women were lost in admiration as Peter's assistant prepared the fifty-five-carat stone for polishing.

'Aaahhh. . . .' Yasmina let out a long sigh and her eyes glittered. 'This first stone will belong to my client's mistress. I can already feel the frissons of love and desire emanating from it. How I admire that woman, her lover would kill to give her the jewels she craves. She has a thorough understanding of the game of eroticism and power.'

'Hmmm. . . .' Brilliant gave her a look of scorn. 'Well, your king's-ransom lady will certainly be tamed by that.' Her professional eye was quick to appreciate the superb quality of the 1F – internally flawless – Rare White. For one moment, the two women, so different, took on the same intensity of expression. Eyes narrowed, nostrils dilated and bodies tensed, like animals waiting for the kill.

'Now, Madame Chardin! Would you like to come to my office to discuss your parure, or shall we display the stones here?' Peter was anxious to uphold the Kempen tradition of cloaking the client's business in the utmost secrecy.

'Oh no, Peter! Please get out the stones. This client has nothing to hide.' Brilliant tossed her head in Yasmina's direction.

'On the contrary, the Comtesse de Tarn Riberac has always done everything as publicly as possible. She wants this new bauble to make all the headlines, she's even given her approval for a piece in the trade press.'

She smiled at Arkady.

'You probably remember, Arkady, all the drama of that jewel theft in the Dordogne last year, where one of the house guests was implicated and later let off? There was a hell of a shindig – a family scandal – and the lovely Adèle was sued for divorce, though they're back together now like turtle doves. Anyway, the insurance claim was astronomical. The diamond parure we are copying had been in the family for generations and was part of Adèle's marriage settlement. I've been waiting for the right rose-coloured stones for months and managed to get them at the last Sight.'

The ghost of a smile hovered on Yasmina's lips.

Peter Verhoet set up a black-covered baize board on his worktop, his assistant pulled heavy curtains over the lead-paned windows, powerful lamps were wheeled into position and in an instant the cosy artisan's shop was transformed into a dramatic theatre where the hushed spectators awaited the entrance of the inanimate star. A battered cardboard box was reverently carried from another room and after much scrunching of blue diamond paper a perfectly graded set of delicate blush-pink fancies was laid out in all its glory.

Yasmina's sharp intake of breath and the further extraction of her personal loupe was gratifying.

'Take a good look at these, everybody!' Brilliant ordered. 'You'll live a long time to see better. I've had all the scouts out, including Carl, but Henry finally winkled them out for me. They're FIs from Letseng-La-Terai in Lesotho, the highest mine in the world.'

Carl looked on with amusement as the assembly of diamantaires raised their loupes in unison and handled the stones as tenderly as a mother with a new-born offspring.

'All the Cs are there,' Brilliant pronounced in triumph. 'Carats, Colour and Clarity, and when Peter has finished, they'll have the fourth one – superb Cut, as well.'

'Personally, I've never held with fancies.' Yasmina sniffed and folded away her loupe. 'These are very fine, of course, but many people consider colour a little *vulgaire*. The number of times I've been offered canaries, champagne, d'oré. . . . Only the other day there was a Senegalese with a gunmetal black, very similar to the Black Orlov, but I had to refuse. It's not my line of business – my reputation has been built up solely on superb quality whites.'

'I think they are quite stunning.' Carl was quick to notice the flash of annoyance in Brilliant's eyes. 'The blush of colour gives them an added dimension. How have you decided to cut them?'

'The Comtesse is letting us do a modern version of the parure, with an eight-sided emerald cut.' Brilliant turned her back on Yasmina. 'Though a traditional rose cut was used for the original.'

Peter wiped his steamed-up glasses energetically and gave his assistant the nod to restore the room to its workaday austerity. In a cosy front parlour Mrs Verhoet and her eldest daughter served them coffee and schnapps. A fire burning in the grate for nine months of the year had given the walls the mellow patina of a Vermeer painting.

Yasmina stood next to Arkady and sipped her coffee from an old Delft cup. There were vibrations from this man that she, of course, could not fail to pick up; an extraordinary animal magnetism that was quite rare and, once directed at a woman, was almost impossible to resist. How fortunate that it was not directed at her – quite pointless anyway, as only power, whether it be money or influence on a massive scale, had ever stimulated her sexually.

'Carl, *chéri*.' She smiled at him. 'If there is no more pressing business I suggest we return to town for lunch, I have an engagement at three o'clock. . . .'

Carl excused himself for a moment to discuss finance with Peter while Brilliant thanked Mrs Verhoet for her hospitality. As Yasmina smoothed on her long black leather gloves she looked inquiringly at Arkady.

'Monsieur Tverskoy! Porthole windows cannot be the only market for your enormous diamonds. Perhaps we could do business together?'

Arkady looked at Brilliant and not at Yasmina as he replied.

'You are correct, some of the finest gemstones in history have been found in Russia, as Countess Curnonsky knows well. . . .'

'But of course!' Yasmina clicked her tongue impatiently. 'We are talking about a legend there – or half of one. But even legends have to be kept alive. I feel the White Tsaritsa is ready for the next exciting phase in its saga. Acquiring the Sierra Siren for Carl has given me an edge. Now he is very well aware that he owes me. I have a feeling in my bones about that jewel and I am not often wrong. It is part of my Eastern mysticism.'

Arkady instinctively avoided Brilliant's eyes. What an extraordinarily fortuitous encounter! Yasmina was mad, of course – she was about as mystic as his chum Sergei Stopich of the Armenian mafiosa.

As Carl strolled back into the room with Peter, Yasmina tucked her arm through his.

'But Carl thinks I'm very naughty – niggling away at him all the time. He tells me the White Tsaritsa is not for sale, but how can that be?' She shrugged her shoulders, inviting the others to share her incredulity. 'My dears, of course it is for sale, everything has a price. Naturally I appreciate the sentimental interest in the stone, but the matter is really not just for one individual to decide.'

Carl gently removed Yasmina's hand from his sleeve.

'While I find it hard to refuse a lady anything, there are some things that are sacrosanct. All the money in the world couldn't buy them.' He looked around the room with an air of finality. 'Now then! We're in Belgium where they take the matter of lunch extremely seriously. Let's get started back to town, we're eating at the Diamond Club.'

As Brilliant walked quickly to the door she found Arkady close behind her. He helped her on with her coat and said in a low voice, 'Countess Curnonsky, would you do me the honour of having drinks with me this evening, I feel we have a lot to talk about. If you could come to the offices of Russelmaz, it would be more discreet.'

The pleading expression in his eyes, together with the urgent secrecy of his whisper, made her smile in spite of her recent dismal thoughts.

'That would be wonderful, Arkady,' she whispered back, just as urgently. 'At seven then? Perfect!'

Carl frowned as he watched Arkady hold the door of the waiting limousine for Brilliant and then climb in after her. Arkady prudently moved to the centre of the seat, in order to keep the two women apart. As they rolled through the manicured suburbs on their way to Pelikaanstrasse everyone seemed engrossed in their own private thoughts.

'I've booked lunch at the Diamond Club, the food's superb. The Bourse and the Diamond Ring are always trying to pinch the chef. It's a standing joke between them!' Carl wondered whether his bonhomie sounded as forced as it felt.

Yasmina, who had been thoughtful for most of the journey, crossed her legs carefully, smoothed her skirt over a shapely knee and smiled sweetly at Brilliant, as though to make amends in some way.

'You know, Brilliant, this is the strangest little town-in-a-town you can imagine. It reminds me in some ways

221

of Koidu, I feel completely at home. The Belgian government completely turns a blind eye to what goes on, diamantaires are expected to declare some profit, of course – for *vraisemblance* – but that's all. It works absolutely charmingly, no one is pressed too hard for taxes.'

'I always knew it was a hotbed of rascally operators.' Brilliant stared morosely into the distance. 'Strange really – I thought the Belgians were such sticklers for fair play.'

'They don't want to kill the goose that lays the golden egg,' Carl said laconically. 'If the government got too particular the dealers would emigrate, they're mostly foreigners and could set up shop anywhere.'

The limousine turned into Pelikaanstrasse and passed the Tourist Hotel, through whose stolid Dutch doors trickled a constant stream of Africans from Liberia, Zaire, Sierra Leone or the Central African Republic. 'All of them with submarine goods, stuff that's escaped the DTC's net,' Carl commented drily.

They purred to a halt outside the tall building of the Diamond Club and Arkady sprang out after Brilliant, leaving Carl to take Yasmina's arm.

'Hurry up, you two, I'm ravenous!' Brilliant called over her shoulder. She looked surprisingly composed and Carl hurried to hold open the double doors. He wondered, with a feeling of intense relief, if his fears over Brilliant's reaction to Yasmina's connivances might turn out to be unnecessary after all.

15

As Carl busied himself signing the visitors' book, Brilliant cast a critical eye over the marble splendour of the Diamond Club interior. Baroque or rococo? She could never remember which was which. One glorified God and the other Mammon, one started in the north and the other the south, both had burst forth simultaneously with unrestrained exuberance and astonishing similarity.

Only good old Mammon here, no doubt about that. Her eyes were drawn towards a large notice-board displaying photographs with detailed biographies of candidates aspiring to membership. She walked up to take a closer look. Several suspension orders were pinned there, together with a large notice which proclaimed the expulsion of one Klaus Vader.

Carl's voice close to her ear made her start. His tanned face over her shoulder, also examining the notices, exuded masculine well-being and the subtle notes of a woody aftershave. For an instant their heads came so close that his hair brushed her cheek. She was conscious of a delicious sensation, a languorous expectation so voluptuous that she instinctively closed her eyes. It was a curious feeling, an experience already lived through, that she had sensed with Carl several times before.

'Aha! So they finally got old Klaus then!' Carl looked down at her. 'Are you feeling all right, Brilliant? You look pale. Need your lunch, I expect!'

She opened her eyes wide. From across the expanse of foyer Yasmina was staring at them, tapping her loupe in the palm of her hand.

'What dreadful crime has Mr Vader committed, that he's to be ostracized? To Brilliant's irritation her voice sounded curiously hoarse.

223

'The unpardonable one of stealing a diamond, or pretending it was his when it wasn't. If you're suspended you might as well pack up and go home, you've no hope of readmission. The whole thing rolls along on wheels of trust and someone like that just doesn't belong.'

'On va déjeuner, mes enfants!' Yasmina lifted her chin and called out imperiously.

Arkady reappeared from the direction of the telephones and they trooped into a much-gilded restaurant that gave directly on to the trading floor. Brilliant and Carl exchanged amused glances as they passed table after table of serious trenchermen, heads down and napkins tucked in shirt buttons. As they sat down a buzz of excitement at one of the trading tables had them craning their necks for a better view.

'Mon Dieu! What's that? They must be showing some extraordinary jewel.' Yasmina's commercial instinct was immediately to the fore.

'Something tells me. . . .' Carl's smile was cryptic. 'Just hang on a minute, let's wait and see.'

'Check-mate!' The tension round the far table suddenly relaxed and the diamantaires dispersed, smiling and wagging their heads.

'I thought so.' Carl laughed. 'Just a tense game of chess. The Exchanges are used more as social clubs these days – people prefer to do their business in private. No one sees what you buy – or who you sell it to.' He smiled at Brilliant with special warmth.

'What do you think of the wine, Brilliant? I chose it with you in mind, I know you have a nose for a good claret.'

'It's very good, Carl.' Brilliant gave the wine her full attention, inhaled the bouquet, savoured it carefully and then replaced her glass on the table. 'You have excellent taste, in wine as in all things. But I prefer to drink claret in the evening, somehow it needs dark and warmth and candlelight to be fully appreciated.'

'And a robust constitution.' Yasmina was forking her

224

food around her plate with distrust, then masticating each tiny morsel as though it were hot potato. She paused to take a sip from a glass of mineral water. 'Red wine is so bloating. You know if a woman drinks it regularly it begins to show. In France we say it gives her a sort of blowsiness, an overblown quality.'

Carl choked on a forkful of food. Yasmina thumped him sharply on the back, her dark eyes shining with concern.

'Attention *chéri!* Really, the way you Americans bolt your food, *c'est une atroce!'*

Arkady applied himself enthusiastically to his plate, his thoughts private and absorbing. Brilliant took another sip from her glass of claret and smiled at the Lebanese woman.

'You know, Yasmina, it's extraordinary how the fashionable image of women has changed in the last few years. Working on publicity, of course, you notice these things. The models we use, the advertising angle, the editorial slant. Thank God the "artificial" type is out, and the big, beautiful, healthy woman, who looks as if she can do a day's work and enjoys her food, is in. The top models spend more time in the gym than they do in the beauty salon – if they go there at all.' Was the animosity she felt towards Yasmina in defence of women in general and the White Tsaritsa, or something much more fundamental?

'*Mon Dieu,* of course, we all know these things are a matter of taste and fashion!' Yasmina shook back her curtain of dark hair, displaying to advantage an unusually modest choker of baguette-cut diamonds and ten-carat earrings. 'Pleasing the man in your life – "*plaire aux hommes*" – is part of the Frenchwoman's philosophy, which seems to have been mislaid in the new feminism. But there are still some men around who like their women to be women.' Her diamond-covered hand crept across the damask cloth and laid itself gently on Carl's.

There was a moment's embarrassed silence. Yasmina

was looking at Carl and a hunted expression appeared in his eyes.

'Everyone has their own views on this emotive subject.' He seemed to be choosing his words carefully. 'But I do think some women today are confused with their role as women . . . and this in turn is reflected in their attitude to men. . . .'

Brilliant swallowed hard, caught the gleam in Arkady's eye and laughed rather awkwardly.

'Of course – you're quite right! I agree with you whole-heartedly. But you'll never make a man happy if you are not happy with yourself in the first place. And I don't mean just external appearances. It goes far deeper than that. But a lot of misery happens when women try to conform to some fantasy that magazines spell out for them.'

Arkady looked up suddenly and smiled. 'What do you do then, change your man or change your image? Easier to change your man, isn't it, and find someone who likes you the way you are. If that's what the new feminism is about, then I'm all for it.'

'I don't think it is as simplistic as that, Arkady, and it's not really what I had in mind.' Brilliant stared at Carl. His eyes told her that he, for one, understood what she had in mind. She looked away with an emotion she found disconcerting to explain.

'I would love to continue this conversation, but I have to leave now,' said Carl. 'Johannes von Rinn is waiting in the Clubroom. I'd like you to meet him too, Brilliant. I think you'd be interested in his marketing strategy.'

As they were leaving the restaurant, Yasmina undulated to Carl's side and took his arm. She gave Brilliant a radiant smile.

'Perhaps we could meet later, Brilliant? For a cup of English tea in the hotel? I do so love the custom.' A patch of intense colour burned high in Brilliant's cheeks.

Carl watched Brilliant covertly as Johannes von Rinn outlined his marketing plan in the Clubroom. As soon as they were alone, he said to her with an air of resolution, 'Look, Brilliant, I feel we have to set the record straight. This whole ridiculous business with Yasmina is the result of a conversation I had with her two years ago. It was based on a complete misunderstanding, and now she has turned it into jungle warfare!' He ran a hand through his hair. 'Yasmina is hooked on diamonds to a quite exceptional degree. . . .' Carl spoke almost to himself. 'The worst case I think I've ever seen.' Brilliant listened impassively. 'She's had her sights set on the White Tsaritsa for as long as I have known her. I don't know if it's for herself or this Saudi client she talks about – but my God, she wants it – no matter what the personal cost!'

'Why shouldn't you sell the Tsaritsa, it must be a great temptation?' Brilliant spoke softly. 'You could retire for ever and devote yourself to your antiquarian pursuits. Diamonds mean very little to you, you said so yourself. Whatever was discussed in that "misunderstood" coversation, Yasmina has assumed proprietorial rights.'

Carl gripped the sides of his chair.

'How can I convince you I will never sell the Tsaritsa – never! To Yasmina or anyone else. It is quite simply not for sale.' He raised his fist, straining till the knuckles showed white.

'And . . . Yasmina?' Brilliant's voice faltered on the name.

Carl's face changed and he avoided her eyes. A muscle worked at the side of his mouth and he seemed to be struggling with something within himself. So. . . . Brilliant let out her breath in a long sight of regret. So there *was* something there . . . a dark side that she thought perhaps she had only imagined.

She felt totally perplexed with the confusion of her feelings. On the one hand she was reassured by Carl's vehement loyalty to the White Tsaritsa; on the other hand she experienced a cruel shock of disappointment and disillusion in his attachment to Yasmina.

She swallowed hard. 'All right, Carl.' Her voice

belonged to a stranger. 'We won't speak of it again. You must do what you think is right.' She looked at her watch. 'I must go. I have some calls to make . . . and then. . . .'

Her face brightened. 'Then I'm meeting Arkady Tverskoy at Russelmaz. I'm quite excited about it. He's rather fascinating – something sad and enigmatic about him, don't you think?' She stood up to go.

Carl touched her hesitantly on the shoulder. 'We'll meet in the foyer tomorrow morning then, about eight. Don't set too much store by what Arkady Tverskoy tells you. Russelmaz is a front – a swarming hive of KGB activity.'

Her mouth opened in surprise.

'But, most definitely, yes!' Carl's expression was serious. 'The office is just a listening post. It's very tough to actually buy anything. Most firms go direct to Central Selling in Moscow.'

Brilliant shrugged impatiently. 'It's extraordinary how the Americans see all Russian commercial activity as spy-ridden. It's a disease with them.'

'Was it just chance that a KGB agent, kicked out of the Russian Embassy in '71, turned up in charge of Russelmaz here?' Carl shrugged. 'Well, anyway, I wish you luck. I hope you find out what you want to know.'

Carl watched her walk down the street with quick, confident strides, then turned back into the foyer and went immediately to the telephone.

A few minutes before seven, freshly bathed and wrapped in a sleek dress of hyacinth crêpe, her eyes emphasized with deeper blue, Brilliant hailed a taxi outside the Tourist Hotel. Three Lebanese dealers on the steps swivelled as one and followed her with transfixed expressions until she was swallowed up in the maelstrom of traffic.

The taxi stopped outside a nonedescript block in Lange-Heventalsestraat. She paid the driver and looked up towards the second floor. A blind twitched and a head moved away from the window. She glanced across the road towards the imposing eight-storey block that bore the De Beers name and set her lips. All this Le Carré nonsense was beginning to make her feel uneasy. It was so typical of the mystique of the diamond trade. She snapped her handbag shut and pushed open the grimy swing doors. Among the nameplates in the anonymous foyer she distinguished the simple brass plate 'Russelmaz. Second Floor'.

She mounted an ill-kept marble staircase and moments later Arkady surprised her with the warmth of his welcome, the firmness of his lips on her hand and the triumphant gleam in his pale eyes.

'Countess Curnonsky, welcome to a small part of your homeland on Russian soil! We are so looking forward to your visit!' He opened the door on a roomful of expectant guests.

Something rather intimate, a *tête-à-tête* with Arkady, would have been more to her way of thinking. She was hugged and exclaimed over whilst being introduced to baffling Dutch names with Russian patronymics. The Embassy personnel, the head of Russelmaz and his staff, local businessmen and so on and so on. . . . Her Russian delighted them, with its old-fashioned formality and slight French accent. After numerous toasts to the lovely visitor – *krasavitsa nasha*; to the illustrious name of the Curnonskys; to the legendary White Tsaritsa; to Soviet-Dutch co-operation; to the surpassing of the diamond quota – her head began to swim, in spite of judiciously not swallowing all her vodka in one mouthful with each toast, as custom dictated, '*volpom*'.

A copious *zakuski* table ran down the length of the room, to which guests repaired between toasts to stock up on tangy morsels of *balik* – sun-dried sturgeon – raw smoked goose, *piroshkys* with sour cream and a score of other dishes.

After what seemed an interminable while her eyes met Arkady's across the smoke-filled room. His lips twitched with amusement and he excused himself and edged round the floor towards her.

'You have very expressive eyes, *maya dorogaya*. They transmitted one thing: it is high time to leave this unbearable place.'

Just as quickly as she had been propelled into the party she was extricated, almost too abruptly for protocol, she thought, but Arkady seemed not at all concerned with the niceties of prolonged farewells. Before she had time to think they were out on the street and into the back of a waiting limousine.

'Only the English are concerned with this business of goodbyes.' Arkady smiled benignly. 'To be seen to have arrived is all that matters. You don't think I could have had a *tête-à-tête* with you without the whole of Russelmaz wanting to join in, do you? Do you realize there is no word in Russian for "privacy"? To the Overidjse!' he commanded the driver in Russian. 'Now perhaps we have earned a little time together! I am taking you to my favourite drinking place on an old canal, which also happens to be an art gallery.'

Brilliant settled back against the comforting country smell of the leather upholstery and stole a sideways glance at Arkady. There was something new in her appraisal – she was evaluating him, as though seeing him for the first time. He was not strictly handsome in the conventional sense, she thought, his face and body were too elongated, his green eyes rather disturbing in their intensity – but it was his expression that made one want to respond to him. His speech and gestures were full of suppressed passion, his mobile face reflected every mood; joy and disappointment passed over it with the unaffected spontaneity of a child.

Within minutes of being seated in a dark corner of an ancient bar, surrounded by wall-to-wall paintings and flickering candlelight, Arkady was anticipating her host of unasked questions.

'I can sense that you are almost ready to revisit your

homeland. The Russians would be honoured to welcome Countess Curnonsky. I don't think I told you that we are distantly related, like most of the ancient families of Russia.'

'Oh! How's that? And please stop the Countess non-sense. I thought you were only joking. The title doesn't exist any more.'

'We in Russia haven't forgotten our titles, whatever may have happened in the Revolution. I am Count Tver-skoy, my grandfather was a disciple of Lev Tolstoy, which fortunately saved the family from a dreadful fate at the hands of the proletariat. Tverskoya is now a Collective, but they left us a hunting lodge and a few acres as a sort of conscience offering. Superstitious lot, the Russians – none too sure about the Day of Judgement. Tverskoya is the most marvellous place, on the shores of a swan-haunted lake, fringed with silver birch. Quite magical – just like the ballet – you must come there and dream with me one day.' Arkady's face was alive with the spirit of his own imagery and she laughed with him, her eyes dancing.

'It sounds so folklorique I might have to take you up on it! My mother always made Russia come alive for me, through her stories and legends. But because of the past, what happened to us. . . .'

'Oh! I'm so sorry. It was thoughtless of me to bring back painful memories.' Arkady's face changed in an instant and his eyes clouded.

'Oh no, not at all! I've no memories, that's just the problem. I wish I did. I've often thought I should go back, but there's been no reason – no one to visit.' She smiled matter-of-factly and prudently changed the subject. 'Arkady, how did you get involved in this crazy world of diamonds?'

'I studied art history at the Conservatoire but, as a non-vocational degree serves no purpose unless you teach, I switched to economics. Later, through my connections – and believe me, that's all that matters in the Russian *nomenklatura* – I was found a job in Russelmaz. It happened quite by chance. I became fascinated and eventually worked my way up to economic adviser – a vastly important post which gives me the opportunity to travel and pursue my first love, which is classical painting.'

'Wouldn't it be easy for you to defect, you could fulfil your love of art so much more in the West . . . ?' She stopped short at his appalled expression.

'Defect! How blunt you are. You have no idea what my homeland means to me. I would no more defect than I would betray or abuse it. I believe in the past and future greatness of my country. . . .' He paused, seeing the humorous twitch at the corners of her mouth.

'I can see you are amused, but let me assure you of this. Fundamentally I am a Russian, not a Westerner. You know, of course, about the Raskol, the great split in Russian ideology before the Revolution? The reason why Russia has lost her way is because of this divide, because we try to emulate the West and not to build on our intrinsic Russianness. When the Curnonsky twins split the White Tsaritsa, removing the flaw from its heart, they symbolized the rift that happened in our country. I want you to understand, Brilliant,' he seized her hand, 'why it has always been my dream to reunite the two halves of that diamond. So Russia can find her own true heart again, through the talisman that protected and nourished us spiritually.'

A curious tingling started in Brilliant's spine.

'Tell me more about the White Tsaritsa, every single thing you know!' She pressed his hand and Arkady's eyes narrowed.

'I'm sure you know more than I do. But I did translate that *Time* magazine article for the Ministry to put on the record. We still think of the diamond as ours. It is "on loan to the West through misappropriation" – like so many of our national treasures that went astray. But it will come back one day.'

'One of your treasures! It belonged to the Curnonskys,

before that unspeakable Vanderberg. . . .' Brilliant's fist clenched on the tabletop.

'Aha! So that's how you really feel. That's the reason someone of your talent is biding their time with Adamantina. I think perhaps we could be of real help to one another.' Arkady ignored her frown of irritation.

'You might be interested to know some ancient chronicles concerning the White Tsaritsa are gathering dust in our National Archive Museum. In my lacklustre early days with the Ministry I was compelled to research lengthy treatises on Tsarist jewels that had been "misappropriated". We make constant efforts to trace such jewels and reacquire them, by whatever means we see fit. One day I was presented with some ancient papers, dating from the Middle Ages, giving indisputable proof of the finding of the Tsaritsa on the banks of the Tura and its subsequent illustrious role in our history.'

To Brilliant's intense annoyance they were interrupted by the arrival of two of the guests from the cocktail party. They had little chance of resuming their conversation until they were in the limousine on their way back to the hotel.

'Most tactless, the Prashvilis' joining us like that. But what can you expect from a Georgian racketeer?' Arkady had been amused by her barely concealed impatience when the unwelcome couple had settled beside them for the night. 'But perhaps for me it was fortunate.' He smiled hesitantly. 'For it gives me the opportunity to ask you out another time. Perhaps we could meet tomorrow?'

Brilliant shook her head. 'I can't, Arkady.' She looked dejected. 'I'm leaving for London on the ten o'clock flight. Carl has to go to New York and I'm covering the Sight.'

'How incredibly convenient! I am also in London during the week, Russelmaz representatives will be there. We can arrange a rendezvous in one of my favourite cities, so cultured and understated.'

The limousine, warm and enveloping, negotiated the turnings of the dark back streets and neared the Pelikaanstrasse. For several minutes they sat in silence, unspoken emotion passing like an electric current between them. On an impulse Arkady turned towards her, seemed about to say something and then checked himself. The beam from a street lamp fell across his drawn face and Brilliant, apprehensive, reached out and touched his hand. She sensed his tremor of hesitation, then in one convulsive movement he grasped her shoulders and began to kiss her, gently at first, then with a mounting lack of restraint. There was no escaping the paralysing determination of his grasp, and after a moment or two she gave up the pretence of trying. Arkady's kiss was like nothing she had ever known, a savage, sensitive language of the erotic that she had yet to learn. Shaken to the core, hardly aware of what was happening, she matched his passion with a wild sensuality that came from somewhere unknown within her. Her eyes opened at last to a discreet cough. The doorman of the Tourist Hotel held the car door deferentially. Behind his back an avid group of Japanese businessmen sheepishly averted their eyes. Shaking, Brilliant withdrew her hands from Arkady's imploring ones and extricated herself, still trembling, with a whispered promise to meet him in London in three days' time.

'Brilliant, Brilliant and then again . . . Brilliant!' Carl's conversation continued along familiar lines. From Yasmina's smoke-obscured viewpoint, the stolidly built forms of Pieter Bruegel's peasants merged with the sleeker contours of the twentieth-century connoisseurs who were appraising the famous painting. She and Carl were privileged guests at a showing of masterpieces of the Dutch School, organized in aid of charity by one of Antwerp's leading diamantaires.

'Of course, Arkady is quite harmless,' Carl assured her. 'He is known in the business as an egghead and an aesthete, very much into the arts, never married. You never know with these Russians, their homosexuality is so much more discreet than ours.'

Yasmina snorted with laughter and gave him a sharp look.

'I do not think there is the remotest chance of Arkady Tverskoy being anything but one hundred per cent male! Haven't you noticed his eyes practically devouring her?' As Carl frowned, she added quickly, 'But I'm sure that in her case the interest is purely academic.'

Yasmina took a sip of champagne and sighed. She must say nothing to jeopardize Brilliant and Arkady's fast-developing relationship. She must be tact and sweetness itself. It was only a matter of time. She was travelling to London tomorrow with Brilliant. Strategic opportunities must never be lost. At the moment fate seemed happily to be taking its course – but one never knew when it needed to be given a gently encouraging hand.

16

Yasmina stole a satisfied glance at Brilliant, sitting next to her on the KLM flight out of Antwerp. The sensual droop of an eyelid, the curve of a tremulous half-smile, the caressing gesture of a hand smoothing down an invisible crease in her skirt told her intuitive woman's instinct all there was to know. She gave a sigh of content. Arkady and Brilliant, now she thought about it, were inevitable. There were certain men that women had to undergo, as a sort of soul-stiffening exercise.

It had been like a family gathering at the airport. Arkady was there to see Brilliant off on the London flight with Yasmina, whose thuggish bodyguard had been despatched at an ungodly hour to await her arrival in London. Carl's flight to New York was at 10.30 and Yasmina had him in tow, struggling manfully with a mountain of monogrammed luggage. Brilliant, in a new mellow mood induced by the proximity of Arkady, watched them together and found it hard to suppress her rising chuckles. Carl was undeniably attractive – she was somehow gratified at the way other women looked at him, a sort of pride by mutual association. But like many so-called 'masterful' men he seemed unable to deal with the tigress-kitten paradox of Yasmina's personality. In a flash of insight she even felt a pang of sympathy. Carl was inherently courteous and could not be openly rude to her; it would be easy for Yasmina to confuse his kindness with affection.

Yasmina had been at her most expansive, utterly charming to Brilliant and praising Arkady. In low tones and when Carl was out of earshot, she had said to her, 'My dear, Arkady has just told me of your interest in some ancient archives on the White Tsaritsa. I had only a hazy idea of your involvement and now I completely understand your point of view. Please forgive some of my earlier remarks.'

The goodbyes with Carl had been brief and automatic, there was a general feeling of tension, a desire to separate and get away.

Soon after take-off Brilliant declined coffee and outsize Dutch croissants from the stewardess and confided to Yasmina, 'Do you know, I think I might finally get to Russia, after all. Who could be a better guide than Arkady – it certainly wouldn't be boring.'

Yes, that's what it is, I've never seen her look really happy before, thought Yasmina. Now there is something new, a radiance, as though someone has got out the duster and polished up something already beautiful, but neglected. Poor Carl! So much for Arkady's harmlessness. Men really were so unbelievably, incredibly naive.

Brilliant's face grew pensive and Yasmina did not press her. The last few minutes at the airport were still corruscating in her mind. Goddammit! The infuriating way Carl was always so controlled with her, so obviously, edgily courteous. But at the last minute that control had nearly snapped and he had practically pushed her away, his eyes stricken as he had watched Brilliant go. At least the Arkady episode would bring the soothing balm of retribution.

The aircraft shuddered through a layer of nimbus and the familiar sombre sprawl of London materialized through the haze. Brilliant could make out the dark mass of Hyde Park and the river, then tried to pinpoint the Savoy and the embankment, home for a few days at least.

During the taxi ride into the city Yasmina's conversation was informed and entertaining. Brilliant joined in for the most part indifferently, but when she kissed her cool cheek outside Claridge's, she found herself wondering if perhaps after all she had misjudged her. There was something gallant yet rather pathetic about Yasmina's improbable way of life. Even her face is diamond-shaped, she smiled to herself as she waved her away, the tiny figure standing so valiantly erect and faintly ridiculous, her glitter reduced by the grey London light.

Brilliant directed the driver to the Savoy. Evidence of English pride in homes and gardens met her eye at every turn as the taxi negotiated the stucco terraces towards the river. Geraniums had won the battle for hardiest perennial in an uncertain climate and ran in a riotous ribbon of colour along the window-sills of the well-groomed Georgian streets.

The familiar verdant smell tugged at her, lured her into dappled parks and half-glimpsed gardens, seduced her with a thousand scented sprays and breeze-tossed blossoms. She sighed. She had so little time and such big problems.

There were Sheikh Yosami problems, multi-million-dollar problems. Sheikh Yosami was one of Adamantina's most prestigious clients, an immensely wealthy Kuwaiti who spent lavishly on important diamonds for the Sheikha, his wife. He was a man obsessed with the acquisition of perfect, peerless gems; not merely for the gratification of his Sheikha, but to satisfy his own indulgent need. He purchased diamonds compulsively, almost slavishly, and handled them with a reverent emotion rarely bestowed on his wife and numerous mistresses. Now the capricious Sheikha, perhaps out of spite for the transparence of her husband's affections, had expressed her dissatisfaction with the set of exceptional F1 flawless gems that Adamantina had acquired for her at the last Sight. The Central Selling Organization had been asked to come up with something very special, very fast.

She must put through a call to Carl immediately. Carl . . . She frowned and drummed her fingers on the battered Gladstone bag she carried, almost superstitiously, on every flight. He had looked so tired and worried at the airport that it still weighed on her mind. She knew there were cash-flow problems at Adamantina. Like most diamond houses they had suffered from the recession and the Sheikha cancelling her order could be disastrous for them at this time. Although she was closely involved in the financial running of the company, there were some things Carl kept close to his chest and chose not to reveal. And now there was Arkady and she wanted time off. Yes . . . Arkady. . . . Brilliant crossed and recrossed her legs, her fingers unconsciously caressing the length of her thigh. She met the driver's appreciative stare in the mirror and looked away in embarrassment, as though he were able to read her thoughts.

There was work to be done and yet. . . . She had worn the excuse of work like a protective shell for so many years, now she longed to throw off the restraining chrysalis and emerge, like nature around her, a frivolous butterfly intent on enjoying pleasures of a purely Bacchanalian kind.

The opportunity for Bacchanalia presented itself sooner than she thought. Arkady had telephoned her very late that evening at the Savoy, as she was preparing for bed. He had just that minute checked in to his hotel in Bayswater, he said; the atmosphere was bohemian, but *simpatishna*. His voice, impassioned and impatient, pleading for an urgent meeting, had made her smile but had also caused a curious knot to form in her stomach.

The next evening she found herself alone with Arkady at their rendezvous on a terrace overlooking the Thames. He leaned nonchalantly against the balustrade and beamed as she buried her face in a huge bouquet of cornflowers.

'When I saw those flowers in Harrods I immediately thought of you . . . and of your eyes. They're a bit wild, untamed – you have that quality, too. A very large lady next to me sniffed and muttered something about "weeds" – so I bought the lot.' Arkady's face was alight with the euphoria induced by his beautiful companion, the grandeur of the setting and several glasses of vodka, downed in one *à la Russe*.

The slanting rays of the setting sun erupted in Catherine wheels of fire in the great windows of the Hayward Gallery, the mauve of a summer twilight began to gather

239

round the dome of St Paul's to the east. At their feet the Thames curved in a glittering ribbon of glass.

'I feel as Wordsworth must have done when he wrote his famous lines on Westminster Bridge. . . .' Arkady inhaled the evening air as though it were his last breath and let it expire in a long sigh of contentment.

'You're very well versed in English literature.' Brilliant's bouquet did not quite hide her broad grin. 'Your speech is full of Shakespearean allusions, you're obviously very much at home here, far more than I am, I think.'

'All Russian schoolchildren can recite reams from the English poets, Shakespeare, Burns, Dickens – the social writers – as they get older. Learning lines by rote is part of our system, reciting out loud gives you the "feel" of a language, its resonance, through the poetry you can find your way to the soul of the people.'

He took her hand and drew her away to a far corner, muttering imprecations, as the terrace began to fill up.

'Twenty minutes of functionalist art is quite enough – what did you say the man's name was – Justin Vavasour? But then the English have always been very liberal with their New Art forms. Nothing like this would be allowed at major art museums in Leningrad, changes in art have to be taken more slowly, it has to be seen as part of the evolution of society.'

'Whatever happened to *glasnost* and the new liberalism?'

'Expediency, expediency . . . crumbs to get us to increase production twenty, thirty per cent. But I suppose Nabokov, Zamyatin, Bulgakov in print are quite big crumbs. And at least Soviet avant-gardism is now officially recognized. But it's skin-deep, only skin-deep.' Arkady brought his face close to hers. His sharp profile was outlined in heavenly fire and his eyes were dark and inscrutable.

'You have not brought me here to talk about art. Our time together is so short. I must tell you all you want to know about your diamond. You have a few days to think

240

over my plans, and I will have the archive material translated ready for when you come.'

'When I come? But surely, Arkady, I don't have to go to Leningrad, you could just send me the translation? I have to be in New York, Carl needs me. . . .' Her voice trailed off.

'Carl needs you!' His smile was mocking in the half-light. 'During the last few days I have perfected the most sensational plan. You are not cold, *krasavitsa maya*? Stay here, I'll go and refresh our drinks and we can sit and talk as it grows dark. . . .' He used the evocative Russian *sumrachnyvach* – to sit and talk companionably until it grows dark – for which there could be no English equivalent. Her heart contracted and she smiled softly after his departing figure.

He came back presently, juggling a tray with several glasses and half a dozen curling sandwiches. He took off his jacket and placed it carefully around her shoulders.

'You seem to be preparing for a siege,' she remarked drily, looking at the reserves of alcohol.

'I'm so sorry!' He looked crestfallen. 'Is it bad form? In Russia we're so used to getting drinks when we can. *Nazdrovya!*' He raised his glass and watched her drink, her face luminous in the fiery after-glow.

'Why should the White Tsaritsa go to that Lebanese she-cat?' Arkady came straight to the point.

Brilliant frowned. 'There's no danger of that, Carl has given me his word.'

'His word! Excuse me, but you're being utterly naive. What does it matter to a man like that? He is a businessman first and foremost, used to doing commercial transactions of that kind every day. He wanted to retire early, the White Tsaritsa would be the sale of a lifetime.'

His eyes glittered. 'If it weren't Yasmina there would always be somebody else. You can't take that risk. You say the ring is yours – I say it belongs to Russia. You must help me return it where it belongs, as part of our heritage and the mystic soul we have lost.'

She felt an impulse to laugh, but seeing the injured look on his face she laid her hand gently on his arm.

'Arkady, whatever you might believe about the destiny of the White Tsaritsa, and perhaps in some ways I do agree with you, there is nothing we can do about returning it, either to Russia or to me.'

'You're wrong! There is a way we can do it.' His eyes blazed with a wild hope. 'You have access to the ring in the Adamantina showroom in New York. Carl trusts you completely. It would be very easy for you to remove it.' His voice had sunk to a penetrating whisper.

'Remove it? Of course I could remove it.' She shrugged her shoulders uncomprehendingly. 'And spend the rest of my days in the cooler, as the Americans so picturesquely put it!'

'Yes, you remove it – and no one will find out! You simply replace it with the perfect replica, which is being made in our factory in Akademgorodok, with the blessing of the Soviet government and Carl Vanderberg of Adamantina.'

She let out her breath in a long sigh of disbelief.

Arkady's expression was triumphant.

'What do you think of my plan? Devastatingly simple – like all good things. And foolproof! I get the fake stone to New York, you change them over, the real stone comes back to Russia where it belongs and would be safe for ever. In New York, no one will ever know the truth. You can rest assured that the replica we are making would impress even your diamond eye. Think of it, the White Tsaritsa would be back among its own people who revere it, it would help heal the schism in the Russian soul . . . and. . . .' he whispered close to her ear, 'you would avenge yourself on the family who cheated your mother.'

Brilliant closed her eyes and swallowed hard.

'Arkady, stop it! You're crazy! How could a mad scheme like that possibly work? And why should I want to be part of it? Certainly not for Russia. As for my feelings of revenge, I don't really have any. . . .' Even as

242

she spoke her heart was questioning the words. The White Tsaritsa would be safe, safe from predators like Yasmina. If it could not be hers at least it would be back where it belonged. The wildly daring scheme, its very simplicity and implausibility appealed to her impulsive nature. It seemed a natural thing to do, and in a way, almost just.

'But in the museum, won't they find out that it's the real Tsaritsa, how can it be kept a secret . . . ?' Her voice faltered and Arkady, sniffing victory, grasped her hand.

'Only a handful of people will know the truth. They are sworn to secrecy, naturally. The new stone will be thought to be a cleverly made fake. Its manufacture in Akademgorodok has already been announced in the Soviet press. In private you will be accorded the highest honours of the Soviet people.'

Brilliant could not suppress her laughter.

'The highest honours of the Soviet people? Something no girl should be without!' She mimicked Arkady's solemn tone. 'Really, Arkady, I'm not sure I want to have the honours of your country.' Her face was serious. 'We have very different views on the paths of freedom.'

'But, don't you see, that's where we have gone wrong; now the White Tsaritsa can show us the way.' Arkady's eyes were pleading. 'Will you at least come to Leningrad? I ask nothing more of you – just to see your homeland and think about what I've said. I'll take you to the Archive Museum to see the manuscript, then we could spend a few idyllic days at Tverskoye. Magical midsummer days that never end . . . hunt for wild mushrooms, enjoy all the country pleasures. . . .'

She smiled at his fervour.

'It's a package that sounds difficult to resist! Well . . . I might just take you up on it, to visit the museum – only that, mind – definitely no other promises at all. And to see Galina again, that would be wonderful.' She looked thoughtful.

'I do need a holiday, I've been burying myself in work for what seems an eternity. Now! I'm feeling chilly and very hungry. Let's go and eat. But first I have to call at the hotel, to see if there's a message from Carl. The Yosami affair seems to be at crisis stage. Our rival Christianou has been trying for years to get Yosami's custom, and I know he's behind all this.'

Brilliant stood up, her white dress glowing in the purple darkness. Arkady adjusted his jacket carefully round her shoulders as a damp chill rose from the river together with the lengthening shadows.

'I have to admire your dedication to duty.' He tucked her arm through his. 'We have only one night together before I leave for Moscow. Let's forget about diamonds and lose ourselves in the hedonism of this fascinating city. You know it well . . . where will you take me?'

They walked back hand-in-hand along the river to the Savoy where Brilliant asked the concierge for her room key. 'I'll change quickly and meet you down here in a few minutes!' Her teeth were almost chattering and she found it difficult to meet Arkady's eyes.

'Thank God I've caught you in time! I thought you might have already left for dinner.' Carl materialized out of nowhere.

'Carl! What on earth are you doing here? I thought you were in New York.'

'I got there more or less, found out about this Kuwait affair and came straight back. The Sheikha Yosami deal is off unless we deliver the new stones immediately. Christianou has been working on her and she wants to cancel the whole order. I thought the only thing to do was to get out there as quickly as possible, and that means tonight. I happen to know that Christianou won't be leaving New York until tomorrow morning.' He ran a hand through his hair. 'It's the only way we have of saving three million dollars. I know you wouldn't have wanted it otherwise.'

'Good God, no! Yosami can't walk out on me now. Not after the time I spent with him, practically recreating the crown jewels for his Sheikha. I know it's got nothing to do with the diamonds. The Sheikha's family have dealt with Christianou from way back and he's promised her the skies if the Sheikh will buy from him. He's an unscrupulous Greek émigré and his stuff is crap! I can't let Yosami buy from him, he'll get a rough deal. We're doing him a favour and he doesn't know it.'

'Check-mate!' Arkady whispered almost inaudibly and touched Brilliant gently on the shoulder.

'I'll leave you now, *dorogaya maya. Da nasha skoro svidanyia v Leningradya!*'

'*Da, Arkady! Mi skoro povidimsya.*' She reached up gently after her promise and kissed him on the cheek, once, twice – and on the third he held her close for a split second and his fingers tightened on her arm. Her heart gave a violent lurch and the blood rose in her cheeks. Great are the pleasures of anticipation. As she watched Arkady disappear into the summer night she experienced an almost illogical feeling of relief.

'I'm sorry, Brilliant, I'm sure you had other plans. It's unfair of me. . . .' Carl's voice was husky. 'I'll see to it you get the holiday you deserve when all this is over.'

'Don't worry about it. Tonight business comes first – but then!' She looked at him with shining eyes. 'When are the White Nights in Leningrad? I've missed them, haven't I? They're getting in the hay harvest at Tverskoya, magical Russian midsummer nights. . . . to Russia! It's so strange, I speak the language but I've never been back, to my own country . . . it's a dream that's now going to come true.' Oblivious to Carl's dazed expression she took his arm and steered him across the foyer towards the gilded elevator.

'I'll be ready in ten minutes. You can fill me in on all the details later. How did Yosami communicate with you, by telex? Have the Sheikha's representatives discussed money? I know it's got nothing to do with the quality of the stones. . . .' Carl stared blindly ahead as they ascended swiftly to the seventh floor.

17

A searing shaft of sunlight falling through the Moorish window branded a fretwork pattern of filigree on the carpet at Brilliant's feet. Carl shifted on his cushions and ran his fingers inside his collar. In spite of the ceiling fans the heat was oppressive. The low room was really an extension of the formal garden outside with its lovingly nurtured greenery and hypnotically splashing fountain.

After their arrival in Kuwait there had just been time for a shower and breakfast at the airport before their appointment with the Sheikh. Brilliant had discussed tactics with Carl, how best to handle the notoriously capricious Sheikha, on the flight over champagne and caviar, more caviar and nothing else but caviar. Licking her lips like a replete feline after the last spoonful, she had put on an eye-mask and fallen into a peaceful sleep. Looking at her slumbering face, etched in profile from his reading lamp, Carl had envied her peace of mind. Sleep had been out of the question. He could only ponder the stroke of fate that had brought Arkady Tverskoy into her life. Surely it was not just masculine rivalry, he frowned, couldn't there be a hint of philanthropy in his very real concern for her happiness?

He could not shake off his despondent mood as he watched her now in the Yosami Palace. Particles of sun-spangled dust shimmered round her head like some ethereal halo. Brilliant misinterpreted his anxious expression and winked at him reassuringly. She had just reappeared pale and composed from a private interview in the women's quarters and the Sheikha had now joined them, a heavily veiled figure who took a seat on a distant cushion.

Brilliant stood up and smoothed her linen skirt decorously. She felt at a considerable disadvantage speaking from the floor. She brushed a stray lock of hair from her pale face and then proceeded to give the bemused Sheikh the charismatic performance of a lifetime. She presented conclusively the case for buying their diamonds and not Christianou's, pacing the room in her high heels, swinging her mane of hair, emphasizing her point with expressive hands and transfixing the potentate to stunned surrender. At last the Sheikh threw up his hands with a gesture of finality, declared the deal concluded and turned his attention to the pressing business of mint tea and refreshments. Yosami then muttered profuse apologies and disappeared for a few moments' consultation with his spouse.

'Well, congratulations, you've done it!' Carl's tired smile was almost grudging. 'That was quite a performance. Now for Pete's sake let's get the contract signed and get out of here.'

'Don't think we're going to get away that easily.' Brilliant tapped him sympathetically on the shoulder. 'Nothing gets done in a rush here.' She shook her head. 'No, no, it simply isn't protocol. He'll be giving orders for lunch at this very minute – endless exotic dishes to impress us with his hospitality – then we'll be joined by countless members of the family and hangers-on. At least that means Christianou's won't be given a look in, even if they get here this afternoon. With a bit of luck I'll have the whole thing in the bag before we leave.'

After a protracted meal lolling on cushions around the feast-on-a-carpet, Brilliant retired to Yosami's office to sign the contract. She emerged a few minutes later with a perspiring Sheikh submissively in tow. Carl felt a curious lack of elation at the triumphant snap of her briefcase. Further meetings, delivery dates and accounting complexities were discussed before they were able to take part in the leisurely and formal farewells.

When they were alone at last in their hotel's shadowy courtyard, fragrant with the scent of orange blossom, Brilliant leaned back in an armchair and confessed to extreme exhaustion.

247

'Thank God that's over! Something strong is called for. What do they drink here – *arak*?'

'Nothing at all, drink is strictly forbidden.' She laughed at his doom-laden expression.

'Well, too bad for them. Order me a large jug of *arak*!' She yawned and stretched her arms high over her head. 'To think that in a week or so I'll be ordering vodka in Leningrad. I'm thrilled to be going back. I realize now how much I always wanted to, but I needed someone to give me the push.'

'I wish that push had come from someone other than Arkady.' Carl's lips set in a thin line.

'Other than Arkady? What on earth do you mean? He's intelligent, charming – I couldn't wish for a better companion. What can you possibly have against Arkady?' Carl's gloomy scrutiny irritated her. 'It can't be the KGB nonsense – all that's a thing of the past. Besides, I didn't think your job entailed the vetting of my friends.' She tried to sound arch but stopped, feeling ashamed, when she saw the hurt expression in his eyes.

'I'm sorry, Carl, I guess we're both tired. I didn't mean to sound like that. I'm going on a kind of pilgrimage, you see.' Her face lit up. 'Arkady's awakened a latent Russianness – I feel it's time I went back to explore my roots. Anyway, the whole point is to look up some old archives on the White Tsaritsa that Arkady is having translated for me.'

Carl looked quickly away. What could he say? He knew with an ominous fatality that she had to go to Russia. There was nothing he could do to stop her. But what of his overwhelming compulsion to prevent her? Was it just irrational or perverse or – worst of all – entirely self-seeking? Their eyes met, there was a moment's hesitation, then Carl murmured some inconsequentiality, his heart heavy with defeat. Brilliant smiled, an incredulous smile of relief – she had thought for one second that he was going to be tiresome over Arkady – and the moment for truth telling was past.

They both sought the pretext of an early night to separate, to ease the tension and the unspoken emotion
between them. The coolness persisted on the aeroplane
to London the next morning, both sharing feelings of
frustration impossible to put into words. Brilliant felt a
need to blow the cobwebs away, an unjustified resentment
that Carl was keeping many things from her, both in his
private and professional life. There was no reason for him
to be otherwise, except that he seemed to assume the right
to interfere in hers. It made her all the more determined to
escape for a while. Arkady made her feel relaxed, carefree,
wanted. More than that she chose not to elaborate on.

Carl had to fly straight back to a hastily convened board
meeting in New York, leaving her to reorganize the
London office. Turnover was down and the board had
appointed a new managing director. Only after a week's
reshuffling in the Bond Street showroom, a pleading call
from Arkady and an equally terse call from her to Carl,
did she set off for the Venice of the North, with hand
luggage only and a heavy cargo of expectations.

Arkady was at the airport to meet her. His anxious face,
craning over the heads of fellow greeters, broke into the
relieved creases of an exultant smile.

'I hardly dared believe you'd come!' He clasped her
close and breathed into her hair. Then he held her at
arm's length and examined her minutely, as though to
convince himself she was really there, muttering broken
endearments in a husky undertone.

'Let's get away from here. I loathe airports.' He suddenly broke out of his apparent trance. 'You had no
trouble, I hope, with Arrivals, they can be such a frightful
bore.' He smiled smugly. Of course. Her fellow travellers
were still standing glumly in line in the rear distance,
enduring the discomfiting experience of Soviet immigration. She had been waved straight through customs,
Arkady's influence had given her priority.

The famous Leningrad White Nights were over, but the northern city still had the feeling of being *en fête*, luxuriating in the brief spell of midsummer heat and perpetual daylight. Arkady had an impressive limousine on hand to take her on a short drive round the inner city, to whet her appetite. Brilliant was surprised, almost shocked, to find the palaces painted in exuberant yellows, blues and apricots.

'I had no idea, I feel I should have been warned.' She was enchanted. 'I'd imagined an imposing granite city and it's like something out of Italian opera, all frivolous and flamboyant.'

Arkady was gratified. 'We owe it all to Peter the Great. He wanted a "window on Europe" and had the sense to employ the Italian genius of Rastrelli. Hence these wonderful palaces and vistas, all part of his grand vision – and his barbarism,' he added glumly. 'Thousands of workers died bolstering his vanity in these fetid marshes.'

They followed the bank of the broad grey Neva for a while, then turned into Nevsky Prospekt.

'This is the real pulse of the city. All the theatres, shops and cultural institutions are here. I've booked you a room at the Berlin on Zhdanov Street. It's the best of the older hotels, nostalgically seedy. They're closing it down any moment and transforming it back into the Savoy. Let's hope they preserve the period details. I thought the decaying grandeur would appeal to you more than modern breeze-blocks.'

'I thoroughly approve.' Brilliant smiled at her first glimpse of the Berlin foyer and was irresistibly reminded of Carl's New York apartment. 'Seedy grandeur is something interior decorators spend a fortune trying to contrive, but they never achieve the patina of the real thing.' She frowned and tried to put an annoying picture of Carl, lounging in his worn plush armchair, out of her mind. Her nostrils twitched and she took a deep sniff. The creaking wooden floors and old panelling were redolent of oily fish, whether it was floor polish or paint she couldn't tell, but it pervaded most interiors and remained with her as an enduring impression of the city.

Brilliant left her bag at reception and they went straight out to enjoy the heady summer sunshine.

'Well, if you want to walk we'll start with Nevsky Prospekt: it runs for three miles and covers most of Leningrad's history.'

Arkady took her hand and guided her through the leisurely oncoming tide of pedestrians. She turned her face up to the sun, half-closed her eyes and felt her heart swell with emotion. Through Arkady's anecdotes and snatches of gossip the city came alive for her – Pushkin, Dostoevsky, Gogol, Lermontov and Gorky all worked along the Prospekt – Mussorgsky, Borodin and Tchaikovsky composed there – and later, he commented drily, it housed the headquarters of the Workers' Revolutionary Movement.

'Time for refreshment!' Arkady suddenly grasped her arm and pulled her out of the seething current of humanity. 'We've already passed Sever's, that's the famous pastry-shop in a basement, haunt of writers and artists. Now it's too much of a tourist-trap for my liking. I'll take you to my *blini* place.' Dragging her along at breakneck speed Arkady dived down an alley, round a couple of dank corners, pushed open a grimy door with his foot and hurried down a stone staircase.

'My God! Whatever is the rush?' Brilliant paused to draw breath from the wooden bench where he had abruptly set her down.

'Secrecy! The sole requirement for membership,' he announced in a stagey whisper, his lips twitching.

She had to admit, once her eyes had got used to the gloom, that a more clandestine-looking venue would be hard to imagine. Every inch of the cellar walls was lined with yellowing posters in various stages of decrepitude. A single oil lamp swinging from the blackened ceiling cast a murky glow over crooked chairs and oak tubs smeared with the grease spots of ages. A few dusty bottles on a counter at the far end were the only indication of the basement's business. Behind this rudimentary bar a half-open doorway gave out a cheerful light and the appetizing aroma of pancakes.

'The very beer shop where Dostoevsky wrote *Crime and Punishment*.' Arkady rolled his eyes dramatically.

'I don't believe a word of it! It can't have done his eyesight much good, though it scores ten out of ten for local colour.'

A lugubrious waiter in a long apron shambled up to their beer barrel.

'Bring us a mountain of *blinis*, your best caviar, sour cream, onion, pepper vodka and *malinova*.' Arkady gave the order curtly. 'And clean up this table, it's disgusting!' The waiter, with silent hauteur, flicked a few crumbs from the tub with the end of a greasy cloth tucked into his belt. Soon the room began to fill up and a pungent pall of cooking fumes and cigarette smoke made it difficult to distinguish faces across the low room.

'I can quite see how the walls acquired their patina!' Brilliant was jostled nearer the wall now, the last delicious *blini* and caviar long eaten, as Arkady plied her glass with pepper vodka and the obligatory chaser, raspberry-juice soda.

The unsavoury waiter returned with reinforcements of vodka, the standard two hundred grammes in an elegant small carafe, but Arkady waved him away with a frown, putting his hand over Brilliant's glass.

'Enough, enough, *dorogaya maya*! There's so much more for you to enjoy. . . . First we shall have our Tsarist supper, private, intimate. . . .' His fingers brushed her arm and she shivered. Surely it could not just be the vodka that made her temporarily lose the use of her legs? Arkady steadied her as they negotiated the steep stone staircase and she swayed slightly on the uneven pavement.

His arm was around her waist and he stared at her, as though trying to make up his mind. Then he grasped her arm in vexation and began to hurry her along. He spoke angrily, almost to himself.

'You are a woman most men would be wary of – there's something unconquerable there. You belong to no one but yourself, or to the past . . . I can sense it somehow.' Arkady did not add that this elusive independent core unsettled him. He wanted to win her, not seduce her. It mattered fiercely to him that this woman should love him. Of all the women he had carelessly wooed this one somehow had the magic touch to vindicate all the others.

'Arkady, don't stare at me like that!' It was some time later and Brilliant tried to smile nonchalantly across the candlesticks in Arkady's Tsarist restaurant. 'I feel like some victim of an ancient rite that you are softening up for sacrifice!'

He smiled, momentarily disconcerted.

'If you like, I am! Well, I'm anxious to impress you, of course. I want you so much to see the good things here, discount the bad, the ephemeral. If I could, I would will you to love Russia. I'd cast a spell on you, just to keep you in my power!' His eyes, set in the high cheekbones, glowed amber-flecked in the candlelight.

Her laugh sounded rather forced in the quiet room. She pressed his hand.

'You don't need to do that! I am already under a spell. I feel perhaps I have always been. And now I've come back . . . home . . . I feel it very strongly.'

It was true. From the moment she had walked out of the airport the immensity of the Russian sky had seemed to enfold her like some friendly, well-worn garment and an uncanny sense of *déjà-vu* greeted her at every view and vista. She could not explain it and did not even want to try. The language, the Cyrillic on shops and slogans was familiar, of course, together with certain aspects of the culture she was acquainted with from her mother's stories. But there was an inexorable quality about her presence here that was profoundly unsettling. She puzzled over it at first, but then chose to ignore it and gave herself up to a hedonistic enjoyment of the inevitable.

'Tell me more about "your" restaurant. I'm intrigued! I didn't know you were such a capitalist at heart.'

Arkady had proudly announced his co-ownership in this elegant and surprisingly Westernized restaurant off Mayakovsky Square. Discreet letters on the tasteful dark green exterior proclaimed: 'Co-operative Café Korotinskaya'. Inside was a restrained and luxurious elegance that was innovative by any Soviet public eating standards.

'We're not all the philistines you might think! As soon as Mikhail Sergeivich Gorbachev gave the go-ahead to private enterprise, certain *bons viveurs* in the city were united in the common cause – to bring back a little glamour and nostalgia to our dinner tables! I hope you like it. I never know with you, *dorogaya maya*, that you aren't teasing me. Our cuisine may still be rather rudimentary, but the decor has taste, you can't deny me that.'

'It has more than taste – it has flair and a sense of the theatrical.' Brilliant examined their little jewel-box of a private room with admiration. It was rather like sitting inside a Fabergé encrusted egg, with its ornate Byzantine wall hangings, lavish mirrors and lush gilding. The glittering reflection from ancient lamps and icons gave the room a fabulous intensity of dark brooding colour and complex pattern. The main room, or rather the collection of interconnecting small rooms that comprised the dining area, was more simply conceived, but still conveyed a stylized period richness. In illuminated niches along the wall a collection of antique samovars was displayed to advantage.

'I managed to sniff out all the furnishings on my travels,' Arkady proudly informed her. 'One of the ten co-owners is a set designer at the Maly Theatre. An individual of real talent – he turned his hand to all this in his spare time. The details were a problem, things like fine china, cutlery, glasses, as we don't produce any quality here. We managed to bring most of them in from Finland.'

Their food arrived in true Russian abundance and soon covered the spotless white cloth. The blue-bordered oval

254

dishes offered samples of the best of Russian cuisine, both hot and cold, from every corner of the motherland.

'I suppose our way of eating owes a lot to the East.' Arkady pressed her with strange dried meats and spicy chicken dishes from the Moslem republics. 'Even with our main courses we like to try several small dishes. If we particularly like something then we order more of it. Our chef is Georgian – they are noted for their fine cuisine – but the food here is eclectic. We've tried to dream up a more exciting menu – from the fourteen different republics – the best of all the Russias.'

Arkady watched her eat, hardly touching his own food, his pleasure compounded by her obvious interest and enjoyment.

'I don't know which gives the greater satisfaction, to watch a loved one eat, or to share a sublime dish, far more sensual and erotic. Here, try this *basturma*, smoked venison from Uzbekhistan – sensational! Or my favourite chicken *satsivi* from Georgia. The sauce is made from chopped walnuts and cumin. Eat, eat! Take it in your fingers – it's the only way.'

His face grew suddenly serious.

'Our main problem here is our popularity. We could fill the restaurant three times over. Unfortunately my astute co-owners prefer to turn away the rouble-paying natives and court the tourists. The mighty dollar reigns supreme, as everywhere in this city. It appals and angers me, and now I'm part of the corruption. Our rouble is worthless, our mighty civilization crawling and toadying for dollars, grasping and degenerate.' He sighed. 'What's to be done? We need currency to pay back our *syuda* – that's our government loan, rather like your mortgage – within three years. You see, we're beginning to find out about capitalist *angst*. Co-operatives have come in for a lot of stick with the locals, they push prices up and rub salt in the wounds of the have-nots.'

'But there *are* Russians here.' Brilliant had passed several tables of garrulous businessmen. 'I would have thought you were doing society a service?'

'Sure, sure, there are plenty of roubles under mattresses – what else is there to do with them? But it's expensive for Russians, a meal for two with vodka and a bottle of Georgian wine costs about forty roubles, a lot of money when the average salary is two hundred roubles a month. Anyway, money burns a hole in Russians' pockets, they like to have a good time, live for the moment, who knows how long this will all last? Will capitalist co-operative owners be first on the hit-list when the showdown comes?'

Brilliant shivered. 'How can you talk like that? Things could never be the same as they were. People are used to new freedoms, they would never endure it.'

'Don't you be so sure. There's talk of difficult times ahead, two years of. . . .' He toyed with a piece of rye bread, rolling it into a ball between his fingers. 'Anything could happen. Mikhail Sergeivich Gorbachev is more popular in the West than he is here; unfortunately the proletariat are blind and senseless. There will be trouble ahead. But we Russians are inured to it. One "Time of Troubles" has followed another since the Middle Ages. We shall survive.

'Kostya!' His almighty roar for the waiter made her jump. 'More wine, Kostya! We're neglected and becoming melancholy.' Arkady turned to her with an almost diffident smile.

'I remembered that you liked red wine. This one's called Black Bear from Uzbekhistan, a lusty brew that helps the natives sire a second family at the age of one hundred!'

She drank and smiled at him over her glass.

'How's Galya, when shall we see her?'

'Galya, Galya. . . . She's absolutely fine, tearing around on some research project, difficult to get hold of. We'll arrange everything in the morning. . . . Come now, it's not quite dark, a magic night.'

The still-light streets were enchanted as he walked her

256

back to the Berlin – so much to laugh at, to wonder at, to be happy for. She held his arm tightly and swayed a little as she put her head on his shoulder. She smiled drowsily, she felt as if the Uzbekh Big Bear were enfolding her right now in furry arms. . . . If she could only go to sleep right there and then. . . .

'*Dorogaya maya*, you are tired, you must rest. Perhaps I should leave you now?'

She opened her eyes with a start. The smiling receptionist was holding her bag and motioning her to follow. She looked regretfully at Arkady.

'I'll be waiting for you in the morning. Sleep well, *nenagladnaya maya*.'

Dearest Arkady. So chivalrous, so thoughtful, so unlike other men. As she drifted off to sleep on the cool white bed, palaces of pink, yellow and blue chased each other through her fading consciousness.

18

When she came down to breakfast next morning Arkady
was already drumming his fingers on a table near the
window. His face lit up when he saw her and he jumped
up to hold her chair. In spite of the wine and vodka she
had slept well and felt clear-headed – and, now that she
had seen Arkady – somehow emotionally supercharged as
well.

'Bright-eyed and bushy-tailed!' he exclaimed. 'That's
how you look. Is it really a compliment in English? I've
often wondered. You never know with the idiosyncrasies
of the language, but it always seemed a dubious remark
to me.' He poured her coffee and motioned to the rye
bread, hard-boiled eggs, jam and curd cheese, obviously
impatient to start the day.

'I have one great disappointment, you wanted to go
straight to see the White Tsaritsa, but the museum's
closed for . . . hmmm . . . refurbishment. That's a
euphemism for weeding out some of our crown jewels
and selling them for hard currency, split up and cleverly
disguised, of course. Galya's up to her ears in paperwork,
so we'll do the Great Siberian Adventure first. But right
now . . .' and his voice dropped dramatically . . . 'there
are the archives. Eat up, *devushka maya*, there's so much
to do and so little time.' Arkady took her arm.

Brilliant drained her coffee cup and pushed back her
chair.

'*You're* impatient! I've been waiting all my life for this.'

Arkady said nothing but increased the pressure on her
arm, his eyes so intense that she swallowed hard and had
to look away. She hurried after him on to the sunlit
pavement and waited while he negotiated the fare with one
of the taxi drivers hustling for currency at the kerbside.

The sepuchral interior of the National Archive Museum contrasted starkly with the shimmering city streets. Serried aisles of rickety shelving were stacked high with crumbling manuscripts, secured with yellowing tapes. Documents spilled on to desks, chairs and tables, every inch of space was infested by a plague of decaying paper in closely written Tsarist script.

Pallid girl librarians in dust wrappers and kerchiefs, faded as the manuscripts they guarded, cast curious glances at Brilliant. Hardly knowing how she came to hold the manuscript, hands shaking, she stared unseeingly at the curling pages. The words on the cover leapt out at her: *Count Fedor Ivanovich Curnonsky. His Journal. 1603–1682.*

Arkady touched her shoulder gently.

'You've no idea of the amount of red tape I had to get through to allow you in. You can't take the manuscript away but you can read it here, side by side with the translation. You'll be happy at what you find there.' He cleared a space on a dusty chair by the window, kissed her fleetingly and then left her alone.

The faded greenish ink of the ornate Cyrillic script danced in front of her eyes. So here was the end of the trail, the answer to the enigma. . . . The pages crackled and seemed in danger of disintegrating in her hands. She sat down shakily and pored over the archaic text. One or two words sprang out at her – names, dates, places. Impatiently, she turned to the translation that Arkady had pushed into her hands.

'I remember well the day I found the large shiny stone, the day the messenger from Moscow came. . . .' The handwriting and language was that of a young man not yet familiar with his craft. Two hours passed like minutes. When at last she lifted her head Arkady was waiting by the doorway. She went to him wordlessly and he folded her in his arms. Her face was pale with the effort of concentration, her eyes shining.

'Fedor's story is more wonderful than I ever imagined,' she breathed. 'I feel that he is part of me, that we have a unique empathy.' Seeing Arkady's lips twitch, she added hastily, 'Well, he is my ancestor! You see, I sensed it was a love story from the very beginning; knowing that the White Tsaritsa was first given to Aisha as a love token makes me so happy.'

'Well, I'm glad you have found some of the answers.' Arkady looked at her thoughtfully, his lips compressed. Then in a sudden whirl of activity he returned the manuscript to the bashful librarian – Arkady Ilich was a minister and one of the intelligentsia – picked up Brilliant's bag and grasped her arm.

'Come on – let's get some air! This dust of ages is bringing on an allergy.'

They crossed the road to the river embankment and Brilliant gazed across the grey expanse of the Neva, her thoughts still focused on an earlier, more savage epoch. All the emotion she had just experienced seemed to be concentrated in her eyes as she turned to Arkady.

'Fedor's "second sight" – what do you make of it? That is the enigma and mystery of his journal, isn't it?'

Arkady plunged his hands into his pockets and stared straight ahead, his eyes fixed on some distant object in the water.

'You know, throughout our history, we have had mystics, in the Church and out of it, who professed this same ability, to see into the past and future. . . .' He shrugged. 'I'm a sceptic anyway, more likely it was just a greater than normal sensibility, a highly developed intuition. But what is uncanny are the claims that the mystic influence carries on long after the subject's death.'

His intense eyes were on her and he took her hands. An electric charge ran from the base of her spine to the roots of her hair. Her nails dug into his palm and she whispered, 'So you see, I haven't been mistaken. All my strange, weird feelings, presentiments of some destiny, of myself and that diamond. . . . Fedor's words – how did they go? "In all my visions of the future there has been

260

a sense of leaping of time, of centuries, a reaching to someone far beyond me . . ." '

'Of course, *lyubimaya*.' He smoothed a lock of hair from her damp forehead.

'Fedor foresaw the White Tsaritsa inside his father's doublet deflecting the assassin's dagger that night they left the Tura . . . the first of an extraordinary chain of incidents. Do you think all those things really happened, that there is some truth in the legend, something really supernatural about the diamond?' Her eyes were wide. 'Poor Fedor, how he must have suffered, a sensitive soul lost in a sea of brutality. At least he lived to see his cousin Michael crowned first Romanov Tsar, with the White Tsaritsa in his hands. But who added that ominous postscript to his story?'

'Bishop Trakhorin – who was at Fedor's bedside when he died.' Arkady's eyes suddenly blazed. 'Now can you understand what inspires me! Those words – "This diamond with mystic power has a Russian heart – in love it was given and through love alone can it preserve that power. If you abandon the White Tsaritsa you abandon truth, you abandon virtue, you abandon the unity of Holy Russia herself." ' Brilliant trembled violently and he held her close.

'Enough, enough! You're with me now, *dorogaya*, and I shall never let you go. And now. . . .' Arkady took a deep breath, his eyes shining '. . . you need diversion – food, drink, Russian distraction!'

He carried her off without protest to lunch at a club near the Maly Theatre to meet some of his artist and writer friends. After an exuberant lunch a tenacious half dozen declared her '*strashna simpatishna*' and volunteered their services as tourist guides. Deciding which famous sights to see, the obvious or idiosyncratic, sparked off heated differences of opinion.

'The Hermitage, of course!' But what next to absorb the spirit of Leningrad in such a limited time?

'Pushkin's House?'

'No more museums,' growled Arkady. 'The weather's too fine.'

'Strelka, on Vasilevsky Ostrov?'

'No, too far!'

'Peter the First's Cottage?'

Marvellous! By unanimous consent they streamed off to the banks of the Neva to see the wooden building made of pine logs, just two rooms and a study, built in three days by the great Tsar himself and used thereafter for his Summer Residence.

Picking up more revellers under the lambent evening sky, the noisy party repaired to Bakhunin's for Caucasian food and gypsy music. Brilliant was introduced to *shashlik* and *tkemali* – sour prune sauce – with fragrant rice pilaff, *karabakh loby* – green beans in soured cream with tomato sauce – and *tarkhun*, long green leaves that when bruised gave out a pungent aroma of aniseed. More wary now of the innocence of raspberry juice, she drank her vodkas and chasers slowly, unlike her companions from the Maly, who were soon cavorting to the wild strains and pouring out their hearts in soul-searing ballads. The strange not-quite-darkness gave her a feeling of unreality as she walked back with Arkady through the quiet streets.

'You know, of course, why I couldn't ask you to stay with me? I have only a few square metres in my grand-mother's apartment near the Summer Garden. She cared for me when my parents were killed in a rail accident. I would hate her to live alone now, so I never bothered to move out.' Arkady gave her a troubled sidelong glance. 'These things are not easy to arrange in Russia . . . and I ache to be alone with you, *nenagladnaya*.'

'Yes, bureaucracy does seem to hedge one in on every side – it's not very conducive to romance. What does a woman do in these circumstances? Am I allowed to ask you to visit me?' Brilliant felt oddly embarrassed. The words came out so flippantly that she could have bitten her tongue.

'Of course! It's quite permissible.' Arkady's hand tightened on her arm. A pulse began to beat at her throat. He stared gravely into the distance.

Brilliant smiled brightly at the blonde receptionist who examined them covertly from under lowered lashes, then took the lift with Arkady to the third floor. Yesterday she had been initiated into the Russian key ceremony. On each floor a *dejournaya* – a worthy watchwoman, usually of formidable proportions – reigned supreme from her desk at the end of the corridor. Here she dispensed keys with baleful glances of the utmost suspicion to the unfortunates who had to pass her to get to their rooms. As Brilliant paused in front of her desk, lips parted in a nervous smile, the white-overalled matron glowered up from her knitting and narrowed her eyes at Arkady.

'Room 37 – booked one occupant only!' she barked. 'You – where's your passport?'

'Passport? Oh, my God, I'd forgotten about that! It rings some sort of bell. . . .' Arkady shrugged his shoulders helplessly, comic frustration on his face. 'I seem to remember friends of mine, an English couple, they weren't married and the tour operator had taken away the group's passports. They were booked into the hotel on separate floors and spent the whole time, without success, trying to get together past the *dejournaya*. Now, Mother dear, be a good sort, what's it to you?' He tried a few blandishments. 'I'm Arkady Ilich Tverskoy, of the Ministry of Non-Ferrous Metallurgy.' He produced his card with a flourish. 'Not one of your fly-by-night tourists. This is Countess Curnonsky, one of us, a Russian. . . .'

The *dejournaya* snorted, rolled her eyes heavenwards and set her lips in a thin line.

'People of your position should know the rules and abide by them, there shouldn't be a law for you and a law for the others – ordinary folk like myself. . . .' They were subjected to a long homily, and the sight of the eminent Arkady shuffling his feet like a schoolboy on the mat made Brilliant struggle to stifle her laughter.

'Arkady!' At length she put a reassuring hand on his

263

arm. 'It can't be helped. Couldn't you go and pick your passport up anyway?' She looked puzzled.

Arkady's shuffling turned into an infuriated stamp.

'Damn the obstinate old *baba*! My passport's buried under a pile of papers at my grandmother's, she's ill and it would disturb her at this time of night.' He looked balefully at the furiously knitting *babushka*. 'I could go downstairs and get her a bottle of vodka. . . .'

'Vodka?' The *dejournaya*'s sharp ears picked up the word. 'No, you don't try that! I never touch the stuff.' Her lips set in an ever more disapproving line.

Now Brilliant could not suppress her laughter. 'This really is the end then. Come here, you sulky boy!' Still laughing, she drew him into the shadows and ignoring the disapproving set of the *babushka*'s stout shoulders, she took his face in her hands and planted a chaste kiss on his lips. She stepped quickly away and held up her hand. 'No! Please don't try to follow.'

Arkady put his hand on his heart and declaimed in mock heroic tones, 'Then I shall pursue you to the wastes of Siberia. In the morning I shall come for you!' His distraught face relaxed. He bowed stiffly towards the stolidly knitting *dejournaya* and followed Brilliant with his eyes until she disappeared into the shadows of the corridor.

Late the next afternoon Brilliant watched the legendary red and cream train with the emotive inscription 'Moscow – Vladivostok' emblazoned on its side, loom through a haze of heat, noise and seething humanity in Moscow's mock fairytale castle, Yaroslavl Station.

Arkady had been all masterful efficiency in the morning, organizing their flight from Leningrad to Moscow and then the short drive to the railway station.

'We could have flown straight to Novosibirsk but you would have missed the great Trans-Siberian experience. There's no point in wasting time in the capital. After

Leningrad, it's a cultural desert. Red Square, the Bolshoi, Arbat – just tourist fodder after all. We also need to get to Akademgorodok before Professor Avsey leaves.'

He helped her climb the high steps to their wagon-lit. She felt transported to a pre-Revolutionary age, no country had been so radically changed by the building of the railroad as the Russian heartland.

'We are incredibly privileged, not only travelling soft class, but having the new two-berth sleeper, instead of the usual four. Can you imagine having to share with devil knows who? Sailors reporting back to Vladivostok – drunken, cursing! Professors returning to Krasnoyarsk – anglophile, philosophizing! Peasants getting off at Omsk – sausage-chewing, belching!' Arkady grew more and more appalled as he reeled off the hypothetical list of horrors. He led her into a carpeted compartment with a bunk on each side, already made up with immaculate white linen. At the window a small lamplit table was framed by crimson tasselled curtains.

'What everyone does now is change into a dressing gown.' He laughed at Brilliant's startled expression. 'Oh, yes, it's a special form of Russian *déshabillé*, seasoned travellers wear nothing else for the entire journey. In winter they seal up the train and heat it to suffocation point with stoves in the corridors. Right now it'll be hot as hell on the Siberian plain. There's supposed to be air conditioning, but it never works. You establish a rapport with your attendant,' he gave her a meaningful wink, 'and order your tea and stronger liquids for the duration. There's a shower and lavatory in between each pair of cabins. The hard-class passengers have no bathrooms, only washbasins at the end of the corridor. It's all terribly *intime* and friendly, rather like a relaxed house-party. I'm just off to see the attendant, so make yourself comfortable, *doragaya*.'

Brilliant smiled uncertainly and examined the little room that was to be their home for the next few days. Arkady gone, she quickly unfastened her bag and pulled

265

out a long silk caftan. She undid the buttons of her dress then, suddenly remembering the outside world, hastily pulled down the blinds at the door and window. Slightly flustered, she slipped the caftan over her head and wriggled it past her hips. She preferred not to think of the intimacy of the situation, sharing a few metres of space with a man she hardly knew, but then such things were normal in Russia; people simply did not have compartments to themselves. She swung round, startled, at a sharp rap at the door. The blind sprung up on a perspiring attendant, carrying a champagne bucket and two glasses. He set them down with a flourish, extracted a pencil from behind his ear, licked it and wrote in a grubby notebook, then swept from the compartment without so much as a second glance.

Arkady, laughing, more expansive than she had ever seen him, followed hard on the attendant's heels.

'Perfect, absolutely perfect!' He clasped his hands and ran amused eyes over her *déshabillé*. 'Though as a rule one doesn't change until the train has pulled out of the station, it might cause comment on the platform, to quote Oscar Wilde.' He laughed at her embarrassment. 'Believe me, *milaya*, I'm only teasing.'

He thrust his head out of the window. 'We're just about to leave – perfectly on time. Sometimes they delay the train for ages, waiting for some dignitary, or for no reason at all, making searches.' There was a sudden cacophony of whistles, shouts and cries rising to a crescendo, then the great train shuddered and moved off smoothly, past serried ranks of tearful, leave-taking Russians, waving their dear ones off into the limitless unknown.

Arkady poured the sweet Russian champagne and solemnly presented her with a sparkling shallow-bowled glass.

'Here's to the Great Siberian Adventure . . . The White Tsaritsa . . . and of course, to us!' He drank deeply, looking into her eyes.

'You will find this the Train of Toasts – and drinking

parties. You will be invited to many, but I am possessive and want to keep you all to myself.' He smiled but his eyes were guarded. 'There is so little time to be together.'

She drank nervously, the golden liquid drumming against her palate. Then they sat and held hands over the little table, watching the vast forests of birch – the beloved Russian *beriozhka* – roll away to a seemingly limitless horizon. As the sun set, puffs of cotton-wool mist formed in hollows, lights twinkled from solitary *izbas*, smoke wreathed up from hidden chimneys.

'Come! It is time to join the rest of Russia at the supper table.' Arkady fussed about, ushering her to the dining car. Brilliant had severe misgivings about the suitability of her caftan, hoping that it might pass for the English eccentricity of dressing for dinner. In the restaurant car she was relieved to find several Russians in dressing gowns of varying degrees of splendour, a few long past their former glory, some quilted and intricately embroidered, others bordered with bold black frogging straight out of a Tsarist smoking room.

The menu was huge and optimistic, but only those items with pencilled prices against them were 'on'. Vegetable soup, breadcrumbed cutlets and sauté potatoes, followed by ice cream, seemed to be the exclusive option. Oblivious of the curious glances cast in their direction they held hands across the white cloth during the interminable breaks between courses and talked soul to soul, existing only for each other. Any fellow traveller who tried, with easy Russian familiarity, to strike up a conversation, was given short shrift, dismissed with curt mutterings of 'later . . . later. . . .' The Georgian brandy and the warmth of Arkady's hand brought a flush to her cheeks as she stared out into the deepening night and awesome expanses of moon-silvered corn.

Long after the last crumb had been flicked from their table by the tired attendants they walked back along the heavy car, rolling gently on its wide five-foot gauge.

Their beds had been turned back, nightlights put on,

a flask of water and two glasses placed on the little table. She sat down at the window and looked out at the primordial forest, spangled like hoar frost in the moonlight.

'There's just one ceremony left before they leave us alone.' Arkady whispered close to her ear. 'The tea ceremony.' A sharp tap at the door announced the red-faced attendant with glasses of tea in silver holders, lumps of sugar and dishes of jam. Arkady drew the brass bolt firmly behind him and pulled down the blind. Sipping the warm liquid, gazing around the cosy compartment with its polished woodwork, starched linen and crimson-shaded lights casting a mellow glow, Brilliant felt all the yearning of a lifetime crystallized into this one moment of happiness.

'What are you dreaming about, *schastya maya?*' Arkady's hand was caressing her arm. Of all Arkady's endearments, used naturally and spontaneously like all Russians, *dorogaya* – darling, *lyubimaya* – beloved, or the heart-catching old Slavonic of *nenagladnaya* – wondrously beautiful – it was this *schastya maya* – my happiness – that summed up the deep contentment of her mood.

'Drink your tea like this, it is so good.' Arkady was holding out a glass of tea. 'Here, take a lump of sugar in your teeth and drink your tea through it, as we do . . .' He laughed at her maladroit efforts as the sugar lump crumbled into a sticky mess.

'You have to judge your moment finely – as in all things in life. When the sugar is just saturated, that is the moment to swallow.'

Laughing, she wiped her lips with a napkin. Suddenly, with a convulsive start, Arkady sprang forward and pulled her to her feet. He began to kiss her insistently, first her mouth, moist from the sugar, then her eyelids, her temples, the hollow of her neck, the dimple in her cheek, until finding her mouth again, he kissed her until she was breathless and dizzy.

Brilliant closed her eyes. She was sinking, sinking in an exquisite unguent tide of sensation . . . But some instinct from the past – warning, constrictive, kept her from submerging. A tremor ran through her and she froze, rigid with apprehension, in his arms.

Arkady released her abruptly and turned away, leaning his head on his hands against the cool window, in an unconsciously histrionic gesture.

'I'm overwhelmed by your beauty, can you blame me? *Krasavitsa chudesnaya!* Beauty like yours inflames a man. But I want you more than that. With you I want to transcend the physical, it can never be enough. I want you to love me as I love you, the love of the soul, the spirit . . . the sublime emotional experience I have always dreamed of but never thought possible. So now, just when I thought love to be our inescapable destiny . . .' He passed his hand over his eyes. 'If you cannot love me like that, then tell me now. I swear I will never touch you! I want the whole of you – your body, your soul, your Russian being.'

Arkady's passion was contagious. She fought down an instinct to deride, reflecting that the West had lost much with progress: the unashamed Russian baring of emotion, a certain innocence. There was a refreshing immediacy of contact with them, physical and emotional, that perhaps compensated for the harshness of their material lives. Whole families walked hand-in-hand across pavements, men embraced and exchanged endearments straightfor-wardly, comrade-to-comrade; women strolled arm-in-arm in warm companionship, confidences were exchanged easily, heart to heart. Arkady's flamboyant ardour might lay itself open to ridicule, but what was the laid-back Western suitor but a coward, frightened of rebuff?

She smiled at him, eyes glowing, then hesitantly echoed his words. 'The sublime emotional experience I've always dreamed of, but never thought possible. Oh, Arkady . . .' Her voice dropped to a whisper, her lips trembled.

'*Ozhivlenya!*' He gripped her hands so tightly that she flinched. 'Anna Karenina's special quality. You have that overwhelming sexual vitality that Tolstoy knew all about, the old reprobate.' He switched off the crimson-shaded

269

lamp. 'Let me see you sitting here in the moonlight, my Anna-on-that-train, full of suppressed longing.' He knelt at her feet. 'Say you love me, *nenagladnaya*! Tell me! Don't turn your back on our happiness.' He buried his head on her lap.

She put out a tentative hand to caress the springing dark-blond hair.

'Arkady, you know I love you. I can't hide it . . . or pretend.' She spoke with simple sincerity.

Too moved to speak, he held her face in his hands and kissed her almost shyly.

'I love you, Arkady . . . Arkady . . .'

'Shhh . . . *lyubimaya maya!*' He put his finger to her lips. 'We belong to each other now, we have made a pact of love a million times stronger than mere desiring.' He smoothed a stray lock of hair from her cheek. 'I want to make what men call love to you, only our bodies cannot convey that love, we are so coarse, so earthbound.' He looked so downcast that she laughed, then shivered.

'You are cold, *milaya*?' He touched her bare arm in concern. 'No . . . I think not . . .' As she sat, unable to speak, his hands moved over the neck of her garment, letting the fabric fall around her shoulders.

'Dearest one . . .' He traced the tender curves and hollows with wondering humility. He took her hands and raised her gently to her feet. 'I want you like a goddess on this magic night.' He shrugged off his own clothes with impatient haste.

'Unbelievable!' Tears sprang to his eyes. He stepped back, his eyes consumed her. The moonlight streamed over his long-limbed breadth of shoulder, a Nordic god cast in silver.

'*Maya lyubov* . . .' The words caught in his throat. 'I want this night to last for ever.' He lifted her effortlessly and laid her on the narrow bed.

The light played strange tricks as he knelt over her, a satyr etched in smouldering moonshine.

He seemed to want to brand her with the indelible

imprint of his eyes, his mouth, his hands. His caresses were urgent, provocative, masterful; his mouth on her lips, her breasts, her thighs, explored her with rhythmic, throbbing insistence. Rippling shudders racked his body as she caressed him, hesitant at first but then encouraged by the intensity of his pleasure.

'Arkady, oh Arkady,' she whispered under the mounting tension of his caresses, but his mouth found hers again and silenced her.

'Slowly, slowly, my beloved . . . I have all this sublime night to love you . . . I want you to be completely mine.'

She shivered, sensing in him a Slavic machismo at once sensitive and savage. 'Arkady, my love, I want you . . .' She sobbed, as he delayed as long as possible the moment of possession.

It seemed her whole life had been a preparation for this moment, her heart and body were a vacuum that Arkady alone could fill. Ageless, primeval, she was locked in a time-cocoon of erotic energy. She grasped him, yearning, straining, arching, brought to an unbearable agony of urgency, until that aching moment when at last he took her and they fused, frozen for one second of stillness, before a mind-numbing explosion of sensation.

Bright sunlight woke her. She looked at the tousled head next to her on the pillow and shifted on the narrow bunk. She ran her hands over her body in disbelief. Had she dreamed their lovemaking, could her body possibly be the same, had she not changed in some subtle way?

Arkady moaned as her hand brushed his side. He turned towards her, his eyes still closed, his hands seeking her in his sleep. She started as though stung. He opened his eyes wide and smiled at her lazily. He looked younger, rumpled, his head more boyish on the pillow next to hers.

'*Anxhel moy, ya lyubly ti, ya obozhaya ti* . . . ' The words of love were full of aching tenderness, the passion of the night softened into caresses of grateful sensuality. He propped himself on one elbow and looked at the body he had made his own, his eyes green and tilted against the sunlight. His naked body flexed and roused itself, sure of its conquest. She was struck again with his streak of Asiatic dominance, arrogance, almost cruelty, that both disturbed and aroused her.

'Yes, I have Tartar blood, my maternal grandfather . . .' He smiled as she touched his high cheekbones and tilted eyes, a rider's tautness of belly and sinewy thigh.

No, she had not imagined their lovemaking. Her pulse beat faster as his fingertips traced the curves and hollows of her breasts, discovering anew the body that the night had screened in asilvery veil of modesty. Sensing her mood, he kissed her reverently, almost shyly, and their lovemaking was chaste, tender and lingering, ending in a bursting glow of satisfaction that echoed the dazzling summer sunlight outside.

After thousands of miles of forest, lakes and farmland the Trans-Siberian approached the grandeur of the Urals. On the frequent stops the more energetic passengers tramped up and down the platform in a variety of eccentric dress and snapped up *piroshkis*, hot meat pies, and *kvass*, home-brewed beer, to supplement the monotonous train diet. Eventually the train passed the city of Sverdlovsk and drew near the Tura river.

Brilliant would not move from the window, every taut nerve concentrated on her impressions. She tried to imagine how it must have been for Fedor all those centuries ago in a virgin land, surrounded by enemies and barbarians, exiled from all those he held dear. And what of his love for the beautiful Tartar girl Aisha, killed by her kinsfolk for hiding his diamond offering of love? Even reading of it years later was to suffer with Fedor the anguish of his loss.

'You see, it is a very emotional moment for me,' she

confided to Arkady with embarrassment. 'I'm actually here, at the shrine of my pilgrimage.'

Arkady took her hand and began to speak, swiftly and urgently.

'We must talk about our dreams. Everything is ready, completed down to the last detail.' Brilliant continued her solemn scrutiny of the landscape. 'Professor Avsey is masterminding the whole project. He is Director of Mineral Science at Akademgorodok. What can I tell you about Avsey – he's a visionary, a bit of a *wunderkind*. There's no point, wait until you see him for yourself.' Arkady chuckled. 'He is even more of a Russophile than me, a man out of his time – or ahead of it,' he added drily.

'Arkady!' She turned, misty-eyed, towards him. 'This journey, as I said, was a pilgrimage. Why are you spoiling it? Do you really think I would be party to a criminal act, stealing a diamond worth millions of dollars?'

'Yes, you are capable of it. Or I have misjudged you?' He looked at her levelly. 'Stealing? That's nonsense! Call it deception if you want, or reappropriation.'

She laughed outright. 'I know what the world would call it, make no mistake! But . . .' She looked pensive. 'Perhaps I am capable of doing it.' She was intrigued to know more of Arkady's plan. 'How do you see me getting away with it? Changing the stones over in New York is no problem, but do I just catch the Leningrad plane with the ring on my engagement finger?'

'Not at all, *schastya maya*. The rings will travel independently between America and Russia. You can leave that safely in our hands. You only function within the Adamantina showroom. We have everything taken care of.'

'Taking care of it must involve an awful lot of people.' She frowned.

'A chosen few, as I told you. The White Tsaritsa will keep her secrets.' Arkady smiled enigmatically. 'Remember one thing. In Russia nothing becomes public knowledge unless we want it to be public knowledge. We have no free press, no snooping media network, no do-gooder

journalists. As far as the Ministry is concerned the repro-
duction of the Tsaritsa will attract the tourists and earn
us a lot of foreign currency.'

'How can you make a replica without having the real
thing? I thought you would start the project when you
came to New York in November. Take photographs,
casts, do some proper research . . .' Brilliant shook her
head.

'That's no problem. You'll be interested to know that
our people have been in and out of the Adamantina showroom, taking photographs with hidden cameras, measur-
ing with microscopic equipment and infra-red. We now
know everything we need to know about the size, weight,
shape and configuration of that stone, including the flaw,
and it has never left the safety of its glass casing.' His
smile was triumphant.

Brilliant's heart missed a beat as she glimpsed for the
first time the chilling bureaucracy behind Arkady's plan.
He grasped her hand again and held it fast.

'That diamond belongs to you – well, yes, perhaps –
but in truth it belongs to us, the Russian people. It is part
of our soul, our heritage. Don't you see, it must be joined
with its other half, part of my plan to make Russia whole
again, our resurrection!' His eyes shone with a fanatic
light.

Brilliant did not answer. She looked out at the forest
stretching away to a limitless horizon, at a small bird
wheeling high and free in the infinite blue, at the immensity of this enigmatic land, strange yet somehow familiar.
Arkady had touched chords deep within her, chords of
emotion she found it hard to deny. She nodded hesitantly.
Perhaps some of Arkady's chauvinist passion had entered
her soul with his lovemaking, perhaps she was too much
under his spell to reason, but for the moment she had
cast off her prejudices and surrendered herself to the
inevitable.

The next morning the train had swung in a great curve
south-east to Omsk on the Irtysh and was approaching

274

the highly industrialized city of Novosibirsk, entering the station via the imposing length of the Ob bridge.

A large black car was waiting outside the station and took them swiftly to the space city of Akademgorodok, thirty miles to the north.

'Akademgorodok's a phenomenon. You've nothing like it in the West,' Arkady announced smugly as they drove through forests of birch and pine. 'They decided to build a science city – *schplot!* – just like that, in the middle of Siberia. It's an invigorating place, the average age is only thirty-three. I feel like a geriatric when I'm here, half the population are children. I've a special affection for it, though, I did a year's research here after university. You see, in the Soviet Union people need to specialize early, to fit in a niche where the state can use them.'

They drove through neat, flower-lined streets, broad avenues, parks and grass-filled squares that gave the town an appealing leisurely air.

'The city's exceptionally well planned, but it *is* Siberia, remember. We have to offer something extra to persuade people to live here. In winter it reaches fifty degrees below and it can be hot as hell in summer.'

Arkady waved at a couple of strolling professors, deep in conversation.

'Ah, but you're breathing rarefied academic air. Sixty-one members of the Soviet Academy of Sciences are skulking about, plus hundreds of PhDs and thousands of students. Quite a challenge to the educated mind. It goes to the heads of some of them. Unusually for Russia, they allow foreign scientists in every year on visits. There aren't too many hotels, so we're putting up at the House of Scientists, we're coming to it now.

'All this is new.' Arkady indicated a futuristic monument. 'There's a department store and a supermarket with no queueing, would you believe? Well stocked, too, with goods you'd never find in Moscow or Leningrad. They even do home deliveries. The centre has its own bar and restaurants and it's very culturally alive. Why aren't they beating back the stampede to get in? Well, it's a very small pond where the big fish eat the small fish. Mind you, it suits these academics, they like the incestuous type of life. Most of them want nothing to do with the real world. They're too busy building up their own little empires. It wouldn't do for me!' He gave a savage shake of the head. 'I couldn't wait to get out. It has a strange sort of effect, saps certain energies.'

They stopped outside a featureless block and the driver sprang out and opened the door. Arkady hurried her up the steps to a desk where a pale youth sat reading. After a murmured exchange Arkady took a key and motioned her down a broad corridor covered in bright matting with abstract paintings on the walls, reminiscent of Scandinavia.

'No accursed *dejournayas* here!' He grinned over his shoulder, pushing open the door and throwing their bags on to twin beds covered with red embroidered quilts.

'The professor's waiting in the bar. Let's go and meet him straight away!'

19

The waxy bookish smell in the university lounge, redolent of interminglings of stale cooking, unwashed sweaters and beer, the earnest faces, the egoistic discussion, isolated words – talk, talk and more talk – made Brilliant feel twenty years old again, back at college and able to conquer the world.

Arkady came back from the scrum at the bar clutching a bottle of wine and some glasses.

'Nearest you'll get in Russia to an English pub – recognition that alcohol fuels the creative processes of the intelligentsia, at least. Try this full-bodied Georgian red, I think you'll like it. Good, here comes the professor.'

Avsey apologized immediately for his lateness.

'My lecture ran overtime, it's these wretched students and their devilish questions. I told them they'd have to buy me a beer if they wanted a minute more.' The professor shook hands and gave Brilliant a disarming smile. The face in the middle of a halo of white hair was unlined, saintly and extremely young-looking, though Arkady had told her he was nearly sixty.

'The bar's much more conducive to inspiration than the lecture hall, don't you think? Why don't you come to my room in half an hour, when you've finished your wine?'

She watched as Professor Avsey was swallowed up in an animated huddle of students, well fortified with bottles of beer. Voices were soon raised in heated debate.

'Avsey's got this marvellous ability to establish a rapport. It's his humility as well as his learning; they hang on his every word. His genius borders on imbalance, of course, in another age he would have been a Yurodivy, a sort of Holy Fool. He's an enigma – an agnostic but an authority on the Orthodox Church, he collects religious relics, manuscripts and icons . . . and as I told you, he's a fanatic Russophile.'

Arkady looked up as the hubbub of voices in the corner rose to a crescendo and then abruptly ceased. The circle of students parted reluctantly and the professor made his way to the door. He waved encouragingly at Arkady.

'We'll go to his apartment in a few minutes – give him time to breathe. He always lives like that, on the run. Never changed as long as I've known him.'

Fifteen minutes later Brilliant's eyes were growing used to the cool half-light of Professor Avsey's living room. Blinds were down to keep out the heat. An old-fashioned fan whirred in a corner.

'We have marvellous central heating and double glazing, but not-so-good air conditioning. I do hope you won't find the heat oppressive.'

Avsey's old-fashioned manner reminded her instantly of Honoré Chardin, ever her friend and champion in her memories, and she warmed to him immediately.

'I didn't think I'd ever have to complain about the heat in Siberia. It just shows you how wrong you can be.'

'Anyushka!' Avsey called out. 'We must drink champagne and nothing else! This is a very special day for me, Countess Curnonsky.' He used the old Tsarist appellation, and she had that strange impression, as she had many times in Russia, of time standing still, despite the Revolution.

A stout woman with deeply ruddy cheeks, her white overall straining at every button, made an impressive entrance with the champagne clinking in its bucket of ice.

'*Zakuski* too, Anyushka! Bring whatever you have, we must celebrate! She's the best cook in Akademgorodok.' The beaming Anyushka bowed out, with a firework display of flashing gold teeth.

'You know, Countess, the White Tsaritsa has always occupied a very special place in my affections. I wholeheartedly support the scheme for making a replica. But if only it were the original, the piece with the flaw is the vital one, the one that really matters. . . .' Avsey folded his arms across his chest and gazed pensively into the distance.

'Well, well!' The Professor recollected himself with a start and smiled apologetically. 'Be that as it may. That is quite another story, as you are perfectly aware, my dear.' His voice had an almost hypnotic gentleness. 'The White Tsaritsa is not my only passion, as you can see!' He waved expansively at the surrounding walls. Icons, ancient tapestries, intriguing artefacts and time-blackened religious paintings jostled for every inch of available space.

'Science is too restrictive, there are things in the universe we can never know and understand. Christ taught us the all-important lesson of humility.' Avsey refilled their glasses and paced up and down the room. 'You know, my father, Prince Anatoly, was in St Petersburg the day they cleft the White Tsaritsa. His report for *The Scientific Gazette* was well thought of at the time. I looked it up and had a copy made for you. He diverges a bit here and there on his pet subject – he was an enthusiastic amateur gemmologist – but the social details are quite fascinating.'

Anyushka had been plying between the living room and the kitchen, throwing a spotless white cloth over a long table and covering it with the familiar collection of small oval dishes.

'Come now! To the *Zakuski* table. Of all Russian culinary institutions, this is the one of which we are most proud. It always impresses my foreign visitors, who think our food is only the appalling stuff they serve up in Intourist hotels. Try Anyushka's preserved wild mushrooms, or her aubergine caviar, or this pâté of wild hare. . . .'

Avsey pressed Brilliant with mouthfuls of food from the dozen or more dishes on the table.

'This, of course, is very modest. For a crowd Anyushka surpasses herself. The *Zakuski* table originated in country houses, where the guests travelled hundreds of versts in dreadful weather – that and notorious Russian unpunctuality meant the hostess had to stop the early arrivals from getting completely drunk before the last guest had arrived. It's very unusual for a Russian to drink vodka without eating something, if only a morsel of bread.' He motioned to Anyushka to bring more vodka.

'The modern method of serving dinner, one course after another, was called "*service à la Russe*". The standard European practice was to put all the dishes on the table together and they all got cold. Then the rest of the world followed our example. So you see, we have made some impact on the gastronomic scene.'

Brilliant laughed, warmed by the ice-cold vodka he insisted she drink down in one gulp.

'Arkady has probably told you, I'm here on a . . . a kind of sentimental journey.' She spoke hesitantly, wondering how much he knew. 'The train journey was a very emotional one, coming near the Tura. How did the White Tsaritsa come to be found on its own, lying in a little hollow?'

'I too have read the moving journal of your ancestor!' Avsey's eyes rested on her warmly. 'The White Tsaritsa's size is quite extraordinary, but nevertheless it was brought down the river from kimberlite pipes, and deposited at that distance during a time of exceptional floods. The Siberian shield between the Yenisei and the Lena is strikingly similar to the African plateau around Kimberley, which I am sure you know quite well.'

'*Ahemmm* . . . !' Anyushka was shifting from one foot to the other in the doorway.

'*Gospody!*' exclaimed Avsey. 'I'd love to continue this conversation, but we've been asked out to dinner and I'm a notoriously bad time-keeper. Let's see. . . .' He peered at his watch in the half-light. 'We should have been there ten minutes ago.'

The dinner, in a colleague's nearby apartment, was intimate and lighthearted. Crowded around the *pièce de résistance*, an enormous steaming dish of *pelmeni* – tiny Siberian dumplings – the talk was sparkling, by turns

jocular, academic, savagely satirical or downright sentimental. Brilliant basked in the warmth of the Russian
welcome and experienced again the disorientating sensation of being cocooned from reality, hermetically sealed
off in a special world of the chosen few.

Towards midnight, tired and thankful to be alone in
her room, Arkady making a phone call from a booth at
the end of the corridor, she kicked off her shoes, stretched
out on the embroidered quilt and took out Avsey's article.

She studied the old sepia photographs with care. The
Curnonsky brothers – Grigor elegant and clean-shaven,
Anton burly and dishevelled – posed proudly alongside the
great diamond-cleaver himself, Theodore Van Rijnders,
resplendent in beaver coat and Cossack hat. Catching the
name Curnonsky under one of the captions, she read
further.

ST PETERSBURG SCIENTIFIC GAZETTE. Dec 1913.

A Report by Prince Anatoly Avsey

On 20th November of this year the celebrated Russian
diamond, the White Tsaritsa, was successfully cleft before a
distinguished audience in the Science Museum of St
Petersburg. The four-hundred-and-five-carat uncut diamond,
the property of Count Grigor and Count Anton Curnonsky,
has until recently been part of the Imperial collection. In July
of last year, following a special scientific study, his Imperial
Majesty, Tsar Nicholas II, gave permission for the cutting of
one perfect gem from the flawed whole. Tsar Nicholas held the
view, together with Count Grigor Curnonsky, that the
superstition surrounding the White Tsaritsa was evidence of a
Russian backwardness ill-suited to this scientific age.

The task of cleaving the White Tsaritsa was initially the
responsibility of the Dutch master-cleaver Joseph Asscher.
However, owing to increasing ill-health after the cleaving of
the great Cullinan in 1908, Mr Asscher was obliged to
relinquish the operation to his fellow countryman Theodore
van Rijnders.

At the invitation of the brothers Curnonsky, Mr Van Rijnders and his family took up residence in the Curnonsky Palace last year, where, the Dutch master-cleaver informed the author, his children played freely inside a huge papier-mâché model of the White Tsaritsa set up in the nursery. Just as the children played inside the model's two equal-sized compartments, Theodore van Rijnders, according to his own reports, played inside the real diamond in his mind both as architect and engineer – not to mention chess player – in order to plot his moves ahead of time. So absorbed were the whole family in the project that they practised breaking their bread rolls at mealtimes into two perfectly intact halves.

The White Tsaritsa, an extraordinary freak of nature found in the Tura region of the Siberian plateau in the sixteenth century, ranks (above the Orlov which is reputed to be of Indian origin) as the largest uncut diamond in the Imperial collection. Its centrally placed flaw has often been likened to a heart or a flame, and its miraculous propensity to save its wearer from harm has earned it a special place in Russian folklore.

Uncleft, the stone was about the size of a hen's egg, with one side rough and frosted, the other smooth and flat as though already polished. Mr Van Rijnders had consulted with leading Russian cutters, notably Mr V I Belasaev and Mr K V Kuznetsin, but their learned opinions as to the best method of cleaving the diamond were violently opposed. Several European cutters were of the belief that the grain of the diamond ran parallel to this flat plane. Failure to cleave along the grain might shatter the diamond into thousands of fragments.

After a year's intensive study, a microscopic crack in the surface of the stone encouraged Mr Van Rijnders to determine the run of the grain. Under the most powerful microscope a tiny ledge was revealed, with a sixty-seven-degree difference between it and the smooth surface, which had previously been thought to be the surface of the grain. The 'heart' of the gem was centralized, about four-fifths into the stone from its smooth side. It was Mr Van Rijnder's intention to cleave one perfect gem at a stroke, leaving the flaw in the slightly larger half.

On the day of the ceremony inclement weather – the first heavy snowfall of the year – hampered the arrival at the Science Museum of several distinguished members of the audience.

Staying at the Lebed Hotel were Mr Stanwell Arkwright, the celebrated diamond merchant from New York, together with Mr C Dobson and Mr R Krantz, his fellow countrymen. French and German dignitaries were guests of the Berlin Hotel, including Count Wittgenstein and Monsieur Philippe Chardin, the Parisian diamantaire. So packed were the foyer, back benches and galleries of the lecture theatre with jewel merchants, cross-cutters and brilliandeers that late-comers had little opportunity of observing the proceedings closely. His Imperial Majesty had declined an invitation, perhaps wisely in the light of the recent attempt on his life, and had likewise graciously declined the offer of the flawless gem for the Tsarina. The twin Count Curnonskys sat on opposite sides of the lecture hall, the great diamond on the dais between them, typifying the divisive factions, Slavophile versus Westerner, which have recently become so manifest in St Petersburg society.

The atmosphere that greeted Mr Van Rijnder's arrival was one of intense excitement. Fortunately he displayed none of the nervous exhaustion that precipitated Mr Asscher's collapse after cutting the great Cullinan. The White Tsaritsa was removed from its casket and placed in a specially constructed framework on top of the cutting table. The diamond had the appearance of a miniature mountain with clearly marked paths and tracks where the outlines for cleaving and sawing had been marked in Indian ink, a technique pioneered by the great Antwerp cutters. Mr Van Rijnders made the first crucial mark, a V-shaped kerf, with the honed chip of another diamond, then inserted a blunt wedge-shape into the kerf. The audience held its breath. Mr Van Rijnders tapped lightly and smoothly on the wedge with a counter-balanced mallet – there appeared to be a flash, perhaps a trick of the light, whilst the observers blinked and gasped – then the White Tsaritsa split cleanly and accurately into two parts. Contrary to much learned opinion, Mr Van Rijnders had correctly divined the run of the grain.

The successful division of the huge stone accomplished, the great cutter took a bow amid thunderous applause. Without further ado, the twin stones were removed from public inspection to an upstairs workshop, to receive the attention of Mr Osip Ossowsky, the great brilliandeer from Warsaw. Mr Ossowsky's 'mathematical formula' of cutting, to bring out the maximum play of light within the gem, has been strongly criticized by some of our native cutters. Many consider that Mr Ossowsky sets the 'table' too high in order to get maximum fire, and consequently sacrifices brilliance. Mr Ossowsky anticipates a 'waste' of approximately 42 per cent after brilliandeering. This is an exceptionally high return, due to the successful nature of the cleaving. His task will take several months and the finished gems of approximately eighty carats each will be set into two identical rings.

Mr Ossowsky, a man of science with little time for 'superstitious hysteria', confessed to experiencing unusual emotion when handling the White Tsaritsa. In his opinion the diamond possesses a unique quality which will inspire him to reach the highest level of his craft. He considers the flaw to be a small speck of carbon, or possibly a crystal formation that is indeed heart- or flame-shaped. Almost miraculous in a stone so large, the diamond is otherwise entirely perfect.

Underneath Prince Avsey's account were more sepia photographs, a blurred print of the rings, the author talking to Ossowsky . . . Ossowsky shaking Theodore Van Rijnders by the hand. . . .

Suddenly Arkady's head was close to hers. She started in surprise and his mouth found hers, forcing her backwards. An avalanche of kisses obliterated her face, her neck, her hair. Breathless and too weak to laugh, she eventually held him at arm's length.

'Don't push me away, darling one! I've endured those hot eyes on you all evening, I've been longing to touch you, to feel your soft skin . . .' He fumbled impatiently with the buttons on her dress, his face set in lines of frustration.

'Wait, wait, Arkady! Here, move these papers . . .' Too late, the loose sheaves of manuscript scattered all over the floor.

'Mmmm . . .' His blissful face had found her breast, her body moved under him in a long shudder, her hands caressed his hair and she lay back in the shadows, an inexplicable tear welling in the corner of her eyes.

*

She was woken next morning by Arkady shaking her shoulder briskly. Freshly shaved and dressed he stood looking down at her impatiently.

'I let you sleep, but we must be at the factory in forty minutes or we'll miss the flight back to Moscow. I'm going to phone now – be ready when I get back, *milaya!*'

She smiled tartly as she hurriedly started to dress. There was something indefinable about the Russian male's treatment of his woman – *muchestvo* – a kind of semi-Asiatic machismo, that Arkady possessed in full measure.

She was ready within minutes, to his gratification, and they drove out to the suburbs for a lightning tour of a grim-looking factory that could have been any factory for all she saw of the operational side. 'It's top secret; making diamond windows for space probes is very hush-hush,' Arkady assured her *sotto voce*, before they were introduced to Ignaty Yurievich Tessorian, the director.

In Ignaty Yurievich's office she was shown a replica of the White Tsaritsa, so like the one in the Adamantina showroom that she caught her breath in astonishment.

'This model is made of crystal, but Ignaty Yurievich assures me that the synthetic diamond will be ready within a few weeks. Then we'll get the publicity moving for the special ceremony, the public unveiling of a national treasure.'

Arkady withdrew for a private conversation with the lugubrious scientist, leaving her kicking her heels among dusty piles of neglected paperwork. After goodbyes and much hand-shaking she extracted a rare smile from Ignaty Yurievich before they were whisked away in the waiting black car to Akademgorodok airport.

After take-off Arkady seemed preoccupied and stared morosely out of the aircraft window. Brilliant knew there was a meeting with his superior in the offing and her eyes gleamed sardonically.

'Who is this minister you have to report to in Moscow? I shouldn't think you relish much subordination!'

'Viktor Terepin is effectively my boss at the Ministry

of Non-Ferrous Metallurgy.' Brilliant's eyebrows shot up in amusement. 'Yes, rather unwieldy, isn't it? And incongruous to have the glamorous Diamond Trust under its wing, which is my concern. My division is pretty autonomous, but someone, somewhere, has raised an objection to the money being spent on the replica.' Arkady lapsed into a gloomy silence and was non-communicative for the rest of the journey.

They arrived at Moscow's Sheremetievo Airport thirty minutes behind schedule. Late for their appointment, they drove straight to the Ministry and sat for a further half hour in a small ante-room. Arkady paced the room moodily, pausing to aim the occasional kick at one of the plastic chairs ranged bleakly along the walls. Just as Brilliant was fearing for the safety of the china dolls on top of the mantelshelf, a clerk stuck his head round the door and summoned Arkady to meet his superior. Almost immediately, the door opened again and the minister himself appeared, with arms spread wide and an expansive smile on his face.

'My dear Countess Curnonsky! I had no idea you were here. How unforgivable to keep you waiting. I've a reception in progress, so let's continue our business with a glass in our hands.'

Viktor's suit was as tightly upholstered as an expensive armchair, his handsome features were already beginning to slacken under a layer of indulgent fat. He took her arm and guided her towards a door marked No Admittance. She glanced over her shoulder at Arkady. From his impassive features it was impossible to tell whether the short interview had been in any way conclusive.

Under the ubiquitous chandelier an exotic collection of visitors from Soviet Central Asia stood about in un-Russian subdued silence. Waiters with laden trays stood idly on the sidelines.

'Moslems, you know!' Viktor hissed in her ear. 'They don't drink, it makes these do's most trying!' He helped himself to two glasses, handed one to Brilliant, motioned the waiter to serve Arkady and steered her away to a corner where he made one or two perfunctory introductions.

Brilliant looked around the group with interest. She had always been intrigued by the people of the Eastern Autonomous Republics, speaking a common language yet poles apart in religion, culture and lifestyle. The delegation was from Frunze in Kirghizstan on the borders of China, and Dushanbe in the south.

There were several stout matrons, but her eyes were drawn to a beautiful young woman who smiled at her shyly and then looked away. Zoya, when Brilliant was introduced, was a Tadzhik from Dushanbe, with waist-length hair framing a perfect oval face. Just as Aisha must have looked, she thought, marvelling at the slant of deep-fringed black eyes and the finely modelled mouth. The legendary lovely women of Dushanbe, reared among their vineyards and lemon groves, had only in the last few decades been persuaded to give up the veil. She was loath to break off her conversation with the fascinating Zoya, learning how generations of women in the same family lived quite different lives in Tadzhikstan now, but Viktor was determined to get her to himself.

'Let me offer you another drink?' He was breathing heavily at her side, his sanguine face flushed an even deeper hue. He took her empty glass and led her away from the smiling Zoya.

'How long are you staying, Countess? I hope you will be my guest at the ballet tonight? I have already spoken with Arkady Ilich and it seems you have no other engagements.' His eyes glittered expectantly over the rim of his glass.

She smiled her acceptance and shrugged slightly. Well, if Arkady had already arranged it. . . .

'You know, Viktor Borisovich, Zoya Semyonova has been telling me that she is the first woman from her *oblast* ever to become a delegate . . .'

'That is correct . . . and if they are all beauties like her we won't have any objections!' Viktor smiled broadly and drained his glass.

Brilliant stared at him, unamused. Curious that male chauvinism should flourish so rampantly in this communist climate of equality.

It would be good to see him lose his smile.

'You know jewels are my business, of course. How do you see the future of Russian diamonds?'

Viktor's moist eyes glittered malevolently.

'We have had our little diamond revolution! We do our own cutting and polishing here, so we can short-circuit the De Beers monopoly. The Ministry used to sell diamonds as if they were shoes, or batteries, or caviar. Every diamond is different, you can't do it that way. We were underestimating the value of our diamonds, being taken for a ride. That's where Arkady Ilich comes in, there's nothing he doesn't know about the world market, who's buying what, where and when.' Viktor drew in his chest proudly. 'Now we operate from a position of strength.'

He checked his watch briskly.

'*Chort!* It's easy to forget the time with you, *dorogaya*. Shall we try to discuss other things besides diamonds tonight? Let's say six-thirty at your hotel, the Savoy, isn't it? Arkady Ilich has such good taste. Until we meet . . .' He bent his gleaming face over her hand.

Waiting in the atmospheric foyer of the newly refurbished Savoy – formerly the Berlin – and sharing the same *fin de-siècle* decor as its London namesake, Brilliant drummed her fingers on her handbag irritably. She supposed she had not really been surprised to find that Viktor's invitation was strictly *à deux*.

Arkady thought she had understood from the beginning . . . tickets for the Bolshoi were like gold dust . . . it was such a privilege. Viktor was really quite harmless, he had added, and would probably fall asleep in the car on the way home. Brilliant had retorted sharply that she was quite capable of seeing off lechers, while reflecting that somewhere between Arkady's wildly

romantic exterior and pragmatic heart lay a perplexing
vacuum.

20

Coping with Viktor at the Bolshoi turned out to be less exacting than she had anticipated. His face was positively turgid with pride as he escorted her during the long inter- val, a pre-Revolutionary ritual where everyone promen- aded and preened, ate and drank copiously at the large buffets and generally spent an uproarious hour having the real fun of the evening.

The ballet was one she had never seen in the West, *Stone Flower*, wildly sentimental folklore, and the warm- hearted audience took the debutante prima ballerina to its heart and would not let her go. Curtain call after curtain call brought back her exquisite dark head and fragile limbs into the limelight. Brilliant was quite dizzy with the lights, the applause and the smells before the huge audience were allowed to pour out on to the streets. As Arkady had predicted, Viktor, already glowing and expansive at the outset of the evening, collapsed like an affable bear in the limousine on the way home. He mumbled a few ardent propositions into her hair before she was able to dodge his embrace and wave him away from the steps of the Savoy.

Sightseeing in Red Square was most definitely not on Arkady's agenda next morning. She smiled as he gave her a perfunctory kiss after breakfast. There were Men from the Ministry to talk dark secrets to, but he had arranged a car and drawn up a Moscow-in-three-hours programme for her.

'What is there to see, *lyubimaya?*' He shrugged his shoulders dismissively. 'You who are used to Saks Fifth Avenue will hardly be enthralled by GUM, and the Arbat is full of hucksters. After Leningrad it is appallingly phili- stine, absolutely the Dark Ages, but there are a few hidden treasures. Don't forget the Novodevichy Convent, where all the noble ladies sought sanctuary at the time of your Fedor, you'll find marvellous relics of that period. Boris Godunov was elected Tsar in the Cathedral. I've told the driver to take you straight to the airport at one o'clock, so don't be late, *dorogaya*.'

She was glad to be alone, declining the attentions of the Intourist guides, to walk inside the austere Kremlin walls. In the Armoury she stared wide-eyed, as Fedor must have done, at the extravagant splendour of his cousin Michael Romanov's coronation robes, encrusted with great rubies, emeralds and pearls. In another room she saw Michael's throne, with its secret cubby-hole where his father Filaret sat hidden, prompting his son's performance at foreign audiences with the consummate skill of a ventriloquist. She had just time to go to the Novodevichy Convent and admire the rare icons, paintings and sixteenth-century costumes before she was reminded of the time by the anxious driver.

At the airport Arkady was waiting in high good humour. 'Good, you're on time! I thought I would lose you for ever to the Smutnaya Vremya. Tell me all about it on the plane, *milaya*, I know you would have liked longer but there will be many more times.'

Brilliant was happy to be going back to Leningrad. This time the streets were familiar and as they approached the Museum of Tsarist Treasures, the colourful palaces seemed like old friends.

'Galya's staying on late for us. It's not easy to persuade the staff to close a minute later than the prescribed time.'

Galina was leaning against a pillar by the entrance, chatting to an elderly attendant who sat with stout legs straddled in a low chair.

'Brilliant! Arkady! I was just going to give up on you.' A patch of colour burned high in Galina's cheeks as she opened her arms wide. 'Welcome to Leningrad! It's wonderful to see you again.'

'Galya!' Brilliant felt a surge of genuine emotion as

she held Galina close, bestowing the ritual three kisses, inhaling her old-fashioned smell of cold cream and soap-washed hair.

'*Golubchik maya!*' Arkady's little dove was quiescent in his arms one prolonged second and then stepped away, shaking her hair back, smiling her wide smile that exposed even teeth. Brilliant felt a perplexing stab of anxiety and frowned, troubled by the beating of her own heart.

'Are there any treasures left then, Galya, after refurbishment?' Arkady glared at her in mock severity. 'You'll soon be curator of an empty museum.'

'Don't worry, we've still got the one that matters! And we'd better hurry, we've kept the museum open specially late. Elena Lyubovna's been working overtime.'

The stout attendant nodded baleful affirmation as they passed.

'Follow me! This way.' Galina called over her shoulder and set off at a brisk trot across the deserted foyer.

They are lovers! Galina walked mechanically through the familiar rooms of her museum. The well-loved objects seemed to give her comfort. She had known, as soon as she looked into Brilliant's eyes she had known. She had seen no happiness in those singular eyes – only confusion and a certain haunted quality. So, Arkady! How much you had to answer for in your pursuit of perfect love.

She felt no malice. On the contrary, there had been compassion in her embrace, a regret that Brilliant should have to share in the sorority of suffering. She glanced over her shoulder, beckoning to them to hurry. Arkady had his arm round Brilliant, sensing by her expression that all was not well.

'Quick now, the light's going. I don't want to advertise to the world that the museum is still open.' I may feel no malice, but that doesn't make me a saint – I am jealous, *jealous!* The blood sang in Galina's temples. His mouth on her body – there was a new voluptuous way Brilliant leaned against him. His masterful-tender blend of lovemaking that was like no other, savage, exquisite, the poetry of the erotic . . . there was no way she could not envy Brilliant that.

Brilliant smiled uncertainly at Arkady. His arm round her shoulder was reassuring, his eyes searched her troubled face. She felt nervous, unaccountably shaky, so many emotional experiences had been crammed into so short a time.

They followed Galina's white overall down a dim corridor, her high heels clicked over the polished parquet. The high-ceilinged rooms of the old palace were deserted, a sense of its former grandeur as a private residence filtered back with the mellow evening light.

They paused at last in a doorway. With a flick of a switch the White Tsaritsa was unceremoniously revealed. Startling, stark and unadorned, it sat alone on a plinth in a darkened cell, probed by the single piercing beam of an overhead spotlight.

Brilliant pressed her forehead against the thick protective glass and stared silently at the extraordinary ring resting against a background of dark velvet.

'It is quite outstanding,' she whispered as if to herself. 'The purity, the brilliance, even without a loupe the quality is exceptional . . . and in a stone so large.'

'That is all you feel, no emotion, now you're face to face with the other half of your diamond? Ah! This Western coldness, you aren't appraising rough at a Sight, you know.' Arkady's voice broke the sepuchral silence. But the tremor in her hands had not escaped him, for all the matter-of-factness of her words.

'The museum only reopened today after some . . . some necessary alterations.' Galina looked quickly at Arkady, wondering how much Brilliant knew. 'The museum is so thrilled to be acquiring the replica of the flawed half! We are going to give the whole jewel maximum publicity – in a larger room but with the same dramatic treatment, darkness and spotlight. It was Arkady Ilich's idea to set it up like this, and now it is the most popular exhibit.'

Brilliant smiled drily. Yes, Arkady had quite plainly

293

copied the setting from the Adamantina showroom, and when the other half arrived it would certainly feel at home on the same velvet and on the same plate-glass plinth.

'Yes, everything seems to be going ahead quite well. We hope there won't be any last-minute set-backs.' Arkady looked quickly at Brilliant, who was reading the potted historical notes inscribed beneath the diamond. 'Listen! Tomorrow's Saturday. I think we deserve a holiday. Galya, we're going to descend on you and drag you off to Tverskoe, we'll go hunting for mushrooms. Ah! It's so long since we did that. I know exactly where to find them near the lower lake. Say you'll come, Galya?'

'A bit early for mushrooms, isn't it?' Galina smiled. 'A day in the country . . . hmmm . . . the weather's perfect. It sounds enticing, but the children – they so look forward to their Saturdays with me.'

'Take them to Babushka Leila's, they adore going to Grandma's and she spoils them like crazy. Give yourself a day off, it'd be no holiday with them along.'

Brilliant looked from one to the other. They could have been husband and wife sorting out the domestic details of a proposed outing. Galina shrugged her shoulders and smiled in resignation.

'When Arkady has his heart set on something he always gets his way! You'll love the woods around Leningrad, Brilliant. You can't go back to America without doing the Russian country idyll.'

'Decided, then!' Arkady said firmly. 'We'll come and collect you, Galya, not too early, around ten.' Laughing and squabbling about the details of their expedition, they walked arm-in-arm with Galina to the main entrance and Brilliant heard the grating of the heavy bolt as she shut up the museum behind them.

On the way back to the hotel, Brilliant looked at Arkady thoughtfully.

'Galina knows that the real diamond is being substituted, doesn't she?'

Arkady nodded calmly. 'Of course! She had to know. She is the one person in my life I can trust completely.'

They arrived at their hotel and spoke no more about it. But as Brilliant lay in Arkady's arms that night the image of Galina's gentle, tired and vulnerable face rose inexorably between them.

'*Chort Vozhmy!* Already nine-thirty!'

Galina flew frantically round the tiny apartment, throwing all Sasha's paraphernalia of soldiers, broken bits of guns and forts, into a box in the corner. Then she began picking up discarded clothing and stuffing it into the laundry bag on a chair. There were days when the twenty-five square metres felt more like one, yet she had made the small area homely and she shared it with no one, even the bathroom was her own.

She was late – the buses had been so crowded with football fans it had taken her an age to get to Arkady's grandmother's, hating the loud-mouthed youths already flushed with vodka, shoving and pushing, but at least Sasha and Alyosha would have a day of cosseting in Leila's plump and capable hands.

She threw the quilted covers over the divans, one for her, the other for the boys, artfully arranged a cascade of embroidered cushions, straightened her grandmother's Kazak rug, coaxed the huge vase of dried grasses into a more pleasing shape, flicked a duster over the lovingly assembled prints and paintings and surveyed the small room that served as bedroom, living room and dining room with a glow of pride. It had warmth, its accoutrements and artefacts were nearly all home-made, it was a very personal reflection of her taste and fantasies and, more important, it was a private haven to which she could retreat from the very unprivate business of Russian city life.

Galina knew she was lucky. Even before she was divorced from Slava she had extracted the promise of the apartment from an elderly lady curator who was retiring to Yalta for health reasons. Finding somewhere to live was problem number one for Russian citizens, bigger even than the problems of food and child care. But she was fortunate to live in the city, and so escape the shortages and boredom of Vishnev's bourgeois bureaucracy.

Every few months she took the children on the train to visit Babushka Elena, when for a few blissful days she could shut her eyes and escape into the nostalgic warmth of an indulged childhood. But she was always glad to close the door again on her small Leningrad world, thankful she had to share with no one, least of all a man.

Slava Milowitz had been impossible to live with, like an amiable bear intent on extracting the maximum from the honey-pots of life. The spoilt son of Igor Milowitz, educated round the world wherever his father was conducting, Slava had forged a career in the cinema through virtue of his connections. Not that Slava didn't have talent, Galina mused. He had an extraordinary ability to bring out the best in other people, an eye for the unusual, aided by his bizarre upbringing and the tenacity to get what he wanted which, in a few meteoric years, had made him one of Russia's leading directors. But the early years had been difficult. After university Galina had got the job at the museum because it paid well and she earned for both of them while Slava made experimental films.

She had been beautiful then. She caught a glimpse of her pale face in the mirror as she passed. They had been happy, too, at first. But when the boys came life had been harder. Slava had changed, or perhaps not changed, she smiled a little bitterly, but become more himself. Her friends told her she was mad to have another child, it was hard enough with no living-in *babushka* to lend a hand. But Galina adored children and wanted Sasha to grow up sharing, to be able to have a real family life. It was true, after Alyosha was born life was difficult; up at six to dress and feed the boys, struggle with them to the nursery and then catch the metro for the museum. The buses always seemed too crowded to stop or didn't run during last winter's record-breaking temperatures.

But her career had brought her solace and fulfilment during the year that Slava had started staying away from home and, finally, when she plucked up courage to tell him not to come back, it didn't seem to matter so much. Moving out of their impressive apartment near the Maly meant there was much less work to do, an end to the stream of friends and hangers-on who sat around and drank, oblivious to the fact that the great man himself was nearly always absent.

In her little kitchen, hardly more than a cupboard, Galina put the smalls to soak, making a mental note that she'd used the last of the washing powder. She was too late now to join the queue at the *gastronom*. She sighed. Her domestic pride was piqued. She had wanted to prepare something home-made for the picnic. But Arkady had a car, they could shop in style at Eliseyev's and drop the washing off at the laundromat on the way.

They would be here any minute. Pulling the dress from Alla's atelier over her head – thank God she had ironed those endless metres of skirt last night – she ran to the bathroom and rummaged in the drawer under the mirror for the lipstick she'd bought in New York. The texture was soft on her lips, its scent seductive, its glossy brilliance so unlike the waxy cosmetics she was used to. On special occasions she unfurled it from its tortoiseshell casing and noted with dismay its rapidly diminishing length.

She stared closer at her face in the mirror. She looked so tired these days! She pinched her pale cheeks, then wiped her finger over the precious lipstick and rubbed it along her high cheekbones. Better! The watchful brown eyes, like a forlorn deer's, began to sparkle. She plucked one or two stray white hairs from her browline – since her treatment in New York they seemed to proliferate daily – and noticed the fine lines gathering at the corners of her eyes. '*Krasavitsa!*' men used to whisper as she passed. Who would look at her now, in her headscarf and galoshes waiting passively in the ubiquitous queue? She filled in the contours of her wide mouth with bright pink, tilted her head coquettishly and smiled at her reflection. Suddenly her face was transformed. She was again Natasha Rostov, Tolstoy's heroine, with her tip-tilted nose, mobile mouth and wide, subtly exotic eyes.

She heard Arkady's voice on the landing and ran to the door, brushing out her hair. Brilliant's frank appreciation of the apartment was intensely gratifying.

'What a wonderful room, Galina, so welcoming and artistic, the sort of room it must be a joy to come home to,' Brilliant exclaimed in delight as soon as she had looked around.

'Thank you! Only don't look too closely. I'm covering up a multitude of sins with this and that scattered here and there.' Galina grinned with pleasure.

'These must be the boys. They look like real rascals.' Brilliant peered at one of the many photographs of the boys that stood on top of the bureau.

'Yes, they're real boys, that's for sure. I'm from a family of girls, so I'm learning a lot of things for the first time. They're with Babushka Leila now, so they'll be spoiled rotten.' She smiled fondly.

'Galina, I love your dress! Did you buy it here?' Brilliant was frankly surprised at the stylish cut and print of Galina's cotton dress.

'No, I didn't buy it, I had it made "Chez Alla" and I wore it specially to show you what we can do. Alla's just opened her own designer fashion house. It's a co-operative, but Alla's the creative one. She's got real talent, a genius with the scissors. She makes one-off dresses for about two hundred roubles. A lot of money by our standards, but worth it to get an original. I felt like a rich Parisienne having my own *toile* made and several fittings of my personal creation.'

'Amazing!' Brilliant smiled. 'I only briefly aspired to the couture in Paris – while in Leningrad evidently it's commonplace!'

'Oh, hardly that.' Galina grinned sheepishly. 'The state dress factories approve about five new models a season and then churn out a million or so of each. No wonder there's no individuality. We remember the years by our dresses . . . "You remember, that summer we all wore the red frock with black spots . . ." Thank heaven for people like Alla – or the second-hand shops. By the way, Arkady! I've had no time to buy anything, I thought we could shop at Eliseyev's and then Brilliant can see it for herself.'

'Of course – the Harrods Food Hall of Leningrad, where else?' Arkady's critical eye swept over the room. 'Yes, you've done a good job, Galya. You can't buy such taste here, you have to make it for yourself.'

'Here, Arkady! Make yourself useful.' Brilliant watched as Galina loaded Arkady's arms with the essentials for a picnic, then with an oddly compressed feeling round her heart she followed them down the echoing staircase and out on to the sultry summer street.

21

At Eliseyev's food store on Nevsky Prospekt, decadently Tsarist in decor and still called after its pre-Revolutionary owner, Arkady gave the orders as the two women zigzagged from counter to counter in the laborious process of Soviet shopping. Queueing to order the goods, queueing again at the cash desk with a ticket to pay, then back again to the same counter to queue for the goods with the stamped ticket.

'It'll be goddamned nightfall before we get a mouthful!' Arkady scowled irritably as he stowed the rough brown paper packages in the boot, taking care with the bottles, as the Russian minor roads were notoriously potholed.

They drove out of the city along the shores of the Gulf of Finland, skirting the town of Lomonosov in the direction of Narva, then turned south on to a small track that wound through wooded hills. After half an hour they left the marshy coastline far behind and were in a pastoral upland area, with the bucolic landscape of a naive painting. Painted wooden houses, contented cattle and picturesque clumps of trees were randomly set against a backdrop of bright green grass and improbably blue sky.

'There it is . . . over there – on the edge of the lake! Tverskoe, lovely Tverskoe. . . .' Galina craned forward from the back seat, her hand on Arkady's shoulder and her eyes shining with anticipation.

Arkady scanned the familiar landscape.

'Look, Galya! Shame! They've cut down half of Tikhon's wood, pulled down his *izba*, built a ghastly silo.' He turned to Brilliant. 'Our grandmothers were best friends, we used to spend the summer holidays here as kids.'

He spun the steering wheel violently and they careered off the road along a potholed track.

'All that's left of ours is the old hunting lodge by the lake. They pulled down the big house when they made the Collective, it had been neglected for so long it almost fell of its own accord. Leila's been ill, so the lodge hasn't been opened up this summer. We'll take a quick look and then eat outdoors, I'm ravenous.'

The interior of the old lodge, overgrown with oak-moss and creeper, was as atmospheric as a stage set. Arkady pulled open one splintered shutter and a shaft of sunlight filtered through the Gothic window onto eerily dust-sheeted furniture. Brilliant peered in and saw sombre paintings, crazed mirrors and dusty patterns on the painted wooden floors. Arkady was instantly seized with a fit of sneezing and hustled them outside.

Brilliant would have liked to have lingered but Arkady shuddered. 'I loathe the dust wrappers, they remind me of a funeral.' Despite her declared interest in the antique furnishings, he was adamant.

Galina remained silent and Brilliant was reminded once again of the curious empathy between them. They had spent holidays together here as children, perhaps Arkady's memories were too personal for him to want to share? He grasped her arm and began to lead her towards the lake.

'I've found my best mushrooms in these woods. All right, Galya, it was in autumn! Baskets of them – *cèpes*, *girolles*, little *bleuets* that melt in your mouth. We ate like kings for days. Lunch first, then we'll take to the woods.'

Arkady marched them to the edge of the lake like a resourceful boy scout, drew the wine corks, plunged the bottles in the water and spread out the rugs. Brilliant helped Galina, the sun warming her back through her thin cotton dress. From the awkward brown paper packages they unwrapped sausage in many guises, smoked fish, vegetable salads liberally mixed with *smetana*, dill-flavoured cucumbers, soft cheeses and *keffir*, aromatic rye bread and a large bag of sugared doughnuts, Arkady's favourite.

Curious, soft-eyed cows drew closer on the other side of the stream and munched reflectively, keeping a respectful distance. The lapping of the water, the steady buzz of countless unseen insects and the Georgian wine had a soporific effect. Arkady withdrew a few yards along the bank, settled down comfortably in a small hollow and whittled away industriously on a birch branch. When Brilliant next stole an amused glance he was asleep, his hair in wisps over his forehead and his mouth open, like an angelic child.

Galina, packing the unused food back into the baskets, intercepted the fond look. She really is in love with him and – amazing – I feel no pain. No. Only commiseration – so I must finally be free! Then a voice of scrupulous conscience seemed to take over. Galya, Galya, enough of lying. Be truthful, now is the time, there has been so little honesty in all our Russian lives.

Loving a man had always seemed to her so much more complicated than loving a child, which was straightforward, a selfless giving which brought its own reward. But was loving Arkady really any different, she wondered; why should she continue to fear it, how could it change or harm her in any way, now? It was true she had always loved him, even in these very woods at Tverskoe, so how could she suddenly cease? It was as deep-rooted as her love for these trees of her childhood, immutable and changeless. Perhaps at last she had grown up, while Arkady never would. She had grown to love him and accept him as he was. He could not hurt her. She would hurt herself more by denying that love.

Galina stole another look at Brilliant's face and her heart contracted with misgiving. It had been a long time since Arkady had pursued her and she had so convincingly rejected him. Why should he change towards her now – she had grown older, he treated her like a fond sister. She frowned, waving away a wasp that hovered over the sugary doughnut paper. She had learned to live without him, without any man, putting thoughts of sensuality and emotional closeness far out of her mind. But she was not yet old. Was the rest of her life to be like this – the endless cycle of work, children and responsibility without the leaven of love; surely it was the only thing that made life endurable or gave meaning to its baffling absurdity?

A little bubble of helpless anger welled up and burst in Galina's consciousness. In a sudden flash of introspective honesty she knew she was resentful, unable to accept Arkady's love because of injured pride. Surely not just that, she thought, seeing herself as faintly ridiculous. But pride is part of self-respect – without that there can be no peace of mind. I have come a long way to find myself, I have changed, so why shouldn't Arkady?

'Galina! I'm so sorry. Let me help – I was miles away. That food was so good, I've eaten far too much. Things taste so much better out of doors. Russian bread must be the most delicious in the world. I have this theory that food doesn't transplant.' Brilliant laughed. 'I'm not being very coherent. I mean that the food of a country tastes best in that country. How many times have you been abroad and brought back some speciality, or tried to reproduce that wonderful paella at home, and it just doesn't taste the same?'

'I've never had that problem.' Galina smiled without rancour. 'Apart from the visit to New York, I've never left the boundaries of the Soviet Union.'

'I'm sorry.' Brilliant frowned. 'That was thoughtless. But you know, it's almost impossible for us to imagine what it must be like not to travel, to have experienced at least one culture other than our own.' She looked at Galina thoughtfully.

'What were we saying in New York about another species. . . .' Galina's pert nose wrinkled in annoyance. They both laughed, the tension between them was broken and they lapsed back into the warmth of their American relationship.

'Everyday life must be difficult for you, Galina, from what I've seen?' Brilliant's voice was gentle. 'You've none of the labour-saving devices we take for granted – instant food, takeaways, laundries, home deliveries. Most of my friends seem to be endlessly complaining about how hard they work, yet they don't really know they were born.'

The wine had loosened Galina's tongue, given it a biting edge.

'You know, Russian women get sick to death of hearing about our image in the West! We're not all digging roads and going about in ankle-socks and headscarves, weighing in at fourteen stone. Some of my friends have never done any housework in their lives. With a live-in *babushka* and a so-called brilliant career, they never need to soil their hands. They eat in restaurants at work, their children eat at school, they never even cook a meal. In the evenings it's bread and sausage from the *gastronom* in front of the television, they dress as fashionably as many a Western woman and their nails are three inches long.' Galina flapped her hands viciously at the persistent wasp that was circling the last of the doughnuts.

'My life was easier when my mother lived with me, but she was a *limitchik* and couldn't get a permanent pass. Eventually she had to go back to Vishnev.'

'Why was that?'

Galina's lips set in a bitter line.

'A *limitchik* is someone who lives outside the city limits and doesn't have a pass. No one is free to travel from one city to another, you need an internal passport. The *limitchiks* crowd into the city to find work but they are despised by the natives, who resent sharing precious food and accommodation. Tension builds up, there are fights – a bit like your race riots – but these are our own people! Mama's on her own now. I visit her when I can.'

Brilliant thought of the parallels of her former anxiety over her own mother, and bit her lip.

Galina's eyes sparked with sudden resentment.

'But you're only in trouble if you have a man to look

after. Men create most work in Soviet women's lives because they don't do a damned thing. Oh yes! They're lazy as hell and demanding, too. The women pander to them, won't let them do anything. Between male and female pride we have a situation like the Middle Ages. Who do you see in the endless queues everywhere? Women, women and more women – women with *avozkas*, "just-in-cases", the string bags we carry everywhere, just in case we spot something worth queueing for. I've got a woman working for me whose husband wants meat every night for dinner. She spends more than two hours a day queueing for it – when she can find it – the whole of her lunch hour. She never eats herself. But she's terrified he'll leave her if she doesn't feed him well.' Galina shrugged despairingly. 'But women are supportive of each other, especially at work; it makes a big difference whether you have a male or female boss.'

Galina sat back on her haunches and clasped her hands in her lap.

'We're all women in the museum now and we've arranged a shift system to fit in shopping, collecting kids, doctor's visits, that sort of thing. It works really well. Women work harder than men in my experience, anyway, and given a sympathetic climate they respond and give their best. I sound like a rabid feminist, don't I? I've surprised even myself, it's never come out before.' She looked down at her hands, embarrassed.

Brilliant leaned forward and touched her arm.

'Galya, I know that anything I say will sound patronizing, but I am Russian, I feel Russian, being here has struck strange chords. . . . But the responsibility for change is a collective one. Hasn't *perestroika* made any difference at all?'

The two kneeling women faced each other across the debris of the meal.

'Materially, not in the slightest. But in other ways, yes, an enormous difference. *Straxh* – fear – has gone. Fear of talking openly to your colleagues, your friends, even your family. And, oh, yes!' Galina's face suddenly lit up with an enchanting smile, 'the *dvori*, the gates, are open again!'

'The gates?' Brilliant looked puzzled.

'The courtyards in the town all have gates leading on to them, even in my block there are short cuts if you know how to zigzag through the alleyways. But the gates have always been locked. People have been afraid. Now they're open, people visit, wander where they will. A trivial notion, you may think? No, a profound indication of *glasnost*. People have come home from the camps, thousands of them, but still not enough.' Galina's smile faded. 'But the biggest change is the feeling of being whole again, human beings, real people. It may seem like a very small step in the right direction but it will break into a run, for once you've given people back that sense of dignity there'll be no turning back.' She looked down at her hands and was silent for a while.

'And now . . .' she lifted her head and the light had gone out of her eyes, 'we'd better wake up Arkady, don't you think?'

She went over and gave the still sleeping Arkady a shake, with that ready familiarity, at once proprietorial and restrained, that had intrigued Brilliant at their first meeting.

Arkady, refreshed and in sparkling form, entertained them for the rest of the afternoon with anecdotes and snatches of song, rifling through the bracken like a well-trained hound, cavorting around the birch trees, beside himself with delight at the perfect weather, the enchantment of the pastoral scene and the two lovely women at his side. It was too early for *cèpes*, but they managed to fill one basket with *girolles* and the ethereal pale violet *bleuets*.

His high spirits were contagious and it was difficult for Brilliant to explain the constricted feeling round her heart, a niggling ache, that she remembered from the past – that pain, that sense of loss. She looked from Galina to Arkady in slow realization. In Galina's whole joking familiarity with Arkady she saw a deliberate distancing, a suppression of affection that spoke volumes. Arkady's eyes followed Galina's every movement with a tenderness she had never seen in him, even in their most intimate moments. There was an unconscious caring in the involuntary way he cleared a path for her or turned to warn her of rough ground.

Suddenly Arkady jumped on a small hillock in front of them, striking a neo-classical pose. His head, garlanded with leaves like a pagan god, was outlined in sharp relief against the sunlight. Amid the laughter it was as if she saw him for the first time. Something in her heart seemed to swell, flow over and then subside. And with it came a feeling of great calm, a blessed peace.

'Galina, could I come with you on Monday when you collect the boys from school? I'd love to see them and it's my only chance, I have to leave on Tuesday.' Brilliant turned to Galina. Her eyes were pleading.

Galina looked at her in surprise.

'*Noo, vot,* of course! They'll just adore you.' Those eyes were telling her many things; how could it be – how could she know? There was something singular about Brilliant, an intuitive sense that gripped one and made one want to be part of her destiny.

In the car on the way home Arkady's effervescence fizzled out and he was uncommunicative while the two women chatted. Suddenly, as if on an impulse, he turned to Galina, frowning.

'See here, Galya, I have work to do tomorrow, something's cropped up. I thought you two could keep each other company . . .'

'No problem!' They exchanged smiling glances. 'We'll let you off the hook.' Brilliant watched him covertly as they emptied the boot of the picnic remains.

Galina crossed the yard to throw the rubbish in the bin while Arkady struggled upstairs with the precious basket of mushrooms and armfuls of rugs. Brilliant waited for Galina and helped her carry the basket of dirty crockery.

307

When they got to the landing outside Galina's door, Arkady was crouching over a figure slumped in the doorway. The blood drained from Galina's face and she forced Arkady aside with unexpected violence.

'Zina, for Christ's sake, what is it? Speak to me!'

The recumbent figure unfolded rag-doll limbs and lifted a dirt-streaked face that was the picture of desolation.

'She's a friend . . . an actress . . .' Galina whispered as Brilliant stared.

'She'll live!' Arkady stood up. The anxiety had left his eyes and was replaced by cynical annoyance. 'Spare us the histrionics, Zina. You're not giving a command performance now.'

Zina scowled and roused herself from semi-consciousness with surprising agility, though it was obvious when she lurched to her feet that she was extremely drunk.

'Shut up, Arkady!' Galina, frowning and spittingly angry, grasped Zina's arm and tried to steer her through the door. Zina swayed against the door jamb, yelped as though she'd been struck and doubled up in pain. An ugly weal was visible just below her elbow, her dirty dress was torn at the neck and more bruises were swelling on her chest and shoulder. The door of the neighbouring apartment opened a crack and two eyes peered at them accusingly above an unsavoury stubble.

'Fuck off!' Zina mumbled thickly and attempted an obscene gesture.

'Quick, get her inside, and put the kettle on,' Galina hissed at Arkady. Brilliant scrabbled at the mushrooms strewn on the chipped flagstones. Her heart pounded uncomfortably and her head had started to ache. She shut Galina's door on the prying eyes on the landing and leaned against it, suddenly weary in every limb. What to do now? Arkady and Galina were bending over Zina, who lay prostrate on the divan. She was muttering incoherently.

'Ulyanov, the bastard, he tried to kill me . . . But I gave him a good pasting first. . . .'

Galina exchanged a look of resignation with Arkady

How many times had it been like this, prodigal Zina returning to the fold to lick her wounds after more self-induced lacerations in the chancy game of life.

Brilliant looked down at a puzzlingly familiar as well as a remarkably unscathed face. Zina's forearms had taken the brunt of the beating as she protected her head with her hands. As Galina bathed her arms with hot water and disinfectant, Zina winced, then grinned stoically.

'Who the fuck's she?' Zina jerked her head a fraction in Brilliant's direction.

'Brilliant Curnonsky – now living in America . . .' Galina intoned quickly, clicking her tongue as she uncovered more bruises.

'Oh yeah. . . .' Zina looked remarkably unimpressed. 'Full of bullshit, American men, worse than most, but they give you a good time while they're at it. . . .'

Brilliant continued to stare at Zina's face.

'Zina . . . ? She's Zina Azerova, isn't she?'

'She? Who's *she*? Something the cat brought in . . . ?' Zina had turned peacefully on her side and looked as though she were preparing to go off into a deep sleep.

Through the blood, the dirt and the tear-streaks Brilliant had recognized the Oscar-winning actress from the Russian box-office success *Leningrad Doesn't Believe in Love*. Impossible not to marvel at that face, striking against all the odds, white-skinned and green-eyed, surrounded by a wildly frizzled cloud of dark red hair.

Zina tossed fretfully, eyes closed, then gave a sudden howl of anguish.

Arkady jumped as though stung.

'*Chort! Zinyushka!* What is it?'

Zina struggled to sit up and Galina restrained her, pushing back damp tendrils of hair from her face.

'It's Baba Sofia, she's dying! That's why I got drunk and we had the row. Timon told me – he went to Vishnev to telephone. . . . She's asking for me, Galya! I have to go, right this minute, right now, she can't die without me. . . .' Tears coursed down Zina's cheeks.

'We'll go, Zina, ssshhhh now, we'll go. . . .' Galina looked hopelessly at Arkady. 'We'll go in the morning, won't we, Arkady?'

Arkady bit his lip.

'Tomorrow's impossible.' He looked uncomfortable. 'Couldn't you go with Brilliant? I'll get you a driver, Galya. . . .' Galina frowned at him and said nothing.

Brilliant shifted her feet on the spot, feeling desperately tired and utterly superfluous. This was family – she felt like an intruder. She should go immediately and leave them to their own lives.

'Please don't be concerned about me,' she said quickly. 'I'll be fine on my own tomorrow, you have enough troubles. But if I can help in any way. . . .' She wanted to get away, back to her cool room, to think, to be alone.

'I'll drop you back.' Arkady's face was stern.

'No, no, Arkady, please don't bother! Galya needs you.' She recoiled from Arkady's hand on her forearm.

'There's nothing I can do now. Zina just needs sleep.' Arkady looked grimly at Zina's apparently slumbering face. 'And so do you and Galya. Let's get you home now, Brilliant.'

When he kissed her chastely goodnight and left her outside the Astoria, for the first time in their relationship he forgot to add a word of endearment.

22

'Let's go, *dorogaya* . . .' Zina rolled over and mimicked Arkady's throaty drawl. 'Let's go and screw each other rotten. Christ, is he going to have a bloody glorious time!' Zina propped herself on one elbow and gave Galina a winning smile. 'She's beautiful. Where did he drag her up from?'

A slow flush spread up from Galina's neck. She turned her back and put the kettle on.

'I'll make some tea. I thought you weren't quite as bombed out as we supposed. She's . . . she's . . . well, you know, the White Tsaritsa . . .' Galina sighed. Zina, of all people! To have to explain Brilliant away to Zina was just about the last straw.

'Ah – that Curnonsky. Lucky Arkady, to be able to combine business and pleasure so conveniently.'

'Shut up, Zina! Brilliant's all right – she's . . . she's *simpatishna* . . . Look, I don't feel like talking about it, all right. If you're going to stay here you'd better get washed. Go and put on my nightdress.'

Zina rolled off the bed and stripped off the torn remnants of her clothes obediently and without inhibition. She made one or two passes in front of the looking glass, striking poses, while Galina rummaged in a drawer and threw her a nightdress, one of her mother's old ones, high-necked, modest and totally unalluring. Zina gave it a withering glance and held her arms high, head flung back, lips pouting and nostrils flared in her 'vixen' face.

Her body had the luminous whiteness of a redhead, and one or two freckles were negligently placed, like errant tea-leaves, on strategic parts of her pert anatomy. Among so much lunar paleness the brightness of her pubic hair seemed somehow shocking. Try as she might to be, sound or look vulgar, Zina's face and body always refuted their owner's single-mindedness. All the finer details, the set of ear, turn of knee, curve of jaw, seemed to have been devised by a zealous craftsman, anxious to create a superior model out of basic peasant clay.

Galina had been several times with Zina to her village, and marvelled that the sophisticated Zina, now an accomplished actress with several successes in popular films to her credit, could have emerged from such a background. Zina was a rarity. Like an orchid growing on a dungheap, she had flourished in the most improbable surroundings. Her father had been a mystery, her mother a drunkard and Galina had searched Baba Sofia's face in vain for any sign of her granddaughter's beauty. Roughened and weathered as the saddle of a packhorse, as wise as her namesake goddess, Sofia's face only bore witness to a lifetime's survival in rural Russia, the outward testimony to nameless suffering and stoic endurance.

'*Da, da*, her mother was a beauty too, a *krasavitsa* like you've never seen!' Sofia had told Galina. Valentina had been as talented, as mercurial of temperament as Zina, but for her there had been no escape. The stifling brutality of peasant life had overwhelmed her. First there had been a disastrous marriage, then a growing instability which led her through drink, men and moral dissolution to the oblivion of suicide.

'For heaven's sake, don't tell me this is the type of gear you're wearing now!' Zina's face, freshly washed and gleaming, emerged pink and indignant through the neck of the nightdress. Suddenly she looked fourteen again and they were in Vishnev; it was summertime, the elderberry branch to ward off mosquitoes was swaying in the window and Zina was sharing her bed and her heart. The transition from childhood to womanhood was shifting in their veins; the world was theirs and the future glorious.

Catching the nostalgic look on Galina's face, Zina catapulted into her arms and hugged her close, trying to insinuate herself back again in her affections.

312

'Galya, Galya, don't be cross with me – I need you to be kind. I've got . . . I've got . . . hell!' Her little face crumpled. 'Let's have tea. I've got a sod of a headache.'

Galina sighed and stroked Zina's hair. Nothing ever changed – Zina could always manipulate her, even her own two sisters had never occupied that special place in Galya's heart. It had been that way from the very beginning at school, when the Sigorin family had moved to Vishnev when Galina was twelve. Zina had been from the poorest of villages twenty miles out – it could have been two thousand for all its remote inaccessibility. The earth was moved to send Zina to school. Rumour had it there was someone powerful involved – her father, the gossips said, after her mother had killed herself. Zina was fostered in the town by a kind, simple family who found it difficult to deal with her capricious moods and undeniable talent. For Zina acting came as naturally as breathing, her whole life was a drama that was not worth living without a wide-eyed audience.

When she had gone with Galina to study in Leningrad they had clung together, provincials in the bewildering city. In the holidays she had stayed in their home, attaching herself to Mrs Sigorin like another daughter, craving love, approbation, the family she had never had. But the focus and epicentre of her life had always been Grandmother Sofia, who had cared for her from birth after her indifferent mother Valentina had set off to town to earn money for drink.

'Well then, Zina, we'll leave for Sofia's first thing in the morning. Sleep now . . . there's nothing to be done tonight.' Galina pursed her lips and thought furiously as she served hot, sweet tea in tall glasses.

'Let's see . . .' Her mind ran ahead. 'Arkady's going to let us have his car and a driver . . . we'll have to spend the night in Vorolivo. The boys can stay over with Babushka Leila. Irina L'vova can cope with Monday – it's a quiet day at the museum – and she's had a lot of time

313

off lately anyway. Oh God! What about the *Amerikantsa*? Arkady's leaving her with me.'

Zina gave a knowing smile.

'Tired of her already is he? She'll find out soon enough. Looks at him with those great melting eyes . . . naive little fool!'

Galina busied herself making up a divan.

'Don't say that – she's no fool. Besides, strictly speaking, she's not an *Amerikantsa*, she's one of us.'

Zina clicked her teeth in scorn, picked up a cushion and threw it affectionately at Galina.

'How can she be one of us – real Russian blood – until some of Vorovilo's rubbed off on her. She'd have to get some of Semyon's potato vodka down her, Marfa's peelings' stew, the sunflower-seed bread . . . Oh, Galya!' Zina clasped Galina round the waist as she leaned over the divan and nuzzled her cheek somewhere between her shoulder blades. 'How I miss those days together in Vishnev, life seemed so simple, so happy and uncomplicated . . . before Kolya and me . . . before I messed it all up.' She collapsed abruptly on the divan and her face crumpled, as white as the sheet she sat on.

'Zina, what's up!' Galya looked at her in alarm.

'I'm not pregnant – any more – with Ulyanov's bastard, if that's what you're thinking. I came out of the clinic last week, except this time I'm done for, fucked myself up completely, bled like a pig for days. No more babies, they said, aren't I lucky, even if I wanted the buggers!'

'Oh, Zina!' Galina held out her arms and Zina snuffled into the warmth of her shoulder. 'That can't be true! But it's far too many . . .' She stroked Zina's hair and tried to reckon up. As far as she knew Zina had had half a dozen abortions, and the real number was probably nearer ten. Although this was by no means uncommon, with no other form of birth control available, women generally resorted to it only when they had had their families. Zina, she knew, in her heart desperately wanted a child.

Her marriage to the respected actor Kolya Konstantin

314

had been a splendid union. They had seemed idyllically happy, made an Oscar-winning film together, travelled frequently to the West and became the darlings of an adoring public. But Zina's senseless infidelities had broken up the partnership. Why? Galina sighed and held her close. She would do anything to stop Zina destroying herself as her mother had done. But Zina seemed to need men for the power she exercised over them; there was undeniable malice in her love of conquest. Perhaps she really hated men for her mother's betrayal at the hands of her irresponsible father – or worse. There was a seed of revenge, a hurt, angry child deep inside Zina that Galina had never been able to understand.

'Look here, Zinochka! You've got to start acting more responsibly, men certainly won't, that's for sure. Take control of your life, you've got everything to live for. Have a child by a man you can respect, or you can adopt one – you'll bring it up alone anyway. Forget about Kolya, be positive about the future. Perhaps you'll get back together, who knows? You won't if you ruin your health and career on these sordid affairs. Why aren't you working now, anyway?'

'Who wants to go on Gastroly? I turned it down because I wanted to be here with Ulyanov. I said I was overworked and emotionally exhausted. What does it matter, I'm paid like all the rest whether I work or not. They've been cashing in on me for years, while those other lazy cows sit on their fat arses. I'm so thin, look at me, my bones are showing!' She held out enviably slim wrists and Galina smiled acerbically.

'You've always been slim, there's no difference. Too much fucking and not enough home cooking.'

'How coarse you are, my dear, it always sounds better coming from me. What about fucking, anyway? Don't tell me since the divorce you've been a vestal virgin . . . though I don't know . . .' She glanced down scornfully at the nightdress. 'You're not still holding a torch for that bastard Sigorin, that's for sure. It's not good for you,

315

you'll get plain. Go out and find a lusty hussar, one with a big . . .'

'Shut up, will you!' Galina pushed her away and stood up abruptly. 'You're obviously completely recovered and in fighting form. What do you know of real feelings, anyway?' She moved away, ashamed but unrepentant. Zina knew she had shut Arkady out of her life long ago. More she would not reveal to her. But ingenuous Zina wore her heart on her sleeve for all the world to see and ached for Kolya with feelings as deep and genuine as Galina's own.

'I've just thought! Why don't we take the *Amerikantsa* with us?' Galina whirled round. The idea sprang instinctively from her feeling of pique. 'You say she needs Russianizing – well, let's give it to her.'

'Yeah – Russianizing, rustication – what's the difference? What about the guards, though? They'll be hanging about at the limit . . . I know, she can lie down on the floor, we'll cover her up with a blanket. I'll chat up the guy and get out a bottle. No problem!'

'Right!' Galina's eyes were sparkling with a combination of righteous zeal and frustration. 'Arkady only wanted her to see the good things – never straying from Nevsky Prospekt, shopping in Eliseyev's, the token visit to my apartment. What can she know of how we live, it's not right, she'll go home with completely the wrong impression.'

'Oh sure!' Zina's shrewd eyes were mocking. 'See yourself as a crusader, huh? Righting a few international wrongs. Well, for whatever reason, it'll be fun, cheer us up on our doleful mission.'

Zina wriggled under the chaste white sheet and went off into a long reverie while Galina telephoned first to Leila and spoke to the boys, then to her deputy at the museum.

'I've been thinking,' Zina confided, when Galina finally returned from the bathroom, wearing a pink striped nightdress to her knees with her hair tied back in a pink ribbon

'If La Brilliant needs to see how the other half lives we'll take her first to my flat, stiffen her up a bit, what . . .'

'Oh God, no! You're not still into that litigation?' Galina insinuated a foot between the cool sheets of the opposite divan.

'Galya!' Zina's wail was heartfelt. 'Don't get in over there, you know I can't ever sleep alone.'

'God help me! You're worse than Alyosha. Move over, then.'

Zina's arm and a leg in their scratchy folds of nightgown twined around Galina for reassurance.

'Well . . . it's like this, Eugenia Timofevna's had the people round from the mental hospital now, but she still refuses to budge . . .' Long before Zina had finished intoning the latest instalment in the saga of her communal apartment, they were both asleep.

Next morning Arkady called at Galina's apartment around nine. In all fairness he wasn't relishing it; he would simply have preferred to telephone, explain away these crucial meetings with the Minister and disappear for two days. But Galya had problems, she had looked exhausted last night – not surprising with that tiresome little bitch Zina – and the least he could do was to fix her up with a car and see that Brilliant was taken care of.

Zina opened the door in Galina's towelling robe, her hair still wet from the shower, a half-eaten apple in her hand.

'Come in, Tartar *moy* . . .' She waved him in. 'You've timed it right, into the kitchen, the tea's just made.'

He followed her into the kitchen, looking warily from left to right in the small living room. The divans were made up, everything was neat and orderly.

'Galya's gone for bread and milk. Just. You must have missed her on the stairs. The *gastronom*'s shut on Sundays, she's gone down to the *boulochnaya* on Pimen Ulitsa.' She darted a sideways glance through her lashes as she poured out two glasses of tea.

'Here, sugar or jam, help yourself. Your Brilliantka

phoned, she'll be here in about fifteen minutes. She was so thri . . . i . . . lled with our invitation to the country – said she'd just lo . . . oo . . . ve to come!'

'Oh . . . good.' Arkady looked surprised and embarrassed. 'Do you think it'll be all right, I mean, you might have trouble getting there. And then, it's a bit, well . . . different, isn't it?' he finished lamely.

'Well, you don't know, you've never been there for a start. Different – for her – it will be. But we don't think that'll be a problem, Galya and me!' She smiled at him brightly.

'The weather's good for it, there'll be no mud.' Nevertheless Arkady stared apprehensively at the patch of blue sky visible from the kitchen window.

'No, just ruddy great potholes. More tea?' Zina perched half her backside on the table and swung her bare leg nonchalantly. She stared at Arkady oddly. The damp towelling robe opened on a lightly speckled thigh tapering exquisitely into the crafted knee, Zina's firm pale flesh giving out a wholesome odour of milk and country things. So good to touch. Zina's head was tilted back, her green eyes slits of mockery, the ends of her curls still wet. He had to have her. She bit off a piece of apple and held it between her teeth, offering it to him. He took it, spat it away, then kissed her mouth hard and hungrily.

'Ah, Zina, it's been a long time . . .' He put his hand inside her robe, touching those immature adolescent breasts; his mouth closed on the delicate pale mauve nipples. With Zina there were no complications, no guilt, no sentiment. She knew how a man could feel on the spur of the moment, she did it for the fun, for the devilment of it. All the same, as he lifted his head, his eyes glazed with desire, he was wary of her. She was spiteful and gave him the uneasy feeling she was judging his performance, something a man found disconcerting.

Zina wanted to watch him, to see his eyes, so she held his head fast between her hands, to see that look, her legs spread wide.

318

'You little bitch, you whore, you trollop . . .'

'Go on, tell me more, you want me, you can't stop yourself . . .'

There was nothing but the flesh of her, no panties to push aside, just the sweet smell of healthy woman on heat that came from her; he groaned, so easy to transgress, to take her, to enter . . . She moaned but still she held his face in her hands, watching him, mocking him. He was all men, vengeance was hers for Kolya who didn't want her, for him who had first destroyed her trust, for all the others who had made her suffer. Arkady wanted her and she would have him. As a lover he was a *chudesny*, a difficult blend that, both sensitive and unrestrained. She almost felt a twinge of compassion as his lips, racked with the convulsions of his orgasm, whispered wild words of love, primitive and abandoned, from somewhere deep within his consciousness. His head, then, was bowed on her shoulder and he felt no comfort, only the desolation that follows loveless copulation.

A taxi drew up outside and she heard Brilliant's brisk tones to the driver, the slamming of doors. She savoured the triumph of having made Arkady hers, until the last possible moment, as he lay crushed against her breast. When she heard the clatter of feet on the wooden stairs she pushed him roughly away and made for the bathroom.

'I'll leave you to be entertaining.' Her face was a mask of derision. 'I'm not feeling so well after last night, of course.' She shut the door firmly on his ashen supplication.

Brilliant was shown in by a whey-faced Arkady and was surprised to find the apartment empty. She looked concerned and assumed his peaky appearance to be indicative of a night of anxiety on the women's behalf.

'Where's everybody?' she asked straight away. Arkady jerked his head wordlessly towards the bathroom, from whence came the sound of water gurgling down the plughole.

'Zina's reviving, she'll be out in a minute.'

319

'Oh, poor thing. How is she? I expect she's feeling ghastly this morning.'

'I couldn't vouch for that. Knowing Zina, I think you'll find she bounces back pretty quickly.'

Arkady gravitated towards the kitchen and put on the kettle.

'Coffee? Tea? I don't feel so marvellous myself.' He studiously avoided those eyes and instinctively calculated that sympathy would get him a long way.

'Galya's gone for bread and milk. She's been a long time.' He looked accusingly at his watch. 'I have to leave in ten minutes sharp.'

He hazarded a glance and found Brilliant paler than usual and frowning slightly.

'I'm so sorry about all this farce with Zina – it's not right to burden you with it. Perhaps you ought not to go with them – it's a bit risky – well, only a bit . . . But with Zina you won't come to much harm.'

'Nothing would stop me from going with them – I've quite made up my mind. Arkady, I want to . . .'

They heard the sound of Galina's key in the door and the crackle of brown paper as she balanced the bag of groceries on one knee. The antiquated lock required two hands, one to turn and one to push.

'Sorry, there was one hell of a queue!' she said, out of breath. 'You'd think bread was in short supply, as well as everything else. Hallo, Brilliant – Zina still bathing?' The emptying bath water gave a final triumphant bass gurgle and stopped. 'Clear a space in the kitchen and let's have some breakfast – who knows when we'll eat next.'

'I'm just leaving – don't bother about me.' Arkady picked up the jacket he had thrown on the divan.

Galina set the brown paper carrier down on the kitchen table and retrieved the bitten-off piece of apple from the floor. She moved the half-drunk glasses of tea into the sink and straightened the table back against the wall. She looked up quickly as Arkady made a move towards the door.

320

'No, we won't be bothering about you! This is women's business.'

'Women's business, women's business . . .' Zina drew the bolt of the bathroom door and emerged in the old dress Galina hung in there and used for housework. Its well-worn folds hung on her forlornly; she looked like a child in grown-up's clothing.

'What's all this about women's business, Galya *maya*?'

'Well, then! Get going, Arkady.' Galina's voice was sharp. 'Leave us in peace. I said real women's business, Zina, so what would you know about that?'

23

Arkady's driver eyed the women suspiciously as they packed themselves and assorted knobbly packages into the back of his smart black Chaika. He was not a man to take a bribe – he frowned darkly as he caught some of Zina's chatter – and considered himself a breed apart from the common riff-raff of chauffeurs willing to take on anyone and anything for the odd dollar or packet of Marlboroughs. He preferred to keep his character and his car spotless. He couldn't abide smokers, and the condition of the Russian streets – when it wasn't mud or dust it was filthy snow – ensured his spare time was fully occupied with a bucket and a fine Kazak goat-skin leather.

'*Chort*! Has Arkady gone out of his mind, sending us him?' Zina had twitched aside the kitchen curtain before their departure and glared down at the little man polishing the car windows at the kerbside.

'What's the matter with him?' Galina had nudged her aside and smiled as she made out the miniature form of the industrious driver.

'Is he some kind of midget? We don't need anything like that or we'll never make it. Vorovilo's no picnic you know, besides, we've got enough of that kind there already.' Zina frowned angrily.

'Whatever's the problem?' Galina eyed her agitation curiously. 'I'm sure you would have preferred Superman, but Ivan Ilich is a tough little guy, he used to be an acrobat in a circus, Arkady says. He assures me he's the best chauffeur the Ministry's ever had – honest, abstemious, doesn't go with women . . .'

'Sure, sure! Just the qualities we need today. Anyway, it's not that, I just can't abide . . .' Zina shuddered and wriggled her shoulders. 'You know, that kind of person . . .'

Galina smiled and pursed her lips. She knew Zina had an aversion to anyone in the slightest way physically abnormal; she made it abundantly clear that even the thinnest milk of human kindness had long ago curdled in her veins.

'The car looks very smart – I'm impressed.' Brilliant was vaguely puzzled by their exchanges and had descended the staircase ahead of them, anxious to start the journey.

The women looked respectable enough. Ivan Ilich surveyed them covertly in his driving mirror. He normally couldn't abide the company of flighty females and only the prospect of promotion within the Ministry, or to be precise the imminent delivery of a new Zil limousine promised by Arkady Ilich, had made him take on the job. It was a mission of mercy, a dying grandmother Arkady Ilich had said. But the women didn't seem too dismal. That was the problem with modern females – they'd lost their modesty and their sense of duty.

'I'm not going back to Vorolivo dressed like this. They'll really think I've fallen on hard times.' Zina was still wearing Galina's worn-out wrapper.

'Could you drive to Ulitsa Lunenko – out by the Dvortsy Garden. I'll change quickly, I promise I won't hold you up.' Zina gave the driver a winning smile. Ivan Ilich's eyelids flickered acknowledgement and his leather-gloved hand on the right-hand indicator was the only sign that he had received her communication.

Zina raised her eyebrows expressively at Galina.

'You'd better both come with me. I've a few bits for Granny for you to carry out.'

The car stopped outside a low-built apartment complex on the outskirts, surrounded by lime trees and with a pleasant small garden in the centre. Some elderly women sat gossiping on the benches alongside swaddled infants in prams and toddlers in leggings and sweaters, though the day was warm.

'This way to my penthouse,' Zina called over her shoulder. 'It's not worth taking the lift, as it's so sordid. It's only seven flights up – my equivalent of your American ladies' work-out at the gym.

'Ghastly, isn't it?' she commented as she leapt lithely ahead of them, voicing Brilliant's impression of the filthy chipped tiles on the staircase. 'No one bothers, they throw all their old rubbish out, usually on the neighbour's door-step. None of your social conscience here.'

The staircase was slightly cleaner as the air became purer. Eventually, puffing from her rapid ascent, Zina threw open a grimy green door and they were met by an indescribably foul smell of cat. Gasping, they pressed their hands to their noses and bolted like hares down a short hallway and through a red door which Zina slammed behind them.

Appalled, Brilliant sat down on Zina's divan and took stock. The large space was filled with rickety old furniture that looked as though it had come straight from an inferior stage set. Boxes of books, clothes and oddments sat about half-packed or unpacked and contributed to the room's disturbing atmosphere of impermanence. The walls were covered with posters, photographs and mementoes of Zina the actress, her life and career. These alone gave the apartment interest and lifted it from the ordinary.

'Zinotchka! You've got to get that awful old woman and her cats out of here!' Galina exploded as soon as she could draw breath.

'There's nothing I can do – we're waiting for a court order. She's mad, you see.' Zina turned to Brilliant with a shrug of explanation. 'Eighty years old and a raving nut case, with fourteen cats who never go out. We're supposed to share this flat, but I never go near the kitchen, the bathroom's bad enough. They've found a lovely place for her in an old-folks' home, but she won't budge. I've tried everything, bribes, the lot, but she's past reasoning with.

When she's gone the place will be mine, I can do it up. It'll be a regular little paradise!'

Zina pranced around whisking clothes out of cupboards. She wriggled herself into a full-skirted red dress, clamped a stiff belt round her minuscule waist, then ferreted in a drawer full of astonishing clutter for lipstick, eyeshadow and mascara.

Seeing the look of restrained distaste on Brilliant's face as soon as Zina's back was turned, Galina explained quietly.

'Getting an apartment here is difficult, you see – well, almost impossible. When Zina was with Kolya they had a four-roomed flat near the Maly. But she moved out and then, of course, a woman's problems start. Money or prestige don't help either, everybody's in the same boat. Besides, she's a *limitchik*, only a Leningradka through marriage . . . It's a great problem . . .' Galina shook her head in sympathy, she had been through it all herself.

'But it's not healthy, you can't go on living here. You should get the authorities in!'

'Authorities, authorities . . . I had a young bloke round here from the Environment the other day. He told me afterwards that I was better off than he was, he shared a much smaller room with two con-men, what was I complaining about? Besides, I'm not here a lot . . . it's just a base. Come on, let's go! Grab these, they're my *"Vorolivo"* bags, all the old rubbish I collect on my travels that nobody wants.'

She thrust a motley collection of bulging plastic bags in their arms and hustled them out. 'Just our luck to have masochistic Tom Thumb with us, never had a woman by the look of him . . .' she muttered balefully. 'Quick – make a dash for it . . .' At the bottom of the stairs Brilliant's face turned a sickly green and she leaned unsteadily against the entrance, gulping fresh air.

'Quick! Over there among the trees if you want to throw up, it happens to all my guests. I lay bets on the ones with the strong stomachs. Now for the delicatessen. Give these bags to Superman, Galya.'

Like most apartment complexes, this one had shops and services incorporated on the ground floor of the block.

'We'll take fancy bread and buns, meat if there is any – and sugar, of course. We'll work together, Galya, or it'll take all day.'

Brilliant followed them inside the grocery shop, which had the drab, unprepossessing exterior of all Russian shops.

'Decisions, decisions, what shall we eat today?' Zina smirked at Brilliant. 'Luckily we're spared the choice and so the *angst* of American shoppers. I just stood and cried my eyes out first time in the supermarket in Los Angeles and walked out without buying anything. How do you know where to start?'

They were in luck, there was sugar and flour, but no soap or soap-powder.

'I've used my coupons anyway, no point stopping anywhere else, and you?' Galina shook her head. 'We've ration books for soap, sugar too sometimes,' she told Brilliant.

Zina seemed cock-a-hoop with her purchases.

'They'll go mad over this fat meat in the village, all we want now is the booze. Ivan Ilich, my good man, could you stop in the *Beriozkha* in Merlaya Ulitsa and I'll fish my dollars out.'

Ivan Ilich inclined his head and intoned, 'Yes – straight away, ma'am!' Things were looking up. She had correctly divined that he would appreciate the antiquated form of address to a valued servant, and now that he had recognized her in full fig, they should get a mite more attention.

The last of the bottles and packages stowed away in the bulging boot, the Chaika sped out through the southern suburbs on the Novgorod road.

Zina settled back against the impeccable upholstery and got out her scarlet nail varnish.

'We'll stop in an hour or so and break out the sausage and buns, I'm famished with all the exercise.'

'*Devushka! Devushka!* Nail varnish is forbidden. Think of the upholstery!' Ivan Ilich's affronted wail broke his monosyllabic silence.

Zina scowled. 'D'you think I'm not used to this? I only ever do it in cars. Finished now. If you think you won't get lost, my good man, I'll doze a bit. It's straight as a die to Vishnev, but wake me up at Kirilov, before the limit.' She rolled up a cardigan and wedged it between her head and the window, closed her eyes and appeared to sleep.

The suburbs ended abruptly and they bowled smoothly along a straight road through serried ranks of silver birch. After about an hour the forest opened on to a broader landscape, dotted with dwellings, and a short while later they approached the outskirts of a small town.

'Kirilov!' Galina exclaimed and nudged Zina, sitting next to her, several times before she woke up.

'Good, good! Here already.' Zina yawned and stretched, her cheeks pink and refreshed.

'Now, Brilliantka, this is where you do your disappearing trick. Get down on the floor like a good girl. We'll cover you up with this blanket.'

'What – hasn't she got a pass?' Ivan Ilich's face and neck swelled up above his collar, like an angry toad's.

'*Nyety* – and she ain't even Russian – a furriner, not one of us.' Zina lapsed scornfully into the accent of her native village.

Brilliant slid down on to the floor obediently and Zina tucked a scruffy blanket around her.

'We'll probably be all right, it doesn't look like there's anyone about, but just in case.' Galina peered to left and right at the town's crossroads. 'I'll dazzle them first with who you are, and if that doesn't work we'll get out a bottle and a lump of meat.'

The back of Ivan Ilich's neck was rigid with apoplectic disapproval.

'Look out, guys, here they come!' Zina eyes gleamed.

Two military policemen stepped out from a covered porch and flagged the car down.

'*Dobry dyen*!' The older, well-built one tipped his cap and signalled the driver to lower his window. Zina peered out of her side with a plaintive smile.

'Papers please, ladies! Chauffeur! Where are we off to today?'

Zina closed her eyes melodramatically and Galina clasped her hand.

'This is a sad day for us, officer. Zinaida Azerova is going to visit her dying grandmother in Vorolivo. We may not arrive in time.'

'Hmmm . . . Ministry car?' The policemen seemed more interested in the Chaika's number-plates, to Ivan Ilich's intense gratification, while the younger fresh-faced officer stared goggle-eyed through the window at Zina.

'Cigarette?' The older man was ready for a chat. 'Nice interior, too, don't get many swanky cars out this way.'

'Let's get out and stretch our legs.' Zina thrust out a shapely leg in scarlet high heels, stood up and smoothed down her swaying red skirts. She accepted a cigarette and looked at the man through lowered lashes as he fumbled for his matches.

The little knot of onlookers had now swelled to a small crowd.

'A teeny bite of sausage and some beer wouldn't half go down well, eh, lads?' Zina exaggerated the local accent and made them all laugh. In a very short space of time they had proceeded through reminiscences and anecdote to toasts and autographs all round. Gnarled hands pressed seedy cake and pickles on them for granny, a posy was presented from a shy schoolgirl and the interlude ended with warm wishes and Godspeed for the local girl made good, her heart still in the right place despite the corrupting influence of the big city.

The Chaika set off again amid a cloud of dust and farewells worthy of a royal progress.

'You can come out now, *dorogaya*!' Brilliant emerged pale and perspiring from the lower depths, while Ivan Ilich muttered curses under his breath and vowed never again to stray from official duties.

'Once past that point we won't be stopped again.' Galina held out a hairbrush and helped Brilliant pick the pieces of dust and lint from her dress.

'That was mighty entertaining!' Zina grinned broadly. 'Pity we're in such a hurry, it was just building up into quite a party. I rather fancied that young one, looked as if he could give good value . . . No, no, Ivan Ilich, turn left! Left here! We don't need to go through Vishnev. We skirt round it to the east, there's about twenty kilometres to go.' She smiled sweetly at Brilliant.

'Vorolivo will be looking its best now, absolutely stunning, a picturesque litter of melon rinds and chewed sunflower seeds in the main street. You've done your homework, of course?' She raised inquiring eyebrows. 'Anyone who has ever read Gogol has Vorolivo down to a tee. Nothing's changed – except for the worse, of course.' She lapsed into a glum silence.

The road, which as far as Vishnev had been in a reasonable state of repair, completely deteriorated after another few kilometres and became a dirt track. Zina glanced despairingly at Galina as the Chaika pitched alarmingly and Ivan Ilich's mutterings became curses of perspiring disbelief. The dry season had set in and the yawning potholes became more prolific as they entered a belt of ripening rye. Suddenly the Chaika came to a shuddering halt.

'That's it!' Ivan Ilich's face was like thunder. 'There's no way we can get round that!'

They all leapt out and stared at the enormous pothole that stretched from side to side like the Grand Canyon.

Ivan Ilich shoved his cap to the back of his head.

'It'll break the undercarriage . . . ruin the suspension . . . blow the gaskets . . .' He intoned a list

329

of threatened parts they did not know existed. 'There's nothing for it, we'll have to go back.'

'Go back, after coming all this way? Not on my life!' Zina's eyes spat venom.

'Can't we drive round it through the field of rye?'

'What, and scratch all my body-work?'

'Damn your fucking body-work! Here, take whatever dollars I've got, that'll pay for repairs.'

The agile driver faced Zina defiantly from the other side of the divide, where he had leapt for a closer inspection.

'No, I won't do it!'

Zina's eyes narrowed to slits of menace.

'I've got a knife in my bag and I swear on my granny's life, you'll do it!' Quick as a flash she extracted an evil-looking weapon and held it purposefully at the ready.

Ivan Ilich smiled in spite of himself and looked at Zina with new approval. She reminded him of the mettlesome girl who used to be the other half of the knifethrowers act. He'd really admired her, even once thought of proposing. He began to measure the pothole with a neat little device he kept in the glove compartment.

'It's too deep for the undercarriage, but we can skirt it with one wheel if we keep all the weight on that side – get over there and flatten down some of that rye. We'll give it a try!'

They all held their breath while Ivan Ilich prepared himself. He managed a taut smile. He was actually almost enjoying himself, it reminded him of the old days. With the natural aptitude of the circus stuntman and a certain love of the spectacular, Ivan Ilich managed to manoeuvre the Chaika round the crevice. The women cheered and Zina wept openly.

The next pothole was even more prodigious and Ivan Ilich's predictions with the tape-measure became ever more ominous. Finally, with dust-streaked faces and aching in every bone, they arrived in Vorolivo just as a scarlet sun was setting.

Zina threw Brilliant a triumphant smile. 'Just as I said, plenty of local colour!'

Dogs barked at the wheels as the ghostly Chaika, shrouded in chalky dust, lurched drunkenly down a wide street of beaten earth. On each side the dilapidated wooden houses were just visible under a tangle of undergrowth as they sank further and further into the roadway with each autumn's rains. It was a familiar sight all right, if not from photographs of rural life, then from the pages of Tolstoy and Solzhenitsyn. Rubbish lay piled up in doorways, disputed over by dogs or the occasional pig, and in the roadway discarded corn husks sprayed up under their tyres with the crackle of machine-gun ammunition.

'Look! That's Vorolivo's pride and joy, our one remaining fretwork treasure.' Zina pointed out a fairytale house, its paintwork faded to subtle gradations of red and blue, the delicate carved detail on roof and porch like the gingerbread decorations Brilliant remembered her mother making at Christmas time.

'They don't build in wood any more, it's all breezeblocks and cement. There's a new concrete village on the outskirts, everyone wants to live there, they've got kitchens and proper bathrooms. No one cares about preserving the old, they'd pull the lot down if they could.'

'There it is! Over there, over there! You can park outside, Ivan Ilich.'

They drew up outside a cottage with a veranda all round and a collapsed roof, looking like a pie that had sunk in the middle. Vegetation fought for dominance and the house seemed to have succumbed, meekly giving up the struggle. The earth was reclaiming its own.

Zina went in alone, into the cool penumbra. The smell of dying, sweet and lingering, filled the room. A pristine sheet was stretched taut to a wasted face, a drift of white hair floated on the pillow like spun sugar. Feeble fingers stirred on the coverlet. There was an icon, a lamp, a little posy of wild flowers. As Zina looked over her shoulder she could see them framed in the glowing doorway, Galina

331

and Brilliant, and behind them the village children and then their elders, their anguished faces like a painting from Hades.

'Get the hell out of here! All of you! Leave me alone!'

Zina turned back to the shrunken figure of the woman she had known in her childhood as lusty and strong, vigorous and capable. Paralysing fear struck her heart. The one immutable thing in her life was being taken away. She took the skeletal paw and stroked it, crooning nonsense, inconsequentialities, words of love she remembered from the past, when their roles had been reversed. The rock in all her shiftless life was crumbling. What was to become of her after Sofia had gone?

She sat with her head bowed over Sofia's hand.

'I can die in peace now you are with me, Zinotchka,' the old voice whispered. 'To love is the greatest blessing. I have never been alone.'

Zina's heart froze in despair. She was alone because she had turned her back on love – out of fear, out of anger, out of much, much more . . . Desperately she began to articulate a confession – was it to Sofia, to her Creator, to her own tormented soul . . . she could not tell. It was as though her own span were running out and she lay there in Sofia's place. Was there still time for her to find a state of grace?

In the room next door, with its ceramic stove and few pieces of wooden furniture, a noisy party was getting under way. Galina set down the parcels in the lean-to extension that served as a kitchen, found plates, cups and bowls and covered the table with an embroidered cloth.

'Here, Brilliant,' Galina muttered in low tones, 'open the whisky, they just die for it. We'll have a visit soon from old Matvei, he's the village elder, I hear he's still alive. Then the other folk arrive in order of importance . . . the kids'll hang about outside.'

Brilliant soon came to understand the importance of stocking up at the *gastronom*. A steady stream of visitors, some carrying their own chairs, shuffled through the door way and sat stolidly round the walls of the small room. All brought a bottle or an offering of food: roast potatoes on a griddle, buck-wheat cakes, honey, radishes, curd cheese and – because it was summer – wild berries from orchards and hedgerows. The long table soon began to look like a harvest festival.

'*Strastvuitye!* Matvei Ignatiev!' Galina inclined her head respectfully and hurried to greet the venerable elder, with a white beard nearly down to his waist, who came supported by two equally ancient henchmen.

'Matvei Ignatiev is . . . how old are you now, Grandfather?' Matvei clasped Brilliant's hand firmly. A fervent light still gleamed in his faded blue eyes.

'Ninety-five, *da, da*, God be praised! I used to sit on the village *Mir* – those were our days of real democracy. We administered our own justice, punished our own kind. Bless you, bless you, my child, a glass of whisky, with respect.'

Women came in, ample mothers, wearing their best floral dresses and with hair neatly combed. They embraced Galina warmly, apologized for the meagreness of their offerings and were cordially invited to stay.

Annoyed at the voices and the laughter in the next room, Zina brought her face closer so she could catch Sofia's halting words. Through the frail fingers clutching hers, helpless as those of a child, the inexplicable happened. The cynical Zina was struck with all the force of a religious experience and the despair in her heart began to evaporate. She had to forgive, to accept, those were the words Sofia was whispering to her. In coming to terms with her lost security, Zina was discovering her own capacity to love. 'Love, love . . . As I have loved you, Zinotchka . . .' Sofia's voice was barely audible. 'Love is the only salvation.'

Zina frowned as the noise grew in the next room, and shouted for them to be quiet.

'No, no! They have come to see you and not to mourn for me.' Sofia's bloodless lips gave the ghost of a smile.

'Go and see them now and come back . . . Don't mind me for a while.'

Zina bent and kissed Sofia's papery cheek and promised to be back very soon. She straightened her shoulders, shook back her hair and made an impressive entrance – Zina would always be Zina – to be exclaimed over, clasped to adoring bosoms, twirled and strutted for their approval and exultation.

'Sonya, Efimova, Eugenia . . .' The smiling, stout women who were Zina's peers came up and were hugged and kissed.

'Now – where's Taneshka? No, no . . . no! Not Taneshka!' Zina wailed and the colour drained from her face. The women looked at each other guiltily and glumly shook their heads.

'She fell down last winter, hit her head on a lead pump . . . she'd bled too much by the time they got her to hospital . . . which wasn't till next day because of the roads.'

Zina collapsed on to a stool, buried her head in her hands and howled for Taneshka. Sofia, with the acute sensory perception of the terminally ill, heard her and muttered a silent prayer. Taneshka and Zina had been inseparable as children, extraordinarily alike, some whispered that they had a common father. Lovely, laughing Tanya had married young and been widowed early with two small boys. Life had been what it always is in the country and Taneshka had found it hard to want to live. She had married again but unhappily and she had started drinking. There had been a small daughter from the union.

'Give me a drink someone!' Zina lifted her head and stared at them with sullen eyes. 'Will someone give that dope of a driver something to eat. He's standing guard by the car, those brats are swarming all over it.' She stood up and drained her glass.

'I'm going out to see the kids, let's get some air.' Brilliant and Galina followed her outside where she called ou to all the children in turn, asking them their names, who their parents were. They answered shyly at first, then jumped around her, beside themselves with excitement, the little ones clutching at her skirts. One small girl stood apart and watched her through narrowed green eyes.

'You're Taneshka's, aren't you? Lara? Don't want to hug me, huh?'

The small girl, about seven or eight years old, shook her head and looked away indifferently. Zina laughed. 'Good girl! Bloody-minded, just like your mother.'

Brilliant caught her breath as Lara smiled. With her red curls, white skin and haughty profile she was a small replica of Zina.

Zina laughed when she commented on it, but looked at the child oddly.

'Come on, Brilliantka, I'll take you over to meet Lydia Andrevna, Matvei's wife. She can't walk, so I have to visit. Hang around, kids, see you later!'

Zina set off across the dusty road abruptly, an incongruous figure in her high heels and swinging petticoats.

'What do you think of our new generation, come on now, honestly?' Spots of colour burned high on Zina's cheekbones and her fists were clenched as she led them down a side road towards Matvei's house.

'We..e..ll – dirty and mischievous as most, I suppose . . .' Brilliant dared not look Zina in the eye.

'A bunch of kids in the Western world wouldn't look like that – and I don't mean the dirt and lice. Look at them! Degenerate, deformed limbs or staring vacant eyes, half-wits. Why? Their mothers are drunks, families are intermarrying, half the people here have the same name. The food's lousy and there's not enough of it. Where's our mythical lusty peasant? Gone, just like our spirit!' She turned to Brilliant with savage anger in her eyes. 'Our country folk are left to rot and the nation is degenerating. My village is dying while I stand here!'

Brilliant swallowed, tears pricking the back of her eyes. She thought she had been prepared for Vorolivo. The reality was far worse than anything she could have imagined.

Zina sprinted ahead of them up the steps of the fretwork house, where a lady with faded cheeks like a pressed rose sat in a rocking chair on the porch waiting for them.

'Lydia Andrevna! Thank God you're well!' They embraced fervently and Zina introduced Brilliant.

'Sit down and don't be so angry, my child!' Lydia, in all her wisdom, patted Zina's hand as she drew up a wooden stool.

'What can you do?' Lydia shook her head. 'They have abandoned us. You know, when Matvei was young and in our local council – the Soviet – the Bolsheviks said "All power to the Soviets" and it seemed to us a natural and welcome step.' She sighed. 'We feel we've been betrayed and manipulated. Before, we had enough to eat, now they take it all and we don't even have our own plots any more. But it is summertime and we're living in clover. Here, Praskovia!' She turned to an old woman sitting quietly in the shadows. 'Bring out the *zemlyaniki* and *smetana*.'

As the velvet shadows lengthened the three women sat at Lydia's knee and ate scented wild strawberries and sour cream out of wooden bowls. Lydia rocked to and fro, watching them with silent contentment, her chair giving the occasional hypnotic creak. Fireflies flew in and out of the fretwork, a cricket chirped, a solitary nightingale started singing for all it was worth.

Lydia had been watching Brilliant intently. 'It will soon be the moment, come and sit here, *krasavitsa maya*, on the corner of the step.'

Zina felt her heart contract in nostalgic memory. How many times as a child had she sat on the angle of Lydia's porch and waited to be turned into a fairy princess, spangled from head to toe in silver lace at the precise moment the rising moon shone through the fretwork?

'*Da, vot*, now!' They breathed in unison as the moon emerged from a bank of cloud and flooded full on Brilliant's upturned face.

'A paper-doily princess!' Zina snorted and then stared, startled in spite of herself at the disturbing trick of the moonlight on Brilliant's pale face.

'A real moon-child!' Galina breathed, wishing that the boys could have been there to see it. Brilliant shimmered from head to toe like a mythical creature, her luminous skin was tattooed with silver filigree, her hair seemed to blaze like a crown of burning silver.

'Come here, child, and give me your hand!' Lydia's voice was hypnotic. Brilliant went and sat at her side.

Zina looked embarrassed. 'You see, Lydia Andrevna is what we call a . . . well . . . I suppose what you would call a medium, a fortune-teller. Only to countryfolk it's a very special power and of great significance. Lydia told me everything that was going to happen in my life, every single thing she saw in my hand has come true.'

'And now, Zinotchka, what of the future?' Galina smiled as she saw Zina clasp her hands firmly behind her back.

Zina scowled. 'It's all a lot of rubbish anyway. I'm master of my own fate!' What if it was her fate to be childless? she thought. She had certainly been instigator of that. There were certain things she did not want to know.

'And you, Galya *dorogaya*?' Zina smiled sweetly. 'I remember last time you wouldn't let Lydia have a look at your little paw!'

Galina smiled nervously. 'I'm not as sceptical as you – besides, what if . . . what if . . .' She was unable to put into words her fears for the boys' future.

The old woman paid no attention to their talk but took Brilliant's hand in silence. Lydia's intense liquorice-dark eyes swept over her and through her to all that was hidden and unknown beyond. She gazed for long seconds into Brilliant's hand, then into her face, then back to her hand again.

'*Gospody!* You are troubled by a barrier, an obstacle.

337

No – it is an object, but it is precious, a jewel. A priceless jewel and it is very, very old.'

Brilliant swallowed and squirmed uncomfortably on her stool. She gave Zina a sceptical look which clearly said that such information was not impossible to acquire.

Zina shrugged and said nonchalantly, 'She doesn't know who you are and why should I have told her? It makes no difference to me!'

Lydia continued as though talking to herself.

'It has special powers, this jewel. Its alchemy is part of you, yes, and it has drawn you into an involvement with someone who loves you deeply, very deeply. You don't believe it, but he loves you . . . the jewel is drawing you towards the man who loves you.'

Zina rolled her eyes melodramatically.

'Ah, lo-o-ve! Let's have more of it!'

Brilliant flushed deeply and closed her fingers tightly over her palm, digging her nails painfully into the flesh. Arkady! Perhaps he really did love her, it was just his extraordinary temperament . . .

Galina had crept closer and was watching Brilliant with shining eyes.

'Yes, he does love you! He can't hide it. No matter how hard Carl tries, when he's with you, it shows in his eyes.'

'Carl!' Brilliant swung round as though she had been stung. 'Whatever made you say that?' Her eyes flashed.

'Carl? Why of course. Did you think that . . . that . . .' Galina frowned gently. 'Brilliant, it makes me sad that Carl daren't hope you can love him, because of the White Tsaritsa. But it is your destiny, don't you see? You can't fight it, there are forces in life that we know nothing about, that control our happiness.'

Brilliant felt shaken, angry and puzzled by turns – also vaguely ridiculous, with Zina and Galina looking thoughtfully at her, as though expecting an answer.

She stood up abruptly and thanked Lydia Andrevna, who solemnly blessed them, making the sign of the cross over their heads, and wished them happiness. The trio crossed the road in rather strained silence. As they came near the cottage they were met by the wild strains of a fiddle and the odd plaintive snatch of song. Zina ran up the steps of the veranda in a temper and wanted to chase them all away, cursing the uninvited fiddler.

She went straight into Sofia's room and found her bright-eyed, her lips stretched in a skeletal smile and her wasted fingers twitching on the coverlet.

'*Davai, davai!* Let them be, let them be! I've always liked a bit of merriment.' Zina remembered when she was a child how Sofia had always led the women's dance, twirling and high-stepping, a strapping woman proud to show off her coloured petticoats.

In their absence the women had roasted a huge dish of potatoes in meat fat, with garlic and dill. They had lit the lamps – there was no electricity in the village – and in the mellow light the convivial company demolished the festive board as though food had been newly invented.

Ivan Ilich had made friends with some of the local lads and got them to wash the car for him, in return for rides up and down the street, first making them remove their shoes. Gratified with his minor celebrity, he had gone to lodge with the motor mechanic, who owned the only garage where he could safely stow the car for the night.

Zina did not feel like eating and went outside for a breath of fresh air, leaving Sofia asleep. The night was warm and groups of children were still playing desultorily in the dust. Small Lara played alone, absorbed in her own game, and Zina, unobserved, drew into the shadows to watch her.

Lara minced up and down the road in a straight line on her toes, then whirled round on herself and smoothed down imaginary skirts, lifted her head and arched her long neck. Then she dipped her chin, parted her lips in a contrived smile, a hand smoothed back a curl behind her ear . . . gestures all so obviously Zina's that she laughed out loud. Lara whirled round, her green eyes defensive.

'Come here, you little monkey!' Zina called softly. 'Who's looking after you now?'

'Auntie Ira and Uncle Petya.' Lara's eyes were downcast.

'Are you happy?'

'No!' The eyes flashed up at her. 'I want to go to the city!'

Zina laughed and held out her hand, palm downwards, as one would to a puppy.

Lara sprang forward with one bound, seized her hand and carried it to her cheek. Zina gathered the girl to her skirts and held her fast, inhaling the intoxicating smell of childish flesh. Taneshka's child. God help them both. Perhaps they could make it together?

When she returned Galina was turning out the last of the hardened drinkers and Brilliant was making up beds around the wide stove.

'Shit-house is out the back here, Brilliantka!' Zina called as she paid it a call. 'That big feller who was the last to leave is our local shit-shoveller.'

Sofia was still sleeping, her shallow breath barely disturbing the taut surface of the sheet. Zina fished out a bottle of whisky from under Sofia's mattress.

'You've got to look after your own here. Those bastards drink you dry and then just shove off.' She glared malevolently at the stack of empties in the corner. She poured them all a large glass, tossed her own back in one, crawled between the blankets, propped herself on one elbow and poured herself another.

'I just caught her outside, little Larotchka, prancing around pretending to be me. I think she's got talent, she could go far! What's to become of her, what's to become of all of them? The boys'll go into the army, like all country boys with large families that can't feed them. No wonder the army's worried about its recruits – take a look at them, mentally and physically degenerate. Christ! What'll happen to Larotchka? She'll be screwed by that bastard Uncle Petya, like I was at her age, a smelly cock and breath that stinks of stale booze . . .'

'Zina, what are you saying, your father . . .' Galina's voice shook.

'My father, someone else's father, how do I know who it was, when you're eight and it's dark and you're frightened.'

Brilliant took a large gulp of whisky and concentrated on the patch of silver moonlight playing tricks on the rough daub of the wall. Her heart pounded and her head ached. Sleep seemed an impossibility.

Zina poured them another pulverizing slug of whisky which did the trick. Within minutes they all slept the sleep of exhaustion.

The next morning the children woke them early, tapping on the window, eyes goggling, bringing fresh-baked bread and still-warm milk. With the sunlight in the window, a fresh smell of mown grass in the air, the nightmare qualities of the day before faded into softer focus.

Sofia had slept well. Although she seemed weaker, she was peaceful.

'I don't think she's got much longer, I'll stay here,' Zina told them. 'You go back with Ivan Ilich, where is the obstinate little sod? He can't wait to get his car home for a spit and polish. I'll get back somehow. If you haven't heard from me in a month, send out the search-party.'

24

Ivan Ilich managed to get Galina and Brilliant back to the city in a fraction of the time it took the day before. More knowledgable about the terrain and anxious to get back to work, he took risks with his body-work in the rye fields and teetered daringly around craters. Galina sensed Brilliant's introspective mood and they drove for the most part in silence. At the checkpoint Brilliant only suffered briefly in the heat under her blanket while they were waved indifferently through.

Ivan Ilich dropped Brilliant first at the Astoria and as she kissed Galina goodbye she said, 'Arkady doesn't get back from Moscow until tomorrow morning and I leave on the late flight. Shall I see you and the boys after school?'

'Of course! It's the Detsky Sad on Naberezhnaya – I'll write it down for you. At six – that's not too late?'

Galina fumbled for a pencil and scribbled hastily, anxious to avoid Brilliant's eyes. She's distraught . . . well – that's not surprising, given the experiences of the last twenty-four hours. She felt exhausted herself, but she had to go straight to the museum to see how Irina L'vova was coping, then sort out the boys. Better not to think too much, just concentrate on work, responsibility, the blessed panacea.

Brilliant ate early in the *fin de siècle* hotel restaurant, avoiding the inquiring eyes of the solitary businessmen. Surrounded by tourist groups and noisy parties she was that Russian rarity, a woman dining alone. The legions of lovely young women obviously touting for trade got no further than the lobby on the ground floor. Wrapped up in her own complex thoughts she was unaware of being a fantasy object for more than one lonely diner.

The next morning she packed early and arranged to

have her carry-all sent to the airport. She left the hotel almost stealthily, although she knew that Arkady's flight would not arrive until lunchtime. She spent the morning walking alone along the Neva, deep in thought. In the afternoon she sat in the Summer Garden, watching the *babushkas* with their plump toddlers playing under the ancient limes, just as Arkady and Galina had once done.

At six o'clock she waited, as arranged, on a seat under the plane tree outside the Detsky Sad. At ten past six she saw Galina running, chestnut hair flying, hand in hand with Sasha whose oversized satchel thumped up and down on his small back as he ran.

'I'm late – we had a meeting!' Galina was breathless. 'They always run overtime, they're an inescapable feature of Soviet life. A friend usually collects Sasha from school and he waits in my office for an hour until the museum closes.'

Hardly slackening her pace she motioned for Brilliant to follow and dashed through the courtyard into a side door. Galina snatched Alyosha from a knot of small boys tumbling like puppies on the floor and smothered his face in kisses. She had a few quick words with his nursery teacher then, tugged impatiently by the two boys, rejoined Brilliant by the door.

The cheerful room, with its miniature tables and chairs and exuberant examples of the children's handiwork, was like any similar establishment in the West, except for the child-sized versions of the slogans that dominated public places, variations on the communist theme.

'It seems so bizarre to have politics enter their lives so young,' Brilliant commented as they walked back to the bus stop.

Galina shrugged. 'All children here go to nursery school, because proper school doesn't start until they're six years old. To us the propaganda is normal, we don't even think about it. What does worry me is that they're being influenced by other women for such long hours, so very young. Many of the girls who do these nursery jobs

343

aren't well trained. But what can you do, there are no choices.'

'*Mamasha, Mamasha*, can we go to the park?' Sasha tugged her arm.

'Ice cream, ice cream!' Alyosha's big eyes were pleading.

'Please! Alyosha, don't forget to say please. Well, why not, *sokolik moy*?' The little eagle's face beamed with pleasure. Galina looked at Brilliant.

'Have you time? We could walk down to the gardens by the river.'

In the shady garden they sat on a stone bench, watching the children play on the sun-dappled grass, Alyosha's face disappearing under a great smear of ice cream. Galina leaned back, half-closed her eyes and sighed.

'These summer days are perfect, it's hard to shut oneself up all day in a museum. Vorolivo – ghastly as it was – has given me an itch for the country. I might ask for some leave and take off for Babushka Elena's.'

'Do you always go to your mother's for your holidays?' Brilliant was careful not to commit her former *faux pas* about foreign travel.

'No, I've travelled quite widely in the Soviet Union. Most people travel in groups, there are travel quotas from factories and schools, that sort of thing. The big carrot for hard work is a holiday on the Black Sea. If you're sick you get sent to a sanatorium, but it is possible to travel as an individual. There are plenty of people who run their homes as a kind of guest house in the summer. I've been all over Soviet Central Asia and the Caucasus, which is so wild and romantic. Arkady and I . . .' Galina stopped in confusion and the colour rose in her cheeks.

'You and Arkady!' Brilliant turned on the bench to face her, her voice trembling. Galina touched her arm gently, her liquid eyes sincere and troubled.

'I don't love Arkady any more, if that is what you mean . . .' Her voice was low. '. . . and neither does he care for me.'

'Don't, Galya! I know about Arkady . . . about his . . . his feelings.' Brilliant swallowed hard. 'But that doesn't matter. What does matter is that he still loves you.' Her voice sank to a whisper. 'And perhaps you still love him.'

Galina shook her head.

'I can't love Arkady . . . I mustn't . . . can you understand?'

Brilliant nodded slowly. 'Yes. I understand.'

'But the ring, the White Tsaritsa, it means so much to Arkady . . .' There was a sob in Galina's voice.

'And it means a lot to you, I hope?' Brilliant smiled. 'So – we'll meet again in November, Galya, at your Tsarist exhibition, in New York?'

She stood up to go and her shadow fell across Galina's face. In her long ramblings along the Neva she had had time to think, time to realize that if she returned the White Tsaritsa to Russia it was not for Arkady but for Galina and women like her. Gentle, selfless, courageous, the future of their country lay in their hands – and their task was formidable.

'Goodbye, Galya! Thank you for everything. In many ways coming here has changed my life and my thinking. But as for the White Tsaritsa . . . as for that . . .' She bent down and kissed Galina gently on the cheek. 'As for our diamond, nothing will be changed.'

A dull ache seemed to start round her heart then, and she had to get away, straight to the airport, board the plane, think of nothing, only escape. What message could she possibly leave for Arkady? Arkady . . . Tartar *moy*, she thought as she watched the lights of the Gulf of Finland drop away through the aircraft window, is it really possible to fly away and leave your love for ever?

Returning to New York was almost as much a culture shock for Brilliant as arriving in Leningrad had been. What had she said to Galina – 'coming here has changed my life and my thinking'? On the simply material level she would never again take her comfortable life for granted. On the emotional level, seeing Carl again she found herself profoundly disturbed by the fortune-teller's words. How could Galina be so sure that Carl loved her – or perhaps it was just her sentimental wishful-thinking? How could she know her own feelings? After the pain of loving Arkady the confusion she felt when alone with Carl was impossible to rationalize.

It was nearly midnight, and the Adamantina showroom was in darkness, except for the permanent searing spot-light on the great diamond. Brilliant pressed her head against the cool glass of the showcase. Through the misty haze of her breath the White Tsaritsa scattered a thousand incandescent sparks.

She had been back from Leningrad only a few days, but already Arkady had telephoned several times. Aggrieved at her sudden disappearance, he seemed to assume that they had accidentally missed one another. He spoke in carefully guarded language, but was pressing her to finalize arrangements to receive the synthetic diamond in New York.

She was to contact a man called Klimov who was in charge of the American side of the operation. Klimov would receive a package from an official, a large diamond ring concealed among a normal delivery of industrial dia-monds. Fairly standard practice for him – Brilliant had suppressed a chuckle at the spy-thriller hush of Arkady's voice – but that was the extent of Klimov's knowledge. The rest was up to her.

To smuggle the real ring out of the country was a much more risky business. For this the other half of the double act took over. A certain Priatkin would make himself useful in disposing of the package, known to him only as top-secret data for the Soviet government's highest echelons. Brilliant would not need to get involved in any of the importing and exporting manoeuvres. She gave a grim smile as she listened to Arkady's clipped commands on the telephone. Klimov and Priatkin's lives were on the line – they knew what to do should there be any danger of discovery. All this skulduggery was set to take place in the few days before Christmas, which sentimental period appeared to be the most advantageous for the serious smuggler.

Oh prosaic Arkady! Was he the same lover who had seduced her with a thousand caresses, sweet words that tore at her heart and made her ache for his kisses, kisses that stirred in her a longing to be loved. *Nenagladnaya maya, krasavitsa, milaya, lyubovtsa maya!* Those words, that voice, that consuming look. Damn you, Arkady! She let out her breath in a despairing sigh. How I loved you . : . loved you. And believed that you loved me.

A light tap on her shoulder made her jump almost out of her skin.

'I'm so sorry, I didn't mean to give you such a shock.' Carl stood in the shadow outside the beam of light. She could just make out the deep creases of his smile.

'It was either that or ringing the alarm bell, which was my first instinct when I saw someone standing there.' The smile had gone now and his face was stern. 'The job doesn't really warrant this amount of overtime – or does it?'

'I'm sorry, Carl. I was a million miles away. I stayed on after everyone had left and started to sort out the Tel Aviv problem. Then I started to daydream . . . and – well – here I am!' She gave a bright unconvincing smile.

Something has happened, thought Carl, she has been avoiding me since she returned from Leningrad. He had greeted her in his office when she had arrived, scanning her face for anything, a look, a sign, but she seemed indifferent and distracted with the business problems that had just cropped up, which Carl had to admit were not inconsiderable.

One of their couriers had been mugged at Lod Airport and relieved of a packet of diamonds worth two million dollars, an employee had been injured in a brawl in Bombay, and last but not least for Brilliant because of the

347

stir it caused in the trade press, the Comtesse de Tarn Riberac had publicly announced her dissatisfaction with her new Adamantina parure.

Carl had tried to draw her out about the Russian idyll but she had brushed all his questions aside. At the sacred tea hour she had feigned an outside appointment and disappeared. He had been in Washington all day with a client and had called in at the office from the airport for some urgent invoices. When he found her with her head pressed against the glass of the White Tsaritsa he knew that he had to find out more.

'Brilliant, why don't we go through to my office and have a talk?'

She was about to decline, then some sort of resolve seemed to crumble and she nodded. Carl went ahead and opened the door of his panelled room. He lit a small lamp in one corner, sensing a mutual need to veil their emotions in shadow.

Carl strode over to the bar cabinet and took out a bottle.

'I don't know why, but I've an irrepressible urge to drink champagne, simply because things can't get much worse at this moment!'

Brilliant watched in silence as Carl eased off the cork and filled two long-stemmed glasses.

'Well? Come on! Why are you keeping me in suspense? It's not every day a mythical princess goes off on a pilgrimage. Did you find the Holy Grail?'

She took a sip of champagne, savoured it against her palate, swallowed hard and took a deep breath.

'There's nothing to keep from you, Carl. I suppose I was a . . . a little disappointed in some aspects of the journey. Though Russia was no different than I expected.'

So that is it. Carl's hand shook slightly as he refilled her glass. Something devastating has happened and she has no intention of telling me. A surge of disappointment swept over him and with it a sense of helpless frustration. Here was another part of her life she was going to keep private, forever suspicious, forever wary.

Brilliant made an effort to sound off-hand.

'I will sit down and talk about Russia one day, Carl, but somehow this isn't quite the right time for me. There's so much to worry about, so much to do. Would you mind if we leave my trip for the moment?' The innocent rebuke against the invasion of her privacy stung him like a lash. 'I wanted to go to Russia because I had got stale. I had to get away for a while, but it didn't really work out. I still feel restless, but it's just something personal I have to work out.' She smiled. 'Oh, by the way, Galina sends her very best regards – she was so kind to me, and Arkady . . . was, too . . .' There was a tremor in her voice.

Carl drained his glass. So there we have it. The trip was incidental, it is Arkady and – by heaven – she loves him.

'Good!' He turned away before she could see his face. 'Let's get you back to work then. We need you as a sort of ombudswoman to sort out our international problems. Who better? I was only telling Wilkie Abrahams in Washington this morning. So it's off with you to France and Bombay and who knows where . . .' The champagne rang in his ears. If only he could get her away, as far away as possible.

'Let's drink then – to your continued travels!' Carl made a supreme effort to smile and for a second their eyes met with a ghost of their former familiarity.

After booking a flight to Paris next morning Brilliant reflected for some time before composing an enigmatic note to Arkady saying that she would be away for a week or two and would contact him as soon as she returned.

When she walked into Adamantina's velvet-lined Inner Sanctum, an evocative scent hung heavy on the air. A cloying scent of musk, or was it gardenia? Brilliant's nose was almost as sharp as her eye, but she stood still for one moment, completely nonplussed. Whatever it was, it struck an unpleasant chord in her subconscious. Then she remembered. Of course! She clenched her fists. It was still early and only one or two customers sat with heads bent over the black baize tables. Molly Rourke got up from a desk and rolled her eyes in the direction of Carl's office. Walking straight up to the door Brilliant tapped briskly and went in. Yasmina's dark head, bent over her loupe close to Carl, jerked up in surprise.

'Ah, Brilliant!' Carl smiled.

Yasmina frowned. 'I thought we weren't going to be disturbed, Carl!' She spread her hands in a gesture of long-suffering irritation.

'What brings you here, Yasmina, buying or selling? I don't think we've got anything big enough for you at the moment.' I can't think why I didn't realize how much I disliked her, thought Brilliant; she's quite odious, and easy to deal with once you acknowledge that.

'Yasmina has brought a superb set of F1 exceptionals. If we wanted to re-do the Tarn Riberac parure they would be just the ticket. Yasmina heard about the fuss and wanted to help out.'

'There's no way we're doing the Tarn Riberac parure again and when I get face-to-face with dear Adèle in the Dordogne she's going to find out why! We conferred end-lessly – *grand'mère*, cousins twice removed, even the new lover was dragged in. To say that the emerald cut is unsuitable is monstrous, and that they were ill-advised and should have had the traditional rose cut is immoral!'

Brilliant's eyes glittered with righteous anger. 'I have a shrewd idea what's going on and I'm going to get to the bottom of it. The whole business of the theft last year and the insurance claim was "*un peu délicat*". But in the end the insurance company paid out handsomely and Adèle's hung on to the money, it hasn't gone back to the family. Now, it's just possible that her marriage settlement, like mine, wasn't a *séparation des biens* . . .' Seeing Yasmina's cocked eyebrow of interest, she continued quickly, 'and therefore Adèle stands to get very little out of a divorce.

The ordering of a new parure was a ploy to get the insurance company to pay out and give the theft story more conviction.'

'*Mon Dieu!* Are you saying that the Comtesse has hung on to the parure *and* got the money?' Yasmina's eyes widened in admiration. Carl frowned from behind his desk.

'Brilliant, what you are saying is very serious. It would involved a lengthy legal investigation and meanwhile we can't make such an allegation without concrete evidence.'

Brilliant tapped the desk impatiently.

'Really, Carl, I'm not that naive! Especially when it comes to the intricacies of "old" French money, marriage and their legal system. I intend to employ the best lawyers here and in France.' She smiled grimly. 'We can soon turn the tables on Adèle with adverse publicity. Just think of the marvellous *scandale* for the French Sunday papers. Do you seriously think we're going to take the parure back because she's "dissatisfied" with it? Look what it has done to our image in the press.'

'That's nothing, people always read between the lines.' Carl still looked troubled. 'I don't think you should get too personally involved, there could be unpleasant consequences.'

'Thank you, Carl, but I can look after myself. So you see, Yasmina, we shan't be needing your F1 exceptionals just yet. Incidentally . . .' Brilliant leaned over the table, 'the second on the left isn't quite up to scratch. I would definitely downgrade it if I had it at a Sight. A VVS$_2$ I should say . . .'

'Hmmm . . .' Carl examined the stone in question through his loupe under a powerful light. 'Good heavens! I think you're quite right! Very slightly cloudy and a minute flaw.' He looked at Yasmina and grinned, shaking his head. 'You have to hand it to her! You can't beat Brilliant's eye at fifty feet – it's quite remarkable, something like that is very, very rare.'

Yasmina's eyes flashed dangerously. 'I don't know what

you're talking about! The stones have all been certified as F1s from the highest source.'

'But not the DTC,' Carl concluded gently. 'Well, as we don't seem to be requiring them urgently at the moment, perhaps we can let you have an answer in a week or two?'

Yasmina shrugged impatiently. 'Really, Carl, they are as good as sold elsewhere. I merely thought I was doing you a friendly service. It's of no consequence, please, let's say no more about it,' she conceded graciously. 'Now, the other matter I telephoned you about in Washington. Since we did the deal on the Sierra Siren I thought we had come to an understanding?'

To her surprise the normally cool Carl jumped to his feet, eyes snapping.

'I don't know what games you're playing, Yasmina, I must have told you a dozen times that the ring is categorically not for sale!'

Brilliant looked from Carl back to the sardonic Yasmina. A germ of an idea sprouted in her mind and burgeoned uncontrollably into life. She heard herself saying, 'Carl, if Yasmina is talking about the White Tsaritsa, I really don't know why you shouldn't sell it to her. I know you think it means a lot to me, but the trip to Russia has exorcized all that. Perhaps it is time it moved from Adamantina, and if Yasmina can find the price . . . Well, why not?'

She did not know whose open-mouthed astonishment gave her the more pleasure – Carl's or Yasmina's. Yasmina was the first to recover.

'There you are, Carl, at last a sensible woman! I think you would have to be very unreasonable to hold out now I told you all you have to do is name your price – my buyer would pay anything you wanted for it – and then double it. Well, what do you say?' Her face was alight with the triumph that was nearly hers.

Carl looked long and intently at Brilliant, his face inscrutable. At last he turned to Yasmina.

'All right! It's a deal. First I need to confer with m

lawyers, then we can fix our terms. But the contract will go through on one premise only, that whatever money you are prepared to pay, and I warn you the price will be a high one, goes not to Adamantina, but to Madame Brilliant Chardin. My personal shareholding will be put up against it.'

Brilliant sat back in the taxi speeding her through the scintillating Paris night and savoured once again those exquisite moments of yesterday. For the first time in her life she understood the thrilling compulsion of the gambler, the seductive surrender to the lure of danger. The pleasure she had felt in offering Yasmina a worthless piece of chemical – which was all Arkady's replica of the White Tsaritsa would amount to – for untold millions had been sublimely sweet, sweet enough to hang for. It could only be crowned by witnessing the fury on Yasmina's face when she found out she had bought a fake. Very sweet, but deeply troubling.

The negotiations had collapsed in confusion, precisely as Carl had intended. She herself had flatly refused such an offer, Yasmina had protested that it put an entirely different complexion on the matter, Carl insisted that he refused to sell on any other terms.

But why had he said it? Could he possibly have been serious? What if Yasmina had taken him up on it? But of course she wouldn't, and Carl knew he was safe. But perhaps she had been unfair to him all along. Certainly, when Carl's lips had brushed her cheek and he had told her to take special care, that he would miss her, there had been a resignation about his shoulders she had not noticed before, and she wished she had told him everything about the White Tsaritsa and its sentimental origins. Quite suddenly she ached to tell him . . . but now, of course, it was too late.

was the first time she had been back to Paris since her

separation from Jean-Claude, and in order to lay the ghosts of her marriage to rest she succumbed to nostalgia and booked in at the Ritz. As she unpacked her suitcase a moaning wind blew the first dead leaves of autumn against the darkened window and she had to swallow hard and straighten her shoulders against the little shiver of apprehension that threatened her resolve. She snapped on the television and called for room service; distraction, succour, anything to keep out the spectres of the past.

Rather than be alone she accepted an invitation from Sylvette LeMarre to a first night at the Académie, and then on to an hilarious backstage party at La Coupole. The actress regaled her with gossip, and Brilliant, watching Sylvette's little *mondaine* face, preening and pouting to the brasserie's clientele at large, realized there was very little of her life, including the people, that she had missed since she left Paris six months ago.

'. . . Jean-Claude was quite heartbroken,' Sylvette was telling her, 'it suited his style so well, one has to admit. The pallor, the distracted lock on the brow, the negligent sweep of cashmere over the shoulder – he was made to play the lovelorn. But there's a new interest in his life now, of course!' Sylvette's eyes were slits of malice.

'Oh, really?' To her intense relief Brilliant felt not a single stirring of jealousy and hardly any of curiosity.

'Perfume! He's got quite maniacal about launching the House's signature scent, Chardin of course, which is a bit, well – androgynous. You heard all about that in the press, naturally, but it was good – the smell, I mean. Now he's going from strength to strength, turning into quite the parfumeur. He's launched Chatelaine, very *exotique* and heavy, and Charlus for men is about to be offered to the young divines of Paris. It really is his niche, almost more than jewellery. I suppose he's going to go into men's underwear and all the paraphernalia like everyone else. People simply don't stick to their metier any more, *n'est ce pas?*' She rolled her eyes heavenwards at a young blond actor who was toying with her foot underneath the table.